To Alison

With very best wishes

Nancy Moore

NEGATIVE SPACE

THE EARTH TONE MYSTERIES

NANCY MOORE

FriesenPress

Suite 300 – 990 Fort Street
Victoria, BC, Canada V8V 3K2
www.friesenpress.com

Copyright © 2014 by Nancy Moore
First Edition — 2014

All rights reserved.

No part of this publication may be reproduced in any form, or by any means, electronic or mechanical, including photocopying, recording, or any information browsing, storage, or retrieval system, without permission in writing from the publisher.

ISBN
978-1-4602-5594-0 (Hardcover)
978-1-4602-5593-3 (Paperback)
978-1-4602-5595-7 (eBook)

1. Fiction, Mystery & Detective, General

Distributed to the trade by The Ingram Book Company

ONE

John Clark steered his black Mercedes-Benz S-Class sedan out of the underground parking and turned south onto Bay Street. The flow of the traffic was in sharp contrast to the sense of panic and foreboding pervading his whole being.

Five minutes ago while he was waiting for the elevator, he caught sight of a reflection in the polished marble wall and instantly he knew. He didn't turn around because he knew Viktor would already be gone. He also knew that somehow it meant the end for him.

He thought back to the meeting in the café. In his mind he reread the typed message his secretary had left on his desk. *Meet me 4pm at the café in your office building, Liu Wong.*

As expected, Liu was waiting when he arrived. He walked to the counter to order his usual from Martha, but Martha wasn't there. Strange because Martha hadn't missed a day of work for as long as he could recollect.

He recalled the nondescript woman behind the counter looking at him as though identifying him out of a line-up. "Martha's off sick! I'm Jean! What'll it be?"

He grabbed his coffee and slid into the booth opposite Liu. His mouth felt dry so he took a large gulp as he eyed the engineer sitting across the table. Liu appeared apprehensive. He remembered thinking that something must really have been bothering him to come all the way to Bay Street from his laboratory in the east end of the city.

He asked: "Aren't you taking a chance wanting to meet me in the open like this? I told you not to contact me. My contact at KZR informed me there's a problem."

Liu turned ashen. "I didn't arrange the meeting. I got a message from you."

Both men immediately knew what that meant.

"Liu, who did you tell about the project?"

"No one, I swear!"

"Then how did they find out, Liu?"

"I told Jiao. Only Jiao! My wife knows I worked for you, but that's all she knows. I didn't tell any of the others at KZR, I swear. I don't know how they found out."

"It had to be through Jiao."

"Jiao can be difficult but I'd trust her with my life. She liked the kind of money you paid when I worked for you. But I swear I didn't give her any details."

"Keep it that way! Tell her nothing more."

"Is the weapon still safe?" Liu asked.

"It couldn't possibly be safer. My wife is the only one with access to it. I must go. Don't call me again!"

Liu whispered, "I know better. I'm afraid now."

As he rose to leave John added, "We agreed it was best to keep this thing out of the hands of the KZR executives. I assume you still feel that way?"

Liu Wong looked him straight in the eye. "I'd give my life before I would divulge anything about it."

John smiled sadly. "If they knew what it could do, they would want it."

John turned and walked toward the door. As he stood waiting for the elevator he spotted the reflection in the polished marble wall. The face of an angel with a heart of pure evil! John Clark knew full well what Viktor was capable of because he'd seen a sample of the monster's handiwork. He also knew why the assassin was in Toronto and in this very building.

He felt the dull throbbing of a headache. He wanted to go home. He wanted to see Emily. More than anything in the world he wanted to feel the caress of her arms, the touch of her lips. He wanted to behold the beautiful sight of his tender elegant wife. She was a beacon in his otherwise dark world.

He scrambled down the stairs to the underground parking and raced to his car. He tossed his briefcase onto the passenger's seat and pulled away before he secured his seat belt.

He thought of the drive ahead of him: the seventy-two kilometres to Dundas, up Sydenham Road and then right onto Victoria Street to his home. He could almost navigate it by rote. He'd done it so many times. His reward was always there. Emily would be standing at the door smiling as she awaited his arrival.

She would look at him lovingly through exquisite pale green eyes. She was his joy, his shining star and he knew full well he didn't deserve her. But from the moment he first saw her, he amazed even himself at the magnitude of his enthralment with her.

He pulled into traffic. He attracted the usual attention from the opposite sex. John Clark could best be described as urbane. He was tall, well-honed with a long straight nose and elegantly chiseled face. His hair was dark though greying at the temples, which gave him an even greater air of refinement. His dark eyes gave you the impression he was ever watchful, careful, vigilant.

He drove up the ramp and merged into the right hand lane on the QEW. Thank God the traffic was moving. He'd be in her arms within the hour. He would tell her all the things she needed to know. He had to tell her about the weapon and instruct her to talk to Detective Turner. He would also tell her about her parents, particularly about her father. Oh God, why hadn't he come clean with her? She deserved so much better.

He had hunted for the missing heiress for years. It was only by chance a client remarked on the resemblance between the owner of a restaurant in Dundas and the photograph on his desk. The minute he caught sight of Emily, he knew he absolutely had to have her for his own.

She was timorous of him from the start. It was as though she somehow on some plane, seemed to sense what he was capable of. He used every ploy in his seduction manual to try to win her over. Finally he played his ace, his son. As soon as she met Paul, he knew she would be his.

She was recognized at that embassy party in Paris. Al Fraih recognized the features and colouring immediately, particularly the opalescent eyes and insisted he bring her to Saudi to introduce her to her father. But as soon as he entered the building the sheik drew him aside and informed him that her father had brought his own candidate for the job he wanted, none other than Viktor. He immediately made Al Fraih aware of the kind of nastiness Viktor was capable of, so they both deemed it wise to secrete Emily away.

A few words in Al Fraih's ear and Viktor was effectively stonewalled. At least he was able to do that.

That weekend marked the beginning of his best work. Enough members of the council supported him to give him an easy win. He should have realized then, Viktor would eventually come after him.

But he was errant in his duty to Emily! Her inheritance was safe and well invested. Only he hadn't told her it existed. She and Paul both deserved to know who they really were. Not knowing could eventually prove perilous to both of them. He shivered as he realized he would no longer be there to protect them.

As soon as he reached home he would come clean. He could trust her to report everything to his son.

But he had spent a lifetime lying. He wondered what she would say when he explained it all to her. What look would cross her lovely face? It wouldn't matter now. He'd soon be dead!

He had to reach home. The things he needed to say to her could only be said in person. But he could phone Turner and if perchance he didn't make it home, the man would see to Emily's safety. Yes, that was the thing to do!

His headache was increasing by the minute. He thought of the coffee at the cafe. Was it drugged? He'd only taken a couple mouthfuls.

He pressed the button on his steering wheel activating his car phone.

He barked out the number and the phone responded, "Detective Greg Turner, here."

John's mouth was dry as he responded: "It's John Clark. Greg, I think I've been compromised. I know it wasn't through you. I'm driving back home from Toronto. It's the only place I feel safe talking to you. I think my office is bugged. Have to tell you about my weapon."

He paused for breath. He realized he was sweating profusely. He loosened his tie.

Turner questioned, "John, are you OK?"

He had to get the words out: "The weapon . . . Liu Wong helped engineer it last year. It's an assassin's dream weapon. Once we tested it and realized what we had, I decided it should be kept out of the hands of certain individuals. Its accuracy is uncanny. The prototype is in a safe place. My wife is the only one who has access to it. I can't remember if I told her where I put it?"

His tongue seemed to be struggling to work. He was straining to breathe. "Emily is unaware of my activities in this area and I prefer she remain so. Above all she must be protected!"

He paused and then whispered, "Oh God. Oh no. Tell Emily I love her!"

Detective Greg Turner of the Toronto Police force immediately contacted the OPP and advised them to proceed to QEW looking for a black Mercedes. His most valuable informant was in danger. Within a minute, sirens were blaring and traffic was stopped but not quite in time.

The black Mercedes had slowed and rolled into the guard rail with enough impact to deploy the window curtain and steering wheel airbags. A black SUV had followed the car from the time it exited the parking ramp on Bay Street. The vehicle pulled up behind Clark's car as soon as it stopped. Both the driver and passenger quickly climbed out and electronically opened the right front door of the Mercedes. One person grabbed the briefcase, which was ironically still sitting on the seat beside the driver. The other reached over, touched Clark's neck and felt a faint pulse. With a quick twist the individual snapped his neck and calmly walked back to the SUV.

Eye witnesses described the SUV to police. One had even written down the license plate. The numbers matched the plates on John Clark's vehicle. Witnesses gave conflicting reports as to the size of the two men. Both wore ball caps and both had moustaches and curly black hair.

Detective Turner was soon on the scene himself. He knew full well this was no accident. He also knew this story was far from over. John Clark may have been an invaluable informant but the man himself was a complete mystery.

He accompanied the officers to Clark's home.

John Clark's dying words were to request he keep his wife, Emily, safe. He would do his best to fulfil that promise. He owed the man that and much more!

They drove up the tree lined street in the small community of Dundas, Ontario. They pulled into the driveway of a tall Victorian home. The three of them climbed out of the patrol car.

He insisted he do the talking.

A tall, very fair woman was waiting at the door. She was lovely and emanated warmth.

Now he understood why John Clark had not told her about the secrets he had passed on. She was a woman any man would instinctively want to treasure and want to protect.

He knew there was no easy way to break news of this sort to a loved one but in this case it was particularly distasteful. He wondered how strong she was emotionally.

But she knew! He didn't need to say a word. Tears were already forming in her eyes.

Turner spoke first, "There's been accident on the QEW. I'm so sorry."

All she said was, "Did he suffer?"

What could he say? He would try to reassure her. "I don't believe so, Mrs. Clark."

She was somehow managing to control her emotions even though she had turned ghostly pale. Her voice was even as she responded: "I'll phone his son."

Turner wanted to offer her some comfort. He had so many questions about John Clark but for now all he could say was, "Shall I stay with you until he arrives?"

She smiled sadly and in a soft but firm tone announced, "Thank you, but no."

TWO

The ringer on the house phone sent out a loud burst of nerve-jarring sound that echoed throughout the bowels of the large Victorian house. The display read 'private caller' just as it had on each of its countless intrusions, which began about seven the previous evening. On the three occasions when she picked up the phone, no one responded to her greeting. Nor did they leave a message in any of the countless calls that had broken the silence of the night.

Emily Clark stood gazing absentmindedly through her kitchen window into her lush garden. Her reverie was interrupted as the toaster made its usual metallic noise releasing its hostage.

She looked down to see her own tired face reflected in the polished metal of the toaster. The oval face of a thirty-three year old woman looked back at her. There was a smattering of light freckles across her nose and cheeks. Her soft flaxen hair hung in riotous waves down over her shoulders. John had liked it long. She hadn't cut it since she lost him.

Her fair hair and skin could only be described as pale, almost colourless. Even her green eyes were unusually light in tone. She'd always considered her unusual eyes her best feature.

Apart from the incessant ringing of the phone, the house was eerily silent as usual, just as it had felt for the past year, a year without John.

It was 7am. She woke up at 5:30 as usual. She rarely slept through the night anymore and last night, even less so. Often she would awaken expecting to hear the sound of her husband's gentle snoring and reach over to touch his warm, well-honed body but feel only emptiness and coldness where he had slept.

So many times in her somnolence she'd sense his spectre as though he was watching her, trying to reach out to her.

All she had left of John was his son, Paul. But Paul was a married man with a young son and a busy career. Laura and Ardi were the focus of his life, as well they should be.

Now she shared the house with Wellington, her faithful whippet and a loneliness she never knew existed.

She looked down at Wellington. "Come boy, let's go to Dad's favourite spot. I'm going away tomorrow but right now I need some time to think."

She carried her breakfast tray to the alcove off the master bedroom. She thought of the many Saturday mornings she and John sat here reading the weekend papers and enjoying a leisurely brunch. This was John's refuge away from the worries of his busy law practise in Toronto.

Wellington anticipated her destination and was waiting eagerly when she arrived.

She looked down at her dog and spoke to him as though he had full comprehension of the English language. "I'm going on a painting trip for a whole month and you'll be staying with Nana and Papa. No doubt they'll spoil you as usual."

Tomorrow Emily Clark was taking her first step forward since becoming a widow. She was desperate to break her grieving cycle before it completely consumed her.

She was looking forward to a month-long group painting trip to Tuscany, Italy under the tutelage of Edgar Morris, her watercolour teacher at Dundas Valley School of Art. She needed to get completely away and a trip with the affable Edgar seemed to offer that opportunity.

As she sat in her armchair and raised her porcelain mug to her lips, the phone sounded again. She didn't bother to examine the read-out. She listened until the answering machine clicked on and the line went silent again.

She desperately wanted to put her thoughts in order but the incessant ringing of the phone was unnerving her. She considered phoning Paul or her parents but decided it was better not to involve them. They had all voiced their concerns about whether she was ready to travel on her own. She'd been enough of a burden to them over the past year. It was time she took control of herself and her life and going away for a month was a good way to start.

She'd had a good life as the adopted daughter or Reverend Alex and Moira MacLean. They'd given her every advantage, even if it had meant mortgaging their house to send her to culinary school in Paris. When she returned she opened her own successful restaurant and repaid them the following year.

Her parents hadn't approved of John Clark at first. They felt he was old for her and too much of a 'city boy' as they called him but they eventually came round when they realized how she felt about him. Ultimately they too came under his spell.

The phone rang again forcing her to pause in her thoughts. A shaky hand reached down to give Wellington one of the treats she always brought along.

"You miss him too, don't you boy?"

She remembered the blustery February morning John Clark walked into her restaurant.

The man exuded a kind of feral masculinity. She doubted there was a woman in the place who didn't give him a furtive glance as she paraded the tall dark man and one of her regular customers to a booth at the rear of the restaurant.

He beckoned her to his table as his friend excused himself. Dark eyes set in a sculpted face seemed to study her as if sizing her up and then coming to some conclusion the content of which she couldn't even hazard a guess.

He was sophisticated and charming but there was something about his intensity that frightened her.

Thoughtful gifts would arrive: flowers, a necklace, a lovely scarf. Still she couldn't seem to make a commitment.

When he brought his son to Sunday dinner everything changed. John stood smiling as she and Paul drank in each other's presence. She was only eight years older than Paul but she had an overwhelming urge to mother him.

John took her to Capri the following week. One evening he handed her a single red rose. A diamond ring sat in the centre of the flower.

She wiped away a tear as she remembered the scene. She could still see the sun reflecting in the depths of his dark brown eyes as they sat enjoying the warmth of the evening sun from their balcony overlooking the Bay of Naples.

Again the phone jangled bringing an abrupt end to her brief moment of euphoria.

Her mood changed as she thought of the strange occurrence on their last day in Capri. They decided to enjoy lunch in one of the sidewalk restaurants. A tall, dark-haired woman approached John and put her business card in his jacket pocket. The woman was attractive in spite of her large hooked nose. A large dark mole over the left side of her upper lip gave her a somewhat sultry appearance. However, when she turned to leave, Emily was shocked to see a long ugly scar running down her right cheek.

It was the only time she had ever seen John lose control. He stood up and ripped the card to shreds. It took a double scotch to calm him down. She assumed there was some history between the two of them but deemed it wise not to ask. He never again displayed such anger, not once. If anything he was abnormally contained and controlled in his emotions.

Her mood slipped even further as she recalled John returning to her hotel suite after a car accident in Paris. He was in terrible shape and refused to go to a hospital. They stayed an extra week while she and a local doctor tended to his needs. Stoic as ever he never complained.

She was becoming teary eyed again. With determination she wiped her tears and looked down at her dog.

"Time to get moving, Wellington."

A half hour later she walked slowly down the elegant staircase, passing her own watercolour paintings adorning the walls. She loved this house but she knew she was slowly dying of loneliness here.

Emily Clark, tall, elegant, stepped outside into the bright sunshine of a late August day. As usual she wore sunscreen, dark glasses and a big sun hat, all typical defences utilized by fair-skinned women.

She drank in the aroma of many blooming annuals and perennials as she slowly descended her front steps and walked down the pathway leading to the sidewalk on Victoria Street. She was comfortable here. She loved Dundas, the little town she'd grown up in.

Dundas, Ontario is nestled below the Niagara Escarpment thereby avoiding the worst of the winter weather. But today there was no thought of the cold winds that would sweep down the hills protecting the little valley town.

Today the warm gentle breezes stirred the air wafting the scent of the many flowers into a delicious aromatic bouquet.

Wellington paused to absorb flavours left by other dogs. They proceeded first to the pet shop where Emily purchased a dog pastry, which Wellington quickly wolfed down.

She was contemplating dropping in to visit Laura and Ardi at the old stone cottage on Brock Street when a strange sensation came over her. She felt as though she was being watched. She tried to appear nonchalant and casually turned pretending to watch a couple on the opposite side of the street. A black car was approaching rather slowly. She wondered if it was following her. She had noticed a similar vehicle before entering the pet store. Perhaps her lack of sleep was distorting her thinking.

How foolish of her, so many cars were painted black. She decided it had to be coincidence and continued on.

When she was about to cross at the next intersection, the vehicle sped up. The driver accelerated so quickly, she heard the engine rev up.

Wellington immediately drew himself back. If ever she was grateful for the sight-hound's keen sense of vision and lightning fast reflexes, it was now. The vehicle missed him by mere centimetres.

She tried, unsuccessfully to read the license plate but it was obscured by layers of filth.

As the vehicle sped past, she saw that the right tail light cover was missing. Her sleep-deprived brain registered immediate and intense alarm.

Later she would recall considering whether she should run to Paul's house, which was closer than her own but deciding against it because she couldn't bear the thought of putting Laura and Ardi in danger.

She would be at a loss to describe the route she took to arrive at her own home. Something from her familiarity with the area from her earliest childhood days clicked in. She remembered going through the churchyard and past the manse where her parents lived but anything more than that was a blur.

Her first cogent thought was placing her key in the lock. Next, she was standing in her foyer trying to disarm the security system. 1 7 0 7, the number miraculously sprang into her mind. It was her wedding date.

It was only after she entered her home that she realized how badly she was trembling. As she bolted the front door she peered through a clear area in the stained-glass window and watched helplessly as the same black car passed her home. Whoever was driving the car knew where she lived.

Her phone rang as she watched the car pull over and stop further down the street.

She checked the display on the phone. Again it read 'Private Caller'. She did not pick up.

She waited a minute and then dialled 911. In a shaky voice she tried to explain what had happened.

A black and white police car arrived almost immediately and parked on the street in front of her house. The black vehicle sped away apparently unnoticed by the officers.

A second police car arrived two minutes later and parked facing the first one.

Four police officers walked up her driveway. Two stood at the front of her house while the others walked into her back yard. Wellington kept her posted as to their locations.

No one came to her door. They walked around the house as if doing sentry duty.

Her phone rang again.

She made herself a cup of tea but she was shaking so badly she had to steady her cup with both hands and even then managed to spill some of the hot liquid. Finally, she emptied her cup into the sink.

An hour later a dark maroon car pulled into her driveway. She watched as a middle-aged man climbed out. He was balding, of medium build and his every step spoke of calm self-assurance.

He spoke briefly to the uniformed officers and then rang her doorbell.

She opened the door to a man, whose easy smile gave her a welcome whiff of calm. Before she could speak, he showed her a badge and handed her a business card and announced: "Hello, Mrs. Clark. I am Detective Greg Turner from Toronto."

She reached out to shake his proffered hand. His warmth permeated through her, dissolving the cusp of her terror.

But his next words completely unnerved her again. "We met once before, a year ago. I've had my people watching you for some time. We need to talk!"

THREE

"Watching me? People have been watching me!" Emily recoiled in horror. The words came out sounding like an accusation. "What on earth for? I've never so much as contemplated a criminal act in my entire life."

The detective stood still as a thin dog raced toward the front door. The dog came bounding with such great speed, Greg Turner wondered if it could stop before careening into him, but at the last moment the sprightly pup came to a halt and began sniffing his pant leg.

She was too preoccupied to notice.

"Mrs. Clark, I knew your husband. It was at his request we were keeping an eye on you. Is there a place we can sit? We need to talk."

She stood silently considering him. When she opened the door her first instinct was to trust the man. Something about his manner made her feel safe. She wondered if he really had a connection to John. Truth be told, she would do almost anything to talk to someone who had known her late husband. She put his death announcement in the Spectator and the Globe but only one of his friends came to his funeral.

"I apologize, I'm forgetting my manners. Please come in. Can I get you a coffee or cup of tea?"

He chose the latter and followed her down the long hallway.

It was only then she seemed to become aware of the dog. "Wellington, stop that!"

The detective was surprised when the stately, fair-haired woman opened the front door. He hadn't seen her since the evening he came to inform her of her husband's accident. He'd forgotten how captivating she was. Now she seemed almost engulfed by her own sadness.

Entering the large nineteenth century house further surprised him. Remembering the polished urbanity of John Clark, he expected over the top opulence. What he found was refined elegance much like the woman herself. In the foyer, a patterned wine coloured rug welcomed him. Bright sunlight streamed through the lace-covered window panes in the adjoining rooms. Curtain treatments, sofas and chairs seemed to blend softly together.

The walls were painted in muted shades and soft watercolour landscape paintings hung throughout the downstairs. He glanced at the signature and read 'E. Clark'. Each one of the paintings appeared to have been done in a different place. Many were from areas not frequented by tourists. He wondered if she had actually been to all these places.

The overall appearance of the home gave him a feeling of welcome and relaxation. It felt like a placid refuge from the outside world. When the phone rang she stopped walking and stood rigidly in front of him. He watched as she appeared to brace herself.

"Mrs. Clark, is something wrong?"

Her voice trembled: "My phone keeps ringing. When I answer, no one responds and they won't leave a message."

"When did this start?"

"The first call came around seven last evening and it hasn't stopped ringing since then. It rang over and over again throughout the night."

"Any other occurrences since the phone calls began?"

"Yes, Wellington was up during the night barking. Normally he sleeps like a log so he must have heard something."

"Did you get up to check around?"

"I did get up. When I looked out front, I saw a car pulling away. I always set the alarm system, so I wasn't too worried. But you never know, do you?"

She paused. "The car from last night had to be the same car that almost hit Wellington this morning. Its right tail light cover was missing."

"You are safe now." His calmness seemed to defuse some of her intenseness.

The dog was actively sniffing the detective's pant legs. She offered: "Wellington always seems to forget his manners the minute someone comes into the house. He's really very friendly. Do you mind dogs?"

The detective indicated he liked dogs and followed Emily along the hallway to her kitchen with the dog's nose firmly adhering to his pant leg.

In sharp contrast to the parts of the house he had viewed, the kitchen was ultra-modern. She motioned him to sit in one of the chairs beside a round linen covered table.

The table was next to a window overlooking a lush flower garden. Like the house, the garden showed signs of meticulous care.

He was a patient man and a keen observer. He enjoyed examining people, trying to decode the inner workings of their minds.

He liked what he gleaned from Emily Clark. She may have appeared sad, but she was definitely in control of her life. Her house, garden and even her person showed no signs of the neglect he often saw in widows. She may still have been in deep mourning for her late husband but she was unquestionably a strong woman, and that was a good thing in view of what he was about to tell her.

As soon as she offered to make tea, she seemed to gain a sense of purpose. She became focused and the trembling he had observed when she opened the front door, all but disappeared.

It was a steady hand that lifted a porcelain teapot and poured Earl Grey tea into dainty Limoges cups. Then she sat opposite him. He could feel her examining him.

He took a sip of his tea. Now that he had her undivided attention he began: "Your husband John Clark, contacted me for the first time about six years ago with a tip about an arms shipment bound for Yemen. He was also instrumental in helping us get some hostages out of a terrorist camp in Somalia. There were others instances, which I won't go into here, but you should know that he has given great service not only for his own country but all members of the NATO Alliance."

He stopped to give her time to digest what he had told her.

This was new information for her. For the first time since he entered the house, she smiled. She sat straighter. She cocked her head. She wanted to know more.

"I had no idea," she said lightly.

"He made it clear from the beginning he required total anonymity and insisted I never investigate him. He told me his position was precarious and he promised further useful information on the condition I keep his identity in the strictest confidence."

Again he paused watching her reaction. He had her full undivided attention.

All she said was: "John?"

He continued with his narrative: "From time to time he'd phone me with information and we would meet. He never wavered in his insistence that neither you nor anyone else be told that he was an informant. He also never wavered in his concern for your safety and well-being."

She opened her mouth trying to think of what words to utter. All she could manage was a few plaintive words. "He risked his life?"

Her body language confirmed that Emily Clark had no previous knowledge of her husband's extracurricular activities. He was opening a new chapter for her.

"John Clark's information was always precise and led to the seizure of numerous shipments of illegal arms and other contraband, plus many arrests in Europe and Africa."

"He had a secret life?"

Again it was a question, not an answer.

"Yes, Mrs. Clark, I believe your husband may have had a secret life."

"He knew he could trust me. Why didn't he tell me?"

"He feared for your safety, Mrs. Clark. Actually his greatest concern was not for himself but for you."

"John sometimes underestimated my strength."

"He phoned me from his car just before he died. I recorded the conversation. Do you mind if I play it for you."

"Please!"

She watched as he placed a portable tape player on the table and pressed the play button. Emily Clark turned white when she heard her husband's voice emanating from the machine. She held her breath.

Greg, I think I have been compromised. I know it wasn't through you . . . I'm driving back home from Toronto. It is the only place I feel safe talking to you. I think my office line is bugged. I have to tell you about the weapon . . . Liu Wong helped engineer it last year. It's an assassin's dream weapon. Once we tested it and realized what we had, I decided it should be kept out of the hands of certain individuals. Its accuracy is uncanny . . . I hid the prototype in a safe place. My wife is the only one who has access to it. I can't remember if I told her where I put it. Emily, is unaware of my activities in this area and I prefer she remain so. Above all, she must be protected—Oh, God. Oh no. Tell Emily I love her . . .

The detective turned off the tape machine and looked at her. "With that the line went dead, Mrs. Clark."

She seemed unaware of the tears running down her cheeks. "We never had the opportunity to say goodbye. His last words were that he loved me."

"I'm so sorry, Mrs. Clark, I realize hearing his voice again must be a great shock to you, but it seemed the easiest and fastest way to get you to understand what we are up against here."

Emily grabbed some tissues and wiped her face. She took a minute to steady herself.

"I am not a child, Detective Turner. If my husband risked his life providing important information, I most certainly will do my part to help in any way I can. But you must answer one thing for me?"

"I'll answer anything I can. What do you want to know?"

"After listening to your tape, am I right in thinking my husband's death was not an accident?"

"Mrs. Clark, it was not an accident. He was murdered."

She took a minute to absorb his information. "And you didn't tell me John was murdered because you were respecting his wishes?"

He nodded.

"John is dead, Detective Turner. My wishes matter now. I want to be involved. I want to find the people who stole his precious life."

Turner sat watching her every move. "Are you sure you can handle this?"

"Watch me!"

"Very well then, I'll try to fill you in on the little I know. Your husband claimed he was approached by two respectable businessmen from KZR Ltd, an industrial tooling firm. They wanted him to do some restructuring, give assistance with their research and development claims and assist with relocating funds offshore. John sensed there was more going on than they were telling him so he ingratiated himself with several members of the staff. I have no idea how or when he came to work with Liu Wong in developing a weapon. Nor do I know the source of the information he passed on to me. But I suspect whoever was feeding him information, was somehow connected with KZR. As you no doubt know, he played his cards close to his chest."

"Yes, he did. But why now and why bother me? I know nothing about any of this and John has been dead for a year."

"Your husband mentioned Liu Wong on the tape. He was KZR's top engineer. Last night, his body turned up in the Toronto Harbour. He was tortured to death."

Turner paused thinking about the condition of the body. Then he continued: "Jiao Wong reported her husband missing the previous day and when the police found his tortured body, she became terrified and told us more about the operations at KZR. Mrs. Wong claims KZR is designing highly sophisticated small weaponry in addition to their regular industrial work. This is a firm with a high level of computer and technical expertise. The president of KZR's Canadian operations denies they have ever designed or produced weapons of any kind."

"Detective Turner, John was a lawyer, not an engineer or any kind of a weapons expert. I don't understand?"

"According to Jiao Wong, her husband worked with John Clark in developing some kind of miniature weapon. KZR is claiming that anything designed by one of their engineers is technically their property. I don't know what your husband's involvement was, other than the fact that he was in possession of the object at the time of his death."

"This is all so strange. John was not in any way mechanically inclined."

"I need your help, Mrs. Clark. Your husband stipulated I was never to ask questions or investigate his past in return for the information he passed on to me."

He paused as if pondering how to continue. "After he was killed, I was uncomfortable asking questions because I felt he was right in fearing for your safety. I could understand his concern. He was aware he was risking both of your lives by passing on information of such a sensitive nature. The bottom line is I know very little about the late John Clark."

She sat silently observing him from across the table, her tea long forgotten.

Turner continued: "It appears that while Liu Wong was being tortured he revealed details of the weapon he gave your husband. In view of what's been happening to you, he must have exposed you as the only one with access to it. That would explain the attempts to frighten you."

Again he paused, giving her time to digest the significance of his last statement. "If they wanted you dead, Mrs. Clark, believe me, you would already be dead. What they have done is launch a campaign to terrorize and perhaps try to kidnap you." He paused and then added with determination, "I won't let that happen."

Trying to draw her into his confidence, he asked softly: "Mrs. Clark, is there anything at all you can tell me about your husband's activities?"

"Officer Turner, I know nothing about any of this. John kept his professional life separate from his home life. He loved living here in Dundas because he felt remote from the hustle and bustle of his law practise. He always brought his briefcase home but I would tease him saying that he shouldn't have bothered because he never opened it."

"Mrs. Clark, it is imperative we find this weapon as soon as possible. As the people who killed Liu Wong are now aware the weapon exists, they want it. They may want to do some damage control and that damage control might include you. To complicate matters even further we know little about who might potentially be involved in this. In addition KZR is stonewalling and denying any involvement."

"I have no idea where John put any papers or weapon or anything of that nature. You are welcome to search through the house if you think that will help."

She reacted as he hoped. He would use the opening to act. "Mrs. Clark, would you mind if I bring in a forensic unit to search your home from top to bottom? If these people find out we have done a thorough search, they may leave both you and your home alone at least for a while. It will mean having several units parked in your driveway. We can explain to your neighbours that there was a break-in and your house was vandalized and the units are here doing some repair work."

"Please feel free to search my home from top to bottom, but I assure you that nothing extraordinary will be found."

He reached for his cellphone and relayed rapid-fire instructions into it. "A unit will be here in fifteen minutes. In the meantime, please tell me more about your husband."

They strolled into the den and sat in oversized chairs. She was gradually becoming more comfortable confiding in him. "John and I lived a very ordinary existence. We were together for about seven years and our relationship was peaceful. My husband loved nothing better than to enjoy Sunday dinner with the family. His son Paul is in his twenties and happily married with one child and another on the way, and my parents live not far from here."

She paused, her mind quickly skimming through the memories of their years together. "I can't even begin to imagine John becoming involved in something nefarious and jeopardizing his own life. He gave the appearance of being happily married. He was a loving husband and caring father. I know it sounds as though I am putting him on a pedestal now that he's gone, but truly that's how he was. I'm at a loss to understand what is happening!"

She began to recite John's history as she knew it: "I was John's second wife. His first wife died of cancer two years before we met. He never talked about her. She apparently was a successful divorce lawyer in Toronto. She left behind a wonderful son whom I have come to cherish. Until we married, Paul was cared for by nannies or sent to boarding schools."

"What about your husband's parents? Any siblings?"

Again she paused considering. Her voice was more highly pitched as she responded: "John never mentioned any family. When we married he invited only one friend from Toronto. He seemed to want to put his old life behind him. Perhaps it reminded him too much of his late wife . . . Mr. Turner, if you'll excuse me. I must phone and cancel my trip."

He looked at her questioningly. "You are planning to go away?"

"I was due to leave tomorrow morning for Tuscany on a month-long group painting trip. I'll call my teacher, Edgar Morris and explain that something has come up. This is just too much to absorb."

Greg Turner raised a hand, "Edgar Morris! Did you say Edgar Morris?"

"Yes, he's my watercolour teacher at Dundas Valley School of Art. He's the leader of our art trip."

"Wait a minute. I understand how you must feel about wanting to cancel your trip. This is all so new to you. I need to talk to a couple of people before you decide."

He excused himself and pulled out his cell phone as he walked out of the room. She strained to hear snippets of his conversation. "Karl, I have a high priority job for you and Burns. Can you drop whatever case you're working on and head to Russ's place in Tuscany . . . . Within 24 hours . . . . Remember the informant, the one who . . ."

He walked out into the front yard. She watched as he ended the call and dialled twice again. He walked to the street and spoke to some men who were doing some road work.

When he returned she looked at him and uttered, "John trusted you."

It was a statement, not a question.

He smiled comfortingly, reached out and touched her hand reassuringly before continuing: "Mrs. Clark, you husband's last words were to ask me to keep you safe. You can trust me. From now on, I will do the all worrying for you."

As if in surprise she said, "The phone stopped ringing."

When the doorbell chimed he motioned for her to remain seated. He ushered a uniformed officer into the room and introduced her as Sergeant Iris McGirr.

McGirr immediately walked over and shook Emily's hand. "So nice to meet you, Mrs. Clark. I'll be co-ordinating everything for Detective Turner. My first bit of good news is that the two guys in that black car are now on their way to Barton Street Jail. They won't bother you again."

Turner addressed Emily: "Is there a room where McGirr can set up her equipment?"

"Use my husband's study. It's down the hall on the right."

As soon as he closed the office door McGirr began: "We caught them on Highway #5 trying to beetle their way back to Toronto. Both of them were down and outers. Said they met a suit in a bar who gave them five grand to harass Mrs. Clark and promised another thirty if they grabbed her."

"Were they the ones making the phone calls?"

"Yea, the dimwits thought it a great joke. Last night the dog really spooked them. They saw Mrs. Clark put the dog out the back door around eight last night but the dog ran so fast it scared the snot out of them. Then they had the grand notion they might break in around two in the morning. Every time they looked in a window, the animal was already there looking out at them. Sounds rather funny, actually."

"They tried to run it down this morning," Turner replied.

"They figured if they hit the dog, they could grab Mrs. Clark but she took off running up an alleyway and reached home before they could catch her. The fools were lamenting they couldn't collect the thirty grand."

"Probably lucky for them they couldn't deliver. Doubt their payment would have been a cash bonus. Any idea who the suit was?"

"Not yet, but we'll try to get a composite as soon as they're booked," McGirr said.

"Doubt we'll find him any time soon."

"Turner, you were right about putting surveillance on her parents' and her step-son's homes. Someone tried to grab the grandson about an hour ago."

"That's not good news! This is heating up. Suggest you put some security on our two prisoners. As of now they're all we've got."

"Consider it done," McGirr responded.

Turner returned to the living room and after apologizing for the interruption, resumed his seat opposite Emily. "Let's talk about the prototype. I have a feeling your husband has somehow left you the whereabouts of this weapon in a familiar place. Do you know if he had a hiding place in the house or a safely deposit box?"

"The safety deposit box was examined after John died. It contained his will and some securities. John wasn't like that. He'd never conceal anything from me. Not the John Clark I was married to. What you're suggesting is out of character for my husband." Her voice grew in pitch with each sentence.

Turner was accustomed to handling difficult individuals and quickly mollified her in a gentle voice. "Ah, but Mrs. Clark the man was passing along information about illegal arms shipments and as you heard, he referred to the weapon on the tape. How do you account for these things?"

"I simply can't account for any of that! All this is so new, I'm having some difficulty understanding any of it."

She was bewildered. "I know how this looks but I lived with John. I never saw any undercurrents of a secret life, not ever."

"Mrs. Clark, your husband had an unusually high sense of duty. He had the opportunity to do something quite outstanding for his country and he stepped up and did it." He paused and waited until she looked up at him. "We all have secrets, things we tell no one. There's no blame to be doled out. It's merely a question of finding the weapon and it all goes away."

"You're right. I'm still mourning my husband. Perhaps I'm too emotional to be objective."

"According to the tape, he left the weapon where you can access it."

She was unable to respond.

He displayed a half grin cajoling her. "Husbands and wives have their own secret world. It's what makes them a couple. One day soon you will realize where to look. On the tape John said he wanted it kept out of the hands of 'certain individuals'.

I promise I'll do whatever is necessary to safeguard the thing once we find it."

"But you don't know the identity of those 'certain individuals' he was talking about any more than I do."

"Right now, I don't, Mrs. Clark, but I promise you I will find out."

"With all due respect, Detective Turner, I don't see how I can possibly enjoy a whole month away with this hanging over my head. If these people are not above torturing and killing that engineer, you know they would not hesitate to do the same again."

"I understand your feelings, however, remaining here doesn't guarantee your safety any more than it does that of your family." He put particular emphasis on the last two words.

A look of sheer panic crossed her face. Whatever she was thinking, she kept to herself. She responded defiantly: "Very well, I'll go, but not because of any weapon and not because you want me to go. I have never held a gun in my life nor do I ever intend to. But if I changed my mind about going away my family would be here worrying about me and I've had enough of that already. I'd prefer my family be kept in the dark about all this."

Turner grinned. She had spunk. "They will learn nothing from my lips and I will advise my staff of a likely story, should anyone ask."

A dark van pulled into the driveway and a four men wearing matching yellow jackets and carrying cases approached her home. McGirr appeared and introduced each one to Emily. She asked Emily to escort them through the house.

Emily led the way explaining about the history of the house as she went.

There were four floors. The top floor had been remodelled into bedrooms for guests and her painting studio. The enormous master suite and two smaller bedrooms were on the second floor. The main floor contained the kitchen, breakfast nook, living room, dining room, library and a large family room. The basement had been completely renovated and held the gym, laundry, pantry and furnace room. McGirr assigned an officer to each floor.

Wellington was most impressed with all the commotion. He loved having new people to sniff. He considered it one of his official duties. Finally Emily decided she should drop him off at her mother's house before he made a complete nuisance of himself.

"I'll drive you there, Emily," Turner offered.

"It's only two minutes from here. Besides Wellington needs a walk," Emily offered.

He looked at McGirr. "It should be OK, sir."

Once outside Emily smiled at the two men who stood beside their van pondering a non-existent pothole.

As they turned the corner, Turner flashed his badge to two surveyors.

He spotted the stake-out car as they came to a stately Georgian home. He slipped into the back seat and allowed Emily to proceed up the walk. "You guys are parked in a tow-away zone."

One of the young officers grinned. "Works for us, sir."

"Let's watch the action. She's exposed here. I don't like it."

The three men watched as the front door sprang open and a short rather roly-poly woman came bounding out. The dog practically did cart-wheels when he spotted her.

She was followed by a small man wearing a clerical collar. His face broke into a warm smile as he spotted Emily. He embraced her as Wellington jumped around and barked and raced through the open door into the house. He returned with a red ball in his mouth, which he promptly dropped at the man's feet.

The second officer commented: "These are good people, sir. Rev MacLean is pastor at my sister's church."

They watched as Emily pointed in the direction of her home and bent down to exchange kisses and hugs with her parents.

McGirr was waiting at the door when they returned. "Need to speak to you privately, sir."

Emily interrupted, "No, I want to be involved. I want to know everything."

Turner eyed McGirr in silent communication.

He looked back at Emily. "You sure?"

"Positive!"

"OK, come along."

McGirr pointed to the items on the desk. "We found a knife taped to the underside of a night table in the master bedroom and another one taped to the underside of the stationery bicycle in the basement. There were credit cards in different names at the back of the desk drawer. We are still looking. So far we haven't found anything resembling the weapon you described."

Emily stood in silence momentarily before replying: "This is so unexpected."

She paused and then spoke with determination: "Do whatever you need to do, but find the damn weapon."

McGirr grinned. "Thank you, Ma'am. In light of finding these things, I arranged for six more officers to help in the search. It's a big house and we need more manpower to go through everything quickly."

Turner nodded. "Well done, McGirr!"

An hour later McGirr found her sitting quietly in the den.

She asked, "You up to answering a few questions?"

She nodded.

"Mrs. Clark, how long have you owned this house?" McGirr asked.

"About eight years," Emily responded.

"Did you do any major renovations to it?"

"Yes, it was quite rundown when John bought it. He hired a company from Toronto to do all the heavy work and I did the decorating myself."

"Do you know the name of the firm he hired to do the work?"

"No, John told me they had worked on his home in Rosedale. He said they were honest and did good work. They were not from here."

"Not from here? What do you mean?" McGirr asked.

"Only one of them spoke much English. John liked old-world craftsmanship."

"Do you know what country they were from?"

"No, John dealt with them exclusively."

"What about the kitchen and bathrooms?"

"The husband of one of my girlfriends specializes in that sort of work. He did those at the same time."

"Do you know what areas of the house these other contractors worked on?" McGirr asked.

Emily thought back remembering the four men. "I was still running my restaurant so I wasn't monitoring their progress, but I would come in to measure for draperies. They were here for several months working all over the house. They spent a long time in the basement. I wasn't involved in redoing John's library."

"Anything else, Mrs. Clark?"

Emily continued. "John designed his own walk-in closet. He wanted to model it after the one in his home in Toronto."

"Thank you, Mrs. Clark." McGirr said and quickly left the room.

For the next hour, she heard tapping noises emanating from above and below her. She sat quietly in the den collecting her thoughts.

An hour later both Turner and McGirr came into the den. It was McGirr who spoke first: "Mrs. Clark, your husband's weaponry—"

Before she could finish Turner interrupted her: "Did your husband ever mention owning a gun?"

"Absolutely not! Why would he need one?"

His tone was gentle: "I'm afraid he owned a great number of them."

She flew out of her seat. "What? I want to see."

As McGirr lead the way she began to explain. "My people thought the basement seemed a tad small for the size of the upstairs area. As they were searching they kept hearing a dehumidifier click on and off and then they discovered the switch that opens this panel. When they looked inside they found an arsenal of weapons and ammunition and some computer equipment."

Emily followed them into the hidden room and gasped when she spotted the vast array of weapons. "I don't understand this at all. Where did all this come from?"

"We don't know but we're checking all the serial numbers," McGirr replied.

The weapons ranged from high powered rifles with precision-made scopes to revolvers. Each weapon had its own slot on the wall and each one appeared to have been repaired.

McGirr commented: "There is some high priced weaponry here."

"We found something else, Mrs. Clark," McGirr said as she handed her a mauve envelope.

Emily pulled a card out of the envelope and began reading:

Dear Johnny,

Thanks for the use of your credit card. May whoever stole my handbag rot in hell!

Mary wiped the room down before we left. She asked me to apologize to you.

Checked out the tortilla con almejas at La Ancha as you suggested. It was superlative.

See you in Vegas next month.

As always,

R

"We were in Madrid two weeks before John died. I discovered La Ancha on one of my walks and brought my husband there to try the omelet."

She hesitated. "I don't have any idea who R might be, but John and I planned to go to San Diego, not Vegas."

"You should see these Ma'am," McGirr said as she held up a manilla folder.

Emily examined the first item. "These are our tickets for San Diego and this is our hotel reservation. We were to stay at the Del Coronado, September fifteenth to the twenty-third."

Emily smiled as she looked at the next page. "Oh how sweet! John booked a private tour of the museum for me. He often did thoughtful things like that when we travelled."

When she pulled out the next sheet her smile disappeared. "This is a hotel reservation for three rooms at The Mirage in Vegas. The rooms are booked for the sixteenth to the twenty-second."

She examined the next page. "Rental for a private plane to be picked up at the San Diego Airport on the sixteenth and returned on the twenty-second. It says John William Clark is the pilot. I don't understand, John couldn't fly a plane. He didn't have a pilot's license."

McGirr handed her another page. "We printed this out from the DOT files. He was highly qualified, Ma'am."

She looked at the next sheet. "Rental of a Porsche Boxster to be picked up at Las Vegas airport. This is signed by my late husband."

McGirr passed her the final two pages. They were stapled together. She read the first page. "It's from Guinon Security. I never heard of them. Account for security for September fifteenth to twenty-third. It's a bill for 15,000 US dollars and it's marked 'paid in full'."

She studied the page before commenting: "John must have feared for his life."

Neither McGirr nor Turner made a comment. Both stood watching her as she flipped over the page to examine the one stapled to it.

She gasped as she read and reread the words on the page: "My God! It's a contract to provide security for me on our trip to San Diego. It includes providing a driver and vehicle and constant surveillance. It also includes picking John up from the airport on the eighteenth and delivering him back on the morning of the nineteenth. Guess he planned to drop by and visit me."

Rivulets began to stream unbidden down her face. "Any idea what this is about? I don't understand."

"There may well be a logical explanation for all of this. It all points to the possibility that your husband may have served as a secret agent for another country," Greg Turner offered.

"Another country? Not Canada?"

"Definitely not Canada!" Turner replied.

"And the security for me?"

"Again, if he was an agent, he may have felt you were at risk when you travelled."

"That sounds reasonable, I guess. But it seems like a lot of money to spend."

McGirr held out a small green book. "We found this ledger taped to the underside of his desk. Have you ever seen this book?"

"No," she replied.

"Is this your late husband's handwriting?" McGirr asked.

Emily examined the handwriting and numbers carefully before answering: "It's definitely his handwriting but it's not written in English. John was thoroughly Canadian or at least until this minute I thought he was. He spoke only English and a tiny bit of French or so I thought. What language is it?"

McGirr was quick to respond: "No one here recognizes it, but we'll soon find out."

Detective Turner chose not to mention that behind a sliding panel in her husband's library they found a garrotte and several assassin's extension knives. He also chose not to tell her they discovered a secret panel behind his suits in his closet where they located a cache of passports and more foreign currency.

He directed her back upstairs. They sat facing each other in the den.

"How often was your husband away from home?"

"We always travelled together. He dealt with international corporations in his law practice so we made numerous trips to

Europe, the Middle East and the United States. I came along and painted while he went to his meetings."

"How long would he be away from you on these trips?"

"Usually several days at a time! Sometimes he'd come back mid-week and then leave again. It would vary. There was no pattern."

As soon as she responded he quickly asked another question: "Did you paint all the pictures in the front hallway?"

"Yes, John insisted on framing one painting from each trip. Mr. Turner, I see the direction your suspicions are taking you and I don't like it. I know how this all must look but bear in mind that John was a family man. I don't believe he would do anything to jeopardize his family. He was not a crazy man. There must be a logical explanation."

"I agree with you. I met your husband and I know he would never jeopardize you or your family. But we're trying to figure out who he was involved with. The serial numbers on the weapons downstairs indicate that most of them are anywhere from four to forty years old, but we still haven't found the prototype we've been looking for."

"I've had too many shocks today to remember details about our travels or anything else."

He was silent for a few minutes, trying to give her time to compose herself. Then he said, "I feel your husband's involvement in this started long before you met him, Mrs. Clark. Tell me what you know of your husband's life before he married you. You may know more than you suspect. Were you ever at his home in Toronto?"

"I helped him clean out the place after it sold. The only furniture he brought here was his library furniture and his armoire and the headboard in our bedroom."

Emily Clark suddenly had an 'aha' moment. She stood and began pacing.

"I lived with my husband for years. I thought we shared our innermost thoughts and feelings. There were no secrets between us or so I thought until now."

Turner did not speak.

"He never once mentioned his parents, grandparents, or brothers and sisters if he had any. He never talked about his friends from school, university or even law school. I have met only one of his colleagues and that was at our wedding and again at his funeral. I have never met or dined with any of his clients. I don't know the name of his secretary. I had no idea he could speak a foreign language. I had no idea he owned a single gun let alone a whole room full of weapons. I'm at a loss to explain how a man who couldn't change a light bulb was involved in designing a sophisticated weapon."

She faced Turner.

He remained silent.

"In short, Detective Turner, I don't know who the hell I was married to."

He spoke: "How well do any of us know ourselves let alone each other?"

"That may be true but in my case it seems to have been carried to the extreme."

He grinned. "Don't take it personally."

"I'll keep that in mind." She chuckled and added: "Mr. Turner, you must be hungry. I'll fix dinner for your squad."

He countered: "We normally get take-out while on the job." But then he saw the determined look on her face and smiled.

She now had a purpose and continued with enthusiasm: "Not in my house! I don't have any fresh food, as I planned to go away tomorrow. Not to worry, I'll whip something together. I prefer pasta sauce from fresh tomatoes but tonight bottled sauce will have to do."

As they passed the open doorway to John's library, Emily saw John's books arranged in piles on the floor. The room was in general disarray. McGirr who was examining the contents must have heard her gasp. "Don't worry, Mrs. Clark. We always clean up after ourselves."

They continued down the hallway to the kitchen at the back of the house. Detective Turner sat at the kitchen table again.

Emily was completely focused on her food preparation. She grabbed a loaf of bread, two packages of ground sirloin and two bags of frozen raspberries out of the freezer. The microwave buzzed as she thawed the meat. Then she appeared with pasta and bottled pasta sauce from the pantry.

He realized this frenzied activity was her way of dealing with a stressful situation. He'd seen his own wife cope in a similar fashion.

It gave him time to think. Greg Turner had risen through the ranks because of his uncanny skill in sizing up people and situations. He was renowned for his investigative abilities.

John Clark had been an enigma since the day they met in an obscure café in Toronto. He received a phone call from a throw away cell phone instructing him when and where to meet. He was told to sit working on a crossword and he would be contacted with worthwhile information. Out of curiosity he had obliged. There was something compelling and authoritative about the voice that told him this was no hoax.

He sensed rather than saw Clark's approach. The guy moved like a second story man. He slid into the seat opposite and told Turner to reach under the table. An envelope was placed into his outstretched hand and he quickly slid it into the pocket of his trench coat.

It was like a scene out of an old spy movie.

"I'm John Clark," he said as he flashed his business card. "I need your word that you will keep my name confidential. Only you are to know about me. You are at no time to investigate me or make enquiries of any kind about me. Do not even think to try to contact me."

With that Clark left the cafe, moving swiftly and silently.

Back in his office, Turner examined the contents of the envelope. He remembered thinking this was a motherlode of information—if it was real. He sent faxes of the papers to his international contacts and within a week received a reply. Yes, the information was good. A ship was boarded in the Mediterranean and a large cache of illegal arms was found in the container as indicated in the papers John Clark had given him.

Clark was dealing with dangerous people to get his hands on this kind of information. Passing it on put him at even greater risk. Surely the man knew his life would be in peril. The fact that he survived so long amazed the detective.

On their second meeting, Clark mentioned his concern for his wife. He insisted that if anything happened to him, Emily was to be watched and protected. She knew nothing about his dealings. She was his utmost concern.

Their future meetings would echo the same themes: anonymity and protect my wife. The information he passed on was always accurate and extremely useful. It involved gun running, terrorist connections, drug shipments and even a European government cover up.

It came as no surprise to him that John Clark had been murdered. Careful examination of his vehicle revealed skillful manipulation of the steering and brake systems. They were designed to fail after twenty-five minutes of driving. What was unusual was that his car door had not been pried open but opened electronically, his head given a quick jerk ending his life, and his briefcase removed. Whoever killed him was a pro.

Only after Clark's death did the detective confide the name of his contact and only to people he could trust. He needed cooperation to have Clark's wife protected until he was better able to size up the situation.

John Clark never had so much as a speeding ticket. The man was squeaky clean. Strangely enough the only involvement with the police was not with John, but with his late wife. A female client laid assault charges against her but later dropped them. No doubt, money changed hands to get the charges dropped.

Turner learned more about the man from the society pages of Toronto newspapers. He researched back twenty years. Clark and his first wife were a social fixture. She was small and curvaceous with a huge mane of dark hair. There were numerous photos of the handsome couple at receptions and balls. She was a real dresser. Her gowns looked expensive. The woman looked high maintenance. Turner didn't envy him with that one.

Within three months of the first wife's death, Clark's photo began appearing again, this time on the arms of wealthy widows and heiresses. He was obviously very much in demand. Not much wonder with his kind of good looks. Two years after the death of his wife, the photos stopped. His name was no longer mentioned in gossip columns. The guy was living the high life, when suddenly he dropped out of sight.

The reason for his abrupt change in behaviour was working away in the kitchen before his eyes. Clark had fallen in love with this strong-willed woman. In their earlier conversation she said she didn't want any of the showy furniture from Clark's Toronto house. The same must have been true for his high-lifestyle. The guy gave up his way of life to drive the long way to Dundas twice each day to spend time with this intriguing woman.

He could have found a cozy place closer to his office.

Why move here?

It was off the beaten track. It meant spending at least two hours each day driving on the QEW back and forth to Toronto.

His wife was from here.

Only one of his acquaintances attended his wedding. Why? Was he was protecting her from something in his past? Maybe but then again he was a prominent lawyer working everyday in Toronto. The man wasn't hiding from anybody. He was keeping his wife out of sight.

Why hire security for her when they travelled?

Clark was afraid for her. He was more afraid for her than he was for himself. As an informant he jeopardized his own life and yet he was more concerned with his wife's safety.

Clark was sophisticated, keenly intelligent but his recollection of the man was different from Emily's. Unless he misread the man, Clark was obdurate. He was unquestionably fond of Emily but there was something more. Everything the man did was calculated, planned. The man wouldn't spend large amounts of money to protect the woman unless he had a very good reason to do so.

He reviewed what she had told him. One miserable February day, Clark had driven to Dundas to meet a client at her restaurant.

Not a chance! He came to meet Emily MacLean. He targeted her.

He was bounced out of his thoughts with the sound of Emily's voice: "Dinner is ready! Do you want to call your people? I set up everything buffet style."

Then she looked directly at him. "Your officers can eat in here while you and I sit in the dining room."

Detective Turner looked at the array of food. There were huge bowls of spaghetti and meatballs, homemade Italian bread and a large white casserole filled with raspberry crumble.

"It's not fancy, but it is better than take-out," she offered.

When Turner tasted the pasta he wholeheartedly agreed. The woman either had uncommon culinary ability or a magic wand. Spaghetti never tasted this good when his wife cooked it.

Over the course of his lengthy career he had seen how people reacted to emergencies. Many women resorted to histrionics, others simply fell apart.

Not Emily Clark! After recovering from her initial bout of nerves, she wanted to know what his investigators had found, and when their findings turned sinister she voiced concern for her family. He had watched her sit in the den and quietly gather her strength. She loved Clark and was slowly reconciling herself to the fact that he had a side she did not know about or even begin to understand.

Over dinner they went from being Detective Turner and Mrs. Clark to Greg and Emily.

"Emily, do you look after this big place all by yourself?"

"I have help. Maria and Steve Deralla do the cleaning and all the repairs."

"How long have they worked here?"

"I used to joke that they came with the house because they started as soon as we moved in. They know the house better than I do. John made provisions to keep them on indefinitely."

"Tell me what you know about them."

"Not very much! Maria told me that John hired them as soon as they emigrated from Macedonia. They love to use the exercise equipment in the basement."

"How can I reach them?"

"I'll give you their number. They never answer the phone. I always leave a message. I told them to take this week off in addition to the month I'm away. They haven't taken any time off since my husband died. I thought they'd go away but I saw them this morning."

"Where did you see them?"

"Steve almost rear-ended the car that tried to kill Wellington. He blew his horn several times. I took the opportunity and ran as fast as I could. Can we talk about something else?"

He smiled and told her about meeting his wife, Angie, while serving in Cyprus. He had also served in other places under the NATO flag and later joined the police force. She surprised him with her knowledge of the Blue Jays. She explained she had to follow their games to keep up with the rest of the family. She spoke sadly about all the baseball games her husband took them to and about the Christmases they spent together in this big old house when Clark was alive.

When they finished their main course, Emily put out a tub of ice cream to go with the raspberry crumble. Greg noted that there were no leftovers when his team finished eating. The bread was gone and the plates scraped clean. The raspberry crumble seemed to evaporate out of its white casserole dish. There was no chance for seconds of that!

His people pitched in and did the clean-up. Soon the kitchen was sparkling clean again and he and Emily returned to the den to chat.

He said, "I spoke to Edgar Morris and he agreed to act as your bodyguard on your trip to Italy."

"Edgar, a bodyguard! He's a sweet guy, but a bodyguard?" she tried unsuccessfully to stifle a laugh.

"You of all people should realize that people are not always what they seem."

"I'm sorry. You're right in that!"

"As I told you, Edgar and I served in the armed forces together. He'll look after you on the flight to Italy. You'll be staying at Villa DiMattia in the Tuscan Hills. The owner Russ DiMattia, is also an old army buddy. Edgar arranges all these painting trips so he can make a bit of money and visit with his old friends at the same time."

"Villa DiMattia looked old and interesting in the brochure."

He smiled reassuringly. "As we speak, the villa is being equipped with surveillance equipment. By the time you arrive, there will be monitors in all the main rooms and hallways, even outside in the courtyard. Once established in Italy, Karl Busch, another friend, now with Europol, will take over your security. Karl is completely trustworthy and extremely capable. He is a highly decorated veteran. He laughed when I told him he may have to join a painting class to be near you."

She considered. They would escort her to the airport in the morning. She was not to worry. They had not yet found the weapon but they would keep looking. Tonight she was to sleep in one of the beds in the spare bedroom and be protected by guards.

She now understood why John had trusted this man but could he keep her safe as he had promised?

FOUR

In lieu of Emily's usual limo to the airport, she rode shotgun beside McGirr at the wheel of a Ford Explorer that looked as though it hadn't seen the inside of a carwash at any time during its five years of existence. Anyone passing them on the highway might notice the yellow Porsche in front of them or the black convertible driven by a buxom blond following them. Chances are no one gave a second glance at the dirty grey vehicle with dark tinted windows.

McGirr flashed her badge and left the vehicle parked outside the sliding doors leading into the airport. She ushered Emily into the building. They were immediately surrounded by other officers. Turner was standing directly ahead and gave a warm smile as they approached.

"Plan went off without a hitch, sir," McGirr announced as she approached Turner.

"Let's hope the rest of it goes as smoothly."

"Security in place, sir?"

"Security is ready and waiting, McGirr."

Turner turned to Emily. "We've rearranged the seating on the plane to help ensure your safety and comfort. You and Edgar will be in first class. We are in the process of doing background checks on all participants in the painting group. Surprisingly, there are several late entrants. We'll have security do an extra close check on all carry-on luggage for your flight."

He paused for a moment assessing her. "Emily, you all right?"

"I'm fine. I'm not accustomed to so much commotion."

"I'm not surprised. It took a lot of courage to continue with your travel plans. Hopefully this will help us flush out the people involved in this. I think you should know that in light of this new evidence, I am now officially reopening the investigation into your husband's death."

This last bit of information took her by surprise. Whatever the circumstances of John's death, he was gone forever from her life. And yet in a way, he was still there. She still felt his love and warmth at times. She had only to think of him and warm feelings would fill her consciousness.

She caught her breath. "John deserves justice. But it's been more than a year. Do you think you can find enough evidence to convict whoever killed him?"

He steadied his gaze on her. "I am more certain now than I was a year ago."

"Now I want to instruct you on how to protect yourself," he continued. "Two female officers will accompany you through the airport. Should you need to use the washroom, they will go with you. Do not accept food or drink from anyone other than Edgar or one of these officers. You are to remain glued to Edgar Morris from the moment you board the plane until you arrive at Villa DiMattia."

Emily listened and nodded as he spoke.

He kept up his monologue: "After boarding the plane, remain seated with Edgar. Alert him if you need to leave your seat for any reason. Wake him up if necessary. He must be aware of your movements at all times. You'll have a three-hour stopover in Rome before boarding your flight to Florence and from there you will be bussed to Villa DiMattia."

Again she signed her agreement as she listened.

"Your time in the Rome airport is of great concern to me. There have been serious security breaches in Europe over the past few years. Karl Busch, the Europol agent who will be in charge of this case, is reluctant to request security for you at the Rome airport. He believes the fewer people who know of your entry into the country, the better. Unfortunately his concern extends to people in law enforcement. He has chosen his staff for this mission with great care."

She nodded. "Can Mr. Busch meet us in Rome?"

He responded: "Unfortunately no! Are you comfortable going through the Rome airport with Edgar and his group of painters?"

"I am fine with that."

Turner pressed on: "Karl Busch and his partner Jerry Burns, are on assignment and are hoping to be available the day after you arrive in Tuscany. Once you reach the villa, Agent Ingrid Soll will see to your safety. Agent Soll is highly qualified. She is from the Central Security Operations Nucleus, which is an elite branch of the Italian police force."

"Sounds impressive!"

"My final point is this: don't allow yourself to be distracted by anyone, not even members of your painting group. Don't take anyone, no matter how sincere he or she may seem, into your confidence. Trust no one unless we tell you we have cleared that person."

"Your point is well taken. I'll be careful. Greg, you've obviously worked all this out with great care. I appreciate all the effort you've taken."

"Just doing my job, Emily. We'll continue searching your home today and as soon as we find the weapon I'll phone you. Then we'll get the word out through our undercover agents and the threat to you will disappear. Perhaps we'll find it today."

"I keep trying to recall anything John said that might help but I can't remember his ever mentioning hiding something and I'm certain he never talked about a weapon."

"I have a feeling the answer will come to you after you've had a chance to relax."

"I hope you're right."

"I feel you'll be safe going on this trip, otherwise I wouldn't have suggested you go. I've known Edgar Morris for years, he is a great guy and will protect you with his life if necessary. So try to enjoy yourself in spite of all else."

Edgar Morris bowed as she approached him. "I see you're wearing your regulation blue scarf."

"Do I have to wear it every day for the whole month?"

"Only if you want to."

She laughed. "I'll take that as a 'no'."

His smile vanished as he leaned close to her. "The artists are behind me."

"I can see them, Edgar."

"They're all wearing beautiful blue scarves."

She laughed. "Beautiful! I think beautiful is a rather extravagant term to describe our scarves, Edgar."

"See that little woman," he said as if he was disclosing a closely guarded secret.

She followed his line of sight. "You mean the lady wearing the brown jacket?"

"That's Jenny Adams. She's one of my veteran painters. If she tries to carry her bag, she could strain her back again. I forgot to tell her I'd carry it for her."

"Don't worry, Edgar, I'll tell her for you."

As Emily approached, Jenny Adams welcomed her into the group and began peppering her with questions. The tiny Irish woman introduced Emily to her friends, all of whom were long retired from various professions. When Emily finally had the opportunity to speak, she whispered, "Edgar told me about the problem with your back. He wanted me to tell you he'd carry your bag for you."

"Say that again."

This time Jenny and her friends were silent as Emily repeated Edgar's offer.

With a twinkle in her eye, Jenny announced, "He said that, did he? This means war, Edgar! Carry my bag! Ha! I may be old enough to be your mother . . ."

One of the others chimed in "grandmother!"

She continued with a gleam in her eye: "Makes me no nevermind! I'll fix him!"

Emily could feel herself blushing and turned towards Edgar who was busy talking to a woman with bright red hair. The woman was dressed in shades of pink and wore two-inch fuchsia heels.

Jenny followed her gaze and laughed out loud: "Well, lookie here! It's wearing a blue scarf! Let the fun begin."

After checking in with Edgar, the red-haired woman pranced in the direction of the other artists. Jenny mumbled, "This should be interesting."

When the lady in question realized her two-inch heels allowed her to tower over Jenny, she locked in on the tiny Irish woman. Everyone else smiled and moved in closer. An elderly gentleman, Emily remembered being introduced as Dr. Ned Jones, winked at her. The others seemed to be stifling giggles, some of them not very successfully.

"Don't you just love airports? They're such wonderful places to meet people," the red head gushed.

"You come here often," Jenny looked at the woman's name tag and added: "Miss Aiello?"

"My name is Gianna Aiello. I'm the manager at Louisa's Bistro in downtown Toronto. I'm sure you've heard of it."

"For sure! But, aren't you the cute up-town gal!" Jenny paused, then smiled. "Did you know that on one of these trips two of the painters fell in love and ran off and eloped?"

Gianna smiled winsomely. "Really!"

"Are you single?"

"Divorced."

"You are the marrying type?"

"Oh yes, I've been married four times."

Jenny's smile widened. Emily looked around at Jenny's friends. They were listening with great anticipation.

"Married four times? What happened to numbers one, two and three?"

"My first marriage was annulled. I was really too young and his mother didn't like me anyway. And my third husband was shot in the back of his head when he was visiting his cousin in Italy."

"What happened to two and four?" Jenny quizzed.

"My second husband said I spent too much of his money. I mean, is that fair? What's his, should have been mine too!"

"I agree with you completely. And number four?"

"Oh, him! He was such a bore. He thought I should sit at home and go visit his family all the time. That's no fun! I'm alive. I want to have fun. So I went out and had fun without him. You understand, don't you?"

Jenny was beaming. "I understand how you feel. I think you should get acquainted with Edgar. The poor fellow is alone in life and he's a real fun guy."

"You mean Edgar Morris, the leader of our group. I understand he's a well-known artist. He's not another pauper, is he? I hate it when I have to pay for dinner."

"He was heir to his grandmother's estate and he has a good job teaching art, plus he sells almost everything he paints. He's probably sitting on a nice little nest egg."

Emily thought of Edgar's tiny house on a back street in Dundas. His grandmother was an artist. If Edgar had a nest egg, he kept it well hidden.

Gianna replied, "Do you think he'd like me?"

Jenny assured her, "You're a shoo-in with your looks and taste in clothes. Wait until after we go through security. Then go ask him to carry your bag. He loves helping ladies with their luggage."

"Thanks. Gee, you're nice."

As soon as Gianna left to check in at the kiosk, Jenny announced in a stage whisper, "This is going to be fun."

The old doctor came over to Emily. He was a tall thin man who used a cane to walk. "Don't look so worried, young lady. This kind of high jinks goes on every year. It's all in good fun."

She looked up into laughing grey eyes, set in a long distinguished countenance. "Every year?"

"Oh yes! We've all known Edgar since he was a boy. We all studied watercolour under Mae Morris, his grandmother. He quit the forces so he could look after Mae when she took ill. After she was gone he starting leading these painting trips. The first year we came more as a tribute to Mae, but we had so much fun we've kept coming. I will admit that sometimes we don't get a lot of painting done"

"So you've come on every single one of Edgar's trips."

"Guilty! He treats us like royalty. We go either to Russ's villa in Tuscany or Alexandros' place in Patmos. You may want to come again next year. The trip to the Greek Islands is an adventure. Alexandros takes us by boat to some of the other islands. It's beautiful there."

Emily watched as an oriental woman who looked to be her age, greeted Edgar and then walked toward her. Ruth Zhou was a Chinese Watercolour painter and like Emily she was widowed. The more they talked the more they found they had in common.

Other people arrived. Emily smiled as introductions were made but she had already found her friend for the trip.

Edgar announced it was time to proceed toward security. The group was directed to the left conveyer belt.

When a small man wearing a beige overcoat and carrying a black valise tried to jump in line ahead of Emily, the two policewomen acted promptly. They grabbed the man. Another officer appeared out of thin air and whisked him away.

Emily was startled but tried to appear nonchalant. She removed her shoes and sunhat and placed them on the conveyor belt alongside her carry-on bag. When she realized her hands were shaking, she slowed her breathing, willing the trembling to stop. By the time she went through the metal detector, she was in control again.

Ruth was behind her. "The world is full of jerks."

As they began the long walk to the departure area, Emily looked for Edgar, hoping she could stay close to him.

She almost laughed out loud when she spotted Edgar carrying Gianna's bright pink carry-on. He had a look of desperation as he politely listened to what the red head was telling him. While Gianna looked glamorous in the two-inch heels, she wasn't able to walk very fast.

Jenny and her friends waved as they passed by on a passenger shuttle.

A man and woman both pulling bags came up close behind her. Again she looked back at Edgar who was too involved with Gianna to notice her concern.

A male voice whispered: "Don't worry, Ma'am. We're both security."

Ruth appeared on her other side again and began talking about her last flight or some such thing. Emily tried to smile or nod at the right time, but she was feeling exposed. Greg Turner was nowhere to be seen.

When she reached the departures area, someone had pulled three tables together. Jenny Adams was carefully approaching the table with a tall glass of beer in each hand. There was a trail of liquid behind her on the floor. She set one glass at the end of the table and then sat down and began to drink the second one. "That's just what the doctor ordered," she announced as she savoured the cool liquid.

A thoroughly frustrated Edgar arrived five minutes later. "I owe you one, Jenny! That was mean."

"Shut up and drink your beer, Edgar. You had it coming. The very idea—carry my bag!"

Emily burst out giggling.

Edgar stood up. "We are off to Italy! Let the fun begin! Let's get acquainted. We'll go round the table introducing ourselves. I'll start. My name is Edgar. If I were a spy, my undercover name would be 'the brush'. I'd be Edgar 'the brush' Morris."

Jenny asked, "We have to be a thing, Edgar?"

"No, you can be a colour or anything you want."

"My name is Jenny Adams and if I was a spy, my code name would be scorpion. I'd be Jenny 'the scorpion' Adams."

Emily listened intently to catch the names of the younger painters.

"My name is Mary Cominski and my code name would be 'the potato'."

"My name is Mary Josephine MacDonald and I already have a code name. It's 'MJ'."

"I'm Gianna and my code name is 'tulipano rosa'. That means pink tulip in Italian. So I would be Gianna 'tulipano rosa' Aiello."

There were three men at the end of the table. Emily wondered if they would take part. They did and introduced themselves as 'the knife' 'the whip' and 'the silencer'.

Last of all were Ruth and Emily.

Ruth announced her code name would be 'the dagger'. And Emily's codename was 'Wellington'.

Edgar announced: "I need six of you to volunteer to double up in your accommodations. I spoke to the hotel owners early this morning and was told that after accepting some late registrants, they found themselves overbooked."

He looked around at his group. "Who wants to volunteer to share?"

Emily and Ruth immediately agreed to be roommates. Actually, sharing a room would give Emily an extra measure of peace. The thought of being alone at all on this trip was rather frightening. With Ruth in the same room, she'd have a friend to chat with at night.

MJ and Mary Cominski agreed to share a room.

The two women couldn't have been more different. MJ was a very large, dark-haired woman with a booming voice. It was one of those voices that carried above the sound of everyone else's chatter. When she laughed, it was with a very loud cackle that reminded Emily of a cartoon character. MJ was the type of person who liked to be the centre of attention. Her loudness might be annoying at times but she seemed to be good-natured.

Mary Cominski was a small woman with a beak-like nose. Her soft tawny hair was drawn back in a chignon and she wore dark-rimmed glasses. She reminded Emily of the librarians from her childhood. She seemed a bit shy but most eager to make friends. Emily wondered if the sweet girl was alone in the world. It must have taken a lot of courage for such a quiet person to travel on her own.

Edgar nodded when two of the men seated at the end of the table agreed to share a room. They, as well, were a study in contrasts. Rolf Linski was white blond with icy blue eyes while Max Connor had darker skin and black hair.

Gianna announced to anyone who cared to listen that she was recently divorced from her fourth husband with a sizeable settlement and was looking to spread her wings. She looked up at Edgar who ignored her.

Jenny pointed toward the three men at the end of the table. Gianna pulled up a chair beside the tall man. He had introduced himself as Dave Rowe but Emily didn't remember seeing his name on the original list of painters. He had to be one of the late registrants Greg had spoken about.

When Emily was about to speak, an announcement from the airline drowned out her voice. Their flight would be delayed at least one hour. While other nearby passengers moaned a cheer went up from the members of the painting group. "Let's order another round of drinks!" MJ shouted.

Emily thought of her many trips with her husband. She had spent many hours waiting in first class lounges while John sat and read a newspaper and sipped a drink. This was new to her. These people were uninhibited. This was fun.

Edgar Morris stood up again and waved. "There's my old drinking buddy. Think I will go join him. You know him, Emily! Come join us!"

He picked up his tote and in a flash grabbed Emily's arm and her carry-on bag. His momentum was so great she was airborne for a short time as he lifted her out of her seat and propelled her along. When she turned around she saw Detective Turner approaching on a passenger shuttle. Security personnel appeared out of nowhere as she and Edgar were surrounded and escorted to the shuttle.

It all happened quickly. She had no idea that Edgar, who normally appeared slow moving, could lift her out of her seat so easily or move so quickly.

They climbed aboard the passenger shuttle and drove in silence for about two minutes until Turner stopped the vehicle. The officer with him grabbed Emily's carry-on bag and extracted a small button from under the handle. Then she used a small scanning device on both Edgar and Emily and produced yet another button from under the lapel of Emily's jacket. Both devices were quickly destroyed under the heel of her boot. She then asked Emily to remove her jacket. The officer scanned the jacket and handed it back to her.

"Both of you, climb back on. I'll explain things as we go. Two members of the cabin crew from your flight called in sick. That is why the delay, and I don't like it," Turner announced.

Then he looked at Emily. "Don't worry about these minor snags. Everything is under control. That man who pushed in front of you in the security queue became quite the talker after a little prodding. We saw him plant the bug on your bag. Word is out about the KZR weapon. Bidding has already started. Anyone with information leading to its recovery is looking at a hundred thousand in US dollars and the actual finder will reap ten times that. That little guy wanted a shot at a fast million dollars."

Emily was nervous again. "Greg, this is insane. Would I be better off at home? I don't want to endanger Edgar."

Edgar quickly chimed in, "I'd love a bit of excitement."

Turner continued, "Emily, my people haven't found the weapon and who knows, they may never find it. If we don't flush these people out, you won't be able to walk your dog or go to the grocery store alone. Next time it may not be your dog they try to run down, it could be you or another member of your family."

She appeared mollified. "Greg, you're right. Please forgive me."

He continued with alacrity: "There is nothing to forgive. Your reaction is perfectly normal under the circumstances. After the incident at security, we decided to transfer the two of you to another flight. You'll have a two-hour stopover in Amsterdam and arrive in Florence at least a half hour before the rest of the group. Proceed as we previously discussed after your arrival at the Amsterdam airport. Go to the first class lounge, and, Edgar, do not let her out of your sight, even if it means going into the washroom with her. Understand?"

Edgar gave a coy grin and said, "This is sounding like more fun all the time."

Turner continued, "Your flight was due to depart ten minutes ago. We delayed it to load your luggage and to wait for the two of you. Both of you will be seated in first class. Be vigilant! When you arrive at Villa DiMattia, Emily, don't get too close to anyone in the painting group. Edgar will let you know who has been cleared."

"I understand. But what will Edgar's group think with the two of us disappearing like this?"

Edgar laughed. "I told them, I spotted an old drinking buddy when I saw Turner driving up. They'll think I'm drinking in one of the bars. In any case, there's nothing to worry about. Jenny will take charge. She's probably bossing them around already."

Turner replied, "I'll speak to your friends, Edgar."

He slowed the shuttle as they approached the ramp to the plane. "Here we are. Say hello to everyone at the villa for me."

Several men stood waiting. Edgar looked serious as he climbed off the shuttle and shook hands and spoke with each of them.

It was a side of Edgar she had never seen before. She heard Turner groan with impatience.

As she approached she could hear part of the conversation. "Draco! At last we meet. It's an honour and a privilege. You ever want back on board, give me a call."

They walked down the ramp toward the waiting plane. As they passed through the doorway they overheard comments from passengers who were annoyed their plane's departure was delayed.

They were directed to the left and sat down somewhat breathlessly in the first class cabin.

"Are you always this exciting to be with?" Edgar asked with a grin on his face.

"No one ever mentioned it before," she responded.

She was beginning to realize there were great depths to this big bear of a man she thought she knew.

FIVE

As soon as Emily Clark fastened her safety belt, memories of her many trips with her husband came flooding back to her. The feeling of déjà vu keep reverberating through her consciousness.

Whenever they flew together John would down several glasses of scotch on the rocks and then doze off. He rarely tried to make conversation. She would feel so alone. She always brought a book to read. Reading helped pass the time on long flights and their flights always seemed to stretch on and on.

She forgot to bring a book this time. It didn't matter. She wouldn't be able to focus in any case.

As the engine roared for take-off, Edgar reached over and held her hand. "I'm afraid of flying. Mind if we hold hands?"

His touch on her hand pulled her out of her reverie and into the present. She tried to appear nonchalant and laughed. "You're telling me you are afraid to fly! You've got to be kidding me Edgar 'the brush'. Why did you give yourself a code name like 'the brush'. Surely you could have thought up something better for an alias."

"What do you mean something better? I think 'the brush' is a good alias for a painter. Can you think of anything better?"

"Something more exotic, like 'the dragon' would suit you. Yes, Edgar 'the dragon'! That's it!"

After Edgar finished choking, he replied, "When you announced your code name was Wellington, Jenny was really impressed. I didn't have the heart to tell her you wanted to impersonate your skinny dog."

As soon as they were airborne a cabin steward handed each of them a steamy hot facecloth. Emily absorbed the warmth into her inner self as she willed herself to relax.

Edgar watched her curiously. "What are you thinking, Edgar, 'the brush'?"

"I know what animal I would be, that is if I had chosen to be born an animal."

"OK, I'll bite. What animal would you be?"

"I'd be a giant black stallion. Yes, I'd be king of the horses."

"Edgar, I doubt very much horses think in terms of kings."

"Have you ever observed horses? Really observed them?"

"Well, no!"

"I have and there is always a boss horse. I would be the boss horse, king of the horses. What animal would you be?"

"Never thought about it."

"I think you might be a newt."

"A newt?" she uttered a loud guffaw and then cupped her hand over her mouth.

Dinner arrived and he continued his banter as they indulged in juicy steaks.

As soon as the dishes were cleared away he asked: "You ever think what you'd do if you had to spit on a plane?"

"Spit? Why would I have to spit on a plane?"

"Well, think about it. Years ago there were spittoons and everybody spit into the spittoons. But nowadays there's no official place to spit. Especially when you're on a plane."

"I can't believe I'm sitting here discussing spit."

"Oh, it's a very important topic. Do you have a lot of spit?"

"I'm not answering that."

"Some people have very little spit and then others, the lucky ones, have loads of it. Now they're the ones who need spittoons."

"Spittoons on planes! I'm going to ignore you and get some shuteye."

She lowered her seat back and listened as Edgar began chatting with the man across the aisle. She hadn't slept well the past two nights and longed to close her eyes and drift off into a dreamless sleep.

Edgar's voice permeated her subconscious. "Yea, I sort of rescued the little lady here. She was married to a pig farmer."

She punched his arm. "What do you think you're doing? Pig farmer! Pig farmer! I was never married to a pig farmer."

"Don't get your socks hot. Women do marry pig farmers, you know," he replied with a lopsided grin.

"You're right. But just what do you think you're doing, telling the man I was married to a pig farmer," she said while poking her finger into his arm.

He rubbed his arm pretending to be gravely injured. "You're too serious for your own good so thought I'd distract you a little bit. You know, give you something else to think about."

"Consider your job done. I'd love another glass of wine."

"I live only to serve your every wish, madam," he said with a grin.

She drank the wine and fell asleep.

She awoke to the aroma of freshly brewed coffee. The tall blond air hostess was standing over them with a tray. Edgar lowered her tray table.

The hostess smiled broadly. "Eddie insisted we let you sleep as long as possible. We'll be touching down in about forty-five minutes."

She looked at Edgar. "You let me sleep that long. I've never slept much on planes."

He smiled. "You looked so peaceful, I didn't want to disturb you."

"So you're Eddie now? What ever happened to Edgar 'the brush'?"

"Trying to keep you on your toes."

"You're doing a good job. Did you manage to grab a bit of shuteye?"

"Nope, I was busy."

"You were busy on a plane. I don't see a book or a laptop. There's nothing to do on a plane but sit and be bored or watch an old movie."

She paused and looked at him suspiciously. "Just what were you doing?"

"You'll see."

"That's what I'm afraid of."

After a smooth landing they rose from their seats.

The woman who sat across the aisle from them came up behind Emily. "Oh Emmy, I've been so eager to talk to you."

Emily looked at her questioningly and then she eyed Edgar who was looking straight ahead, not at her.

"I'm Carol and that's my hubby, Bill beside your Eddie. He told us last night how much you love fly fishing. I can't wait to have you both up to our cabin on Gods Lake. We'll take you over to Answap for some great walleye fishing. Bill also loves fishing at Aswapiswanan Lake. Maybe we can take you there as well. Last year he caught three giant bulldawgs in a single day at Aswapiswanan."

Emily eyed Edgar who was still fixated on a spot in front of him.

As soon as they were off the plane another passenger approached her. "Oh, Emmy, we're finally able to talk. My name is Charlene and this big guy is George. Eddie told us about how good you are with horses. Why, you're a real natural. I can't wait till you come visit our ranch. George works at the acute care centre in Fort McMurray and our ranch is just out of town."

When they were in line at passport control Edgar was beside her. They were still surrounded by their new best friends so she couldn't really talk.

Edgar or rather Eddie chatted happily with everyone, inviting them to come visit them in Dundas. If they came at the right time, he promised to fly some fresh lobsters in from Nova Scotia.

As they handed over their passports she quizzed him: "So Eddie, when did all this happen?"

"People like to talk."

"Since when did I go fly fishing. Fly fishing in Gods Lake! Where the hell is Gods Lake?"

"Northern Manitoba and don't forget Lake Aswapiswanan. There's good fishing there too."

"Yea and I'd probably need my body weight in bug repellant."

"I admit there is that."

"And riding horses?"

"Guess I kinda exaggerated your abilities there. But it was for your own good."

"My own good, my own good! How can you say that?"

"Think about this. We walked all the way from the plane to passport control and then we stood in line with everyone else for at least ten minutes and you never once worried about your own safety."

"My God, you're right. You are right. No one could have come near me with so many people crowding around us. But what happens when they phone and want to come visit 'us' in Dundas."

"Not my problem!"

"What do you mean not your problem? These are nice people, Edgar. It is your problem."

"I gave them your phone number," he responded with a grin.

She punched his arm as soon as their passports were stamped.

He rubbed his arm as though nursing an injury. "Ouch, Emily! You pack a wallop. You're bruising my beautiful body."

"You deserved that!" she replied.

After passing through passport control they saw a man waving a sign: MORRIS. Edgar ignored the sign and kept walking.

Emily missed a step and felt Edgar's arm go around her.

He whispered to her: "Emily, don't make eye contact. Security is just ahead. Above all, stay calm. Try to breathe normally. There's no need to panic. Keep walking."

Emily did as instructed. She held Edgar's arm and walked stiffly beside him.

A burly man walked up to the sign carrier and in a rough British accent announced, "Jason Morris here. What do you want, mate?"

When they reached the security area Edgar could feel Emily shivering so he drew her into a hug to reassure her. "Emily, it's all right. That sign wasn't meant for us. Relax! Nobody knows we're here. I'll keep you safe, my dear. Besides, I promised Paul I wouldn't let anything happen to you."

"You promised Paul?"

"Yes, I did."

"I bet Paul made you promise that."

"Your step-son insisted you needed looking after," he said barely suppressing a grin.

"That night you had dinner with my family, he did that, didn't he? I'll bet he waited till I wasn't there listening. Did he tell you to phone him if anything happened to me?"

"Yea, the guy was worried about you, so I bravely stepped up to the plate and promised to take extra good care of you." Then while trying to hide a grin, he added gently: "He thinks you're fragile."

A high pitched voice responded: "Fragile? Fragile! They've all been taking extra good care of me since I was widowed. That is precisely why I wanted to get away."

She stood straighter, grabbed her carry-on bag and tossed it onto the conveyer belt with determination. Then she removed her shoes, hat and jacket and loaded them in a pile behind her bag with equal determination.

Edgar grinned when he saw the stubborn look on her face.

As they progressed through security the burly man who had responded to the placard came up behind Edgar. Emily tried to listen hoping to prepare herself for whatever story Edgar was concocting now. The exchange was short and they proceeded towards their gate.

She knew they had a two-hour wait before their plane was due to depart and about thirty minutes of that two hours had already elapsed.

As they walked down the concourse past some shops, Edgar stopped. "Remember what Turner said about not letting you out of my sight even if you needed the washroom?"

She looked up at him. "I'm OK, I don't need the facility."

"Well, that's you. It works both ways. If I need the washroom, you—" he paused.

Realizing the implications of what he was saying, Emily tried to think of what to say. She eyed the men's washroom in front of them and watched as men came and went from inside the room. When she turned to look at Edgar, he gave her a wink and raised his eyebrows twice in quick succession. Edgar's effort at humour was immediately rewarded. Emily's laughter erupted from deep inside her.

They reached their appointed lounge area and sat in the corner against the wall so Edgar could scrutinize their surroundings.

Emily watched as the same burly man passed by several times. His sandy hair was cut close to his head. He had a faded scar that ran down the left side of his face bisecting his eyebrow and continuing down his cheek.

Seemingly oblivious to the menacing person who appeared to be stalking them, Edgar checked for messages on his cell phone and then looked at her. "Emily, when Gram died I had no one. Love passed me by in life. I realized then I could spend the rest of my days feeling sad or take a page from Gram's book of philosophy. She found humour in everything around her. Sometimes we'd go to parks or diners together just to people-watch and we'd make up stories about whoever we saw there. It was escapism, but fun. Want to grab some chocolate fudge sticks and do some people-watching?"

At the kiosk the man with the scar came up behind Edgar. Emily could have sworn he slipped something into his pocket. She wondered if it was a bug like the ones the man had planted on her at Pearson Airport. Edgar seemed not to notice but then he reached into his pocket and nodded.

They sat down and began their people watching. They didn't have to wait long for an interesting subject to arise. An old man with an attractive much younger lady sat three rows in front of them. Were they married? Was she his daughter? His mistress? His nurse? Emily bet one coffee that the woman was his mistress and when the lady in question kissed the doddering old man on the lips as she handed him a latte, they looked at each other and simultaneously mouthed the word 'mistress'.

They looked around for other interesting passengers for their little game. Anyone seeing them would never have guessed the circumstances surrounding them.

"Emily, don't you think it's amazing that we pass thousands of people in airports and never know what drama they're experiencing in their lives? Really, so much of the world is hidden from view."

"Yea, life is like that. Sometimes when you think you know someone but you find out later you don't really know them at all."

Edgar didn't respond because he knew she was referring to her late husband.

The mystery man with the scar reappeared as soon as their plane was announced.

"Edgar, who is that man? Don't pretend you don't know him. I saw you talking to him when we came through security."

"What man?"

"That man with the scar, that's who."

"Who? Him?" he said as he pointed to a businessman in front of them in the line-up.

"Edgar, stop it! You know who I mean. Tell me or I'll scream."

"You're scaring me now."

"I will scream!"

"Don't get your socks hot, Emily. I'd introduce you to the guy but he's afraid of women."

"He doesn't look like he's afraid of anybody or anything. What nonsense!"

"He is afraid of spiders, Emily. If I held up a spider, he'd run and hide. I wish I had a spider, I'd show you."

"I've had enough. John kept me in the dark all the time we were married. Things were happening around me and he never told me. I've had enough! I want to know. Edgar, tell me who he is." Her voice had risen in pitch.

She hesitated. "Oh my God, I'm sorry Edgar. You didn't deserve that!"

Edgar was grinning broadly when she finally looked up at him. "Good for you, Emily MacLean Clark! OK I will tell you who he is. I didn't tell you earlier because I didn't want you watching him. I didn't want anyone to think the three of us were together. His name is Jerry Burns and he and Karl Busch are partners at Europol."

"Karl Busch is the man Greg told me about. He'll be looking after me once we reach Villa DiMattia."

"That is correct. Now do you feel better?"

"We are safe here, aren't we? You look worried."

"I need you to do something."

"What's that?"

"Wrap your arm around me."

"What? This isn't one of your tricks, is it, Edgar?"

"We, you and I are going to pass by the ticket taker and then walk down the ramp to the plane attached at the hip. You understand?"

"You aren't kidding, are you? You have your reasons for this?"

"It's of no benefit to you to know the why or wherefore. You are in good hands. Simply do as I suggest."

She laid her head on his shoulder and put her arm around him. "Should I kiss you too?"

"That's carrying it a bit too far, don't you think?"

"You're probably right. I'll whisper sweet nothings in your ear, instead."

"And I thought this job would be a piece of cake," he muttered to himself.

Jerry Burns was behind them as they presented their boarding passes to the waiting attendant.

They followed the other passengers into the passageway leading to the plane. The ramp sloped downward. Several muscular men dressed in maintenance coveralls were milling around an open door about halfway down the ramp.

A voice with a thick British accent said, "Keep moving, Emily. Look straight ahead."

Edgar tightened his hold on her until they boarded the plane. Then he directed her to the back row of the small plane. As soon as she sat down, she realized Jerry was no longer with them. The passengers sat quietly for the next ten minutes. The three women who made up the cabin crew chatted with each other at the front of the plane but didn't make any effort to close the aircraft's door.

As soon as Jerry came on board, one member of the crew closed the door. The three women gathered around him and listened attentively to whatever he was saying to them. All of them giggled several times.

Emily poked Edgar. "You said he was afraid of women."

"Maybe I exaggerated a little bit."

"A little bit! Look at him! They think he's a matinee idol and he's eating it up."

"OK, so I lied. But it was only a little lie."

"I'm never going to believe you again."

"Not even if I tell you to use the washroom now because in five minutes, they're going to announce that the ones near us are broken."

She looked at him, undid her seat belt and ran into the washroom.

She was back in her seat by the time Jerry walked down the aisle. He winked at her before taking his seat across from them.

One air hostess picked up the microphone and began introducing herself and the other members of the cabin crew. She proceeded to go through the safety procedures and ended by informing the passengers to use the forward washrooms only.

While Edgar was chatting with Jerry, Emily drifted off to sleep. Edgar envied her, he was feeling somewhat sleep deprived, still he wanted to take stock of the events of the past 24 hours. Like Emily, he had been pulled out of his comfort zone. For anyone other than Emily Clark, he would have refused when Greg Turner phoned and asked him to act as a bodyguard. He wondered if Emily had any idea of the gravity of her situation. He wasn't about to frighten her with the details he'd gleaned from Turner. His sole involvement in this was to transport her safely from Pearson Airport to Villa DiMattia. He had a feeling that what she was involved in, wasn't going to end anytime soon. When she awoke he planned to give her some coping tactics.

She looked like an angel as she slept. Her, soft pale blond hair fell in gentle curls about her face. She was polished and sophisticated, yet completely natural.

A month ago she invited him to one of her Sunday evening dinners. She told him that he absolutely must attend so he could convince her son she'd be in good hands when she went to Italy.

When he arrived at her spacious and elegant home, he was further surprised. He had walked by the towering residence many times and was excited to receive an invitation to go inside. He expected all the trappings of wealth but found the home was low-key and comfortable. He expected her family to be a bit on the highbrow side and was surprised again.

The meal he was served, beat his own cooking by a country mile. After dinner, while Emily and the women were in the kitchen cleaning up, her son took him to the den to quiz him about the trip.

They sat in large comfortable chairs while a fair-haired toddler raced about on a miniature tricycle. When Edgar commented about the baby's resemblance to Emily, Paul immediately corrected him. "Oh no, she's actually my step-mother.

My father married a much younger woman after my own mother died."

The young man obviously cared very deeply for Emily. He explained that his 'mom' as he called Emily, had been in deep mourning for his father and he was very concerned for her well-being. If there was any problem, Paul insisted Edgar was to phone him immediately. When Edgar promised to give Emily special attention, little did he know things would take a rather ominous turn.

Emily awoke and smiled. "Did I snore?"

"Yes, very loudly! I was so embarrassed. Everyone was looking back at us. Jerry was pretending he didn't know us." That brought a smile to her lips.

"You know you're a sweet guy, Edgar 'the brush'."

"Hey, Em, you and I rub along pretty well together. You don't mind if I call you Em?"

"Edgar, you are the only person in the world I would ever allow to call me Em."

"We land in Florence in about ten minutes then we'll have at least an hour's wait before the rest of the gang arrives. I want you to stick to me like glue while we're at the airport."

"Got it!"

After another soft landing they made their way to the luggage carousel. The burly man whom she now knew to be Jerry Burns was never far away.

They retrieved their luggage and sat waiting in the morning heat for the arrival of the flight from Rome. Meanwhile the conveyor belt continued to circulate laden with a solitary bag. The battered unclaimed, old brown suitcase kept reappearing. It would vanish at one stage in its orbit to the outer part of the building and then return again to the passenger area, making its lonely trip over and over again.

The airport was almost deserted so they decided to walk down the concourse to stretch their legs. When a strange little man approached them, Edgar reached out and shook his hand in a friendly fashion. But the man seemed to crumble before her eyes. People began running both away and towards them. Edgar grabbed her arm and pushed her into a café.

"What happened, Edgar?"

"Guess he fainted. We don't need to be involved."

Edgar picked up lattes and biscotti at the counter and joined her at a table near the front of the restaurant. Jerry Burns stood directly across from them on the concourse. When Edgar held up his cup as if offering him a coffee, he shook his head.

They watched the news on the small TV on the wall behind the counter.

Finally, they heard a familiar cacophony of voices, distinguishable by the exceptionally loud sound of MJ's booming burst of energy, "We're here, at last we're here. What a long trip!"

The others followed ten feet behind her. After spotting Edgar and Emily sitting comfortably at the café, MJ rushed over with barrage of questions: "What's going on? You two are sitting here looking like you've been here for hours. How did you get here before us? We heard you were drinking like a fish with some old buddy. We thought you missed the plane."

Edgar held up his hand, in a gesture designed to quiet MJ. "Yeah, guilty of bending my elbow with an old friend. We missed our flight so they stuck us on another one and lo and behold, we raced you lot here."

MJ seemed pleased with his explanation. It was clear looking at their faces, some of the painters had imbibed copious amounts of spirits during the long flight. They were a faded replica of the once vibrant group Edgar had welcomed at the Toronto airport.

MJ gave Edgar a brief rundown of her flight from Toronto. It was more information than either Edgar or Emily cared to hear but they sat and listened attentively. Then she decided she would take control of Mary Cominski. The big lady grabbed Mary's luggage off the carousel while proclaiming in a loud voice, "Let me help you. Don't want you hurting yourself."

Mary replied in a determined voice, "I am quite capable of handling my own bags. Thank you." She pulled her large suitcase away from MJ and began walking down the concourse.

MJ was quick to repent, "Oh, please forgive me, Mary. I become over-exuberant at times. When I was growing up my brother used to tell me I reminded him of a tsunami. I don't mean any harm. You'll still be my roommate, won't you?"

Before Mary could respond, a shout rang out, "Rinaldo, darling! Hello, you beautiful man! I didn't expect to see you here!" Gianna, with her unruly mass of bright red hair looking uncombed, pulled off her two-inch heels and ran ahead of the group. She threw herself into the arms of a tall, darkly handsome Italian man. "Everybody, meet Rinaldo, the cousin of my late third husband. Oh, Rinaldo, you are more handsome than ever. How wonderful to see you again! I'm so glad you came to meet me."

The tall, dark Italian responded in a voice that reeked of sexual innuendo. "For you, sweet pet, I would go anywhere. I have time to drive you to your hotel in my new Ferrari."

Gianna was bubbling with excitement. "Oh Rinaldo, that would be fantastic. We'll have plenty of time to visit along the way. Let's put my luggage on the bus. I doubt your fancy car has enough room for all my bags."

Rinaldo looked at the redcap pushing an airport cart loaded with four pink suitcases piled high and rolled his eyes: "Some things never change, do they, sweetness?"

They all smiled and welcomed Gianna's friend Rinaldo, but on closer inspection there was a certain oiliness about the man. He was strikingly handsome from afar, but up close his features appeared much less refined.

Edgar pulled Emily aside. "Em, this guy is trouble."

"I guessed that as soon as I saw him. Don't worry I'll be careful around him."

They continued walking down the concourse towards the exit and the awaiting bus. Emily was careful to stay beside Edgar. He texted Turner to let him know they made it safely to the Florence airport and were now on their way to board the bus for Tuscany.

When they reached the bus Edgar directed Emily to climb on board while he spoke to the driver.

Jenny Adams was already on the bus and informed Emily and Ruth that Edgar always sat in the first seat and the next five rows on both sides were reserved for her friends. She and Ruth were welcome to sit anywhere but there. They obliged by sitting a couple rows behind them.

Edgar helped the driver load the luggage into the belly of the bus. He seemed intense as the two men talked.

Dave Rowe and his two friends, Linski and Connor had disappeared somewhere inside the airport. The luggage was now loaded but there was still no sign of the three men.

She could hear Jenny grumbling. "Where are those three clowns?"

As soon as Dave Rowe appeared, Jenny commented, "Here comes that long drink of water, but where are black and white?"

Someone ventured, "They do have names, Jenny."

Jenny continued grumbling: "What good are names when they only talk to each other? Why'd they come on the trip anyway? They're not the least bit friendly."

Max Connor and Rolf Linski finally appeared and nodded to Rowe who was standing beside the bus. The three men climbed on, followed by Edgar and the driver.

Ruth was looking weary. She told Emily how difficult it was to sleep on their flight from Toronto. Apparently Gianna and several others were drinking and decided to amuse themselves by singing. "They actually thought they could sing in harmony. Can you imagine? No, you probably can't. You had to be there to get the full effect. I suspect at one stage the flight attendants might have considered opening the hatch and tossing a couple of them outside. I know it crossed my mind."

Ruth was happily married to an executive with an electronics firm and together they had travelled the globe. When he died of cancer three years before, she went to work in her family's flower shop and took up Chinese brush painting. This was to be her first painting trip and she was eager to take lessons from the renowned Edgar Morris. It surprised Emily how many things she and Ruth shared in common.

Ruth's parents emigrated from Hong Kong and integrated into the Canadian way of life. She sometimes returned to Hong Kong to visit cousins. When Emily asked about her life with her late husband, she said she was still mourning him and didn't want to talk about him.

As she relaxed into her seat, Emily hoped that by now Turner had found the KZR weapon and the nightmare surrounding it would be over. Then she could go back to being of interest to only her family and closest friends, and her quiet small-town life would be restored.

She didn't want to think of the consequences if Turner could not find the weapon.

SIX

Their bus followed an identical bus as it departed the Florence airport. Five minutes later they turned right while the first bus continued straight through a traffic light. For the next ten minutes the passengers were treated to back alley views of Florence. The driver didn't reduce his speed when the bus went through an alleyway where the buildings were so close, you could almost reach out and touch them. Then as if a door had been opened, they drove into the bright sunshine of the Tuscan countryside.

Now there was only a smattering of yellow ochre stuccoed houses beneath terracotta roofs. Intense blue skies posed as a backdrop to soft green olive trees, and grasslands broken up by the occasional mountain. The vibrancy of the landscape caused all but one of them to feel somewhat rejuvenated.

Loud snores erupted from the rear of the bus. MJ was informing everyone within ear shot she was asleep. Her snoring was punctuated by episodes of snorting.

Ruth offered, "Should I wake her up?"

Emily laughed, "She's tired like the rest of us. Let her sleep."

Ruth replied, "But Edgar said the trip will take over an hour. I don't want to listen to that all the way there."

Mary Cominski moved up and sat opposite Emily and Ruth. "I volunteered to share a room with MJ. What'll I do if she snores like that every night?"

Jenny Adams, who was snooping as always, supplied a solution. "Ask Edgar to buy you some ear plugs. That's what you'll do."

The bus turned right and followed along what looked more like a cow pasture than a road.

Emily knew that whatever detours the driver was taking were for her benefit alone.

Jenny called out, "This isn't our regular road to Villa DiMattia, Edgar. Where are you taking us?"

Edgar picked up his mike. "We are traversing the pristine countryside of Tuscany. I asked Mario, our driver, to take us to areas where tourists never go. I'm looking for some new places to paint."

Edgar turned off the mike and picked up his cell phone. As he listened Emily realized she had never seen him look so serious.

The man, Jenny had nicknamed Black came to the front of the bus. Edgar put his cell down. They all strained to hear the conversation over the noise of MJ's snoring.

Black was obviously complaining about the route they were taking: "Why aren't we using the highways? This is a needless waste of time."

"Take it easy, Max. It's a painting trip not a race."

"Why is your cellphone working? I can't get any reception here."

Everyone watched as Edgar stood to his full height and faced the dark-haired man. "It's a satellite phone, Max. I'm using a satellite phone."

Edgar reached into his right hand pocket. It was the same pocket into which she had seen the Europol agent put something. His left side was facing her so she couldn't see if he pulled the object out of his pocket or not. Black looked down in the direction of the pocket, nodded and pivoted to return to his seat.

His eyes were focused on his travel companions at the back of the bus. He didn't notice a cane and an art bag quickly jut out and then disappear at the level of his feet. Emily noticed them. It was a concerted effort because the cane was resident with eighty-year old Dr. Ned Jones sitting on the left side of the bus and the art bag belonged to seventy-five year old Jenny Adams, on the right side of the aisle.

Black hit the floor just as the bus went over a particularly nasty bump.

She heard Jenny intone. "Oops!"

Then she added in an almost motherly fashion. "You all right, dear?"

Black picked himself up off the floor of the bus and disappeared into his seat beside his friend, White.

Edgar resumed his seat. His expression was stern. He continued to talk into what they now knew to be a satellite phone.

Ruth had fallen asleep and missed the whole scene.

Emily sat watching as beautiful areas of the Tuscan countryside were paraded before her.

Her trips with her late husband now seemed austere, even sanitized. There was a time when she had revelled in the sheer luxury of their extravagance. Now as she sat watching the concern on Edgar's face, listening to the excited chatter among Jenny's friends, trying not to listen to MJ's loud snoring from the back of the bus, she felt alive. Crazy as it sounded, she felt more alive than she had in years.

As the bus eased its way over another pothole, Jenny called out, "I remember that store. We're almost there, folks."

They could see the villa from a distance. It shone golden brown in the dazzling sunlight. As the bus slowly drove up the steep hill, the building came into view just as Ruth woke up. One of the men gave MJ a shake and the loud snoring stopped.

Villa DiMattia is a fifteen-minute drive from the old walled city of Lucca and stands on thirty hectares of land beneath Mount Pizorno.

They passed olive groves and vineyards as they neared the villa. The air was clear and fresh and the afternoon sun, unusually warm and bright.

The villa is a renovated monastery which holds twenty guest rooms, all with beamed ceilings. It is a favourite holiday spot for many German and Austrian vacationers.

In contrast to the tranquility of the surrounding area, the painting group boisterously descended from the bus eager to stretch their legs. Emily wondered what the other guests must think of this noisy troop disturbing their serenity.

Gianna and Rinaldo had arrived ahead of the bus. They stood leaning on a dark green Ferrari. The two were engaged in an animated conversation and appeared to be enthralled with each other.

A man and woman came out of the villa to greet them. The older members of the group rushed over to exchange greetings with the couple.

Edgar introduced them as Russ and Pia DiMattia, the owners of the villa.

MJ was the last to exit the bus. When she reached the lowest step, she trumpeted, "I'm gonna be sick. I gotta puke! Where can I barf?"

She ran in the direction of the green Ferrari. They all watched in amazement as Rinaldo stood firmly in front of his vehicle and held out his arms. He began shouting, "Not on my car! Go puke somewhere else! Over there! Not on my new green Ferrari! Go away!"

"Aah!" MJ gave a loud retch as she ran past him. She made it as far as a large planter and stood over it making loud retching noises.

Meanwhile Rinaldo was examining his previously pristine shoes and pant legs and making disgusting snorting noises.

Emily felt as though she was being watched and looked around. While everyone watched the commotion around MJ, Edgar's eyes were firmly fixated on her. His eyes barely wavered when Ruth left her side and went to help MJ.

Ruth tried to offer some wipes to MJ. "I don't want those. They're bum wipes. I need a facecloth and towel."

Ruth spoke gently, "Mary, I mean MJ, the wipes are moist. I use them whenever I travel. Here let me help you."

Edgar's focus did not waver. Occasionally he would do a sweep of the area but then his eyes would come back to rest on Emily.

When she heard the noise of an engine straining as a vehicle climbed the steep hill to reach the plateau where the villa stood, he pointed to a space beside him. She nodded and stood next to him.

"How are you doing?"

"Better than expected, actually."

"You're looking more relaxed."

"Edgar, now that you know the people involved in this, is it all necessary? Can't you just arrest them?"

"Em, Dave Rowe and his pals Black and White as you like to call them, are the tip of the iceberg. To grab them now would serve no purpose. We want to find out who they're working for. Don't worry it'll all be over soon."

"What happens if Greg can't find the weapon?"

He touched her arm reassuringly. "Trust him, Em." He paused and then continued: "You know, when Gram died she promised her favourite locket to Gladys Johnson, our next door neighbour. I searched for months trying to find it."

"You ever find it?"

"Gram left it on my own dresser. It was in plain sight all the time."

"You think I'll find the weapon like that? In plain sight?"

"Something like that unless your husband was some kind of a joker."

"He was anything but."

Pia and Russ DiMattia joined them.

Pia was a short pretty woman. Her dark hair was drawn back into a ponytail. Her husband was taller, but not by much.

Pia's dark blue eyes almost seemed to dance and she hugged Edgar. "You brought us an interesting group this year, Edgar. I'll bet the trip here was fun."

Edgar laughed. "You don't want to know!"

Russ shook Edgar's hand. "The guys worked through the night putting in the security system. Karl was able to cut short his stay in Geneva and is flying in now. I expect he'll grace us with his presence later this afternoon. Meanwhile, Agent Ingrid Soll is in charge."

Emily asked, "Agent Soll?"

Pia responded, "She's a high-level Italian police officer. I guarantee you won't like her."

Emily chuckled, surprised at her comment. "Is she that bad?"

Pia and her husband responded in unison: "Worse!"

Edgar collected the group together and suggested they'd adjust to the Tuscan time zone faster if they didn't sleep until after dinner. The artists exchanged smiles and agreed, but all headed to their rooms and closed their doors.

As weary as Emily and Ruth were, their eyes danced when they opened the door to their room. They examined the Italian provincial furniture set in a spacious room with beamed ceilings. The dressers and night tables were painted a soft cream with medium blue trim and hand painted bouquets of roses. The bathroom boasted two porcelain sinks raised above a marble countertop. At the end of the bathroom stood an ultra-modern enclosed shower with large white towels that were soft and absorbent to the touch. The tall elegant windows featured ecru lace under gold and black stripped curtains, held back by black silk swags. The overhanging gently scalloped valance was also done in gold silk. The three paintings in the room were antique in appearance and featured scenes from Renaissance Italy. The paintings had a sort of faded appearance, which added to their look of authenticity.

Ruth whispered, "This room could only exist in Tuscany."

Emily replied, "Let's check out the balcony."

They opened the door to the balcony and stood there in silent wonderment. They were both delighted with the prospect of spending a whole month in this charming room with its breathtaking view. They could see Mount Pizorno in the distance. The air was fresh and clean. The Villa's elevation was so high that the sunlight appeared almost lemon-yellow in colour.

Finally Ruth announced, "I want to take the first shower. I hope you don't mind! After the long plane ride, I'm feeling rather desperate to clean up."

"Go ahead, so long as I can have first choice of beds. I want the one closest to the sliding door. You shower and I'll unpack," yawned Emily.

While Ruth was showering, the phone rang. As Emily picked up the receiver, an accented voice announced, "Hello, is this Mrs. c-c-c-Clark?"

"Yes," Emily responded.

"I am Agent Ingrid Soll with the Italian police. I am in charge of all Italian police personnel on this case. I will be overseeing your security. You are to come to the dining room immediately."

Emily was surprised at the officer's abrupt manner. She spoke with a pronounced Italian accent. Perhaps she didn't realize how she sounded when she spoke in English.

Agent Ingrid Soll was pouring herself a cup of coffee when Emily entered the room. Emily thought herself tall at five-foot eight but Ingrid Soll was three or four inches taller. Ingrid Soll's face was long and dark in tone. Her glossy black hair framed features that while not individually perfect, together made her appear attractive. Her large dark brown eyes were widely spaced and emphasized with black eyeliner. Her nose was straight and even. Her full lips were covered with a thick layer of intense red lipstick. A dark mole strategically located over the left corner of her upper lip enhanced her already seductive appearance.

"Hello, I'm Emily Clark. You must be Agent Soll."

"Mrs. c-c-c-Clark," the police woman seemed to struggle with her name. "We meet at last. You are the widow of John c-c-c-Clark. He chose you as his wife."

She emphasized the word 'you' as she scrutinized Emily.

"Yes, I am. I lost my husband a year ago."

"People die every day."

Emily's breath caught in her throat. She saw the creases around Soll's mouth deepen as she watched her discomfort and realized the woman was enjoying her reaction. She vowed not to give her the same opportunity again.

"Detective Turner believes my husband was murdered, Agent Soll."

"That is not my concern."

This time Emily didn't flinch. She tried to appear nonchalant. "I know that. If we're going to be working together, please call me Emily. Do you mind if I call you Ingrid?"

The vehemence of Agent Soll's response surprised Emily. "Soll! I am known as Soll. You will call me Soll. If you have any questions, you will come to me."

"Detective Turner told me Karl Busch would be looking after me?"

"Detective Turner may know how things work in Canada but not here in Europe. I am a special agent with the Central Security Operations Nucleus under the Minister of the Interior and I am the one in charge here. Agent Busch will involve himself with important matters as part of a Joint Investigative Team, only. You should know he is a formidable investigator and will want to focus on gathering facts not babysitting you. I will not permit you to annoy him. You are to stay away from him. Do you understand?"

"But I thought . . ."

"You will stay away from him." This time Soll's tone was almost threatening.

The intensity in the room was almost palpable.

Thankfully Pia DiMattia chose that moment to waft into the dining room humming a Puccini aria in a soft low voice. She stopped humming and walked purposefully to their table. She pointedly ignored Soll as she placed a small tray in front of Emily. "Emily, Edgar told me you prefer tea so I brought you a fresh pot of my favourite blend. He also tells me you're a chef. We must compare notes. Tell me what you think of my almond cookies. It's a new recipe."

Pia looked over at Soll and added, "I won't interrupt any further."

Emily deliberately took her time pouring her tea. She picked up the tea strainer and placed it over her cup. Then she gently shook the pot and slowly poured the dark brew into her porcelain cup. Normally she drank her tea nude but this time she added a few grains of sugar and a tiny bit of milk and then slowly stirred the mixture. Meanwhile Soll's face had gone from normal to carmine.

Emily looked at Soll and smiled. "I understand Karl Busch is due to arrive late this afternoon."

Soll seemed to grow less rigid as she began to tell Emily about Karl Busch's many decorations in the line of duty. She spoke eloquently about how wonderful he was to work with. Unfortunately he often preferred to work alone. This assignment was ideal because they could spend as much as a month together.

Any question about Karl Busch seemed to deflect Soll's anger. She would bear that in mind when she dealt with Soll in the future. The thought crossed her mind that maybe she could survive a month dealing with Soll but that thought was jettisoned when Soll abruptly changed the subject: "Where is the KZR weapon? You are the only link to it. You must know where it is."

Emily tried to appear blasé as she replied, "I first heard of the thing two days ago. In fact, I had no idea my husband owned a gun until then. The police were scouring my house for the weapon when I left. I wish they'd hurry up and find it. I really don't appreciate all this attention."

Soll studied Emily intently. Emily sensed the officer didn't believe her, but she refused to let her old shakiness return.

Soll led Emily on a tour of the villa and pointed out the location of the newly installed security cameras as they walked through the hallways and down the servant's back stairway. "You will be safe while you are here. I never slip up."

Emily didn't doubt her. Who would dare cross the woman?

Emily returned to her room and chatted with Ruth until just before seven o'clock. Then the two of them made their way to the dining hall. They spotted some of their fellow travellers already sitting around two tables. The painters looked less like the derelicts who had climbed off the bus several hours before and more like the human beings who boarded the plane in Toronto.

Edgar was standing at the door and directed them to a table in front of a window. Gianna and Rinaldo were seated at one end and Dave Rowe, Black and White, were at the other end. It didn't take a psychic to determine that Rowe was not pleased as he watched the interplay between Gianna and Rinaldo.

Edgar informed them, "Pia reserved two tables for my group. Both of you are to sit there."

She asked, "What about that other table, Edgar?"

"That's reserved for the 'Over 75 Club'."

"The Over 75 Club? What's that?"

"Last year, it was the 'Over 74 Club' and I expect next year it'll be the 'Over 76 Club'. In other words you can only sit with them if you are as old as the youngest member of the group and neither of you qualify."

"And the youngest member of the club is Jenny?"

"You got it. She sets the rules. Occasionally, she'll adopt someone and declare them an honorary member, but to my knowledge neither of you have been adopted by her so you'll have to sit with Gianna and Rinaldo." With a grin he added, "Have fun!"

Ruth joined MJ and Mary Cominski as they made their way to their table.

When they were out of ear shot, Edgar said, "Hey Mrs. c-c-c-Clark, I understand you had the pleasure of meeting Countess Dracula."

Emily rolled her eyes. "You obviously mean Soll and yes, I met her, though I wouldn't use the word 'pleasure' in referring to our meeting."

"Her weak grasp on sanity is challenged whenever she thinks of you. Were you mean to her?"

"Me? Mean to her? Edgar, you know bloody well it was the other way around. If she thinks I'm going to put up with her nonsense for a whole month, well, she's out to lunch! She was abrupt on the phone when she called and asked me to meet her. At first I thought it was a language barrier thing, but when we talked, I couldn't believe how callous the woman was."

"You know what, Em, the woman is hitting high C for no apparent reason. I have a feeling there's more going on here than you or I are aware of. Think of it as a painting. Sometimes things come out of the background that help define the foreground or subject matter. Try looking at the negative space."

"How do I avoid her for the whole month?"

"Stand up for yourself. I'll see what I can do to intercede with Karl, but it's really up to you."

Edgar indicated a table in the corner. "The blond guy sitting with Jerry Burns is Karl Busch. Tomorrow morning after our first art lesson, I'll introduce the two of you. He wants some time to get up to speed before talking to you."

Emily followed Edgar's line of sight to the blond man sitting opposite Jerry Burns. When the man in question looked up, their eyes met. The intensity of his gaze took her by surprise. She stood there like a deer caught in the headlights. He lowered his eyes as if responding to something Jerry said and she felt herself released.

She said to Edgar as they walked toward their table, "Your friend seems intense? What's he like?"

"He's devoted to police work, perhaps a bit rigid but all in all he's one of the finest people I know. You can trust him, Em. Come on, let's grab a seat. I'm starving."

As soon as she sat down, Emily quickly realized that almost everyone at the table was making an effort to avoid looking at

Gianna and Rinaldo, who were huddled together at one end of the table cooing in each other's ears. The one exception was Dave Rowe who sat rigidly at the opposite end of the table. He was glaring at them with such intensity that his closely spaced eyes took on a very narrow appearance. Empty glasses were lined up in front of him.

Emily whispered to Edgar, "What's going on here? I feel like I'm sitting on a firing range."

He countered, "Apparently Gianna was glued to Rowe on the flight over and dropped him like a hot potato the minute she spotted Mr. Oily at the airport."

"That explains it."

Antipasti was served first and consisted of *prosciutto di Parma* with fresh melon. Next a plate of squid and clam risotto was served, followed by cappone in agrodolce, which featured walnuts, steamed figs, green olives, cloves, cream and Tuscan wine. This was followed by a salad of radicchio and field greens to cleanse the palate and lastly, fresh fruit sliced and served in a white wine to finish off the meal.

Coffee was essential at the end of the meal.

Rinaldo ordered the most expensive white wine on the menu for Gianna and himself and made an extravagant ceremony of sniffing the cork before insisting he be allowed to fill Giana's glass himself. His boasting took on epic proportions as he talked about his great financial successes. He was clearly trying to antagonize Dave Rowe and succeeding masterfully. By the time the salad arrived, Rowe had clearly had enough. He rose from his seat and swayed. Black and White jumped up and helped their friend out of the dining room.

Rinaldo found the scene immensely entertaining and looked around for someone new to torment. He turned his dark eyed focus on Mary Cominski who was sitting beside him. "Aren't you the lovely ray of sunshine."

It was at this point that Mary jumped up and ran out of the dining room.

Edgar followed after her.

Rinaldo and Gianna made a strategic exit from the dining room shortly afterwards.

A couple minutes later, an annoyed Edgar returned. "That guy has roving hands. Keep away from him."

"How is Mary?" Emily asked.

"She's fine. I'm going to have a talk with Rinaldo Rizzi. He wants to join our painting group for the next week but, after this incident, that's not going to happen."

MJ responded, "Edgar, be careful. He's a dangerous man. Don't annoy him. If he's going to be with us for only one week, we'll all keep away from him."

He was surprised. He hadn't expected words of caution from one of the late registrants: "Thank you, MJ. I appreciate your advice."

MJ continued: "Don't worry about Mary. We'll keep him away from her."

Ruth was nodding in agreement. Considering both women signed on late for the trip, Edgar wasn't sure if this was a good thing or a bad thing.

He escorted Emily and Ruth back to their room while MJ made her way to the bar.

Emily and Ruth were both suffering from jet lag. As soon as they closed their door, they wasted no time climbing into bed. This time they didn't delight in the luxuriousness of their bedroom nor did they even bother to re-examine the view from their balcony. The lights were barely out when they fell asleep. They missed the loud noises emanating from the room below them; the room occupied by Gianna and Rinaldo. They also missed other noises in the night. But Edgar heard those noises and took action.

SEVEN

The following morning both Ruth and Emily breathed a sigh of relief when they entered the dining room and saw no sign of Gianna and Rinaldo at their table. They loaded their plates with goodies from the buffet table and found seats beside MJ, Mary and Edgar.

Dave Rowe was sitting rigidly at the far end of the table. He was making eye-contact with his coffee and occasionally with a piece of dry toast. Five empty tomato juice cans were lined up like soldiers in front of him.

After exchanging the usual niceties with Emily and Ruth, Edgar looked up and grinned. "This gets better all the time. Don't look, they'll come to us."

Black and White pulled up chairs on either side of Dave who scowled as he eyed them. Both men appeared almost terminally hung-over.

Black was wearing a T-shirt that read 'Kick Your Ass Boxing'. White's shirt was equally as interesting. It read: 'Pot Here' and featured an arrow pointing upward. Below that were the words 'No Pot Here' with a downward facing arrow. Their T-shirts strained to contain their enormous pectorals and biceps.

White looked directly at Mary and winked. "Where's the coffee?"

Edgar responded: "Food is buffet style for breakfast. The waiters will bring coffee over to you."

Both men rose and headed toward the buffet tables. They returned with a whole carafe of coffee and a jug of cream but no food.

Black poured coffee for both of them. White added cream and enough sugar to cause tooth decay. Neither one of them looked particularly healthy as they gingerly tasted their drink.

Emily watched as Edgar put his hands over his face and mumbled, "Oh God!"

Jenny was smiling brightly as she cheerfully placed a plate laden with food before each of them. "I thought you boys needed a bit of protein. See, I even broke open your eggs for you. I knew both you boys would like nice runny soft boiled eggs. And that blue cheese was meant for one of my group but he didn't feel like it today. So I gave it to you."

She returned to her table amid the occasional titter.

As the sulphuric aroma of the eggs and even more pungent fragrance from the blue cheese wafted up the table, Black's pallor took on shades of something between moss and Hooker's green.

Edgar focused on his wrist watch.

As soon as Black and White headed for the door, Edgar looked up and announced, "Thirty-seven seconds. Not bad. I would've given them thirty at tops."

Five minutes later Dave gave a low growl as Gianna entered the dining room. She smiled as she locked in on him. "Rinaldo and I ordered room service. I love breakfasting in bed. Don't you?"

Then she announced to the whole table, "You have to go where the money is."

Edgar rolled his eyes as she flounced out of the dining room. No one ventured a comment but Dave Rowe rose unsteadily from his seat. Then he stood ramrod straight and walked out of the dining room like an automaton.

An hour later, the artists followed Edgar to the terrace. The golden brown stone covering the exterior walls of the villa seemed to glow in the morning sun's brilliance. Emily slowly breathed in the fresh air, scented with the aroma from the many flower pots.

As soon as Edgar stopped, Jenny and her Over 75 Club arranged their stools in a neat semi-circle around him and promptly sat down. The others arranged themselves behind them.

Edgar grinned as he watched Gianna and Rinaldo try to slip in unnoticed.

When the commotion died down Edgar began. He pointed to the planter on his left. "We will be painting this planter today, but first I want to go over some of the ground rules for those of you who are new to all this."

In a stage whisper MJ spoke to Ruth, "Tell me that's not the one I puked in."

Edgar heard and tried to hide a smirk. "No, it's not, MJ. They sent that one out to be sand-blasted. Let's get started. Show respect for your fellow painters by always arriving at the times designated on the calendar. If you miss the bus, you must find your own way back to the villa. Raise your hand if you understand what I just said."

Hands promptly shot up.

He looked through the group. "Max? Rolf? What about you?"

Everyone turned around and looked at Black and White. Under intense scrutiny, two muscular arms were raised as far as their shoulders but no higher.

"Good! So I will assume if any of you are not at the bus at the designated time, you'll find your own transportation back."

Emily thought his warning a bit stern but then he knew who he was dealing with. Besides artists are notorious for doing their own thing and on their own timetable.

"I want you all to welcome Rinaldo Rizzi who will be joining us for the next week."

Jenny turned around. "Welcome, Rinaldo. Looking forward to seeing your work."

Ignoring her comment Edgar continued: "For your comfort, we will travel in an air-conditioned coach with Mario as our driver. On this trip we visit Lucca, Pisa, Florence, Cinque Terre, Barga and Sienna. We will also attend an opera in Lucca as well as several concerts in churches and at Teatro del Giglio, the Lucca concert hall. There will be free days when you can take the shuttle into Lucca, a train ride to Florence or relax around the swimming pool. Any questions?"

He looked around and when nobody responded, he continued: "I will be giving lessons Monday through Friday. I promise to keep my lectures short. At the end of each week, there would be a 'bring and brag' session. Artists are welcome to display what they consider their best works. I will try to make myself available for individual instruction if any of you want it, as I realize there is a great diversity of training levels within the group. I will also give private critiques to anyone who requests them."

Gianna raised her hand. "What if some people need paint?"

"You can buy art supplies in Lucca this afternoon. We will meet in the courtyard after lunch for our trip to Lucca. The bus will depart from the main gate of the city at 4pm. When we return you can change into your swim suits for our pool party."

MJ's voice rang out: "A pool party with free drinks?"

Edgar nodded. "One free drink only, MJ."

"I don't have a bathing suit. How can I go to a pool party without a bathing suit?" MJ asked.

"Pick up whatever you need when we go to Lucca. Right now, I want to take a ten-minute coffee break. When I come back I'll review some to the basics of painting with watercolour with you. If you are a beginner, don't miss this lesson," Edgar announced as he surveyed his students.

As soon as he could separate himself from the group, Edgar came to Emily. "Come with me. Karl Busch is waiting in the office to meet you."

She followed him to an office which overlooked the front courtyard. The blond man Edgar had pointed out in the dining room the previous night, now sat upright behind a polished mahogany desk. Two men sat on either side of a maroon leather sofa against the opposite wall.

Edgar made the introductions: "Emily, this is Karl Busch and you have already met Russ DiMattia and Jerry Burns."

She shook hands with Busch and pivoted to face the other two. Both stood to acknowledge her. Jerry held out his hand. "We haven't actually met. More like we eyed each other at the Amsterdam Airport."

He spoke with a British accent so thick she struggled to catch every word. When he smiled, she wondered why she had ever been afraid of him. She barely noticed the long scar which she had fixated on the previous day.

Edgar sat on the sofa between them.

She turned to face Busch.

His enormous size and air of authority amazed her. He was handsome in a very masculine sort of way. He was a very physical man.

He looked past her to the three men lounging at the other side of the room.

"Don't you guys have some place you should be?"

There was no response.

"Russ, I thought you had a hotel to run?"

"My day off!"

"What about you, Jerry? Isn't there somebody you can go shoot?"

"Can't think of anyone at the moment. Thought I'd hang around here till the sun comes across the yardarm."

"It must be getting close. Perhaps you should head to the bar and wait there."

"It's still a bit early," Jerry replied.

"Edgar, your job is over. I'm looking after Mrs. Clark now. Go play with your old people."

Edgar looked at his watch before responding: "Got nine and a half minutes left in my coffee break. If I rush back they'll make me work."

Karl Busch shook his head in frustration and then looked at Emily.

"Mrs. Clark, Greg Turner called me after the incident near your home and asked if I'd see to your safety on this trip."

He seemed annoyed. Emily wondered if he was unhappy because he was asked to protect a mere woman. No doubt he was usually chasing after major criminals. He probably considered this assignment inconsequential. She was willing to wager that he had obliged to take it on as a favour to his friend. Clearly, he was wishing he was somewhere else.

He spoke in a deep baritone voice with a slight hint of German accent. "I have heard a lot about you from Greg Turner. He really sang your praises. How unfortunate to find yourself involved in all this drama."

Emily could feel herself colouring. "Greg also spoke highly of you. Is it a habit of his to expound the virtues of all his acquaintances?"

An actual smile. "Both of us seem to be among the few he approves of. And by the way, please call me Karl."

"Only if you will call me Emily."

"I want you to wear this security necklace and bracelet. They will enable us to track your movements, should you go astray. There is also a listening device and an emergency button, which you can activate by sliding this little lever."

He handed Emily what looked like an innocuous gold filigree pendant with a matching bracelet. Emily obligingly put both on.

Karl continued in a military tone: "One of the individuals involved in the killing of Mr. Liu Wong has surrendered to authorities in Toronto. He suffered a gunshot wound and decided he liked his chances better with the police."

"Have they found the weapon?"

"Unfortunately, no," he paused before going on in the same deliberate manner. "It seems information about this KZR weapon was leaked by one of the men who tortured Mr. Wong. Now there are several other parties interested in acquiring it."

He emphasized her name as he continued: "Emily, the consensus is that somewhere your husband must have left you a clue as to its whereabouts, if in fact it does exist."

She glared at him. "My late husband did not deal in fiction, Mr. Busch. If he said there was a weapon, then there was a weapon and it had to be a very special weapon for him to want to hide it."

He let her comment pass and paused while taking a sip of his coffee. "Do you have any idea where he may have hidden the weapon?"

As soon as he stopped speaking he looked directly at her. She felt as though his intense cerulean eyes were boring a hole through her.

"No!" She wanted to say a lot more but restrained herself. His officiousness was beginning to irritate her.

"Your life may depend on our locating the blueprints and the prototype before some extremely unsavoury people get their hands on you. Liu Wong not only told his interrogators that he passed the weapon to your late husband, but that your husband put it into your hands for safe keeping. Surely you knew the man you were married to well enough to know where he might have put something so important."

Inured to hearing about the same topic, she responded impatiently: "Mr. Busch, my husband did not give any weapon to me. This is all utter nonsense! The first I heard of any of this was three days ago when Detective Turner played a tape of his phone conversation with my husband just before he was killed."

She struggled to contain her frustration. "I allowed Detective Turner and his people to inspect my home from top to bottom. They found things I had no idea existed. Where those guns they found came from, I have absolutely no idea. I don't know why John bought even one gun because we lived in a safe community. People in Dundas do not run around with guns. This whole business is insane and has gone much too far. Besides, you should know all this. Surely Greg Turner filled you in."

Before he could respond she continued her rant: "To begin with, if I had the ability to read the mind of a man who has been dead for a full year, I would most certainly tell you and everyone else where John put the damn thing. Please tell those people who want it that I don't have and never had the silly weapon. Nor do I want anything to do with that weapon or any other weapon for that matter."

Karl Busch responded in a calm, controlled voice: "If only it were that simple! Number one: we do not know who all 'those' people are, yet. That is why we wanted to isolate you here. We wanted to see who would follow you here."

He stopped for effect, and continued to speak slowly and deliberately. "Number two: even if we did know who they are, they would not listen. They believe your husband passed the weapon to you and won't stop until it is found."

He took an annoyingly slow sip of his coffee before continuing: "Yesterday your husband's former office was thoroughly searched and nothing relating to this weapon turned up. We do know his briefcase disappeared when he was killed, but we feel that if the information was in that, it would have made it to the street long ago. Arms dealers don't wait a year to manufacture a weapon with this supposed potential."

"What is so special about the weapon?"

Karl Busch looked down at a report before replying: "We are beginning to find out what all the fuss is about. From what the Toronto police were able to learn by interrogating one of Wong's killers, the weapon is apparently inoffensive looking but features face recognition technology. The ammunition has some sort of guidance system. In other words, if you pre-program it to recognize a certain face, it will find its target even in a crowded room. We suspect it is disguised as a camera or cell phone or other innocuous looking thing. At this time we have no idea of its accuracy or viability. However, Wong apparently alluded to the fact that it was your husband who performed the preliminary tests on it."

"I don't understand why my husband was involved in this. John was a lawyer. It makes no sense to me. Now he has put my life in danger."

"We don't understand that either but we will continue to search for the weapon and to try to discover your husband's involvement. As soon as the weapon is found, this will be over."

He continued in the same rigid tone, which she was finding increasingly officious and annoying. "We are holding the passports of all the villa patrons. We already uncovered some irregularities in a couple of them. Rinaldo Rizzo is known to us. On at least several occasions he was charged with various offences but the Italian police had difficulty getting a conviction because the witnesses against him kept disappearing."

He looked at her. "I understand Edgar has already warned you about the man."

She nodded.

"His girlfriend is also a person of interest. I advise you to be careful around the two of them. They are up to something."

"Don't worry, I'm not about to befriend Gianna and Rinaldo."

"I am arranging for more security around the building. You are to trust no one other than the people in this room and anyone else I designate as safe. Do you understand?"

"I know I should feel secure with so much protection, but I don't think I'll be able to relax until that dreadful thing is found."

"Point taken! While you are in Lucca this afternoon we will install a few extra surveillance cameras in several blind spots we discovered on the balcony of your suite and throughout the villa. So be careful where you undress. Do not tell your roommate about the cameras."

"But Ruth and I have become very good friends and I trust her. We have so much in common. We are both widowed and love to paint. I liked her as soon as I met her."

His brow was furrowed. He was clearly losing patience with her. He rose and spoke to her as if he was addressing a recalcitrant child.

"I believe Turner counselled you not to confide in anyone in your painting group. Am I not correct?"

"You are correct. He did mention that at the airport but Ruth and I don't talk about the weapon or anything like that. Just women's things! I wouldn't expect you to understand."

"Do not trust anyone until we have cleared them. Give me two or three days to do that. Do not go anywhere on your own or with anyone other than the people in this room or Agent Soll. Do you understand?"

"Got it."

He sat back down again. "Today I have some work from a previous case to finish up so Agent Soll will be on duty with you. She will go everywhere with you until this is over. You will do some playacting and tell everyone how the two of you have become friends. The two of you will be painting buddies for the duration of the month. I assume you are agreeable with this?"

"I am not!"

EIGHT

An uncomfortable look rippled across Karl Busch's face. He articulated his next words slowly and precisely. "What do you mean you are not happy with this? You have no choice in the matter. You will do as I say."

Pale green eyes focused on him with an intensity he wouldn't have thought possible yesterday when he first saw her in the dining room. "Mr. Busch, you are obviously accustomed to ordering people around. I may have had a fright with the events of the past few days but I am not an imbecile. I appreciate your concern for my safety but you must allow me be part of the process."

Karl Busch examined the woman standing rigidly before him. Her pale green eyes were no longer focused on him. Instead they were now looking out the window above his head.

My God, was she was dismissing him? Didn't she realize who he was? How respected he was in law enforcement circles?

Turner had exacted a promise from him to personally see to her safety. It was a promise he was beginning to regret making. He remembered Turner telling him that Emily Clark wanted to be part of the process when they searched her home.

Turner also warned him not to underestimate the woman. It was a warning he should have heeded.

He considered his options. Emily Clark was the key to finding the weapon. This woman's husband had provided the international community with invaluable information in the fight against terrorism and until three days ago the man had been an unsung hero. If someone of that calibre announced in his dying message that he worked on an experimental weapon, then the thing not only worked but it had to be extremely dangerous. That had to explain why he was so secretive about its location.

Some things were beginning to coalesce. That Clark maintained a sophisticated armoury in his basement meant he had a special interest in weaponry. Every weapon had been fired. Every weapon was kept meticulously clean and every one had been expertly modified.

The logical extension was that Clark was merely a gun fanatic or perhaps he may have had a legitimate use for weaponry. Regardless of his interest, he had gone one step further in helping test the prototype.

If the felon Turner's people apprehended was telling the truth, the prototype represented a crucial innovation in close range weaponry.

There were a number of people in the law enforcement community who were already excited at the possibilities this thing might be offering.

Why give particulars about the weapon to this woman?

Turner spoke of her as though she were next in line to be sainted. Nobody was that perfect.

Clark was married to her.

Obviously he trusted his wife to do the right thing but that is true for at least half the married men in the world. But why entrust the weapon to her? It made no sense or did it? There had to be a reason.

Turner met Clark on numerous occasions and declared him to be cultured, astute and a bit self-possessed. In other words the man was no fool.

Pity he hadn't told her where he put the damn weapon.

After an extensive search of Clark's house, Turner's people didn't turn up a whiff of the thing. Nothing! No hint of it! Absolutely nothing!

As far as everyone in law enforcement was concerned, the ball was now in his court and the woman standing in front of him, was the one and only link to finding it.

Karl Busch eyed Emily Clark. He needed her help.

He'd blown it badly. She was still calling him Mr. Busch and now she was deliberately ignoring him.

Usually his good looks and impressive size gave him an advantage when dealing with women. Not this time! Not with this woman!

Let's face it, he'd grovel if that's what it took to get her co-operation.

His three buddies were sitting quietly across the room. Damn them! They were probably having a good chuckle at his expense and he had to admit he deserved that. This was humiliating!

He eyed Jerry who was busy studying a spot on the carpet. He reminded himself of Jerry's call from the Amsterdam airport when he spotted Edgar with this woman. Jerry sang her praises to excess. If there was such a thing as 'a blond a month' club, Jerry could probably qualify as a charter member. Could Jerry handle her? No! This woman already had enough to cope with.

Edgar was studying the same spot on the carpet. Edgar had a run-in with Soll yesterday and last night had begged him to keep 'that monster' away from his friend, Em. Edgar even offered to come out of retirement to guard the woman. That wasn't an option.

Didn't they realize his forte wasn't personal security? He needed to focus on the bigger picture, not babysit a woman. He should spend his time tracking down leads. With young Rizzi showing up here, they could potentially open the door to a major investigation of that whole family.

Soll had already agreed to take charge of this woman. In fact, Soll was eager to take over so he could focus on other aspects of the case and then head back to Geneva to finish up the case he should be working on there.

He watched as she slowly lowered her eyes and looked at him.

Words sprung out of his mouth almost unbidden: "Mrs. Clark, my apologies! Shall we begin again?"

She eyed him cautiously.

He softened his tone, "Emily, I'm sorry. I get a bit high handed at times. I forgot myself. Please forgive me and please call me Karl."

He had the feeling that he reddened as her pale green eyes examined him. He wondered if she had that kind of effect on all men.

"I don't like Agent Soll and I don't trust her."

"She's a professional. She one of the best! I used her on other cases and there's never been a complaint."

A furrow formed between her eyebrows as she looked above his head again.

She was dismissing him again. He wanted to fix this but he'd blown it again. She was unnerving him. Those damn green eyes were almost hypnotic.

"Mrs. Clark, Emily, I would be most honoured to act as your bodyguard. I'm not sure I can pass myself off as an artist. I'm not even good at drawing stick figures."

"If you are as bad an artist as you claim to be, I suggest you become my painting partner. You can do some playacting yourself and pretend we have a little thing going, to conceal our real reason for being together. Though I suspect that anyone wanting this weapon will see through any schemes we devise."

Karl stood to his full six-foot four inches. His blond hair displayed a few strands of grey. His face and bearing implied strength and control. This was a man who was accustomed to being in charge of all situations and he was clearly not the one in charge here. He cleared his throat, "Does this mean you are going to be difficult to protect?"

"Absolutely not! I am considerably more interested in my well-being than you are."

Pia suddenly appeared in the doorway. Karl wondered how long she'd been standing there listening.

"Emily, come join me in the kitchen. Greg raved about the meal you prepared for his crew. He told me your raspberry crumble almost evaporated out of the dish."

The two women left the room in a flash, which left three men still sitting, looking at him.

Karl Busch looked angry and a bit confounded. "What just happened here? When did I lose control of the situation?"

Russ began to chuckle. "When did you lose control?" His chuckle rose in volume as it turned into a loud laugh.

"What's so bloody funny?"

"Karl, you never had control. I believe, you've just met your match, my friend, and I have a feeling that my sweet little wife is somehow complicit in what just happened here. I don't know how she's involved but I do know that Pia was mad as hell last night when you told us of your plan to have Soll act as Emily's bodyguard. Pia kept me awake half the night trying to figure out a way to send Soll packing."

Meanwhile the two women in question were happily wending their way through the back halls toward the kitchen on the lower level.

Pia was the first to speak, "Men! With all their cloak and dagger stuff! It's enough to scare a person."

"I agree. Women put things into perspective. Can you imagine, he wanted me to spend a whole month with Soll as a bodyguard? No, thank you!"

"I knew you were too smart to go for that. I'm so glad you stood up for yourself. Karl really is a fantastic guy. What a great idea to pretend to have an affair. Quick thinking!"

"I know it sounded lame but it was the best thing I could come up with at the time. I was desperate to avoid Soll and her unpredictable temperament. She can be nasty."

"I couldn't have come up with a better idea myself. You should know that Karl is not only gorgeous but is also technically available."

"Pia, I'm not interested! Say no more! I'm still reeling from the baggage my late husband left behind."

As they turned a corner Pia suddenly held out her arm to stop Emily and motioned for her to be quiet. The two conspirators peered down the hall in time to see Soll entering the room of the DiMattia's German maid, Gerta. After she was safely inside the two continued quietly along the hallway. When they were safely out of earshot they began to chatter again.

"She led me to believe she had a thing for Karl. What is she about?"

"Emily, she's a modern woman! We're the old-fashioned ones. I knew about Gerta's proclivities soon after she started with us and I'm glad she's found a friend."

"Doesn't Karl know about Soll's temper?" Emily asked astounded. "Just being near her would be enough to put a saint on edge. Even Edgar crossed swords with her."

"If I know Karl, he sees things in terms of police work only. After his wife died, he became a workaholic. I think he only relaxes when he's with my husband and his other army buddies. They've been close since their days in the military. We all get together every two or three years either here or at Alexandros's and Iola's hotel in Greece. Edgar, Greg and his wife Angie come over from Canada and we collect a few more from around Europe. I'm so glad they've kept so close. Now if only we could find wives for Edgar and Karl. I've given up on Jerry. He's always showing up with a different girl, and they are all blonds. What about you, Emily? Are you sure you're not ready for another go?"

"Absolutely not! I was happily married to John or at least I thought I was until three days ago. Besides, what if I remarried and was miserable? Think about it. If you lost Russ, would you take another chance?"

"I'd find myself a toy boy." With that the two friends burst into gales of laughter. They entered the kitchen arm in arm still chuckling.

Pia explained that she was in charge of the kitchen and housekeeping. Russ, along with their sons who were now in their teens, looked after repairs and maintenance and ran the extensive farm, which included olive trees, a vineyard and the market garden that kept the kitchen supplied with fresh produce. They also sold produce to restaurants in Lucca and several other surrounding communities.

Emily loved the old-fashioned fireplace and the mixture of new and old in Pia's kitchen. Like the rest of the villa, the kitchen area was spotlessly clean and efficiently organized.

Pia and Emily discussed recipes for preparing fish and salads and soon found they had much to share. Pia was working as a chef in a large restaurant in Rome when she first met Russ. Like Emily and John, the attraction was immediate. They married a year later and had now raised three boys.

Emily spent the rest of the morning in her favourite place: the kitchen. When Pia requested some of the bread Greg raved about, Emily happily obliged. She explained her method of using very little yeast and allowing the dough to rise overnight.

The morning flew by with Emily and Pia working side by side arranging plates and discussing ingredients. In Italy, chefs had a year-round supply of many items that must be imported into Canada because of its colder climate.

At noon Emily joined the other painters in the dining room and sat beside her friend Ruth.

"Emily, where were you? I looked all over for you."

"Edgar introduced me to several of his friends. Then Pia DiMattia showed me the hotel kitchen. I used to run my own restaurant so I was interested in seeing first-hand how they do things here in Tuscany. I simply lost track of time. How did you spend the morning?"

Ruth answered: "First I attended the painting session. Edgar is such a wonderful teacher. His explanations are easy to follow. I think I learned more from him this morning than I did all last winter taking lessons. I could have sat and watched him paint all morning."

"Whenever I've taken one of his courses I've thought the same thing."

"After the lesson I sketched for about five minutes. Then MJ decided I should join her and her roommate on a bicycle ride. We borrowed bikes from the villa and rode down the road about a mile. It was so hot, I didn't know if I could make it back up the hill again. I was desperate for a cool shower when I got back."

Emily tried to suppress a laugh thinking about MJ on a bicycle. "Ruth, you poor dear! You'll know enough to hide out the next time MJ approaches you to ride bikes together."

"There won't be a next time, I promise you that. Now I have a blister on my heel to deal with."

After lunch, both women freshened up, gathered their painting gear and stood in line waiting to board the bus for their first excursion into Lucca. Edgar did a head count. Soll climbed on the bus seconds before it pulled out but as expected, Karl Busch was nowhere to be seen. Perhaps he was looking after the paperwork from his previous case as he mentioned or maybe he was patronizing her earlier when they spoke. She had no way of knowing.

The ride into town took about fifteen minutes. The painters chatted as they observed the colours and shapes of the passing countryside.

The old walled Italian city of Lucca is three thousand years old and features countless churches, cobbled streets and retains an old-world charm. Emily was spellbound as Edgar led the group down the narrow lanes laid out in an ancient Roman road pattern. There were towering medieval and renaissance palaces and a very impressive renaissance wall encircling the whole city. This was a feast for the eyes and the mind.

They followed Edgar to the art supply store. He went over the directions to the store in case anyone wanted to buy more supplies later in the month. As soon as they entered the store, Edgar explained they would be using copious amounts of earth tones in their paintings: "If you don't have a good supply of yellow and red ochre, sienna and umber, buy some before we start painting."

Art supply stores are like candy stores for artists. Even though Emily had a good supply of everything from the list Edgar had sent her, she knew she couldn't possibly leave the store without buying something. She began checking out the watercolour brushes and spied a Russian blue squirrel mottler in a glass case beside the other expensive brushes. She looked at the tiny price tag pinned to the wall below the brush and gasped. Yes, she could afford it, but it would be an extravagance. If John were here with her, he would have insisted he buy it for her. She turned sadly away and found a liner in one of the bins.

As expected some members of the group bought everything on Edgar's supplies list. She was about to make a comment to Ruth about that but realized that Ruth was also carrying a large bag of art goodies. When the store ran out of yellow ochre, Edgar gallantly offered to share his supply with anyone lacking it.

She glanced out the window and spotted Jerry Burns standing sentry across the street. But he wasn't there when they came out of the store. She looked around and finally spotted him looking in a store window further down the street.

Edgar led the way to a secluded spot on the side of the wall. "You have to come here to visualize the magnitude of the wall. On Sunday mornings, you're likely to find loads of people walking their dogs on the roadway on top of it. The wall may have been built for protection, but today it is used for leisurely walks and affords great vantage points for us artists."

When the last of the group had settled into their newly acquired stools he began his lecture.

"Red ochre is made of hematite or a form of iron oxide. It was used prehistorically for rock painting, pottery and human tattoos. Red is the colour of blood. Red ochre was associated with human burials in ancient times. The 'Red Lady' found in Paviland Cove in the UK dates back 23,500 years. Another burial site was found in Arene Candide on the Ligurian coast not far from Savona, Italy and the third was found at the Maya site of Copan. Ochres range in colour from yellow to brown and finally red.

"Now look across the city of Lucca. From here you see about a thousand terracotta roofs. Walls are painted in various shades of yellow. You will be using your ochres, siennas and umbers plus a smattering of other shades to get the tones you want in order to capture the feeling of the place. We'll start with some simple things today. I'll do a quick demo."

After working for a few minutes he announced: "I'm cutting my lesson short for this afternoon but I will be here painting if you have any questions. If you are in dire need of a bathing suit, I suggest you begin your search by heading back the way we came and turning right. Don't forget that the bus will be leaving promptly at 4pm. Be at the front gates at least five minutes before that. Capiche?"

Emily chose to sit in the shade of a large tree and carefully sketched out a simple scene of the street below. After a year of loneliness, she was happy to be interacting with people again. The warm afternoon breeze wafted up to her vantage point above the city. She was covered with a long-sleeved cotton shirt and linen slacks and her large sun hat. With her fair skin, she wasn't taking any chances of ruining her holiday with a severe sunburn.

She sketched for at least a half hour before she heard the languid voice of Rinaldo behind her. As usual he was oozing sexuality.

"Beautiful lady, here you are. You always look so poised and lovely. I love fair women. You and I should get together. I can show you how Italian men make love."

She had tied her hair back into a ponytail and could feel his breath on the exposed part of her neck as he dislodged her sun hat. She looked around. Edgar was busy talking with Mary and Soll was nowhere to be seen. Emily was deciding what action she should take to ward him off when suddenly Rinaldo went flying through the air and landed with a loud thud three feet below her on the side of the hill. He continued to roll to the bottom. When he finally looked up at her, he appeared somewhat dazed.

Emily turned around to see Soll standing beside her with a pleased look on her face.

She smiled up at her rescuer. "Soll, can I buy you to a cappuccino?"

To her surprise, Soll accepted.

As she packed up her art supplies, Emily began to have misgivings. Karl Busch had told her Soll would be here to protect her this afternoon so there was really no need to reward the woman for doing her duty. She couldn't very well back out now, so she rose and followed Soll to a trattoria. They ordered cappuccinos and biscotti and sat waiting while their order was prepared.

It was obvious Soll was not about to engage in small talk so Emily began the conversation by thanking her: "I know it's not your job to protect me from lechers, but I want you to know I am grateful for your help back there. I was hoping to avoid Rinaldo but he came up behind me while I was painting."

"He is nothing."

"But Karl Busch told me he was dangerous. He warned me to stay as far from him as possible."

"He's a stupid man! Ignore him!"

"But what about his father?"

"Another stupid man!"

Emily watched with trepidation as Rinaldo walked down the cobbled street toward them and stopped five feet in front of their table. He stood for a minute looking at both women. Then he made a sign with his hand indicating a knife slash across his throat.

Not trusting Soll to react reasonably, Emily whispered to Soll, hoping to distract her, "Poor man, I think he's trying to tell us someone cut off either his tongue or his dick. I'm not sure which."

For the first time since she met her, Soll burst out laughing. Her elegant face displayed a row of perfectly formed white teeth.

Rinaldo pointed at Soll and said, "You'll pay for this."

Soll whispered to Emily. "It wasn't his tongue." Her deep rumble of laughter echoed up the alley. As she stood up and faced Rinaldo her laughter took on a sinister tone.

The already angry Rinaldo became deeply flushed. To Emily's surprise, he turned and ran down the cobbled street.

Soll sat down. "Don't worry about him. He won't bother us again."

Emily shivered, knowing they had just made an enemy and Rinaldo wasn't a man she wanted as an enemy. She suspected he could potentially be violent.

Wanting to distance herself from the scene that had just played out, she gulped down her coffee and announced, "Edgar should still be on the hill with some of the others. I'm going to head back there and join them."

Soll grabbed her arm before she could rise. "Do you think anyone believes you? You claim you are ignorant of your husband's affairs. The police found an arsenal in your own house and you claim you knew nothing about it. How stupid do you think we are?"

Emily found herself on the defensive. With Soll holding her arm in a vice grip, she couldn't rise and the pain was increasing. She tried to answer evenly: "Soll, the gun collection was hidden in a secret room in our basement. It was a room I didn't even know existed until Detective Turner showed me. As for knowing about my husband's affairs, I know only what John told me and he never once mentioned owning any guns. John was a lawyer not some kind of gun runner."

"Who was his client? It is well known he had one specific client who hired him to do many jobs."

"Soll, as a lawyer, my husband had many clients. Lawyers practice law. That's what they do. And what do you mean it is well known he had one specific client. It is not well known at all. You never met my husband. I was married to him. I don't know what you're talking about."

Soll looked as though she wanted to say something but instead eased the pressure on her arm as she paused. Her next words were precise as though she had given careful thought before voicing them: "But the man had to be meticulous. He wouldn't have left any loose ends."

"There you are, Em! I've been searching high and low for you. After you left us I remembered I promised to buy you a gelato. Come, old girl," Edgar said as he walked up to their table. She hadn't seen him approach. But there he was and he wasn't looking at her as he spoke. He was focused on Soll and he was looking quite menacing.

Before she could respond Edgar came around the table and grabbed Emily's backpack and slung it over his shoulder, then pulled her out of her seat forcing Soll to release her arm. He put his arm around her shoulder as he led her forward.

"Been watching that little scene! Em, dear girl, you wear your emotions on your sleeve. I figured Soll was practising her interrogation techniques on you from the look on your face. Is your arm in need of medical attention?"

"I'll probably have a bruise for a couple days but I'll be OK."

They stopped as soon as they were away from Soll. Edgar handed Emily her backpack. "Sure you're all right? There's a clinic not far from here."

"I'm fine! Just annoyed at myself for letting Soll get to me."

"If it's any comfort to you, when she had a go at me yesterday, she really pushed my buttons. That woman takes herself way too seriously, but then again we're laid-back Canadians, so what do we know?"

"Tell me what she said when you met with her," Emily replied.

The old Edgar was back as he lowered his voice and spoke as if he was revealing a conspiracy. "She quizzed me about our trip from Toronto. Wanted to know if you met with anyone on the trip here? Did you talk on your cell phone? Did you behave suspiciously?"

Emily was drawn in and angled close to hear his words. "And you answered?"

"I told her that you and I had a thing going on and how you tried to follow me into the men's washroom and offered to strip nude for me."

"You said what?"

She looked at him. He was wiggling his eyebrows at her just as he had done in the Amsterdam airport. Again Edgar drew her in. But this time he actually looked serious. "She asked me if you passed an object to any one we met at the airport in Amsterdam."

"And what did you say?"

Edgar gave his head a little scratch and paused for effect. "Well, let me think. I believe I told Soll you may have handed something to Jerry Burns, but I wasn't sure what. Maybe it was a spider."

"Jerry Burns, the Europol agent? Edgar, you really are too much. But you're right."

"I'm right?"

"You may not realize it but you have a talent for putting things into proper prospective. I love you, Edgar, 'the brush'."

An inveterate showman, Edgar grinned as he threw his big arm around her shoulder. "Yea, yea, I know. You love me like a brother! By the way, I heard about the Rinaldo incident on the wall and I caught a glimpse of his less than charming display back there a few minutes ago. I asked around about him. Em, he is one scary dude. He has connections with the worst kind of people. What actually did he do before Soll intervened?"

"Well, he came up behind me. Something about his kind makes my skin crawl. He started his usual gushing sexy talk and I was trying my best to ignore him when Soll literally sent him flying through the air. I knew that if I didn't get her out of there fast, Rinaldo would want to retaliate so I offered to buy her a cappuccino. Rinaldo looked angry enough to kill her. But why would she want to provoke him like that."

"My guess is that there's more going on here than you and I are aware of. From what I saw, she's not intimidated by him. In fact, it's almost as though she's daring him to cross her."

"I thought so too, Edgar."

"By the way, let me check your neck. Remember the bugs at the airport. Here give me your sun hat."

Hidden to the underside of Emily's collar was a small round grey object. Edgar pulled it off and tossed it away. "Was your paint box open?"

"Yes, it was open and sitting behind me."

In mock sincerity he continued: "Sorry to disappoint you. Em, but the handsome Rinaldo was not after your beautiful self. That was a tracking device. He's after the weapon, like the rest of them."

"Edgar, you promised me a gelato. Do you realize we passed two gelato stores?"

"That's because we're going to the one directly ahead. I need a chocolate fix. What flavour for you?"

"I'd love strawberry."

They found a seat under one of the umbrellas. Emily sat quietly for a moment while she sampled her gelato. "This is delicious, Edgar. Do you know that when I first met with Soll she raved about your friend Karl Busch. You should have heard her gush over him. She is a beautiful woman, but she told me he seems to ignore her. Maybe if she had a boyfriend . . ."

Edgar chuckled. "You think she might change? Em, dear, you are a treasure, that's why I love you—like a sister, of course. You have much to learn about men. Karl would never fall for that squirrelly creature no matter how beautiful she is. Besides, Karl lost his wife and children a few years ago under tragic circumstances, I doubt he'll ever remarry."

"Oh, I didn't know about his children. How sad."

"Most men, myself included, would prefer to mate with a python before going to bed with a creature like Soll. Can you imagine trying to kiss that one? She might give you that look she gets, you know it, when she wants to interrogate someone." She laughed as he squinted his eyes and barred his teeth. "That woman could give lessons at an inquisition school."

As it was approaching four o'clock Edgar and Emily strolled in the direction of the bus. Organizing painters is often as successful as herding cats, but this time all members of the group with the exception of Mary were standing in line waiting to board the bus at four o'clock sharp.

"Oh, oh! One member of my flock has disappeared," he said to Emily.

MJ announced: "My roommate went shopping. She said to tell you she'll join us back at the ranch."

"Any idea how she's getting back to 'the ranch' MJ?"

"Oh yea! I'm sorry! I was supposed to tell you that she went shopping with Pia. You know Pia, the woman who runs the hotel."

"Thanks, MJ."

Rinaldo and Gianna climbed on the bus first and sat in the back row. Rinaldo's mood was apparent from the look on his face. He was practically incandescent. Gianna looked acutely uncomfortable.

Soll arrived just as the driver was about to close the door. She handed Emily a bag from the art store as she walked down the aisle. Emily was surprised when the beautiful Russian blue squirrel mottler she had examined at the art store and a note saying *Sorry* tumbled out of the bag. Soll nodded when Emily turned to acknowledge the gift. She would let the little scene at the trattoria pass into unwritten history. Soll clearly realized she'd been overzealous and apologized. End of story!

A weary but happy group arrived back at Villa DiMattia fifteen minutes later. Other than Edgar and Mario, none of the occupants of the bus were aware of the two vehicles travelling with them. Jerry's team followed them at a discrete but close distance. Another car preceded them by about the same distance. There were video cams set up in the bus, one of which faced forward out the front window. The second was behind the driver and kept a constant vigil on the movements of the occupants within the bus and the third faced out the rear of the bus.

As soon as the bus returned to the villa, the artists hurried to their rooms to don their swimsuits and then headed to the pool area for the much anticipated pool party.

The bathing suits were as varied as the bodies that wore them.

Drinks and food were in great abundance. Emily was feeling hot and after removing her cover-up, she slid into the water hoping no one would notice the whiteness of her skin. An obviously intoxicated Rinaldo watched her and made his way to the edge of the pool. He tottered there for a short time before falling in. Gianna jumped in to retrieve her drunk friend and with MJ's help got him out of the water and sat him down on one of the chaises.

Like everyone else Emily was watching the drama unfolding beside the pool. She didn't see Karl until he surfaced beside her.

He spoke close to her ear to avoid boing overheard: "Soll told me about Rizzo's antics this afternoon. Don't worry about that jerk. If he acts up again, I'm not afraid to send him packing. His mother may be related to old Italian nobility, but his father is evil as they come. It is his father's connections that keep him out of prison. Soll plans to have a word with him just as soon as he sobers up."

"Don't do that on my account. There was no harm done. Besides, I think she's punished him enough already."

He looked at her as if expecting her to elaborate and when she didn't he dove under the water.

Gianna and MJ were waiting for him as he swam to the end of the pool but their prey adroitly outmanoeuvred them and was out of the water as quickly and silently as he entered it. Emily could see him towelling himself and chatting with Russ.

Then MJ and Gianna made their way toward Emily.

MJ swam up beside her. "Who is that gorgeous hunk? I want his room number."

"I don't know his room number, MJ. He's Edgar's friend. Go ask Edgar about him," Emily replied somewhat evasively.

She wasn't about to tell any of these women the man was her bodyguard.

"Oh no you don't, Emily Clark. I've seen the two of you eyeing each other in the dining room," MJ persisted.

Mary swam out to join them just then. "She's telling the truth, MJ. He's an old army buddy of Edgar's. I met him as well."

MJ groaned, "So if I want to meet the hunk, I gotta ask Edgar. No way! Which one of you will help me meet him?"

They all screamed as Edgar cannonballed into the pool displacing copious amounts of water. He insisted they join him for a game of water polo. It was really Edgar's version of water polo and it was fun. He was an expert swimmer and skillfully evaded them all until Mary and MJ ganged up on him. Then he walked in the water carrying Mary on his shoulders. High atop his shoulders Mary carried on a sword fight with MJ using noodle floaties.

Rinaldo decided he wanted to join in the fun and walked precariously to the edge of the pool again. He was clearly too drunk to swim. The game stopped as they watched him start to sway back and forth. Soll rushed over and grabbed him. Everyone cringed as she unceremoniously poured the contents of an ice bucket over him. It probably helped sober him up because he was more sure-footed as he raced toward the hot tub.

As the noise level rose, other villa guests came out to investigate.

When Edgar declared the party over, they returned to their rooms in time to prepare for dinner. The party had been a wonderful diversion. Emily smiled as she thought of Edgar's magnificent cannonball into the pool.

Dinner was an elaborate affair and featured *fagiano alla fiorentina* (pheasant, Tuscan-style). Emily was pleased when one of her own recipes was used for the salad. It brought back memories of the days when she ran her own restaurant.

Rinaldo was sober enough to join them at the dinner table though he continued to slur his words. Gianna talked to MJ throughout the meal purposely ignoring Rinaldo's attempts to get her attention. She wore a long sleeved shirt and kept rubbing her left shoulder.

Karl nodded to Emily from across the room. She wondered if he would put in an appearance tomorrow when the group travelled to Cinque Terre.

As soon as they returned to their room Ruth put on her pyjamas and climbed into bed. She sat waiting for Emily to shut off her reading light. Emily wanted to finish one last paragraph in her journal, but found she was simply too tired.

She closed her book, removed her necklace and bracelet and gently placed them in the drawer of her night table. It was a habit she had adopted years before, in an effort to prevent her thieving whippet, Wellington, from filching her things while she slept. She smiled as she remembered the time John found her watch and a collection of her jewellery inside his slipper in Wellington's bed. She relaxed and tried to find that elusive thing—sleep.

NINE

Her mind wandered as she eased herself into the stages of sleep, waking up at times and then drifting off again. Some nights are like that. Her thoughts trailed through the events of the day in a haphazard way.

She was feeling safer now that the surveillance cameras were in place throughout the villa. She may not have cared for Karl Busch's high handedness but she trusted him. Turner said Karl would look after her. Turner wouldn't lie. John had trusted Turner.

She liked Ruth. Funny how after all the disturbance at home, she came on this trip and instantly connected with Ruth. Only another widow could understand how lonely life was when you've lost your soul mate. They had so much in common. When they returned home she'd invite Ruth to spend a weekend. She'd introduce her to her family and they could find some interesting places to paint together.

The trails would be magnificent in October. The temperatures would be cooler and perfect for hiking. The autumn leaves would have begun to change.

She began to dream about John. She was transported back to the first time she took him hiking in the woods. He wore a pair of polished boots and declared them to be his walking boots. It had rained heavily the night before so the ground was muddy. In her dream she could see him stop and pour a stream of muddy water out of his boots. The steam of muddy water went on and on.

Then suddenly they were standing in early morning sunshine. Steam was rising from the waters in Coote's Paradise. A flock of geese took flight through the mist and rose into the bright sunshine above. John was trying to photograph the birds, then he smiled and turned his camera on her. He began to fade away.

She tried to call him back but he kept fading. She tried again to bring him into focus. She tried to reach out and pull him into the warmth of Tuscany. She wanted to show him the colours. She wanted him to feel the softness of the breeze.

Emily awoke feeling a gentle breeze on her cheek. The balcony door was open.

She froze.

It was not quite dawn. Why was the door open?

Perhaps it was a dream. Perhaps she could roll over and allow sleep to overtake her again but as she was about to move she heard Ruth's voice.

Instinct told her to remain still. Ruth was standing just outside on the balcony.

Emily tried to tell herself not to worry. Her roommate was her friend. She was safe.

But the door shouldn't be open now. The surveillance cameras, the danger . . .

Ruth was talking on her cell phone to someone.

Perhaps Ruth had a family emergency? Yesterday she mentioned her elderly mother was not well.

Ruth was standing only a few feet from her bed. If she focused, she might be able to catch her words.

She could hear only one side of the conversation. Ruth would speak and then there would be periods of silence as she listened to the person on the other end of the line.

"I was worried she'd wake up when the phone rang, but she's still out like a light. What about your roomie?

"Good, we can talk. The group got together in Lucca as planned?

"Sounds like a good place to meet. Wish I could have been there but I have to keep my distance. Tell me what happened.

"Nobody expected Viktor to show up here. It makes everything a whole lot more complicated.

"I'm not surprised everyone is nervous. We still have to get the job done. The client wants the weapon back. He says it belongs to him. I'm not going to be the one to tell him we didn't get it because of Viktor.

"He knows what we're dealing with. He used Viktor to off Johnny. Pity someone didn't find out where the weapon was before that. Tell me something, I heard you were there and grabbed Johnny's briefcase.

"Why didn't you open it? I would have.

"Tell them it's going well. I watch her like a hawk. She managed to slip away a couple times. I won't let it happen again. I am making progress. She's starting to confide in me. It takes time.

"I looked through her belongings and found nothing. She's a real sucker, Mary. She wasn't hard to con. I told her I was widowed and lonely like her and in a flash, I was her new best friend.

"She could be the poster girl for naivety which goes far to explain how she lived with a contract killer for years and didn't have a clue what he did for a living. I kid you not."

Emily wanted desperately to reach over and open the drawer of her night table. If only she could pull out her security device so she could let someone hear this. She didn't dare move a muscle for fear of discovery.

"She knows nothing. I asked her some leading questions, and I know just by her nature she's not holding back. Think about this. All those trips to Europe and every time some embassy official or executive would disappear. She thought they were travelling so he could see his clients and do a bit of sightseeing. I mean, the woman didn't have a clue who she was married to. Wonder how many women were widowed thanks to him? Couldn't even hazard a guess. He set things up so well, the cops never had a clue.

"Funny how he kept her away from us. Guess she provided him with a good cover. Rumour has it, he had round the clock protection for her. He certainly squirrelled himself away in nowhere's land as soon as he hooked up with this one. What a waste! He was one great mover until then. Do you remember his first wife? She was a real bitch. She and Viktor were lovers for years. Then the stupid thing started asking too many questions so Viktor gave her a shot of a carcinogen. Took her three months to die. What a beautiful form of torture.

"I figure Johnny knew what kind of money he could get for the weapon. He wanted it for himself. I heard he hid it so well, not even the cops can find it. Apparently their place was swarming with cops the minute the word got out. I'd say Mrs. C lived a charmed life. The joy ride is now over.

"With the kind of money involved in this weapon, I'm not going to take any chances. I'm sticking to her like glue. Yes, I realize there are several other players snooping around. Don't worry, nothing we can't handle. Viktor is the one I'm worried about.

"Yea, I know Viktor's been around her more than once. Our little Emily won't stand a chance if that monster decides to beat information out of her. I'll try to intervene before Viktor grabs her. I'll watch to see what happens. If need be, I may have to get the ball rolling today. I owe it to Johnny to keep Viktor away from her. You remember that time in Paris. I'd have been a goner, if not for Johnny. We weren't even working together, but he got wind I was in trouble and got me out. He took a terrible beating in the process. Wonder what his little wife thought after we delivered him back to her hotel. She probably believed every lie he told her.

"I intended to give her a couple more days to see if she lets something slip but after talking to you I've decided to proceed today. Can't do anything here because the place is wired. Even our bloody bedroom has a camera. I spotted it by chance. No one can move without being watched.

"You're kidding. Who tried to?

"Who caught him?

"You've got to be kidding! Edgar, the painting teacher did that? Come to think of it, he always seems to be in the way.

"With all this huge police presence here in addition to Viktor, I'm thinking I will definitely make a move today. I'll start quizzing her as soon as we get on the bus. The minute I get her to one of those villages at Cinque Terre she's mine, all mine. She is in for a bit of a surprise . . . of course she may not remember much afterwards.

"No, she may not remember but a bit of sodium pentathol may jog some of her brain cells.

"A bit of truth serum will also help Emily remember more details of Johnny's activities. I find it hard to believe she didn't meet his big client. Why else would he drag her around with him. Johnny made an absolute fortune out of the connection.

"Your roomie's starting to wake up? Bye for now!"

Emily lay very still. She knew she had to feign sleep. She remembered her yoga breathing exercises and forced herself to ease the pressure in her chest. She breathed in slowly and out even more slowly. She did this over and over again. She had to keep herself under control.

I can handle this. I can do this. Yes, I can. Yes, I can. Yes, I can, Emily said to herself.

Ruth eased the sliding door closed and slipped back into her bed.

Emily was careful to keep her breathing loud and even. She shuddered at the thought of what might happen if Ruth knew what she had overheard. She would have to lie here and pray. Soon it would be morning and she would find Karl and Soll and tell them.

Every minute seemed to stretch out. She wanted time to rush by, but instead, it seemed to stand still. She needed to reflect but it was hard to think. She had heard things about John that were almost beyond comprehension. Ruth called him Johnny. The note Turner found in the basement was addressed to Johnny and signed R. The note had to be from Ruth. She mentioned Mary in it.

This was real. It was happening.

It was hard to think of her husband as some ruthless contract killer. John Clark was no assassin.

The man she had lived with, loved his family. He liked to don his apron and man the barbecue. He enjoyed brunch in the alcove off their bedroom. He told her many times how he loved to sit and read the weekend papers there. He insisted they take Wellington for a long hike every Sunday afternoon.

He'd reach for her as soon as he opened the door every night after work. He'd put his arms around her and tell her how much she meant to him. He made love to her so tenderly and sweetly. They never had a fight. Not once! Even when she was tired and cranky from a long day of travelling, he'd smile and find a way to mollify her.

The John Clark she knew loved his son. He was a doting grandfather to little Ardi.

She refused to believe he was some kind of criminal. He was a respectable Bay Street lawyer.

Then again, the police found a cache of weapons and some computer equipment hidden in the basement. He never told her those things existed.

They also found a book written in a foreign language in John's handwriting. John couldn't speak any foreign languages. He spoke only English, she was sure of that. He didn't even have the whisper of a foreign accent. But the evidence was there in his own handwriting.

Why had John kept secrets from her? Why hadn't he trusted her? They always found time to chat about anything and everything. He told her about his court cases, where he had eaten lunch and many other details of his working day. She updated him on what Paul and his family were doing, the state of the garden or Wellington's latest antics. On weekends, they invited friends for dinner or a game of bridge. John certainly did not behave like a man with dark secrets.

    She began to think about the many trips they'd taken together. John made the travel plans and on occasion would surprise her with tickets. He always provided for her comfort wherever they journeyed. He was the ideal travel companion. His business meetings gave her plenty of time to paint and explore. Certainly they visited some interesting places. But Turner's people had found evidence he hired security for her on their trips together. Why?

    John never told her where he was staying when he was away from her. He never once mentioned the name of any hotel. There were never any keepsakes such as little soaps or fancy shampoos.

    She never thought to question him because she trusted him. She knew that you couldn't make a man be faithful to you. Either he was faithful or he wasn't.

    She attended functions with him when they travelled. He seemed so proud to show her off to his business associates. Strange he never took her to social events in Toronto, only when they travelled.

    They met interesting people at these lavish affairs. During the time they were together they mingled with politicians, royalty, writers, diplomats and many wealthy older men. She thanked her lucky stars she had a gift for fitting in. John told her about the positive comments his clients made about her and how she had become a huge asset to him. Once he joked that he was extremely clever in choosing her as his wife. She hadn't paid much attention at the time because she considered it one of the small ways he was telling her how much he loved her. She never imagined it would end so abruptly.

    Was she somehow part of an elaborate scheme to cover up the real purpose for his trips?

When they went to Paris on their honeymoon, they roamed through parks and museums. While John attended meetings, she visited her old friends from cooking school.

My God, did the man murder someone on their honeymoon?

Near the end of the first week they attended an embassy reception. He explained how important it was to meet potential new clients at these events. She wore a slinky midnight blue gown with matching shoes and purse. The night of the event he wrapped a magnificent sapphire necklace around her neck.

While John was deep in conversation with his clients, she roamed over to the food table and was sampling some of the hors d'oeuvres. She tried one dip which she thought was quite vile and uttered a loud, "Yuck!"

Unfortunately, she was overheard by a distinguished looking Arab gentleman who immediately left the people he was chatting with to join her. When she apologized for her rudeness, he laughed and commended her honesty. They got into a discussion about dips and sauces and she soon learned the man was quite the gourmet. They stood there swapping ideas for recipes until John came and stood between them and introduced himself.

The man was tall and dark but the details of his face eluded her, perhaps because it had been just one more face at a reception long ago. In any case, it was of no importance now.

That night in their hotel room, John lifted her in the air and danced around the room, elated. "You are unbelievable, my sweet love. Do you know how hard I have tried to hook up with this guy? You, little girl, did it on your first night out and not only that, you got us an invitation to a crucial meeting at his home. You are my good luck charm. I love you so much."

They did go to the man's home. In fact, they flew by private jet to somewhere in the desert. John never told her why the meeting was so important to him.

Ruth talked about John's big client. Could that man have been John's big client?

They travelled so much. Was it possible John murdered people on every trip? It sounded like a plot for a book. But this was about her life. It was no book.

What explained his mood when he returned each time from his business meetings? After each absence he presented her with an expensive gift. He would seem almost euphoric and made vigorous love to her, sometimes over and over again. She would certainly never complain about that.

Once when they were in France he returned to the hotel bruised from head to toe. They stayed an extra week to give him time to heal. He said he was in a traffic accident. Ruth talked of an incident in Paris in which John had been badly beaten in her defence.

John fussed over her paintings and whenever they travelled he insisted she bring her painting equipment. When he returned from his meetings he'd choose his favourite painting and ask her to sign and date it. A month after returning home, the painting would reappear framed and matted and be hung on one of the downstairs' wall. All the paintings had identical cream coloured mats and thick black frames. When she thought of it now, she didn't even know the name of the framer.

When they visited the Turkish city of Antalya, she contracted a stomach ailment and wasn't able to paint. John cancelled their flight home and sat beside her bed and nursed her until she was well. When she was well enough, he escorted her around the city until she found a scene she wanted to paint. He was kind but insistent she do one painting for him. She obliged. That painting was hanging on the wall in his study.

Could Karl possibly be Viktor? Ruth said Viktor had been near her. But so had all sorts of other people including the dreadful Rinaldo.

Ruth talked to a woman called Mary. Unfortunately there were two women on the trip bearing that name. MJ's real name was Mary Josephine MacDonald. There was also Mary Cominski. Which one could it be? The two women shared a room.

One of those two women witnessed her husband's murder. One of those women had removed his briefcase, like a thief.

She was at this stage in her thinking when her alarm went off. Emily was so deep in thought that the sudden noise made her flinch.

She had to keep control of her nerves. She didn't want to give Ruth any clue she had overheard her.

One thing was clear: Ruth was not her friend. She led her to believe they had a lot in common but it was all lies. Ruth was a ruthless, hardened criminal.

While Ruth was in the shower Emily quickly retrieved her necklace and bracelet from her night table and switched on the audio on the bracelet. That might at least alert someone that she was concerned with her safety.

Emily spent extra time in the shower. She tried to relax as she allowed the hot water to quell some of her shivering. She had to appear calm. The key to her survival was clear thinking. She told herself she could be clever and resourceful.

She thought of her family and young grandson. She resolved to return home at the end of the month. All this insanity would be behind her. She would hide the truth about her husband from Paul and her parents.

Emily and Ruth made small talk about the day ahead as they made their way to the dining room. Emily tried to feign nonchalance but she was rigid with tension.

In sharp contrast to Emily's mood, the dining room was filled with excited painters. Everyone was enthusiastic about going to Cinque Terre.

Edgar stood up and waved to her when she entered the room.

He was beside her by the time she reached the buffet table. "Are you ill?"

"No!"

"I know something's wrong. I can tell just by looking at you. Are you up to coming on the trip today? I can cancel it. Just say the word."

"Don't cancel it."

"We'll look after you, Em. Karl will be on the bus with us and Jerry and his crew will follow behind us in a van."

He carried her plate to a table in the far corner and sat down opposite her. "You can carry this off, Em. Remember what Karl said about playacting. That's really what it's all about. Think of it as though you've got a part in a movie. When the filming is over, you go back to being you."

"I thought I could do this but there's too much going on in my head. My husband . . ."

"Is dead and whatever people say he may have done or not done has nothing to do with you. Em, I've known you since we were kids. You haven't done anything wrong."

"But, what will people back home think when they find out?"

"They won't find out unless you tell them. I'm not telling anybody. I've got my own secrets as you have probably guessed. No one needs to know anything. Em, John Clark is dead and gone."

"Why didn't he trust me? He kept me in the dark."

"Probably for your own good. Em, the man adored you. I saw the two of you together many times. A guy can't fake the way he looked at you."

"I was so stupid, so naive."

"Em, don't beat yourself up over this. It's not worth it. Think of your family as your anchor. They're good folks."

"You always make me feel better, Edgar."

"I tell you the things any big brother would say to his little sister. At the moment, your friend Ruth looks about ready to flay me. She's the one who upset you, isn't she?"

She nodded. "She's not who I thought she was."

"I know."

After breakfast Ruth stuck to her like glue. There was no way she could easily get away from her. She would bide her time.

They boarded the bus. Ruth and Emily sat behind Jenny. Karl was the last one to climb on the bus and sat somewhere behind them. She could almost feel his watchful eyes on her. He didn't look his usual debonair self. He was wearing a shabby

T-shirt and carried a large overloaded backpack. He sported the ugliest baseball cap she had ever seen. Was this his idea of impersonating an artist?

Ruth wasted no time. "I'm getting tired of having so many people in my face. I'm going to find a quiet spot in one of the villages and sit there and paint the whole day. I've heard that Vernazza is lovely and has a great restaurant. Are you game? Want to join me?"

"I want to hear Edgar's lecture and see what he has planned for us first."

"Sure, once he's done we'll head out together. Don't tell the others or they'll want to join us. I want this to be our special day together. I don't want anyone ruining it."

The traffic was light as the bus wended its way towards Cinque Terre.

Edgar made a few comments into his mike but for the most part, he was quiet. When Ruth fell asleep, he came down the aisle and crouched beside her. "Gotta show you these, Em."

He pulled out his cell phone and displayed picture after picture of his dog. "The Magster sent me a bunch of selfies."

"Edgar, I'm not that naive."

"If you must know Mrs. Johnson, my next door neighbour, is looking after Maggy. She took them and sent them to me. But it was probably Maggy's idea. See, this is a real dog, not like that skinny thing you own."

"I'll have you know, that on behalf of Wellington, I take offence to that."

"One dark snowy night I met his lordship taking your skinny beast for a walk."

"His lordship, are you referring to my husband?"

"Who else? He walked down the street like he was trying to take in the view from Toronto. I used to wonder if he ate caviar for breakfast."

"Edgar, you're bad. He wasn't like that at all."

"In any case he had Wellington dressed up in a fur coat and cute little booties. The Magster could hardly contain herself, she was laughing so hard."

"Edgar, you are really too much. Dogs don't laugh. You're making this up."

"How can you be so sure? They probably get together and laugh at us all the time."

He returned to his seat, as the bus exited Brugnato-Borgetto Vara. Not long afterwards they arrived at Riomaggiore.

Cinque Terre consists of five villages named: Riomaggiore, Manarola, Corniglia, Vernazza and Monterosso al Mare, all of which hang over cliffs by the sea and are accessible by a train which allows travellers to shuttle between the villages at will.

Edgar planned to bring his artists here three times during the month. They could paint in any of the villages on the first two days and on their third day they would travel up and down the coast by boat. The views from each of the five villages were breathtakingly beautiful. The villages themselves were laden with old-world charm. In other words, it was an artist's paradise.

They climbed off the bus and milled around waiting to retrieve their painting equipment from the storage bay under the bus. Ruth was beside her.

Edgar announced in a loud voice that everyone was to follow him. He began walking toward to a grassy knoll.

After Emily identified her backpack, she felt it being lifted from her hand and looked up to see Karl Busch standing beside her. He smiled down at her. "May I join you today? I need extra help with my stick figures."

She thought of Edgar's instructions about playacting and smiled up at him. "I would be delighted. I'm sure we can improve your drawing skills."

Ruth groaned. "But you and I were going to spend the day together. Remember!"

Karl said, "And deprive me of the lovely lady's company? I can't let that happen."

Ruth stood firmly in front of Emily blocking her way up the hill. "Emily, don't you remember? You promised to spend the day with me."

"But I . . ." Emily began.

Karl interrupted: "You won't mind if she joins me today, will you Po-Ling Yanmei?"

Ruth turned pale. "Forgive me!" she whispered as she stepped aside.

Soll had insinuated herself into the painting group. She sat with Dave Rowe on the bus and was now standing beside him. She looked as though she had eaten something rancid as she watched Karl take Emily's backpack and lead her up the hill to the back of the group. Karl showed no indication he was aware of her intent and nodded back to her.

They sat or rather Emily sat. Karl struggled to angle his large frame onto a three legged stool.

Ruth placed her stool beside MJ's and sat down. She was ghostly pale.

Edgar looked toward the parking lot and then up at Karl. His worried look was back. Something was wrong.

He began his lesson: "Today we'll talk about clouds. Why? Because we're on the coast and have loads of them as you all can well see. What colour are clouds?"

MJ's hand shot up. "White!"

"White? Will you point out a white cloud for me?"

"They're all white. Clouds are always white. Everyone knows that," MJ announced as she looked confidently around the group, certain that all the artists would agree with her.

"White and black do not occur in nature," Edgar replied.

"What other colour could they possibly be? Ask anybody. Clouds are white, end of story," MJ countered.

Edgar looked at Mary. "Mary, please hand out one paper to each participant."

Mary did as requested and soon each artist was in possession of an oblong piece of white cardboard perforated with two round holes, one large and the other small.

"Now everyone hold up your piece of cardboard and when you come to a cloud that matches the white of the paper let me know."

MJ stood up. "My God, you're right, Edgar. There isn't a single white cloud up there."

Emily watched as Edgar tried unsuccessfully to stifle a chuckle when both Black and White seemed to become mesmerized with their own study of clouds. When Dave realized everyone was watching them he gave Black a shove.

"Do clouds have shadows? Are they darker on the top or bottom? At present they are darker on the bottom because the sun is above them. At sundown, the reverse is true. What colours can we use to paint the cloud formations we see here today? Decide how intense you want your sky to be? Try using ultramarine with maybe a touch of an earth tone to start? If you want to try some other tones, feel free. Take out your brushes and let's experiment."

He stopped and looked around. "Does everyone have paint, paper and brushes? Anyone need some water? You don't have equipment, Rinaldo?"

Rinaldo pointed at Gianna. She glared back at him but then offered to let him watch as she painted. The two had indulged in a loud argument before Gianna boarded the bus at the villa. Rinaldo then drove his Ferrari to Cinque Terra while she travelled by bus with the rest of the group.

As Emily listened to the lesson she realized that Karl had edged his stool closer to hers. He was so close she could feel the heat from his thigh through her pant legs.

Edgar looked in the direction of the parking area again. He seemed a bit distracted. He began his final instructions. "Please do not travel alone. Go in pairs or better still, in a group. Hold onto your handbags at all times. The bus leaves at 4pm. Please be on time. It's a long walk back to Villa DiMattia from here."

Karl leaned over and whispered: "Emily, something is not right here. I want to get you away as fast as possible. Prepare yourself! When I say to move, we'll run. Pack up all your equipment now. We'll leave the stools and your backpack here. Edgar can grab them later. Hand me your little purse. Is your passport in it?"

She nodded as she loaded her art supplies into her bag. He grabbed her purse and stuffed it into his own backpack.

He didn't move.

Emily suddenly felt as though she was the centre of attention.

Ruth was watching her.

Rinaldo was now standing and looking at her. He nodded to some men standing about twenty metres down the hill from where the painting group had set up. Earlier Edgar had told them to either pay to listen to his art lesson or move away. They turned as a group and began walking up the hill.

Things were happening so quickly. She felt as though everything was spinning out of control.

Jerry wasn't here. Edgar told her he would follow the bus in a van with several officers. He wasn't here. Something must have happened to him.

Edgar nodded to Karl and pointed to Mario, their bus driver, who was standing close by. Mario nodded as well.

Edgar trusted Karl. She had no choice but to trust him now. When they were alone she would tell him about the conversation she overheard last night.

Karl checked his watch and whispered: "Turner told me you can move fast when you have to. There's a train that should be pulling out of the station in one and one-half minutes. It's at least a hundred metres behind us. Think you can run fast enough to catch that train?"

Emily nodded.

He took hold of her hand. His warmth permeated through her coldness.

As soon as his grip tightened, they jumped up in unison. His stride was longer than hers but she made up for it in speed. They ran toward the train.

The whistle sounded as they reached the stairs leading to the platform.

TEN

Emily hesitated at the bottom of the stairs when she heard the train whistle blow.

"Keep moving!" Karl panted. "Don't slow down!"

He wrapped his arm around her, propelling her up the stairs.

The train door was still open when they reached the platform.

The door was less than five metres from the top step. To her mind, it appeared a vast distance away.

She could feel her chest heaving. She was flagging.

With his arm still draped across her back, Karl actually picked up his pace and used his momentum to impel her forward with him.

The train whistle blew for the second time as he thrust her onto the lowest step and jumped on beside her.

The train doors slammed shut.

They stood there holding each other. Both of them were panting.

The train began to pick up speed. They watched through the window as the landscape began to pass by at an ever increasing rate.

"You OK?" he asked.

She nodded but he held her for a moment longer.

Karl waited until her breathing had returned to normal before he looped his arm around her waist and together they climbed up the steps to the platform.

Then he opened the door and allowed her to enter the car ahead of him.

They were met by a wall of harmonious sound.

It was as though they had walked out of one reality and entered another.

The coach was filled with excited school children. Several school buses had followed their bus into the parking area. The students filed by as Edgar was giving his lesson. Judging by the noise level, the children were delighted about having a day of adventure at Cinque Terre.

She could feel Karl close behind her as they looked for a seat. The first car was full. He pulled open the door at the far end. As they navigated to the next car they could hear the metallic music of the wheels as they threaded their way along the tracks.

He pushed open the door to the second coach. She edged past him and began again looking for an empty seat. This car was filled with older children. They were noisy but it sounded different somehow. It lacked the harmoniousness of the first car.

In the third car, they were presented with a choice of seats.

"Emily, there are seats in the middle of the car. Let's sit there."

The train lurched as it began to slow for Manarola, the second of the villages. With Emily's tension at such a high level, she lacked her usual agility and stumbled slightly backwards.

An arm shot out to steady her. It was a strong arm with a large hand that gently rubbed her upper arm in a reassuring way.

She dropped into a seat and he sat facing her.

It was the first time she had the chance to examine him up close. He was handsome in a rugged sort of way. His hair was golden blond with streaks of grey at the sides. His eyes were a warm shade of blue.

As she scrutinized him, she realized she was now dependent on this man alone for her safety. Edgar was no longer there to tease her and cajole her when things went wrong.

She felt vulnerable and began to shiver. Her mind began racing.

Had she made a dreadful mistake trusting him?

Was it possible this man was Viktor, the assassin Ruth had alluded to?

Was his reason for separating her from the others to extract information, even under duress?

He seemed oblivious to her thoughts as he scrutinized their surroundings and checked items in his backpack. "Are you OK?"

"A bit winded, but I'm fine." She lied.

"Are you up to answering a few questions?" he asked perfunctorily.

His question was enough to make her realize she had to get control of herself. Now was not the time to panic. She tried to relax. She could feel him studying her. She didn't want to answer his questions. What she wanted to do was tell him about what she overheard from Ruth's phone conversation last night but she couldn't seem to put those things into words, so she nodded her head and acquiesced.

Details of anything she overheard the previous night evaporated from her mind as soon as she heard his first question.

"Emily, are you aware your late husband resigned from his partnership at his law firm immediately after he married you?"

"Immediately after he married me?" She wondered if she heard him correctly. "I don't understand. John continued to work there. He never changed his business number or address. That can't be right."

"Emily, according to his former partners, he did in fact resign at that time. He then rented his former office from his old firm and referred prospective clients back to them."

"Are you saying that as soon as we were married, he quit his position? He was a partner in a large Toronto law firm. He quit that?"

"Yes, he was paid out for his partnership interest not long afterwards. You seem surprised."

"I am surprised. But he continued to work there. He always seemed to be busy. Did he set up his own practise? But then why would he refer prospective clients back to his old firm, not keep them himself? I don't understand."

"He told his former partners he would be working exclusively for one or perhaps two major clients on his own. Did he mention the names of his clients to you?"

She hesitated. In her mind an image was forming of meeting a tall man at an embassy reception in Paris. She could now see his nameless face. This was the man John had rushed over to meet.

"I beg your pardon, Emily. Are you all right? You look a bit pale."

"I'll be fine. There's been a bit too much excitement, that's all." Her mind was racing, trying to come to grips with another important piece of information about her late husband. Another thing he neglected to discuss with her.

"I understand. Are you up to continuing with some more questions?" Karl asked.

She nodded.

"Very large sums of money started being transferred into Mr. Clark's business account after he separated from his partnership. Were you aware of any major change in his financial circumstances around that time?"

She wondered if the revelations about John would ever cease. She was attempting not to concede to the notion that was forming in her mind, but the facts were piling up forcing her to question everything about the man she had loved, the man she thought she knew.

"From the time I met John he was uncommonly kind and generous to me and to his son Paul. He bought our house before we married and gave it to me as a wedding gift. I'm not a woman who spends great amounts of money but he gave me a more than adequate allowance for house and personal expenses after I sold my restaurant. He invested the money from the sale of my business in my name and gave me regular updates on the status of those investments. Those were the only monies invested in my name. Those were the only ones I knew anything about while he was alive."

"I see," he said slowly as he continued eyeing her.

"Is there a problem? I was told by our accountant that all income taxes had been paid."

Realizing the enormous stress the woman must be trying to cope with, Karl spoke much more gently. "He picked up all transfers into his bank account as income and paid out large sums in taxes."

"I have no idea of the size of his annual income. I don't know how much most lawyers make in a year. One of his clients introduced us. He later told me John was highly successful and commanded huge fees. He said he was worth every penny of it."

"Didn't he keep you informed of his financial situation in the years you were together? He built up a large portfolio during that time. How could you possibly not know?"

"If you mean, did he show me statements from his brokers or his income tax returns, the answer is no. We never discussed finances, not even once. I never thought to ask how much money he was making or what his net worth was. I'm sure he would have told me if I had asked. We didn't keep secrets from one another or so I thought until a few days ago. In retrospect I suppose it was naive of me to hand over the reins so unquestioningly, but I trusted him implicitly."

"You were behaving no different from any other loyal wife. Trust is the basis of marriage. But didn't you wonder at the size of the estate he left you?"

"I did wonder about it. I spent the past year living in our empty house wishing I could trade all the money just to have him back with me."

"Do you still feel that way?"

"Perhaps, not. But why is it, no one wants to believe me? I know absolutely nothing about any of this. It's all been a great shock to me. I didn't know there was an armoury hidden in my own basement, let alone some mystery weapon stashed away somewhere else."

"I believe you, Emily," he said gently. "That's enough questions for now. All of this can wait. I'm more concerned with your safety than anything else. You seem to have attracted some heavy artillery from both sides of the Atlantic."

"I wish Greg would find the damn weapon so this would all go away."

When the train had pulled into Corniglia, they watched as troops of excited school children along with their already weary teachers and chaperones appeared on the platform beside the train and began descending into the village below.

At Vernazza, older children lined up like little soldiers and followed their teachers.

The residents of Cinque Terre had long ago perfected the art of cliff dwelling. The villages are built on magnificent rocky formations that seem to climb out of the water. Somehow the precariously perched dwellings are serviced by the railroad. The beauty of the area is so intense that had her situation not been so dire, Emily would have loved to photograph or sketch almost every scene. The residents added to the ambiance with their local cheese shops and seafood restaurants. Emily had once toured the area by boat but never had she experienced the sheer grandeur of it in this fashion.

There was a smattering of British and German tourists left on the train as it pulled into Monterosso al Mare, the last of the five villages. Emily and Karl were the final passengers to climb down the steps to the pavement below.

"Viktor!"

"Viktor?" Karl repeated, and then comprehension began to set in. His blue eyes ratcheted up several degrees in intensity.

"Are you Viktor?"

Karl almost choked. "Am I Viktor? Absolutely not! How and where did you hear of Viktor?"

"Ruth talked about this Viktor as through she knew him."

"Ruth, your roommate at the villa talked about Viktor? Your roommate knows Viktor? Pardon me if I sound surprised. She talked to you about Viktor?"

"Not really! I overheard her talking to someone else. She didn't know I was listening. I heard her say she wanted to keep Viktor away from me."

"I'm not surprised. What else did you overhear?"

"Ruth said this Viktor person is staying at the villa and has been near me on two occasions."

"Viktor is staying at the villa? And was near you? Are you serious?"

She nodded.

"Emily, what do you know about Viktor?"

"Nothing, other than what I overheard from Ruth. What's so special about him?"

"Emily, Viktor is known in Europe as the assassin's assassin. More often, he is called 'the monster'. He's eluded police for the past ten years. The man is like a chameleon, blending in wherever he goes. He is a man of infinite disguises, usually appearing as a man but occasionally he disguises himself as a woman. We do know he is about six feet tall and of slight build. Has anyone like that been near you?"

"I can't remember. There are so many people at the villa. It could have been anyone staying or working there. He must have found out about the weapon."

"If he's at the villa, he not only found out about it but he wants it for himself. Emily, Viktor is insidious. He has shown himself to be capable of accessing inside information and has severely compromised our security systems. We know there is a leak at a very high level, but no one has been able to find it."

"Greg Turner told me there was a security problem. I was surprised when he insisted Edgar act as my bodyguard."

"You may not have known it at the time, but you could not have been in better hands. I insisted only Edgar and my partner Jerry, be involved in escorting you to Tuscany for a very good reason. I knew you would be safer entering the country undetected. Emily, Viktor has killed witnesses on several occasions and more than once when they were in transit."

"You're frightening me. How dangerous is he, really?"

"When Viktor goes after a target he is indiscriminate about collateral damage. That's what makes him a real hazard. He once blew up a classroom full of children when the target was one of the children and the killing was meant to intimidate that child's father. It was a senseless loss of life. He seems to take a perverse delight in torturing some victims before he kills them. In the past few years, he has left behind a grizzly trail."

"If this kind of person exists in the world, I'm starting to understand why Greg Turner wanted to get me away from my family as fast as possible!"

"He was right to do so and your roommate had good reason to try to keep Viktor away from you, as well. Anyone who has heard details of the kind of depravity he is capable of, wouldn't allow any living creature near the man."

"Rinaldo Rizzi has been near me a couple times. Could he be Viktor?"

They had picked up their pace and now were running down the pathway toward the waterfront. Emily was trying to keep up with Karl's much longer legs. She was shivering badly.

Karl slowed and began pulling his jacket out of his backpack. He stopped and carefully draped it over her shoulders.

"Anything is possible. In some ways Rizzi fits the profile. He is the right height and certainly has a mean streak. With his father's connections he feels he has a free hand to do as he pleases, legal or otherwise. But Viktor is fastidious. He has shown himself to be the consummate planner. From what I observed of Rizzi's behaviour in the past couple days, he tends to act impulsively. I'd rule him out for that reason."

Karl seemed intent on scrutinizing the surrounding area as they made their way through the village. He pointed to a small round table outside a trattoria on the road that ran along the waterfront. "This looks perfect. It has an unobstructed view in both directions. We'll wait here until I can arrange transportation to move you to a safer location."

It had rained the night before and the streets still retained some dampness. Umbrella-toting tourists were busy photographing the scenery around them. A cool breeze blew in from the water.

As soon as they sat down, Karl dialled his cell phone. "Jerry, call me as soon as you get this message."

He dialled again. "Red alert! Viktor! I repeat Viktor is in the vicinity. Soll, I need backup immediately. I want to get Mrs. Clark out of here. Can you arrange for a helicopter immediately?

"No, Soll, I don't need you to do that. I prefer to see to her safety, myself. We are at Monterosso al Mare in front of a trattoria by the sea. Can you arrange transport out of here immediately? Thanks!"

Karl waved the waiter away when he came to take their order. The waiter was about to object but Karl held up his badge. The man nodded and went inside.

"If Greg Turner could find the KZR weapon, all these people would leave me alone," Emily lamented.

"There is more going on here than just that. Finding the weapon is not my immediate concern. Keeping you safe is."

"I thought of something last night. Can you ask Greg to check the watercolours hanging in my house? Whenever we travelled, my husband would select one of my paintings and take it to a framer in Toronto. He always insisted I write out the location where it was painted and sign and date it."

"I'll pass the word on."

He looked at his watch. "Why is it taking so long to get back-up?"

He stood up and waved to the waiter. "Please call the local police station. Tell them I am a Europol agent and am requesting immediate assistance in protection of a witness."

Emily was still trembling. He knew the minute he spotted her this morning something or someone had spooked her. He had a feeling she overheard a lot more from Ruth Zhou than she was admitting to.

If Viktor was now involved, she had good reason to be afraid. Viktor loved to pick off the families of his victims first. Then he'd go after his target. He had told her about some of Viktor's killings but not the full extent of the man's brutality.

If Viktor was bold enough to stay at the villa, he had made his first mistake. It was the chance everyone in law enforcement was waiting for. As soon as this business with Emily was over, he would pour through the guest lists, and the names of everyone at or near the villa or the painting group again. He would scrutinize every tape from the surveillance equipment. He'd also look at the surveillance tapes from all three airports she'd been in. He'd get the bastard.

Karl scanned the road for movement in both directions. Other than the odd tourist, there was no one. He couldn't make sense of the delay in getting backup. The situation was fit to go critical at any time.

"Karl, there's Ruth. She looks terrified and she's yelling something."

Ruth came running towards them. Emily's first thought was that Ruth had figured out where she was and was intent on maintaining her hold on Emily.

"GET EMILY OUT OF HERE! NOW, QUICKLY!"

They heard a popping noise as Ruth seemed to falter and fell to the pavement, her beige pants suddenly displaying a bright red patch. Her paint box went flying.

"VIKTOR IS HERE! VICTOR IS —" There was a second pop and Ruth's head seemed to burst open.

It took Emily – who had never in her life heard the discharge of a weapon – a few seconds to understand the gravity of what had just happened before her eyes.

Karl grabbed her by the arm and propelled her inside the trattoria. Picking up his phone he yelled, "Soll, we have a shooter! I need your help! Where the hell is the transport I asked for?"

Karl ordered everyone in the trattoria to sit on the floor behind the counter.

He spoke to the waiter: "Did you call the police as soon as I asked?"

"Yes, sir, I did. As soon as you said, I came in and phoned as soon as you told me."

"They should be here by now."

Barrage after barrage of gunfire was being exchanged outside.

They could hear several sirens in the distance. The sounds rose in pitch and then one by one stopped. Several Italian police officers entered with their revolvers drawn. Emily could see their images reflected in the glass casing above where she was sitting.

Karl held up his identification and chatted with the officers. He explained the importance of removing his witness, as he called her, from this danger zone.

Emily, was huddled behind the counter with several employees and a number of patrons.

She was trying desperately to maintain control of her emotions. She was trembling and wrapped Karl's jacket more tightly around herself. One woman was whimpering as her husband held her in his arms. A young mother strained to comfort a three year old. One of the waiters slid open a door in the counter and pulled out a chocolate-filled pastry which he handed to the mother.

She thought of John. It was John who had put her in this situation. None of this would be happening if not for him. Any man who loved his wife would never risk her safety in any way. He would protect her, not put her in danger. What if other innocent people were killed?

She watched as the woman continued to whimper while her husband stroked her shoulder and whispered. "Ti amo, Maria. Il mio amore."

Over the din of police radios and multiple conversations, she could hear Karl's deep baritone voice speaking calmly and with utmost control: "Jerry, what the hell happened? An accident?

Who cut you off? Are you all right? How many dead? Viktor is in the vicinity and right now we're in the midst of a shootout. Soll promised to send back-up but it hasn't arrived. She may have been hit. I think Viktor is trying to put the finishing touch on the Rizzi's plans. I'm getting Mrs. Clark out of here ASAP. Arranged for a safe house last night. We'll be incommunicado for a few days. I'll phone you Saturday morning first thing."

The gunfire outside continued.

A uniformed police officer came around the counter and pulled her up to standing position. It took a few seconds for her to grasp that the officer was Karl. He spoke in a low voice, "I am getting you out of here now. Put this on."

A police woman removed her uniform jacket and hat and handed them to Emily. She obediently pulled on the jacket, tucked up her light hair and pulled on the cap. The jacket was a bit large but it would do under the circumstances.

"We will take the police car in front of the trattoria. I've arranged for cover until we're out of this area. Police vehicles are moving in and out of the area with all the shooting going on. Hopefully, we shouldn't attract any undue attention."

Emily climbed into the passenger's seat. She sat erect and tried to breathe normally, praying not to fall victim to one of the many bullets being fired simultaneously behind them.

Karl accelerated slowly from the scene. Once on the highway he picked up speed. After three minutes the vehicle was proceeding at such a high speed that Emily reached up for the grab handle.

After cruising along winding roads for fifteen minutes they pulled to the side of the road under a bridge and sat and waited.

She let go of the grab handle and looked at Karl. He had not uttered a single word since he drove away from the melee at Monterosso al Mare. "Karl, I'm beginning to realize you enjoy being tight-lipped, but we are in this together. I want to know where we are going and if I'll be safe there."

"I'm not used to dealing with civilians. I'm sorry! My mind was elsewhere. I was trying to fathom how things got so out of control back there. I have a safe place where I can hide you away until the authorities get a handle on what just happened in Monterosso al Mare. We intended for you to be used as a decoy to see what interest this weapon might generate but at no time did any of us consider the possibility of the free-for-all you just witnessed. Nor did we think Viktor would be front and centre in this. I apologize that you were allowed to be exposed to this kind of danger."

"This was not your fault. I don't blame you. The only one at fault in this is my late husband."

"I am sorry about your friend Ruth. Seeing a friend mowed down like that, right before your eyes, can be traumatic. But you should know that her life was over. I sent her photograph and prints to a guy from Beijing I met at an anti-terrorism conference in Macau. Her real name was Po-Ling Yanmei and she was wanted in connection with the Ürümqi bus bombings in China. Nine people were killed and over seventy were injured. My associate believed she was tied to some other things, as well. He was most eager to get his hands on her."

"I met Ruth for the first time at the Toronto airport. We seemed to have so much in common. I didn't know her well or for very long. If she knew who Viktor was and didn't turn him in, she had to be evil, herself. However, in the end Ruth gave up her life trying to warn me about Viktor. I'll never forget that."

"I can understand why you might have mixed feelings about her. In my business, you never know who you can trust."

"I'm beginning to feel the same way. No one is who they appear to be, not even Edgar."

He chuckled. "Especially not Edgar!"

"Where are we going?"

"I phoned an old buddy who lives near here. He'll provide us with a car, food and a sanctuary until the authorities capture Viktor and whoever else is involved in this mess. We'll lay low for a few days. It'll be you and me holed up together. Hope you're all right with that."

"Greg Turner told me you'd keep me safe."

"And I will do everything in my power to do so. I can't allow any communication with the outside world for at least three days. Remove your security devices. Here, give me your necklace and bracelet. Viktor has found witnesses in safe houses before. I have no idea how he does it. He obviously has access to classified information. I didn't know the location of all those witnesses, but Viktor found them."

"How do you know it is Viktor every time?"

"Assassins have signatures. There are always similarities, Emily. We have people who specialize in profiling lawbreakers. Criminals have thought patterns like the rest of us. Profilers zero in on identifying similarities in cases. As I mentioned before, Viktor is fastidious about every aspect of his work. There's never a fingerprint or a hair left behind. The man is like a phantom. I'm curious. Tell me what else Ruth said about him? Sounds to me as though Ruth may have been acquainted with Viktor on a personal level."

"I got the impression that both Ruth and her friend Mary worked with Viktor before, but it sounded as though Ruth was afraid of him." Her voice trembled as she added: "I can't remember anything else she said. I'm sorry."

He eyed her. She knew more than she was willing to tell him at this time. She was terrified. That wasn't uncommon for someone caught up in a situation such as this.

He'd try to reassure her: "Emily, I will bring you safely through this. I give you my word. You made quite an impression on Greg Turner. When he phoned me from Canada and told me your story, he insisted I drop my other cases and focus on you. You've been caught up in a horrendous situation and have been very cooperative. We want the weapon before it gets into the wrong hands. And now that I know Viktor is interested in the thing, it is even more imperative we get our hands on it and quickly. However, at the moment, my highest priority is your safety."

He observed the dark shadows under her eyes. "You'll have the next three days to relax and get your energy back."

He looked up and began to open his car door. "Here they are! You'll like my friends."

Two Audis, one old and the second one new, pulled up behind them. A short dark Italian man climbed out of the first car and limped over to talk to Karl. A smiling, rather heavy set woman climbed out of the older car carrying several bags of groceries. She yelled to her husband to grab the rest of the bags.

"Emily, please meet my old friend Vincenzo and his lovely wife Antonia"

With a loud laugh the jovial man responded, "Nice to meet you, Emily. Call me Vince and my wife is Toni."

Vince's melodious voice reminded Emily of Italian opera. Almost every word seemed to have an 'a' attached to it.

Vince looked at Karl, "She's a beauty, Karl! You should hang onto her! Toni's gonna like her, you wait and see. It's time, my old friend."

"Business only, Vince! Not interested."

"A few days with such a woman and you may change your mind."

"Don't even go there, Vince."

"See my nice shiny new car. I won't let you forget what you did the last time you borrowed my car. You had to buy me a new one. That's what happened! Hope you're more careful this time. Don't drive like a maniac! Don't shoot holes in my new car. Don't even think of putting one scratch on my shiny new car."

Karl laughed out loud. "That wasn't me, Vince. I would never shoot holes in your car. You know I'm careful where I aim."

Vince's voice rang out again. "You can stay at my cousin Luigi's house near Pistoia. Luigi's gone to Australia to see his daughter. Here's the key and directions to his house. Now get on your way with this lovely lady and remember, no scratches, no dents, and no bullet holes this time."

"Vince you have me all wrong! I was an innocent bystander." With a laugh he added, "Trust me, it was the bad guys."

In a more serious voice he went on: "Vince, stick to the plan we discussed. Stay with your brother in Umbria. Did you close up the shop? Good! Even jewellers can take a week off. Plus the two of you could use a little holiday. I will be in touch as soon as the coast is clear and thanks."

Vince's Italian accented words continued to sing out: "I trust you, Karl. Actually it's exciting to be involved in all this secret spy stuff. Like some television programme, you know, going into hiding."

"We are dealing with a really nasty one this time, Vince. Don't take any chances. Don't use your credit cards and hide your car when you arrive at your brother's house."

Vince laughed merrily. "Actually it gives me a good excuse to visit with the rest of the family. Toni is all excited about getting away and she loves the intrigue. You shoulda heard her when I told her you were hiding away with a lady. You know, she's been trying to find you a wife for years. She was positively glowing when I told her you would be with a widow of a certain age. Then when she saw the lady in question, well, you shoulda heard her. Look the two of them are already talking away. How women love to talk! Watch out Karl, women are the real ones who make the decisions. They only let us think we decide things."

"No one decides anything for me, Vince."

Meanwhile Toni had already told Emily the story of how Karl saved Vince's life back in their army days.

"There won't be much food at Luigi's house because they are away all this month," Toni went on. "I hope I picked up enough to last the two of you for a few days. I didn't have much time but I did my best. There are herbs and some vegetables growing in the backyard. With all the rain we had, the garden should be in good shape. Vince and I drop by each week and check on the house. You'll like Luigi's place. It's old but completely modernized where it counts. The kitchen is great."

Emily tried not to show her nervousness. Her usual gregariousness had deserted her. All she could mutter was, "Thank you so much!"

Toni looked up and then added: "The boys are looking impatient. I pray you'll be safe at Luigi's place."

Karl indicated they had to rush so she hurried toward the car.

Emily wanted to reassure Toni that she would be fine but words seemed to fail her.

As they drove off they heard Vince shout, "And no shooting guns in cousin Luigi's house either! Any damage and you gotta fix it."

ELEVEN

Karl relaxed as he careened down narrow back roads.

Emily was growing progressively more nervous as they passed blurred landscapes. He seemed so comfortable she wondered if he always drove like a maniac or waited for special occasions such as this. She was amazed the tire walls didn't split open. She didn't dare say anything for fear that if she broke his concentration he might miss a jog in the road.

He smiled with satisfaction as they came to a screeching halt in front of a two-storey stone house with a large mahogany front door. All the large windows were covered with intricate metal grills. The outside was painted deep ochre beneath a terracotta roof. Under other circumstances Emily would have thought the place charming.

Karl climbed out of the driver's seat and unlocked the front door. He disappeared inside carrying two bags of groceries and came out to grab the rest of the bags. He remained inside longer this time and then came out and walked around the perimeter of the building. When he returned he looked at her questioningly.

Emily had opened her car door and unfastened her seat belt but when she tried to lift her legs to climb out of the car, her legs didn't seem to want to move. She sat in the seat feeling unbearably exhausted. When Karl walked around to her side of the car, she whispered, "I want to rest a few minutes and then I'll go inside. I need to get my bearings."

The events of the past night, the gun fight, seeing Ruth killed before her eyes and finally a road trip at lightning speed had all taken a toll on her. She was trembling badly. Karl sensed she had depleted her emotional resources. Her face was ghost white and she looked as though she might pass out.

He bent down and gently but easily lifted Emily out of her seat and carried her into the house. He carefully placed her on the sofa, grabbed a blanket and threw it over her. He boiled the kettle while stowing the meat and fish in the refrigerator. He arrived at her side with a cup of hot tea laced with honey and a biscuit. Her hands were shaking so badly she couldn't hold the cup so he held it for her.

"I know what you need." He disappeared into the kitchen and returned with a bottle of brandy and added some to her tea.

"Try this."

He held the cup to her mouth and helped her drink. Meanwhile he helped himself to a larger drink.

"Take your time. You've had quite a day." He held her cold hands in his and rubbed them. She looked up at him and was suddenly whisked off the sofa onto his lap.

"I started the heater but this old place will take a while to warm up. As soon as there is hot water, I'll run a warm bath for you. In the meantime you need my body heat so snuggle close. You had a bit of a shock today. It is not unusual for someone unaccustomed to gunfire to experience this sort of reaction. Relax, just relax."

He continued to gently rub her back and shoulders trying to soothe the tension in her muscles.

He spoke smoothly: "No vehicles followed us here. I deliberately broke every speed limit and took a rather circuitous route to ensure no one could. Once we arrived I did a quick check of the perimeter and was pleased with what I found. Vince's cousin, Luigi, must have been troubled by break-ins because he fortified this old place. All the windows have solid metal grills and are shuttered from the inside. The back door can only be opened from the inside."

He took a sip of his brandy laced drink before continuing: "The patio in the back is completely enclosed and has a strong door. When you're feeling better, you can sit out there and be concealed from the rest of the world. Hopefully we won't have any worries about your safety so long as you remain in the house or the patio area."

She nestled into the warmth of his body as he continued speaking: "I put the groceries away. All the perishables are in the refrigerator. Toni bought us enough food to last a week. I'll reimburse Vince for the groceries and wine and anything else we use. By the way, can you cook?"

She was beginning to feel more relaxed and answered him in a steadier voice, "Yes. I once ran my own restaurant."

He continued gently massaging her shoulders trying to release her pent up tension as he spoke: "Music to my ears! I love good food but am a lousy cook myself. Jerry and I usually eat out."

Soon his gentle rubbing on her back began to feel sensual. Her shivering subsided and she began to feel deliciously cozy. Her breathing returned to normal.

"Feeling better?"

"Yes, thank you. I'm usually in control of my emotions. I don't know why I was so overcome. Normally I am a very sensible woman. My apologies."

She reached up and gave him a gentle peck on his cheek.

Taken by surprise, he eyed her carefully. "What was that for?"

"Just a little thank you. That's all."

"A little thank you?" he asked as he finished the last of his drink in one gulp. "What does a guy have to do to get a bigger thank you?"

She looked at him surprised, thinking his words were out of character.

"I barely know you but after all you have done to protect me and calm me down, I'm very grateful. I didn't mean to be bold."

"I would never have thought anything like that," he offered as he watched her. "We should eat. We both had some brandy on an empty stomach."

Neither of them moved. If anything, she snuggled closer to him. Instead of rising to go to the kitchen Karl tipped her head back and kissed her, at first lightly and then more intensely. Whether it was the rush of adrenaline they had experienced earlier in the day or the proximity of a sexual body, they were both aroused. He ran kisses down her neck, up the side of her face, across her forehead, down the other side of her face and finally kissed her lips again. Emily responded by writhing on his lap, exciting him even more. She looped her arms around his neck and began returning his kisses.

Emily looked up into his blue eyes. She sounded dubious as she whispered, "You know we really should get some dinner."

With a grin, Karl murmured, "We should, but I think I have a better idea."

Karl picked her up and raced up the stairs in search of a bedroom. As soon as he found the master bedroom he rolled her onto the bed and was immediately on top of her. He kissed her while unbuttoning her blouse. Simultaneously she unbuttoned his shirt. He kissed the soft skin on her neck and then gently suckled her breast. She began to breathe loudly and kissed his shoulder. She ran her tongue along his neck and down his chest ending by gently nibbling at his nipple.

His words were no longer certain. He softly drew out every syllable as he whispered in her ear, "Emily, say no, if you don't want this. Say no, now."

But she did not say no. Instead, she kissed the side of his neck, then his cheek, then his lips.

He implored her, "Emily, I should not be doing this. I am here to protect you."

"Karl, I have the greatest need I have ever felt to be loved. Please love me!"

They stripped off their remaining clothes and were soon entwined. Their lovemaking was intense and when they climaxed, Emily felt as though she was suspended in mid-air. The feeling was new and seemed to resonate throughout her body. She wanted the sensation to last and last. They were panting and covered in sweat as a feeling of contentment descended on them.

"Emily, never in my life have I experienced anything like that. What just happened here? How was it for you?"

"It was the same for me. It was ecstasy," she replied as she felt the newness of relaxation overtake her body.

When Karl's breathing eased he rose and ran a bath. He returned and led her to the tub and then climbed in behind her. He caressed her as he bathed her.

When the water cooled he helped her out of the tub and wrapped a towel around her shoulders. He dried himself and found matching terrycloth robes for them to wear.

As Emily finished drying herself she contemplated their lovemaking. No doubt her desire was brought on by her emotional need to be held and loved after the harrowing events of the past few hours, but Karl was right: something special had happened here. It was something indefinable. She had never experienced anything so potent and Karl said he felt the same way. How was it possible to feel something so intense with someone she met only yesterday?

She watched as the tall muscular man finished drying himself and donned Luigi's short robe. She couldn't help but admire his physique. He had an outstanding build: six foot four, broad shouldered and muscular.

Edgar had told her that Karl lost his wife and children under tragic circumstances years ago and since then had never shown any interest in remarrying. Not that she was seeking a husband, but she would have to guard her heart and bear in mind that this could only be a short interlude in her life. He would be an easy man to love. He had shown her great kindness and gentleness. Oh yes, he would be very easy to become enamoured with.

He followed her to the kitchen area.

"I'll make dinner," she said as she began rearranging the food in the refrigerator.

"Music to my ears!"

Emily opened a bag containing two sea bream. "Karl, I need some rosemary and sage from the garden and some dry white wine for cooking as well."

"I'll find the wine but may need help identifying the herbs. They all look like green plants to me."

She rinsed a cup of rice under cold water and then put it on to cook. Then she followed Karl outside to the patio in search of the herbs. The herb garden had been well cared for by Vince and Toni during Luigi's absence. Emily bent down and took snippets of rosemary and sage.

Back in the kitchen, she crushed some garlic, carefully placed two pieces of bream onto a sheet of foil and seasoned them with herbs, salt, pepper and some lemon zest.

The fish cooked in minutes and was served on a bed of seasoned rice. The side dishes included steamed broccoli and a spinach salad with grated parmesan.

Emily set the table in the back patio. She found a white table cloth and napkins and completed the scene with two candles. Karl opened a bottle of vintage white wine and poured two generous glasses.

They dined with eyes riveted on each other. Both of them were still reeling from the intensity of their lovemaking. It had been a spur of the moment inclination for each of them, but the fire it kindled had astonished them both. Now as they sat facing each other, there was the promise of more passion to come.

They ate slowly, savouring the flavour of fresh herbs mixed with lemon on the fish. They talked casually as new lovers often do, not wanting to probe too much for fear of an answer that may end their euphoric mood.

They sat afterwards sipping wine and enjoying the succulent fruit Toni had thoughtfully bought for them.

When she rose to clear the table Karl declared himself the king of the clean-up. He quickly washed up the dishes and pots.

They chatted about the events of the day. She was grateful to have a respite from what had begun to feel like an endless stream of disturbing events. Danger was new to her. It wasn't something she wanted to become accustomed to.

"Have you done this sort of thing before?"

He looked up from his stance above the sink. "This sort of thing? You mean wash dishes? All the time, I live alone."

"No, I mean hide away with someone like this?"

"Usually Jerry and I do it together so we can spell one another. And normally we're protecting a big scary guy who is afraid of the mafia or some such thing. This is the first time I've had a beautiful woman all to myself. Jerry will be jealous, he loves blonds."

She flinched. Being here with her was work for him, nothing more.

After cleaning up the kitchen, they examined the house in detail. The main floor had been gutted and completely renovated. It was the ultimate in open concept design. The kitchen was separated from the large living room by a long bar with a number of stools along one side. Where the partitions once stood, there was the occasional pillar painted pale yellow ochre to match the surrounding walls.

The living room featured numerous soft toned leather sofas and small tables. A large fireplace bisected the wall on the far side. The house was redesigned for ease of entertaining. Emily could imagine a large family enjoying each other's company without the usual barriers of walls. It was quite different from her own home but she was delighted with what she saw.

Karl was even more pleased with the security measures Luigi had installed. "He is a man after my own heart. You must check out the locks on the grills and in the patio."

He instructed her how to use the lock on the backdoor and the outside grill. "This door opens from the inside only. See how sturdy it is! Now watch while I show you how to open the grill. The grills on the windows open in the same fashion."

He showed her how to lift and flick a small lever to the left before using the handle to open the grill work door. "Here, you try it. I want you to be able to get out quickly in case of emergency. Good!"

The patio was covered with flagstones and surrounded by a high stone wall. There was a large metal door dividing the right side of the wall.

"The key to the door on the patio is hiding here. Lift this and it can be pulled out on a pulley. Now open up the door. See, it leads to the side alley where I parked the car. Because the patio is so completely enclosed we should be quite safe out here. It is a shame to be cooped up all the time but we really have no choice."

That evening they sat on the sofa watching the flames in the fireplace, enjoying another glass of wine. They felt mellow, that comfortable feeling that comes from forgoing purposeful thought. His arm was draped loosely along her shoulders. They talked about their childhoods, he was Belgian and she was Canadian. They had nothing in common other than the case they were involved in and a huge sexual attraction for each other.

Unexpectedly Karl's tone became serious: "Emily, I sense you are not telling me everything. I have a feeling you are holding something back."

She looked away evasively. She deliberated for a full minute before responding, "You don't really know me at all. Why would you think that?"

"Humour me, my dear! When I first saw you this morning, you looked as though you had seen a ghost. When we were in Monterosso al Mare, I got the distinct impression you were distracted. Care to talk about it? I promise you I am a very good listener."

"You're very observant."

"They pay me to be observant."

He sat patiently waiting while she pondered what to say. Still refusing to look at him she spoke: "I told you some of what

I overheard Ruth say last night but there are some other things I am finding difficult to digest. If you will give me some time, I promise to reveal all I overheard. I think I may have figured out who she was talking to."

He turned her around and gently raised her chin, and looked directly into her eyes. "I can't do my job properly without all the pertinent facts. You have to come clean with me."

She wanted to look away but the intensity of his cerulean eyes kept her spellbound. "I understand that. Nevertheless I am asking you to bear with me. How many days will we be here?"

"Today is Tuesday. I told Jerry we would be back in touch early Saturday morning. That gives us three more days."

"I promise you this: on each of the three days I will divulge one of the things Ruth spoke about. Please understand that some of the issues I am dealing with, have a significant impact on my own life. I am requesting your patience."

"Request granted, but I will ask first thing each morning. I won't forget!"

She was grateful for the forbearance Karl was showing her. Emily knew he was the kind of person who was accustomed to exercising control in all situations and yet he was bending for her. He was giving her the time and space she felt she needed to digest the appalling information she had overheard. She needed time to allow herself to begin to heal. She wanted the numbness to go away. Karl had no way of comprehending how deeply these fissures ran throughout the essence of her life with John. Until recently she considered her unblemished husband to be an outstanding pillar of the community. Now she was facing a new and grim truth about the man.

As the fire died down they rinsed out their glasses and headed to bed. What would it be like this time? Would they create sparks again? Had what happened been a singular occurrence?

They climbed into bed careful not to touch but as the bed sagged somewhat in the middle, Emily, the lighter of the two, rolled into Karl. That was all it took. The feeling of skin on skin ignited their passion again. What began with soft gentle kisses escalated to explosive heat.

Within a minute Karl had removed her borrowed nighty and was kissing her from head to toe. She revelled in his every touch. She began to caress him first on his chest and then she worked her way down to his private parts. As soon as she felt the tip of his penis he became rigidly erect. Her touch seemed to ignite a fire in him.

He felt the gentle moisture between her legs and rolled over atop her and entered her. He waited a moment and then slowly began the dance of love. He wanted the rapture to last and last so he lengthened each thrust. Finally with both of them panting and covered with perspiration he quickened the pace and they climaxed in concert. It was a beautiful sweet high, one that seemed to go on and on. Her feeling of pleasure was even more intense than before.

Afterwards she lay awake thinking about this wonderful man. His lovemaking was beyond anything she could have imagined. He epitomized masculinity. He was ruggedly handsome, incredibly well built and unbelievably considerate. She drifted off to sleep dreaming about the man who made love to her, a man she barely knew. For the first time in years her thoughts and dreams were not about John Clark. A new reality had entered her world. A kinder, gentler reality and its name was Karl Busch.

The next morning Emily showered and found one of Luigi's old shirts to wear while she laundered her own clothes.

She smiled at the delightful sight that met her eyes when she descended the stairs. The sun was slanting through the shutters and gave the whole space a warm glow. The pale yellow ochre of the walls seemed to shimmer with warmth.

She thought it might be nice to serve breakfast on the back patio. She put up the umbrella and set the table before going to the kitchen.

She skinned and seeded tomatoes and then pureed them after adding a bit of fresh oregano from the garden. She would serve them with olive oil over fresh biscuits. She waited until she heard Karl turn off the shower before cooking the eggs.

Karl smiled warmly when he found her seated on the patio behind a table already laden with breakfast goodies. "I've never stayed in a safe house where the food was so good and the company so lovely. Even the coffee tastes fantastic. Did you sleep well?"

"Unbelievably well, considering the events of yesterday. And you?"

"Never better."

Then he became more serious. "Now remember your promise. You said you would reveal one thing each day. I am listening."

He had just revealed something about himself. He was first and foremost a policeman and his prime interest in her was business and only business. She instructed herself to remember that. She swallowed. Then she gave a half smile and responded: "I did promise and you said you would ask first thing. I didn't realize that first thing meant before you ate your breakfast. Your eggs will get cold."

His intense cerulean eyes were riveted on her.

"Fair enough! John, my late husband, was married for about fifteen years to a very successful Toronto divorce lawyer. She died about two years before I met him. I overheard Ruth say Viktor had an affair with John's first wife and then injected her with a carcinogen, which apparently ended her life within three months."

"Viktor killed the first wife of the man you were married to? And in such an inhumane way! My God! I can now understand why you needed time to think about this. What a monstrous way to kill another human! Although when I think about it, this is in character for the individual we know as Viktor. He is capable of unfathomable cruelty."

"I know very little about John's first wife other than that her name was Helen. John never talked about her."

"Even if you didn't know the woman or very much about her, this really hits home. Both of you were married to the same man. Do you realize what the implications of this are?"

"Not really!"

"If John's first wife was personally connected to Viktor, it raises the possibility that your late husband was acquainted with Viktor as well. How many children did the woman have?"

"She left behind a boy. Paul was seventeen when John and I got together. He is very dear to me and has grown into a wonderful young man."

"Did this murder happen in Canada or Europe?"

"I don't know. John never talked about his life before we met. They lived and worked in Toronto. As soon as we married, John moved to Dundas and commuted to his office in Toronto."

"Think, Emily. Did Ruth say anything else about Helen Clark?"

"Ruth did say something else. I think she must have known John's first wife because she called her a real bitch and commented that after he married me, he hid me away. Wait, there was something. She said John's first wife began asking too many questions. She said it as though it justified what Viktor had done."

"Think back to your early days with Clark. Is there anything you can remember he might have said about his first wife?"

"John sold his house in Toronto after our wedding. I was trying to find pieces for our home so he invited me to pick out any furnishings I wanted. The place was massive. Judging by the sheer volume of gowns Helen Clark left behind, I would say she and John lead a very active social life together. Their house and furniture were elaborate and not to my quiet taste, so I helped him dispose of most things. I insisted Paul be allowed to go through everything. In fact, I drove Paul there myself and together we went through his mother's jewellery and collectibles. Strangely enough there was nothing Paul wanted, not even her jewellery."

"Tell me about the son."

"I think of him as my own child. He is now a young doctor. I have one grandson and another expected early next year. I know I must sound like a boastful grandmother."

Then she looked up sadly. "That poor woman never lived to see what a fine upstanding young man Paul would become. Her life was stolen from her!"

"The woman was murdered nine to ten years ago. Am I right?"

"Yes, two years before John and I met. That would make it about ten years ago."

"We think Viktor got into action two or three years before that. We have some evidence indicating he started in Italy, which makes me think he could be an Italian man. With all the travelling the two of you did, surely Clark took you to Italy? Tell me about your first trip there."

She thought back to her first trip with John. She remembered sitting on the sunlit balcony overlooking the Bay of Naples when John proposed to her. But she kept her voice business-like. "Our very first trip together was to Capri, or rather he left me in Capri and went off to do his business elsewhere. I'm not complaining because that was our arrangement."

"I see. In that case, it's possible the first Mrs. Clark had the same arrangement. The woman may have become bored when left to her own devices in a strange place and met and had an affair with Viktor while Clark was off doing business. When we catch Viktor we may be able to put the pieces together. We will catch him. Sooner or later these people slip up because they become brazen. That's when they make a mistake and get caught. In Viktor's case, it can't happen too soon."

They finished breakfast and talked about the possibility of going for a walk. The house was somewhat remote with nothing but a hilly wooded area behind it. Occasionally cars would whiz by on the road. Thus far nobody had stopped to investigate their presence in the house, possibly because they had seen Vince's car parked there before when he and Toni came to water the plants. They evaluated the risk involved in being seen by any of the local people.

Emily looked at the golden giant beside her. "Karl, this is Italy. How many Italians look like you?"

"I agree, but that goes for you as well. I've never ever seen anyone with eyes as beautiful as yours. They are such a soft green."

She thought wistfully about his comment. But no, their liaison could not possibly last.

Karl disappeared into the back bedroom to work out on Luigi's exercise equipment while Emily cleaned the kitchen and tidied up the main floor.

After working out, he went through the drawers and found some computer paper, several pencils and an eraser and brought it all downstairs to her.

"I realize none of this is ideal for sketching but it'll give you something to keep your mind busy."

Emily was immediately exhilarated. "Would you pose for me? I took a portrait class in the spring and I'm trying to hone my skills. You can read a book or doze while I sketch."

Karl couldn't imagine himself posing and was about to nix the idea but seeing the excited look on her face he relented: "I'm not going anywhere, so I'll be happy to oblige. No one ever asked me to pose before."

"That's an error which I intend to correct. You are extremely handsome. Your features are strong and your eyes are an amazing shade of blue."

As he posed they chatted amiably. They were surprised to discover how comfortable they were in each other's presence. Conversation was a relaxed give and take interspersed with chuckles. Emily found herself at ease and at times she forgot the horrific circumstances that brought them together.

As she sketched Karl's strong features, she was mindful of her growing attachment to him. She prodded herself to guard her heart or risk being hurt when they parted. Lunch consisted of a delicately seasoned Mediterranean shrimp salad and a fruit cup. Karl marvelled about how she could convert a few bags of groceries into gourmet feasts. After spending a year living alone

Emily was happy to have someone other than herself to cook for and even more pleased not to have to eat alone.

As she began to gather the dishes, she felt his arms go around her and a gentle kiss on the nape of her neck.

"I have a special dessert in mind."

She rotated in his arms and kissed him. Soon they were entwined and made it as far as the large sofa before stripping out of their clothes. Emily writhed beneath him. She couldn't fathom how he could thrill her over and over again. His lovemaking was addictive.

That afternoon she sketched his face from a different angle. She wanted to ask him to pose nude. What was she thinking?

At night, she felt his gaze from across the room as she laid dinner on the table. The mere sight of him was causing her to lose her focus. She'd heard girlfriends talk about having short torrid affairs. Was this how it felt to have one? Was it because she was the daughter of a minister, she considered herself above that. No matter what her previous thoughts might have been, she wanted to glory in every tantalizing sensation.

Was she in denial? She no longer wanted to deal with the fact that this was a very short-term arrangement. She wanted to lose herself in the moment and live it to the fullest. His loving was like a salve to her injured emotions. She wanted to lap up his warmth after the abominations she had heard from the mouth of her former roommate.

It was never like her to behave in such a wanton fashion. Was she exploring a side of herself she didn't know existed?

She mourned a man who in reality didn't exist. The John Clark she loved and cared for was not real. How much of their relationship had been a charade? He used her to camouflage his activities and she was an unsuspecting fool. Their wedding had been the high point in her life. She placed her trust in him, never once suspecting he was not what he appeared to be.

"A penny for your thoughts?" he said as he handed her a glass of red wine.

"They're not worth even a penny. My thoughts run from dreadful to confused. There are times when I want to shut out the world and pretend you and I can stay here forever. And then reality dawns and I tell myself to get a grip and grow up. There's much I have to face."

"Emily, this is temporary. We're here for three days. I am not in any way interested in a long-term relationship. I had hoped we could enjoy each other's bodies without anyone getting hurt. I'm sorry. I should have realized how vulnerable you are before I made love to you."

Her mind was racing ahead. She needed his closeness. Even if it lasted only a couple more days. She needed it to help rid herself of all vestiges of her late husband. Every time he held her, John's hold on her slipped further away.

"You misunderstood me, Karl. I wasn't referring to our relationship. I feel safe here. It's the first time I've felt safe since this all began."

He held her hand and began kissing his way up her arm. "In that case, I made some plans. I booked a room for us tonight."

"A room?"

"Yes, a room with a view of the hills! It's not far, just up the stairs."

"Does the room come with room service?"

"Perhaps that could be arranged."

That night Karl laid her on her stomach and after massaging her and kissing her, he gently entered her. From this position he was in control. She loved being under his gentle care. After making love, she was instantly asleep.

She awoke to the smell of freshly brewed coffee. She opened her eyes to find Karl sitting on the edge of the bed smiling down at her. "Hello sleeping beauty. You ordered room service."

He presented her with a tray of fried eggs, ham and fruit. "Can I interest you in some breakfast? I live on my own so I can manage to cook eggs and a few other things. I know it isn't up to your usual standard."

"It looks and smells fantastic."

"You slept peacefully last night. You didn't toss and turn like the night before."

"I'd no idea I was so restless."

She listened while he described the latest news from the morning television broadcast. Then he fixed her with a direct look. "What information are you revealing today?"

She looked at him sadly and began her story.

"I met John Clark about eight years ago. Both Paul and I saw him transform from an uncaring and distant father into a man who displayed great affection and compassion for his son. From the beginning he was always a thoughtful and considerate husband. He put us ahead of all else and we both loved him dearly. I remember how devastated I was that night when the police came to my door and told me he was killed in a car accident."

She took a slow sip of her coffee as if infusing herself with the strength to continue her story.

"Two nights ago, I overheard Ruth tell her friend Mary, that Viktor murdered my husband. She casually asked her accomplice what was in John's briefcase after she retrieved it from his car."

The look on Karl's face mirrored his thoughts. He put the tray aside and gently lifted her onto his lap. "Emily, I am so sorry you had to find out like that. I know Turner knew from the beginning it wasn't an ordinary road accident, but to wake up one morning and hear an acquaintance discussing you husband's murder is deplorable. And to think they would talk about removing his briefcase in such a cavalier fashion is unforgivable."

She moulded herself into his body, enjoying his nearness and warmth. "I was horrified when I heard Ruth talking about the murder of my own husband as though it was an everyday occurrence. She was standing only a few feet from me. I must be ludicrously stupid or naive. I keep wanting to trust people, but . . ."

He tipped up her chin so she was looking into his eyes. "Emily, you've been caught up in a web of corruption. You have my word that I will keep you safe from Viktor and whatever other people Ruth was associated with. Clark's murder was not random. Viktor usually works in Europe. If he murdered Clark in Canada, it's because someone paid a lot money to lure him out of his comfort zone."

"Ruth said her client had John offed. That's the way she put it, she said 'offed'."

"Calm down, Emily."

"Greg admitted he knew all along John had been murdered but he didn't tell me until after he played the tape."

"In view of the information Clark provided, Turner was probably erring on the side of caution. He's a very astute man. He had his reasons."

"On the tape John said he had been compromised. Greg thought perhaps John was a secret agent for some foreign country. Is that possible?"

"Emily, the information he passed on wasn't available to anyone else. We still have no idea who his source was. Clark gave us precise details about shipments of arms and other key information. We were able to liberate a British businessman who was being held for ransom in Somalia using his information. And that's just part of what he gave us. He had an inside lock on something and he had to know what information he wanted and where and how to get it. It points to someone who was trained in espionage. There is no possible way he wasn't in danger once he handed the information on. From what Turner has told me about him, he was too smart and too sophisticated not to know it."

"He kept all this away from me. I thought back to what you said about his resigning from his partnership. I remember John telling me he'd be going abroad more frequently. But at no time did he tell me he resigned from his law practise."

"Calm yourself, Emily. You're justifiably angry but it won't change anything."

Her words almost fused together as she continued: "I asked him how a Toronto lawyer could practice law in other places and he said he was usually involved in negotiations. He assured me that his greatest skills were in negotiating and in settling accounts."

Karl refilled her coffee and poured a cup for himself. "I wonder who Ruth was working for. Think back, if you can. You said she was talking to someone called Mary. Did it sound as though she was taking orders from Mary?"

"No, she talked about 'the client' so I got the impression they worked together. The client wanted the weapon back. Ruth said it belongs to him."

"This all seems to relate back to Canada. Even though your husband travelled on a regular basis, Viktor was told to kill him there. Whoever ordered the hit was either from Canada or wanted it done in Canada to send a message to someone Clark was connected with. By the time we come out of hiding Jerry will probably have sorted out the mess. Sometimes I think my partner is uncanny. He almost seems to have second sight."

As he spoke he was gentle massaging her shoulders. "Give it a rest, Emily. You need to relax before we head back into civilization."

"This is the perfect place to rest up. I love this house."

He looked tenderly into her eyes. "Emily, it is OK to cry now and then. I promise not to tell anyone. No one can hold all this inside, not even someone as strong as you."

As much as she wanted to maintain control over her emotions, a few tears escaped and trickled down her cheeks. She needed a clear head to think. Crying would solve nothing.

His deep voice caressed her ear: "Try not to be afraid, you're in good hands now. I promise I will look after you and see this through to the end."

Ever the policeman, his mind went back to the situation with her late husband. He walked over to the window and opened the shutters allowing the bright sunshine to enter the room. He inhaled the fresh air as he opened the windows. "Regardless of what we find out about your husband, it took great courage for Clark to come forward the way he did and he took no glory for himself. No one knew who he was until Turner requested protection for you. But we knew someone risked a great deal to pass along such vital information."

He turned around just in time to catch a glimpse of Emily trying to wipe away a tear. "Enough of this for today. Come downstairs, I opened all the shutters and windows downstairs. It's a glorious day! How about a game of chess or would you prefer to sketch again?"

She showered and dressed in another of Luigi's oversize shirts and came downstairs.

He agreed to pose in the nude for her after she explained that in her pastel class she regularly depicted nudes. After a few minutes of chatting about anything and everything, he relaxed into the pose she wanted. None of her previous models possessed Karl's magnificent physical attributes. Emily forgot her troubles as she outlined his pose.

For lunch she made up a pasta salad. She skinned and seeded tomatoes and peppers and again retrieved herbs from the patio garden. After preparing a dressing made from olive oil, anchovies, mustard and lemon juice, she poured it over the pasta mixture and served it in a large bowl.

They dined sitting on a couple of the large leather seats. Emily set out a medium sized table between them and they sat back sipping chilled white wine and eating their lunch.

That afternoon Karl posed again to allow her to finish the sketch. In the afternoon light she could see numerous scars on his golden skin. He explained they were merely battle wounds. He spent his life as a soldier and then in law enforcement. He had been injured several times.

When he began to shift his weight thereby subtly changing his pose, she knew he was uncomfortable. "Why don't we stop now? You must want to stretch. At home our models always complain if they have to sit too long. My apologies!"

He winked at her. "I have something else in mind."

She looked questioningly at him and he nodded downward. He was fully aroused.

She dropped her pencil and ran into his arms. They hurriedly removed Luigi's shirt. She sat on his lap on the leather sofa and carefully mounted him.

He murmured into her ear, "I never seem to get enough of you, Emily. You're so easy to get used to."

Her response was to hold him close and run soft kisses along the length of his neck. There was danger here, danger to her heart. She wanted to take what she could from this sensual interlude and damn the consequences. She'd cry her tears when she returned home.

They showered and decided a game of chess was in order.

For dinner she turned a chicken into a gourmet feast. They closed the shutters and dined by candlelight. Karl found another bottle of Luigi's vintage white and they sipped as they chatted and savoured their meal.

After dinner Karl lit candles on the patio. "I have a special treat for us. I found a bottle of Mandarine Napoleon. It is one of my favourites."

"A brandy with the flavour of mandarines? Sounds interesting."

The evening breeze was warm and gentle. They were learning about each other little by little. They were like ships passing in the night, aware of each other but trying not to get close. They both knew this could only be an affair. It would last a short time and then they would go their separate ways. There was a bitter sweetness about it.

That night he kissed her nether regions before working his way up her body. "Darling, you taste like honey to me."

He made passionate love to her. She thrilled all over again. Her orgasm reverberated through her body. She soared.

"Emily, tomorrow I am not going to touch you."

She looked at him uncertainly.

He kissed her fingers. "Tomorrow will be your day. You will come to me. I see how you hold back. I know you'll enjoy yourself more if you are an equal participant. Remember no one will know, only me. Soon our time together will be over and you will return to Canada, never to see me again. I won't tell anyone what you do. Tomorrow I give you carte blanche. I will be yours to do with as you wish for the whole day."

The words *and soon this will be over and you will return to Canada, never to see me again,* echoed in her mind for several minutes.

That was the reality of her situation. No matter how much she counselled herself against it, she was falling progressively more in love with a man who just told her it would very soon be over and they would never see each other again. That was exactly how it was supposed to be. That is what they had agreed to.

She paused for a moment to digest the reality of her situation and then resolved that if she had only one more day to enjoy Karl, she would make it the best day possible. She would give him a day he wouldn't soon forget. Then she closed her eyes and slept.

They awoke together the next morning and she headed for the shower but suddenly stopped. "Why don't I lather you up and we can shower together?"

Karl grinned broadly. He was out of bed in a flash and allowed her to gently lather him all over. She rinsed him with the shower nozzle turned down very low, taking extra care in his genital area. She gently messaged his balls and lowered herself to the floor while she took his large member into her mouth.

Karl began moaning. She continued to gently suckle him, taking care to run her tongue along the tip at times. Then she began to rhythmically suckle his penis while massaging his balls. He was extremely hard and erect.

"I need to feel you." Still dripping wet from the shower he picked her up and carried her to the bed.

"Oh, no you don't."

She disentangled herself.

"Emily, you're driving me mad."

She began again.

"I think I may have found heaven this morning. You, little girl, are addictive."

She smiled and thought, *the day is not over yet. I have more surprises in store for you.*

They invaded the kitchen together. She cooked a vegetable omelet while he made coffee and toast. While he delivered the food to the patio she whipped up a special smoothie with amaretto, apricots and orange juice. She brought out a pitcher of her concoction and sat opposite him in the warmth of the morning sun.

For a couple minutes, they made small talk.

As expected his mood became somber. "Emily, I hate to change the subject, but you promised me one last revelation."

Her own mood reflected his as she considered what she promised to tell him. "Yes, I did. I will tell you more of what I learned from Ruth about my late husband. As you already know John and I travelled a great deal during our time together. He told me that many of his clients lived in Europe and the US and he needed to deal with these people directly rather than by phone."

She stopped speaking and looked at him. "This may take a while. I'll pour some of the smoothie."

Karl waited patiently for her to continue. She filled two wine glasses with the alcohol laced smoothie and then continued speaking: "It began on our honeymoon. John told me I helped him acquire a new and extremely lucrative client so he considered me his good luck charm. After that he insisted I join him on every single one of his business trips."

She paused, drew in a breath and then continued: "Ruth said that wherever we went, John was there to complete a contract killing."

She bent down cradling her head in her hands, trying to keep control over her emotions. She took shallow breaths as she continued: "In other words, I was living and travelling with a murderer. Ruth called me incredibly naive, because I never figured out that every time we went someplace a diplomat, vice president or some other important person was killed or simply disappeared. I spent years living with and a whole year mourning a murderer. I had no idea the man was killing people during our time together and I have absolutely no idea who he might have murdered."

Karl looked at the woman sitting across the table from him. He was only beginning to understand the depth of her passion and her hurt. "I am not surprised you had difficulty getting out of the car when we first arrived here. How have you managed to hold yourself together at all? You poor dear girl! We must talk about this. Why did you keep this bottled up inside yourself?"

"Was I living with a hit-man?"

"Emily, you are innocent of anything John Clark may have done at any time in his lifetime. It is possible Clark was a professional hit-man. If so, I'm certain he was that long before you knew him. You are much too innocent to have been his accomplice in any way so rid yourself of any guilt you may feel in connection with his actions."

He refilled both glasses with her tasty concoction. Handing her a glass, he chuckled. "As my partner Jerry would say, you don't fit the profile."

Then he turned more seriously: "You said his first wife was murdered by Viktor. Viktor is a professional assassin. Perhaps the two were acquainted for Viktor to hook up with his first wife. If this is the case, and Clark was a contract killer as Ruth suggested, then for certain, he was that long before you came on the scene."

"But there was so much John held back from me."

He swallowed his drink in one gulp and continued speaking: "He kept you in the dark for your own protection, Emily. Now it makes sense why Viktor was hired to kill him. Remember I said Viktor is considered the assassin's assassin? Viktor likes to eliminate the competition and has killed off several other contract killers. However, in view of the leaks about arms shipments, the possibility still exists he was exposed and taken out."

"But why all the subterfuge?"

"Emily, Clark did a very noble thing by acting as an informant. Whatever else he may or may not have done, he saved thousands of lives. What I am trying to say is that the man was not all bad. He reached out to do some very noble acts. I'm uneasy with treating Ruth Zhou or should I say Po-Ling Yanmei as a credible witness."

She interrupted, "Greg Turner thought perhaps my husband was working as an agent for a foreign government."

"It's entirely possible he was an agent under deep cover, very deep cover. Sometimes it's hard if not impossible to get information on people like that. It's all very complex. The more I think about it, it makes no sense that a man who would put himself at risk as he did, would travel around indiscriminately murdering people. It seems far more plausible that he was an agent. Anything I say now is pure speculation. I am more comfortable with Turner's version than with what you overheard from your roommate." He paused and then added with certainty, "We will find the truth, my dear."

He realized she was closing down. "Whenever you want to talk about this, I am here to listen. I'll clean up the dishes and then we can have a game of chess or if you want to draw some more, I'll pose for you. You need to get your mind off this for a while."

They decided to exercise. Karl used Luigi's equipment while Emily practiced yoga. She focused on her sun salutation. It felt so good to stretch out. Then she went through her usual routine of poses.

For lunch she served leftovers from the previous day plus a fresh lettuce salad.

After lunch she said, "Karl, I need to talk."

"I'm not going anywhere."

He poured a glass of white wine for Emily and grabbed a beer for himself. They sat opposite each other in large leather chairs and she began: "Karl, there's a memory at the back of my mind, that I can't seem to formulate. I wish I could figure it out. I keep thinking but can't quite pull it together."

"Sometimes our minds suppress memories until we're strong enough to deal with them, Emily. You have experienced a string of traumatic events in the past week. Give yourself some time. Relax and maybe after a while, it'll come into focus."

Her eyebrows knit together as she pondered what he was telling her. "For some unknown reason, I have a great urgency to remember something. I know I'm not making any sense."

He smiled and spoke very gently: "Emily, just talk to me! Relax and say whatever comes into your head. If it is a suppressed memory, it may come to the surface with some prodding."

She laid her head against the back of the large armchair and relaxed. After about a minute, she began. "Until Monday night when I overheard the telephone conversation, I thought Ruth was an ordinary person. She gave me every indication we were becoming good friends. I even considered inviting her to my home in Dundas."

She spoke slowly wanting to ensure she remembered everything correctly. "At no time did I suspect my husband could possibly have killed another human being, let alone many. I was flabbergasted when Greg Turner's people found a cache of weapons in my basement. I recall going to sleep that night thinking that perhaps John worried about his safety or maybe he kept the guns on behalf of clients, but at no time did I consider the possibility that he could have killed another human being."

She was still trying to come to grips with the reality of what had happened. Defensively she continued: "John wasn't a man with a nasty temper. He was kind and considerate to myself and to Paul and he treated my parents very well. We played bridge with friends, hiked in the woods and spent Sunday dinners with the whole family. They all came over to our house and John loved to man the barbecue. I don't know what the profile is for a contract killer, but I do know none of us had any indication that he was carrying on a secret life. I naively thought that sort of thing happened in novels not in real life, especially not in small towns like Dundas. I know it sounds like I'm rambling."

"I'm not complaining."

She smiled ruefully. "Who ever heard of a Dundas assassin? It sounds like an oxymoron."

She bit her lower lip. It was an old nervous habit. "You will go through all the paintings with me?"

"I'll request photos of the paintings. Maybe when you look at them, something will jog your memory to help us understand how the man operated. Someone was paying him large amounts of money to 'settle accounts' as he put it."

Unaware she wasn't listening, he continued: "Another thing is this: law enforcement agencies were not aware that this man existed. If he was a contract killer as Ruth suggested and was taking out high profile individuals, it's strange that no one was aware of his movements. The killing of an ambassador wouldn't go unnoticed. At the moment the man is an enigma to me."

She pulled herself out of her reverie. "Karl, I'm remembering more of the scene in Riomaggiore when Ruth was so angry. You were trying to sit on that ridiculous little stool. Soll was standing to the side with Dave Rowe and his two buddies. Jenny nicknamed those guys Black and White. MJ, Rinaldo and Gianna were sitting in front of us to the left. When Ruth came up the hill later. She looked frightened."

As a visual artist, she was replaying the scene in her mind. "Ruth looked toward the trio in front of us. I could see her nod to someone there. It must have been MJ because that's who looked back at us. Then Ruth looked to where Soll was standing with those men. No one looked at Mary Cominski. Ruth wasn't talking on the phone to Mary Cominski as I thought. It was MJ. Her real name is Mary Josephine MacDonald. Ruth's accomplice is MJ. It was MJ who was there when my husband died."

He poured himself another beer and refilled her wine glass. "You surprise me. It's as though you have a panorama of the scene in your mind."

Emily closed her eyes remembering the scene. "Rinaldo nodded at the group of men on the far side. I wondered what they were doing there. Do you remember Edgar asked them to move away before he started his lesson? They were with Rinaldo. All of them kept watching him and then looking up at us."

"Anything else?" he asked.

"Yes, there is. MJ looked frightened when she turned around but I now realize she wasn't looking at us."

"There has to be a chain of command. There were other people there. Some of the guests from the villa decided to tag along for the day."

She waited until she visualized each person and their location. Then she replied, "I remember them. They weren't far from where Dave Rowe and Soll stood. They were all standing as well."

"Emily, if Viktor was at the Villa, he would most certainly have followed us to Cinque Terre."

She nodded. "I thought of that. Viktor had to be someone in the group beside Soll. Perhaps he was among the other guests from the villa."

He sat quietly assessing the woman sitting before him. She had just been describing a scene to which he himself had been witness and she had picked up nuances of non-verbal communication, some of which he himself had missed. She had narrowed down the identity of Viktor. Of course, by the time they came out of hiding, Viktor would have covered up his tracks. But it was a start.

He spoke quietly, "I thought it wise to remove you from the scene as quickly as possible. The reward offered for the return of the weapon was high and we were aware several parties were continuing to bid it up even further. That was before you told me Viktor was in the vicinity."

She wasn't listening. She was lost in thought.

Finally she looked up at him. "I keep thinking back to my time with John. He was a methodical type of person. He began dressing more casually because he knew I hated the stuffed shirt lawyer image. He was fastidious about everything else. Everything with him was planned down to the smallest detail. Even the trips we took."

She took a sip of wine and continued; "Sometimes he'd surprise me with tickets but the truth was that everything had been arranged with great care. I often wondered how he managed to orchestrate everything so well. I mean we would check into a hotel and my favourite dinner would be served within the hour. It had all been pre-ordered. I've been trying to recall who John introduced me to or what I may have seen early on in our relationship."

He spoke softly, his officious demeanour had long ago disappeared. "Emily, don't rush this. The memories will come back when you are more rested. Wait and see!"

But she persisted. "If John's first wife had an affair with Viktor, they had to be together on more than one occasion. How did they meet Viktor? Did they travel together? Was his first wife aware of John's other activities? Did she know that the man she chose to have an affair with, was an assassin as well? I can't help but feel there is something I am trying to remember but can't quite put into words. I'm sure it'll come to me, given time. Sometimes you wake up during the night and remember things. You know what I mean."

His voice was soothing but insistent; "Emily, stop punishing yourself like this. You aren't to blame for the behaviour of John Clark. We all exercise our own free will. Clearly Clark was very much his own person. Whatever this memory is, it will be there for you when you need it and are strong enough to deal with it."

Emily had talked herself out. "Thank you for listening. I should start preparing dinner."

He remained sitting on the sofa. Again she had surprised him. He admired the honesty of her thought processes. She was a woman who insisted in dealing with truths no matter how painful those truths became. Turner was right when he had warned him not to underestimate Emily Clark.

Karl was beginning to consider what would happen when she was no longer a part of his life. In a few short days he had discovered a woman who was passionate beyond his dreams. She was his intellectual equal. They would soon part company. Was there a way he could keep her in his life? He never considered remarrying since losing Marta and the boys. The pain had been too acute. But that was long ago.

His brothers had encouraged him to go on with his life. He had insisted he was happy living as he was. But now, three days with Emily was changing that. Having tasted Emily's sweet lips and made love to her, he had to ask himself if he wanted to spend the rest of his days without her? The thought of lying beside her every night for the rest of his life filled him with a contentment he hadn't known for a very long time.

His mind went back to the scene at Riomaggiore. Emily had picked up some of the things he had missed. He needed to check his notes. He excused himself and went to the back bedroom where he was compiling a file on the case. He was always methodical and quickly found details for the day in question.

There it was! He had tried to follow the interactions between the various factions. The whole purpose of this exercise was to draw out the parties who wanted the weapon but there was much more going on at Riomaggiore.

Emily observed things he'd missed. As she had mentioned he struggled to sit on the ridiculous excuse for a stool. Then he tried to pull himself closer to her. He had momentarily lost his focus.

He had spotted Ruth giving a concerned look to the trio in front of them. Gianna, Rinaldo and MJ were together as she had said. Earlier everyone had been distracted because the lovers had a very loud argument before Gianna boarded the bus and Rinaldo drove off in his Ferrari. But Rinaldo didn't disappear. He arrived at Riomaggiore on time, which meant the fight beside the bus was staged. He not only drove straight there but also brought reinforcements. That meant Rizzi's father was planning to make a move then and there. Chances are the old man was sitting in a vehicle nearby.

What Emily had spotted and he had missed was that MJ had looked towards where Soll was standing with Dave Rowe. She was right now that he thought about it. The hotel guests who had joined the excursion were beside them. In fact they had slowly walked up to stand next to them. Was Emily right? Could one of the hotel guests be Viktor? Why didn't Soll send back-up when he phoned her? Maybe something had happened and she was unable to respond. Still it was strange that she could answer her phone and was quite vocal when he phoned her and yet she didn't order a helicopter as he requested. She was dependable. Something happened to her. She would have sent help if she could have. Perhaps someone was holding a weapon on her, preventing her from acting. He prayed she was safe.

Emily didn't mention that Jerry wasn't there. One of Rizzi's people had forced his van off the road. She saw what was there but didn't think about who was missing, namely Jerry. Strange how she could replay the scene in such detail but omit something that significant. Perhaps it's because she was a visual artist. That wasn't something he could identify with.

As he duly recorded all the information Emily had given him today, he considered phoning Jerry and ending their stay prematurely so that he could get back on the case. He still didn't know if Turner had uncovered the KZR weapon. However, he had a lead on the identity of Viktor and that brought a smile to his face.

The aroma of food cooking in the kitchen wafted upstairs to the back bedroom where he was working. Whatever she was cooking smelled heavenly.

This was to be their last night together, his last chance to hold her and make love to her. The business of apprehending Viktor could wait for tomorrow. Tonight he belonged to Emily Clark.

Meanwhile Emily busied herself in the kitchen grilling lamb chops for dinner. She made a red wine reduction sauce liberally seasoned with herbs and served it all on a bed of rice. She served this with grilled tomatoes and an arugula salad.

They dined by candlelight on the back patio. The night was warm and welcoming. The sky was filled with a million stars as the two lovers ate their final dinner together.

Tomorrow morning they would venture out into the world and hope the news was good. Tomorrow their affair would be over and they would probably never meet again, but tonight was a different story. They savoured another vintage red from Luigi's wine cupboard and lingered on the patio enjoying the gentle breeze. There was a bittersweet sadness about tonight. No words were spoken by either of them about the future. In fact, they spoke very little.

Finally they collected the dishes and Karl doused the candles. They went inside and he secured the back door.

After cleaning up the dishes they climbed the stairs for the last of their lovemaking.

Emily began by kissing Karl in the groin area. She worked her way around his private parts and gradually up his body until she was on top of him. Gingerly she encased him in her warmth. He moaned.

"A guy can easily get used to this kind of treatment."

She knew these were just words, sweet words, but nonetheless just words.

She began to ride him slowly, ever so slowly. Little by little she picked up the pace and then eased off. She kissed his nipples further exciting him. He revelled in every nuance of movement. At times she lowered herself down and used her abdominal muscles to massage him from within her. He moaned even louder.

She picked up the pace. They both became frantic to climax. They screamed in unison and then fell to the bed in an exhausted sweaty heap.

"Emily, we both need a shower after that. Wait till I find my legs again."

She smiled thinking she had given him a day he wouldn't soon forget as she planned.

They showered together. She laughed when he lathered her back and insisted on drying her.

They climbed back into bed and were instantly asleep.

When she awoke the next morning Karl was sitting up in bed looking down at her. He had a smile on his handsome masculine face. "If I didn't have to get back to work, I could make love to you this minute."

"Are you always so in—?"

"Is the word you are looking for . . . insatiable? Only with you, my dear, only with you!" he said as he climbed out of bed.

Emily yawned and snuggled deeper into the plush bed. She peeked up at the large golden masculine body silhouetted against the morning sun.

He stretched as he walked to the window and opened the shutters. As he started unlocking the windows, he began, "Emily dearest, I'm going to phone my partner Jerry—" He stopped speaking in mid-sentence.

As he uttered his last word, glass from the window shattered and he was simultaneously pushed back into the room. Karl had been shot.

TWELVE

Emily was shaken out of her lethargy by two sharp cracks and Karl's groan as he fell to the floor.

She screamed as she jumped out of bed.

"Stay down! Stay down!"

"Karl! Oh my God, Karl! Oh my God, you're bleeding! Someone shot you. Tell me what to do!"

"Stay low. Get me some towels and grab my cellphone from the night table."

"The clean towels are in the linen closet. I'll be back in a minute."

She crouched as she made her way to the hallway. By the time she returned there was a circle of blood oozing onto the cream coloured carpeting.

"Forget about the blood. Get my cellphone."

She crawled over to the night table and reached into the drawer.

"I have your cellphone. Should I dial 911?"

"Dial Jerry Burns. Hit *23."

She could see he was already very pale. His words were beginning to slur.

A voice with a pronounced British accent came on the line, "Jerry Burns here!"

"It's Emily Clark! I'm with Karl! He's been shot. I think he's going to lose consciousness. I don't know what to do?"

"Bloody hell! Emily, where exactly was he hit?"

Then she gingerly removed the towels and examined his wounds. "There are two wounds, one is in his upper left arm and the second in his left shoulder. Both are bleeding but neither is gushing now."

"Emily, where are you?"

"At the Luigi Morello's house! Vince's cousin's place!"

She grabbed a piece of mail she'd seen on the desk and read out the address.

"Emily, help is on the way. Can I speak to Karl?"

"I don't think he can talk. He lost a lot of blood. I got clean towels and applied pressure to try to stop the bleeding. Perhaps if I ran downstairs and get some ice. Would that help? I've never been in a situation like this before. I don't know what to do."

"First of all calm down, Emily. Panic is only an option when you're being chased by a bear. Now, where is Karl's revolver?"

"I think it's in the bedside table."

"Get it! You've got to protect yourself until the police arrive."

She opened the drawer again and carefully picked up the gun. Her hands were shaking. "I'm now holding his gun."

"Do you know how to shoot?"

She was shaking all over, even her voice was tremulous. "No!"

"Is it loaded?"

"I don't know."

"Is the magazine in it? Check the handle."

"It's empty."

"Reach in the drawer and grab the magazine and slide it into the handle."

"Done."

"Karl's weapon is a Belgian-made FN five seveN MK2. The safety is ambidextrous. Look for the little lever above the trigger."

"I see it."

"When you push it, you'll see a red dot."

"Yes, I see the dot."

"When you see the dot, it's ready to fire. So push the lever back so it doesn't accidentally go off."

"Karl needs to get to the hospital right away. He's lost so much blood."

Jerry responded smoothly. "I'll have someone there as soon as I can but in the meantime you have to protect yourself. Whoever shot Karl wants you. Don't be afraid to use the gun if you need to. Try to remain calm."

She went over to where Karl was lying.

"Karl, darling, don't even think of getting up. You'll only cause your wounds to bleed more."

"Viktor!" he gasped.

"Yes, Viktor must have survived the gun battle. He found us, darling. I'm going downstairs to try to fend him off. I'll stand a better chance if you promise not to move."

Karl nodded. The shock of the wounds and sudden loss of blood had stunned him but he was trying to rally.

"Karl, promise me you won't try to move about! If I have to worry about your sneaking downstairs and trying to be gallant, I won't be able to focus. You must stay put up here."

He groaned and nodded trying to force out words. "Emily, I feel so bad. I am here to protect you."

"It's my turn to protect you. Now please, dearest, rest until help comes. Jerry alerted the authorities. It's only a matter of time until they arrive."

Emily thought about how Viktor had shot Ruth twice while she was running. The second shot had killed her. Viktor was too good a shot to miss. For whatever reason, he intended to incapacitate Karl but not kill him.

Emily was in control of her own fate. She could sit in the bedroom and wait for Viktor to find his way into the house or she could take a stand. Either way she might lose. If what Karl had told her about Viktor was true, he would torture her to death for the sake of a weapon that meant nothing to her. Her only option was to take a stand. But she'd be no match for an assassin. No match unless she could find an advantage.

Karl's eyes were closed. She kissed him gently on the forehead and whispered, "Please lie still, dearest."

She left the room barefoot, dressed in a borrowed nightgown and for the first time in her life, holding a revolver. She stood on the landing and looked down the stairs. As she descended every stair seemed to creak as she eased her way down. The fourth step from the bottom always gave the loudest creak whenever someone stepped on it. She angled her foot to the side edge of the stair and it was mercifully silent.

Stepping silently across the floor on the balls of her feet, she slowly made her way in the direction of the front door.

She remembered Karl's words after he checked the old stone house for security. *Luigi must have been bothered with break-ins because he turned this place into a fortress. All the windows and the back door have grills. In addition the back door opens only from the inside.*

That meant Viktor could only enter the house through the front door. She knew that but Viktor didn't. She knew the layout of the house like the back of her hand, Viktor did not.

Karl had closed the shutters the night before. The two lovers were often indiscrete about wearing clothing around the house, partially due to the fact they had only the clothes they were wearing when they arrived.

The morning sun shone through the slats in the shutters giving the area in front of each window a soft glow. Emily threaded her way past the furniture with ease. Someone entering from the brightness of outdoors would require a minute to adjust to the dimness inside.

She thought of the many hours of peace she and Karl had enjoyed here. There were magical moments when she had allowed herself to forget about the danger she was in. Their short respite here had given her a chance to regain her equilibrium after the shocking events of the past week. She thought of the man lying injured on the floor upstairs and her resolve increased.

She wanted to stop and pinch herself. Was this actually happening? What had led to this?

She thought of her late husband. It was because of John, she now found herself here. This was a life or death situation and he was completely to blame.

If John truly loved her, none of this would have happened. He should never have associated her with his odious weapon.

She stopped beside the long bar that separated the kitchen from the rest of the open space. She stood there and looked around. She could hide behind the bar. Karl had told her and the others to hide behind the counter during all the shooting at Cinque Terre. The bar was to the side of the building. She could crouch low and maybe peek out.

What would happen when Viktor came inside? The bar area would give her some protection. But Viktor had shot Karl through the upstairs window. He might think she was still upstairs, too frightened to come down. If Viktor went upstairs, he would find Karl lying there. In his present condition, Karl was defenceless.

She turned toward the front door.

Karl had told her it was the only entrance without a metal grill. Sooner or later, Viktor would try to come in through this door.

She examined the door. It opened inward to the right. She wanted to make sure she couldn't be seen so she bent low and moved along until she came to the wall. Then she stood erect and flattened herself against the wall to the left of the door.

For once Emily was pleased with her tall lean body. She had always been her own harshest critic about the scant size of her breasts and her general thinness. Her pale skin and flaxen coloured hair would help her blend in with the light yellow ochre toned walls.

She was so focused she'd almost forgot about the revolver in her hand. She looked down at the gun, carefully running her finger over the safety release switch. She tried it once and the red dot appeared. Then she slid the switch back down.

Emily stretched out her right arm parallel with the floor. Then angled it up. She tried various angles: fifteen degrees, twenty degrees, thirty degrees.

She thought, *I am five-foot eight. Karl told me Viktor is about six feet tall. From this angle I could possibly hit his head.*

Then the waiting began. The gun was too heavy to hold at that angle for long so she rested it by her side. She would wait until she heard something. Then she would angle her arm upwards and pause until Viktor was exactly in line with her hand before she attempted to fire.

No, she would release the safety first. She had to remember to do that or the gun wouldn't fire. As soon as she heard a noise, she would release the safety. But she would be careful not to touch the trigger until she had to.

If she fired prematurely she would miss and Viktor would have the advantage. This was Viktor's line of work, not hers.

She would have only one chance, one shot and that would mean the difference between life and death for her and possibly for Karl.

Waiting for your own executioner to arrive was not going to be easy. She had to stay focused. She couldn't allow her mind to venture down any distracting pathways. She never dreamed of killing anyone. If someone had told her she would actually want to take the life of another human being one week ago she would have dismissed that person as insane. But here she was, Emily Clark from the little town of Dundas, hiding inside a stone house in Italy, gun in her hand and hoping to shoot an assassin.

She heard footsteps going to the back of the house. That meant Viktor had come down from the wooded hills and was now near the house. He would try to enter through the back patio. She knew he couldn't. The gate could only be opened from the inside by using the key hidden in the wall. He would have to climb over the wall.

She continued to wait and listen.

She wanted this over with. The longer it went on, the more blood Karl would lose.

If the police arrived, there could be another shoot-out. The paramedics wouldn't be able to enter the house until it was safe. It would delay getting help for Karl.

She wanted it over with, now.

A calm settled over her. She was a woman on a mission.

In that moment of tranquility she began to put her thoughts together. The reflections that lingered on the edge of her mind the previous afternoon began to come into focus. It was a sort of olio of memories but suddenly it was coming together. She had struggled with these thoughts yesterday when she sat in one of the big chairs and droned on while Karl sat patiently listening.

Negative space . . . that was the key. Edgar devoted several painting classes to the subject. She thought of his demonstration. He painted the background only and several white daisies took shape in the foreground.

Yesterday she concentrated on what she saw.

What if what she saw was only the background? What or who was missing?

Jerry was not at Cinque Terre. Edgar looked several times toward the parking lot before signalling to Karl to proceed. Later Karl mentioned there had been an accident.

She had focused only on what she saw. Thoughts are like key chains. You need every link to form the chain.

When she first spotted Jerry at the Amsterdam airport, he scared her half to death. She had focused on the foreground. If she now thought about the background, she would have noticed Edgar's subtle acknowledgment of Jerry. Jerry was behind them going through security. He and Edgar had chatted, no doubt planning their strategy.

She focused on the scar that ran down the left side of his face. She observed what she could easily see and drew her conclusions from that.

The following day when she met Jerry at the villa, she wondered how she had allowed herself to become so fixated on his scar. The minute he smiled, the disfiguration seemed to vanish.

The scar! That was it! It had vanished. It had to be plastic surgery.

Things appear differently if you change your focus.

That day in Capri, the first time she travelled to Europe with John. They were dining in the patio restaurant. The sun was intense. She was hot. It was all new to her. Her life with John was new to her. John had proposed to her and she had accepted. Her mind was full of ideas for planning their wedding.

That sultry Italian woman came to their table and put a business card in the pocket of John's jacket. She had a scar, a long scar, like a knife wound down the side of her face.

Thoughts of that day floated back to her, now more vividly. At the time she presumed the woman was one of John's former lovers. The very way the woman ambled up to him and completely ignored her seemed to indicate a degree of ownership. When the woman reached over and slipped what looked like a business card into his pocket, John became furious and tore the paper to shreds. There must have been a lot of history between the two of them.

She had focused on the scar, just as she had done at the Amsterdam airport when she met Jerry. It wasn't about the woman's scar. It was about the woman.

That little scene in Capri was not about lovers as she thought. It was about business. It was about the business of assassination. These were two people who killed for money.

Karl's words echoed in her mind. *If Clark was a hit man, he was that long before you knew him.*

Viktor was a woman. That's why the authorities hadn't figured out who she was.

She heard the sound of the back door metal grill rattling. It was impossible to open either the metal grill or the back door from the outside. Karl had insisted both were secure.

Viktor would have to scale the stone wall again and walk down the driveway to come around to the front door. She would probably be fuming because she couldn't enter the house as easily as she hoped.

Emily could hear the sound of her boots as she proceeded back up the driveway.

She heard a spray of bullets being fired off. From the direction of the shots, Viktor had just shot up Vince's car. Emily winced at the sound of bullets hitting a metallic surface.

The barrage lasted what felt like a long time. Viktor was angry and impatient. Hopefully she would make a mistake. Emily recalled Karl saying how these people get caught because they slip up. They become too sure of themselves and then they are vulnerable. She hoped that time had come for Viktor.

Emily slid her finger up and released the safety on the revolver. The red dot became visible.

She stood flush with the wall. She raised her arm. She steadied herself. She could hear the sound of her own breathing as she slowly inhaled and exhaled.

Her mind was focused.

Her arm was not shaking. Her vision was clear. She was ready.

She thought of the pain Karl was suffering in the upstairs bedroom and she allowed herself a little bit of anger.

She thought of John's last words, *Tell Emily I love her.*

This monster murdered her John. This monster had murdered a man who, despite his flaws, had been a wonderful father and grandfather. And he had left unfinished business.

Emily put all extraneous thoughts out of her mind and focused on the task at hand.

It was as though time stood still. She felt intense calm descend on her as she began to aim the revolver and think only on what lay ahead of her. She knew exactly what she had to do and she was prepared. She brought her finger to the edge of the trigger.

Viktor shot out the lock and kicked the front door in with such force that the door flew open and banged on the wall on the opposite side. Light flooded into the room. Viktor had not yet entered the room. She sprayed a round of bullets into the house from her position on the outside step.

Not even the sudden sound of the Victor's gun being fired caused Emily to flinch. She was focused. She listened.

Emily could hear the noise of the scattered impacts throughout the downstairs. She heard the sound of glassware being broken in the kitchen, a large lamp fell off its table and hit the floor with a crash. Another senseless act of vandalism! Her assailant had lost her composure. Hopefully this would make her an easier target.

She was grateful Karl stayed upstairs and hadn't tried to be heroic.

Emily was plastered to the wall beside the door. Her colouring camouflaged her. She blended in with the surrounding walls almost as though she were invisible. She told herself she had the advantage. She knew where Viktor was. Viktor had not yet sensed her presence.

Emily watched as Viktor's shadow slowly began to proceed into the house. She had expected her to take a running leap inside. Had she done that Emily would have been at a loss to defend herself. Never having shot a gun in her life, it would have been almost impossible for Emily to track and shoot a moving target.

Emily realized she had to shoot before Viktor got far beyond the threshold.

Viktor cast a shadow as she stood ready to enter. She was attempting to accustom her eyes to the dimness inside the house.

Viktor slowly started to enter looking around cautiously.

Emily's hand was beginning to shake ever so slightly from the weight of the gun. She fired and fired and fired and then dropped the gun.

She was in shock unable to know whether or not she had hit her prey. She needed a minute to breath. She wrapped her arms protectively around herself and tried to inhale slowly. Her hand hurt from the recoil of the revolver.

She waited to feel the pain of a bullet but the pain did not come.

Her first thought was, *I'm still alive!*

Finally she looked down and saw that the lovely Agent Ingrid Soll was lovely no longer.

THIRTEEN

Emily bounded upstairs. Karl lay inert on the floor. He was pale and barely conscious.

She knelt beside him. "Karl dearest, I am here. Stay alive for me! I love you. Please don't leave me. The ambulance is coming, I can hear it in the distance. Please darling just stay alive for me. I love you so much!"

She looked down at her blood-stained nightgown. "My God, I've got to change."

She went into the bathroom and looked in the mirror and quickly grabbed a cloth. She scrubbed her face and arms and dressed in her own clothes.

The sound of sirens became more intense. The noise stopped abruptly. She could hear voices coming from downstairs.

The police arrived to find a car riddled with bullets and a dead body in the doorway. The sound of her voice drew them upstairs and they appeared at the bedroom door with guns drawn. The officers surveyed the scene on the floor.

Karl nodded toward the bedside table and Emily retrieved his Europol credentials and passed them to the officer who appeared to be in charge.

The young officer announced himself in heavily accented English: "I am Officer Lombardi! Sir, we found your service revolver downstairs next to a dead body in the doorway."

The officer looked puzzled. "Sir, I don't understand. It appears you were shot up here and the body is downstairs."

He looked suspiciously at Emily. "And who are you, Madam?"

She pointed to the broken window. "Karl was shot through the window. He's been losing blood for far too long."

He went to the landing and yelled down in Italian.

The paramedics appeared and began tending to Karl's injuries. They hooked him up to a drip and loaded him onto a stretcher.

"Just who are you, madam?"

Karl tried to speak. "Witness. Needs protection."

"You're under protection, Madam?"

She nodded.

"I'll have some men assigned to you until we get this mess cleared up. Judging by the bullet holes in the front door, I assume the intruder was attempting to break-in. Any idea of her identity?"

Karl was trying to say the body belonged to the notorious Viktor but the dryness in his mouth made it difficult to form his words. He looked at Emily as he realized the officer had said *her* not *his* identity.

Emily replied: "Agent Busch will give a full statement after his wounds have been attended to. Surely this can wait until later. I believe his partner Jerry Burns is on his way here."

"Yes, Madam, Agent Burns is due here shortly."

"He will explain everything to you."

Karl struggled to speak. His parched mouth made his voice sound raspy but there was no doubting the urgency in what he was trying to say. "She is under my protection. She is a witness! She must be protected at all times. I need to talk to my partner immediately."

Emily grabbed his right hand and tried to reassure him. "Calm down, Karl! We are surrounded by police officers. No one will kidnap me here. Now relax!"

As they passed the front door Karl caught a glimpse of the body of Ingrid Soll being loaded into a body bag. He tried to remove the oxygen mask from his face. The paramedics realized he was struggling and stopped.

He looked up at Emily. "You didn't tell me it was her! Are you sure you got the right person?"

"I'm certain!"

Karl was becoming more agitated. When she realized one of the medics wanted to give a shot to put him out, she held up her hand. "But she had top clearance. How could this happen? I chose her to protect you!"

"There was no way you could have known."

"I don't understand. How is this possible?"

"She was an associate of my husband long before I married him. I finally recognized her. I will explain more when your wounds have been properly attended to. Now can we get you to the hospital?"

He relaxed and allowed himself to be transported out of the building and into the waiting ambulance.

As she passed out the doorway, Emily looked down at the dead body. She remembered the exquisite smile Ingrid Soll flashed at Karl at Riomaggiore. Soll never intended to kill him. She must have known he was left handed and aimed for his left arm and shoulder to incapacitate him instead. She loved him in her own twisted way.

Emily rode in the back of the ambulance with Karl. As soon as they arrived at the hospital, a medical team surrounded Karl and moved him through the long corridor to the elevator. She followed along.

She found herself sitting alone in the waiting room. She knew these things took time.

A half hour turned into an hour and still she sat alone.

Her mind began to wander.

Now she was in no doubt John had been an assassin. He was associated with Viktor long before they met. Viktor was a monster. Was John as ruthless? She wanted to distance herself from his memory. It would take time.

She felt angry and cheated now that she understood how completely he had deceived her. She brought an assassin into her hometown. She treated him like family. Why could she not have sensed something? Was she willfully naive? Had she been trying to live out a Cinderella fantasy?

She thought back to the day they met in her restaurant. Once she looked into his dark eyes, she couldn't seem to break his spell. His gaze was hypnotic.

When he invited her out she was flattered beyond words. She was so busy running the restaurant, she'd almost forgotten about a life of her own.

She looked at her diamond ring. She basked in the attention he paid her but something about him intimidated her. She should have realized then and there he was not the man for her.

As soon as she laid eyes on Paul, everything changed. Any doubts she may have harboured about John paled in comparison to the immediate bond she felt with his son. She would have done anything to keep Paul close to her. She wanted to mother him, to protect him. She thought back to the night they met: Paul followed her into the kitchen as she was putting the finishing touches on their dinner. He offered to help but stood there watching as she worked. There was an unspoken connection between them, more than mother and step-son. She knew full well that Paul felt it also.

The engagement ring still glowed on her finger. She held it up and examined it. The stone was clear and very large. The inscription inside read *I will love your forever.*

She slipped the ring into the deep pocket of her jacket.

Next she examined her wedding ring. It was elegantly ornate. She thought of her wedding day. The garden was full of flowers and friends. Her father gave her away with tears in his eyes.

As he walked her down the flower strewn aisle she saw John for the first time that day. He looked devilishly handsome. Emily couldn't believe her good luck. She was about to marry a wealthy lawyer with the added bonus of his son, Paul.

There had never been even an inkling of unhappiness. It was as though her every unconscious wish came true from the instant John walked into her life.

She never questioned the frequency of his business trips. On every trip he went out of his way to provide for her comfort. There would be a limo waiting with a guide to take her on a private tour. She was chauffeured around like a princess.

There was always a thoughtful gift when he returned from his meetings. Whether it was a box of paint brushes, an expensive gown or even jewellery, there was always something. They would dine and afterwards he would make love to her.

Then they would return to their quiet life at home. No one knew they had just come back from Antalya, Cairo, Dubai, or Copenhagen. They would resume their unassuming existence, walking Wellington along the streets of Dundas and greeting their neighbours as though they had never been away.

At Christmas, they threw a huge party and invited their friends and neighbours. The house would be filled. John would hire a group of musicians and Emily would prepare a buffet for their guests. The party always went on until three in the morning and ended with the singing of carols.

It all came flooding back to her. His tiny caresses when he came in the door at night. He would whisper that he was putting a down payment on his loving making later that night.

Had John scripted their life together?

Their life together had been idyllic. Apart from the incident in Capri she couldn't ever remember seeing him angry. That alone was strange! Most couples fight the odd time about something. John was methodical, he seemed to anticipate her every need and desire. It was as though she was married to the perfect man. Except he wasn't the perfect man. He was a murderer.

Was she manipulated to help conceal his other life, as Ruth had suggested? He made her life feel so wonderful she never questioned him.

Then suddenly it was all over. John was dead. She was left in the big house, all alone.

She held up her wedding ring, fingering the detailed etching.

She looked at the inscription. Where she expected to see letters, there were numbers. She held the ring up to the light and began to read the string of numbers.

Slowly she rose from her seat. There was a contingent of police officers at the end of the hallway. She pointed in the direction of the phone booth. One of the officers smiled and nodded.

She walked the length of the hall and entered the phone booth, dialled the phone number on the card she withdrew from the pocket of her jacket. It was the card she had carried with her since the incident in Dundas.

She requested the charges to be reversed. She heard a familiar but tired voice on the other end of the phone. "Greg, I have some numbers for you. I found them etched inside my wedding ring."

Carefully she began reading the numbers.

"What do you think they mean, Emily?"

"I recognize some of the numbers. 01565-004 is the transit number for my bank in Dundas. Perhaps John had a safety deposit box there, he didn't tell me about."

"If the prototype is in there, this could be over."

"It can't happen too soon."

"How are you, Emily?" Greg Turner asked.

"I'm fine but I'm at the hospital. Karl was shot and is now in surgery."

"Shot?"

"Yes, when we got to Cinque Terre, Karl was worried about some of the people with us so we ran and jumped on the train. I didn't think we'd make it because it was about to start moving."

"He had you jump on a train as it was about to start moving?"

"We went to the last village and there was a bit of a shoot-out."

"A bit of a shoot-out?"

"So Karl took me to a hideaway. We stayed there several days but he was shot first thing this morning."

"Where was Jerry Burns when all this was going on?"

"Someone hit his vehicle on the way to Cinque Terre."

"Is he well enough to work?"

"He sounded fine this morning. I phoned him to get instructions after Karl was shot."

"I assume he arranged for back-up until he arrived on the scene."

"Yes, he phoned the police and told me how to shoot Karl's revolver," she responded.

"What? You seemed rather terrified of guns when you were here. Did you actually use the weapon?"

"Yes, I had to. This assassin called Viktor came to the front door and I had to shoot her."

"You had to shoot Viktor?"

"I'm afraid, I killed her."

"Her? I thought Viktor was a man." Turner was surprised.

"No, Viktor was the Italian police officer who was helping guard me."

"Who the hell picked her?"

"Karl said he worked with her before and she was fine, but Edgar and I didn't like her."

"I'm not surprised. How are you holding up with all this going on?"

"I'm doing my best under the circumstances. I sometimes feel like I borrowed someone else's life. That must be how actors feel. If the KZR weapon is in the safety deposit box, then the nightmare is all over. Really, there's nothing to worry about now."

"Glad you're holding your own. I'll be in touch as soon as we check the safety deposit box."

She felt she had just closed the loop. Soon all this attention and furor would be a thing of the past and her life would be her own again. It would never be the same. But at least, she would be free to decide her own future.

She walked back to her seat and resumed her waiting. She would have liked to close her eyes and rest but couldn't. The events of the day were still stark in her mind. She did what she had to do. She put duty first. Now a numbness seemed to fill her. She was in a state of limbo.

Once the KZR weapon was located, the world of guns and assassins would be only a memory. Maybe one day when the newness of it all went away she would make up stories about it to tell her grandchildren on their sleepovers. No one would ever guess Emily Clark could possibly have killed anyone, let alone the notorious assassin Viktor.

She prayed Karl would make a full recovery. Their affair had been so hot. But it was over now and it was time to go their separate ways. It was just as well because she'd become far too fond of him for her own good. She didn't need or want another man in her life.

She'd wait to see him after his surgery, thank him for his many kindnesses and then wish him a fond farewell.

Why had she fallen in love with Karl? It was such teenage thing to do—fall in love with your protector. She should have shown more restraint. What was she thinking? She was remembering the touch of his hand on her breast as she fell asleep. The events of the day had exhausted her. She hoped to close her eyes for just a little while but her tiredness pulled her into a deep slumber.

Jerry Burns smiled as he gently placed a pillow under her head and a blanket over her body. She stirred slightly and immediately fell back to sleep.

Then he proceeded to the private room where Karl was resting after his surgery.

"Bloody hell, Karl, you look awful!"

"You don't look so great yourself."

"Other than a few bruises from the accident, I'm fine. Just wrapped things up at your little hideaway. What a hell of a mess! Viktor or rather Soll fired a volley across the downstairs and Vince's car looks like it was parked at a shooting range. I had no idea the woman was so nuts. Edgar said she was and he was right."

"Don't remind me."

"Yea, the truth hurts."

"How's Emily?" Karl asked.

"The lady is asleep in the waiting area," Jerry replied.

"I must have lost consciousness. I have vague recollections of Emily telling me to lie still."

"I'll try to fill you in. Emily took your gun and put a bullet in Soll's head."

"Where was she when Soll was shooting up the place?" Karl asked.

"My guess is standing like a statue beside the doorway. We found her blood-stained nightgown in the bathroom. She had to be standing at point-blank range when she fired your revolver. She'll probably get a medal for this."

"Any way we can hush it up?"

"Why would we want to do that? Wait, I've got an incoming call. It's Turner. I'll put him on speaker phone so you can hear. Hey Greg, how's the weather in Canada? Any snow yet?"

"Ha, ha, ha! If that's the best of your jokes, Burns, I suggest you stick to your day job. Sounds like you and Busch have been enjoying the Italian version of the Wild West. Don't make me sorry I let Emily go over there. Give me a rundown on everything."

Jerry grinned as he began: "We took her to Cinque Terre with Edgar's gang of old people. Emily and Karl went to Monterosso al Mare to get some peace and quiet and all hell broke out. So Karl took her to a safe place to get some peace and quiet and all hell broke out again. I think that about sums it up. Right now I'm here with Karl in the hospital. He's finished in surgery. He looks like hell right now but he'll recover."

"What about you? What happened to you?"

"Someone working for a local hoodlum forced my van off the road. I was only banged up but we lost a couple good men when it happened."

"What about Emily? She sounded OK when I talked to her. Is she safe?"

"We have a small contingent of Italy's finest watching her but now that we put Viktor and certain other individuals out of action, there is less to worry about. She's safe."

"No, she's not! That's why I'm calling. I finally tracked down the couple who look after her house. Turns out their domestic chores are a cover for their security work. They're highly qualified. They work for an agency out of Eastern Europe. There's a whole team here to give her twenty-four hour protection. Clark hired them as soon as he brought Emily back from their honeymoon. There's all sorts of surveillance equipment skillfully hidden around the house. Whoever wired the place knew what they were doing and then some."

"Why are these guys still working? Clark died a year ago. Who's been paying them since then?"

"Good question! They were contacted a few days after Clark was killed and instructed to stay on. They said they were asked to tell Emily that her husband provided for them before he died, but that's not true. They're paid via bank transfer. They send reports to a site in the UK and the reports get relayed from there."

"Someone has a vested interest in keeping Emily safe," Jerry replied.

"They were set to take action when the two guys tried to grab Emily here in Dundas. They backed off when we got involved."

"How were they going to protect her on this trip with Edgar?"

"This is where it gets interesting. They knew about Edgar's undercover work, even knew his code name. They knew about that job in Somalia," Turner explained.

"Bloody hell, so they knew she was in good hands. Any idea why all the protection?"

"Not a clue, but I think it relates to someone she met on her honeymoon. When she's rested, I'll have a talk with her and see how much she can remember."

"So, do some of these highly paid security people want to take over? We have other cases to work on."

"I'm going to text you a number. Anytime you need help, use it."

"I'll talk it over with Karl."

"Tell Emily, I got the search warrant. We'll know within the hour! Gotta run! Bye!"

Jerry clicked his phone off and looked at Karl. "What's he talking about, Karl? What's this about a search warrant?"

"Don't look at me. I've been busy having surgery," Karl replied.

"You were with her for days, any idea who is threatening her? She say anything while you two were sharing that big bed?"

"Careful, Jerry! She was too stressed to talk much so we played chess most of the time we were together. She beat me three times."

"Ouch! That had to hurt. Chess is your thing."

"Let's err on the side of caution and take measures to keep her safe while she's on our watch," Karl said.

"What do you propose?"

"If she takes credit for killing Viktor, every newspaper on the continent will want a piece of her."

"Say no more, I know just the guy. The young officer, the first one on the scene is perfect. His name is Lombardi," Jerry replied.

"Jerry, let her agree to it. I know she will, but give her a choice."

"I know what to say. She's a woman isn't she?"

"No, you don't, Jerry. She's off limits to you."

"I promise I'll be on my best behaviour when I tell her but we can't protect her here. Any suggestions?"

"I need a few weeks off to give my shoulder a chance to heal. I'm thinking that if I were to bring her to Patmos with me, she'd be safe there."

"Want me to break it to her?" Jerry asked.

"No, let me, but you can make the travel arrangements. I don't want a vapour trail."

"Got it! You look like you're about to fall asleep. I'm starving so I think I'll mosey on down to the waiting room and take sleeping beauty out for a bite to eat, then we'll come back here and bother you."

Emily came awake to the smell of coffee. Jerry was sitting beside her, smiling.

He was holding two coffees. He spoke in his rough British accent; "Thought you could use a bit of company. Want to join me for a bite to eat?"

She nodded.

"There's a café not far from here. I'll drive you there."

"How is Karl?"

"Karl's resting after his surgery! Mind if I ask you a few questions?"

"Ask away."

"Later we'll get a formal statement from you about the events of this morning. Needless to say we're all very grateful for your courage. You rid us of a notorious menace."

"I had no choice. It sounds rather like a cliché but it I felt it was a 'Do or die situation'."

The small restaurant was crowded when they arrived but they managed to find a quiet table at the back.

Their drinks arrived within minutes. As they sat waiting for their food, he spoke: "Emily, we're trying to put together the events at the scene. By the time the police arrived, you were upstairs with Karl. Care to tell me what happened."

"Karl was shot when he opened the shutters in the . . ."

"Don't sweat it. It didn't take a genius to figure out the two of you were sleeping together."

"I heard a sound and he fell backwards and then he was lying on the floor bleeding. It happened so quickly."

"Where were you at the time?"

"Still in bed! He got up and intended to phone you to see if it was safe for us to leave Luigi's house. That's when it happened."

"What happened next?"

"I ran and got some clean towels for him. Then he told me to call you."

"Why did you go downstairs?"

"I figured the police and ambulance would take a while to come because the place is a bit remote so I felt I had to do something to protect Karl and myself."

"Tell me where you were standing when you shot Soll?"

"By the front door!"

"Why there? Why not behind the bar in the kitchen area?" Jerry asked.

"I considered hiding there but I'd never shot a gun before and I was rather scared of the thing. I knew that whoever shot Karl had to be a crack shot. So I figured I would have only one chance to shoot and I wanted to be close so I didn't miss."

"Smart thinking! But you had no protection when you stood by the door."

"I was flat against the wall. I felt I blended in with the colour of the room. I was wearing a beige nightgown and my hair is light so I hoped I'd be sort of invisible."

"You thought she'd enter through the front door?"

"I knew she would. Karl explained how the grills and the back gate locked. The only way into the house was through the front door, I knew that."

"So you figured out ahead of time how she'd try to get in. She made a hell of a mess of Vince's car, not to mention the inside of Luigi's house. You had to be scared out of your wits."

"I was at first, but then I realized if I didn't do something both Karl and I would be dead."

"So you shot her at point-blank range."

"I just shot as soon as she crossed the threshold. My hand still hurts."

"I'm not surprised."

"Can we keep all of this away from my family? Do they have to know about this?" Emily asked.

"That depends on you. You killed a notorious criminal in self-defence. You'll probably get your name in the headlines and be hounded by the press. By tomorrow, you could be quite the celebrity."

"No, I don't want that. Please, can you help me?"

"You sure, you don't want to be famous?"

"No, I don't, Jerry. I want it all to go away. I want to go back home and forget any of this ever happened."

"Tell you what, I'll prepare a press release and name that young officer, who was the first one on the scene, the hero of the day."

"But he may not want all the notoriety."

Jerry grinned. "Trust me, he'll love it."

Jerry looked at his watch. "Karl should be ready to see you now. Let's go."

She followed him down the long hallway in the hospital, then through several sets of doors.

The thought of seeing Karl again reminded her that their affair was over. "Can someone drive me back to Villa DiMattia? Now that all this is over, I want to go to Paris to visit with some old friends and then I'll fly back home. But first I'd like to thank Karl for all he has done to protect me and of course say goodbye to him."

Jerry Burns let out a loud guffaw. "Goodbye? Go to Paris! Bloody hell! This should be fun!"

FOURTEEN

Karl dozed off after Jerry left. He awakened to find a doctor standing beside his bed.

He looked around the room. Jerry and Emily were standing further back. The important thing was Emily was finally here, albeit she was standing by the door and looking pale and somewhat withdrawn.

A physician dressed in scrubs began telling him about the surgery. It had gone well. The wound to his arm had created a lot of bleeding but not much damage. His left shoulder would require rest and then physiotherapy but within three to four weeks it should be fine again.

He looked up at his old buddy.

"Jerry, I'm still trying to put the pieces together. Any idea how Soll found us? I thought we were safe. I never once turned on my cellphone and we disposed of Emily's tracking devices."

"It's possible she used satellite imagery. Your race-driver habits probably gave you away, my friend."

"I doubt that. Have you any idea how many race car drivers are from Italy?"

Jerry chuckled. "I don't but I bet you do."

"Over 4,000 of the best came from here."

Jerry's phone rang. "What can I do for you, Turner? Yes, Emily and Karl are both here. I'll put you on speaker phone."

"Hand the phone to Emily," Turner ordered.

"Your command is my wish. Here Emily, the detective from the great Canadian north wants to borrow your ear."

"Any luck, Greg? Did you find it?" she asked.

"Congratulations, Emily! We found the prototype. The number you gave me was for a safety deposit box at your bank in Dundas as you suggested. It took us a while to get a search warrant but the important thing is that we found it."

"So this is all over now?"

"Emily, your husband was a man with many secrets. There were other things in the box. I'll get back to you later when we've had a chance to process everything."

She hung up. "It's over. I'm free."

Jerry responded. "Not quite yet! We'll use our undercover agents to get the word out that the weapon has been found. Don't go taking any long walks by yourself for a few days."

Emily was still standing near the door. Seeing Karl again made her heart ache. When she looked at him she was almost too emotional to speak.

"I'll keep that in mind," she whispered.

She wanted to say goodbye to Karl and leave quickly. It was tearing her apart to be in the same room with him, knowing she'd never see him again. Their eyes met. "Emily, it's far from over," he said.

"Karl, what are you talking about? The KZR weapon has been found and Viktor is dead. What more can there be?"

"Are you forgetting the activities of your late husband? Turner's people began examining the paintings in your home as you suggested and discovered some information. We have to go through all of that with you. Plus, and equally as important, is the fact that someone was paying John Clark enormous amounts of money to possibly eliminate high profile individuals. You're the only connection to all of this."

She wanted it to be over. She wanted to give her beloved one last kiss and disappear before her tears began to fall. "Can't all this be done in Canada? What about the computer in the basement? Didn't it reveal who hired John? Can't you trace his cheques or bank transfers?"

"That computer self-destructed when they turned it on. Apparently it was password protected. They're trying to reconstruct what they can of the hard drive."

"So this is not over."

"Not by a long shot! By tomorrow Turner's people will have begun to examine and possibly test the KZR weapon. We'll soon find out why it could fetch such a high price. Also by tomorrow, word will get out that the item is safe and secure with the Toronto police."

"I'd like to visit with some friends in Paris and then return home. Surely I can answer all your questions just as well from my home in Canada," Emily said.

"Emily, please come closer to me," Karl pleaded.

Her feet seemed to move of their own accord. Now she was standing too close.

Karl continued: "I plan to spend a few weeks with my friend Alexandros on Patmos. I'd really like you to join me?"

She didn't need more togetherness with Karl Busch. Her heart was already breaking. She was trying so desperately to hold back her tears. And she didn't want him to see her cry. She wanted to turn around and ease her way out the door, but her traitorous feet refused to budge.

"Karl, your job is done. It's because of me you're lying here in the hospital. I came in here to thank you and say goodbye. Besides, after tomorrow I won't need any protection."

Jerry cautioned: "Emily, don't be hasty."

She ignored him and addressed Karl: "I'm grateful to you for everything. I'm sorry you got hurt."

"Emily, I'm a cop and sometimes cops get injured in the line of duty. You are the last person in the world I'd blame if I were the sort of person who likes to place blame for things."

Then he looked over at his partner. "Jerry, I need some privacy."

Jerry understood and left.

Karl looked up at her hopefully. "Emily, dearest, I heard what you said to me before the medics arrived. I may have been groggy but I heard your beautiful words. Our time together was almost magical for me and I believe it was the same for you as well. I refuse to let you slip away from me without a fight."

Tears began to stream down her cheeks.

Karl continued his monologue in a soft voice: "We may find there is nothing between us other than a three-day affair, but we could discover a lifetime of love and happiness."

He looked up at her tear-streaked face and continued speaking tenderly: "Please join me for a few weeks in Patmos? If you and I aren't meant to be, we'll go our separate ways. I lived seven long years alone and now when I have a whisper of happiness, I don't want to let it slip away. Come to Patmos with me. You need time to heal just as much as I do."

Through her tears she looked down at her golden warrior. His beautiful blue eyes seemed to be begging her to remain with him.

What did she have to return to? An empty house filled with memories of a man who deceived her? Her family had worried about her too much already. She didn't want to grow old living her life precariously through the lives of Paul and his family. She promised herself before she left home that this trip would be a new beginning for her.

"Very well, I'll come with you. But you must promise to rest and allow your injuries to heal."

"Lady, I promise to be the ideal patient."

She opened the door and Jerry came back in the room.

Karl's deep baritone voice seemed to resonate off the walls of the hospital room. "Jerry, she is coming with me! Can you make the arrangements?"

"Consider it done." He paused and then added: "This will be easy. I'll use the number Turner gave me."

Jerry disappeared, which left Emily alone with Karl again. She watched as he fought to stay awake. She curled up on the chair by his bed and relaxed listening to the sound of his breathing.

An hour and a half later Jerry poked his head in the doorway. "Better wake Rip Van Winkle up! The troops are on their way to get him ready for transport. Your luggage is on its way from Villa DiMattia as we speak. The helicopter will be landing on the roof in less than an hour. I'll be back to get you in a little while. Make sure the big guy is ready."

She barely had time to nod when he disappeared again.

Half an hour later Jerry reappeared. "Come on people, the helicopter will be landing within minutes. Your luggage is already up there. A couple I know was already headed to Patmos. I was able to piggyback with them. They also plan to stay at Hotel Alexandros, so it worked out well."

As soon as Emily excused herself to go to the washroom, Karl asked his partner, "Your friends? You're starting to sound like Edgar. When you meet one of his so-called friends he could be a bearded Afghani mountain man toting a bazooka. Who the hell are these friends of yours who just happen to be flying to Patmos at this time of night and just happen to be staying at Hotel Alexandros?"

"Part of the deal, my friend. I phoned the number Turner gave me. They set everything up to get the two of you out of here. They'll be your back-up in Patmos at least until I get there. Man, are you cranky."

"I don't need any back-up to look after Emily. I'm quite capable of handling things, myself."

"If I weren't pushing you around in a wheelchair, I might be tempted to believe you."

"I don't want them hanging around us all the time."

"I think you'll find they'll be like ghosts."

"I hope you're right."

"You're really cranky!"

"No, I'm not!"

NEGATIVE SPACE

Jerry mumbled under his breath, "Whatever you say, intrepid warrior."

"I heard that and I'm not cranky."

They reached the rooftop helipad in time to see a black helicopter approach the building. Emily covered her ears to block out some of the noise. A couple in their mid-thirties climbed out and helped assist Karl inside. In fact, they lifted him out of his wheelchair and loaded him into the seat beside the pilot.

Jerry tried to introduce them but she couldn't hear above the noise of the rotors. As he helped her up into her seat he whispered, "Tell the invalid, I'll be down is a couple days. Have some loose ends to tie up here, first."

He closed the door. The sound from the rotors changed in pitch as they lifted off the building and rose into the dark sky.

As soon as they were airborne Jerry's friends introduced themselves as Flori and Konstantin Cana. Physically, the Canas were an unlikely couple. Flori was short and of medium build while her husband, Konstantin was much taller and leaner. Considering the ease with which they had picked up Karl and carried him to the helicopter, they were both very strong.

They seemed content to chat quietly with each other, which left her free to pursue her own thoughts.

The group was helicoptered to a private airfield. The pilot turned off the engine and instructed them to wait.

Emily watched as she saw the lights from a plane approach from a distance and then descend onto the airstrip. The small plane taxied until it was within twenty feet of the helicopter and stopped.

A minute later the hatch was opened and a tall man dressed in a thawb and ghutra stepped onto the runway.

Konstantin opened the helicopter door and he and Flori helped Karl climb down. Emily followed them toward the plane.

The pilot bowed and ushered them onboard. His English was halting. "We fly two hours and land on Island of Leros. Then you take a helicopter to Patmos."

Stepping inside the plane was like walking into the lap of luxury. Konstantin and Flori helped Karl ease into one of the extra-large off-white leather seats. The pilot adjusted the seat so Karl was almost lying flat. Then he brought out several blankets and handed them to Konstantin. Emily helped cover Karl and took a blanket for herself as she stretched out on one of the adjacent seats.

The pilot pointed to a small fridge. "Water, here or make tea or coffee there."

Konstantin thanked him as he disappeared into the cockpit.

Karl fell asleep before the plane lifted off. Konstantin and Flori seemed fixated on an iPad.

Emily sat and tried to organize her thoughts. She felt as though her whole world was in a state of flux and at the moment she was at a loss to make sense of it. She must have dozed off because she was suddenly aware the plane was making its descent. She nudged Karl awake.

They landed at a small airport. The plane taxied until it came abreast of a white helicopter.

The helicopter pilot was waiting for them as they climbed down the few steps from the plane. He was a tall thin Greek man. "Welcome to Leros, the jewel of the Adriatic. My name is Stefanos, I will be your tour guide for tonight, ladies and gentlemen. I understand we have an injured passenger."

He spotted Karl's bandages. "You, sir, will sit beside me. The others can climb in the back."

Stefanos took his duties as a tour guide seriously. He began his monologue as they were lifting off. "You should be pleased to land on Leros because it is such a famous island. The goddess Artemis lived here in ancient times. She was the daughter of Zeus and Leto and her brother was Apollo. She was the 'goddess of the hunt' and the Romans called her Diana. Thucydides, he was a Greek general and historian, he came here. He was famous for writing 'The History of the Peloponnesian Wars'. He was like a philosopher. My favourite quote is: 'Most people in fact, do not take the trouble in finding out the truth, but are more inclined to accept the first story they hear.' What do you think of that? He had many more. When you come back, I'll tell you some of the others.

"Julius Caesar came here also. He was kidnapped by pirates and held on our neighbour Farmakonisi. After he was ransomed he came back and killed every single one of his captors. That's true. It was written in a book by Plutarch."

The helicopter ride lasted long enough for Stefanos to finish two more stories.

They landed somewhere on the coast, judging by the sound of nearby waves lapping the shore.

Stefanos climbed out of the helicopter and began handing out his business cards as he helped the others out.

As soon as Emily stepped off the helicopter she inhaled the freshness of the Aegean night breeze. The night air was pleasantly cool.

She turned around to find that Flori and Konstantin were already helping Karl. They were carrying him in the direction of a waiting vehicle.

She didn't spot the man standing beside the vehicle until Karl yelled out to him.

"Hey, Alexandros! It is great to see you again. I think this is the second time I came here wounded. You must be getting tired of me!"

A deep voice erupted from somewhere inside the Greek man's chest as he responded: "Old buddy, it is the third time you've come to be patched up but who's counting. Jerry already filled me in on all the details, so rest!"

The deep voice then spoke to her: "Emily, I'm Alexandros! Welcome to Patmos. Karl and I are old comrades-in-arms. My wife and I operate a small hotel here. I'll have you there in no time."

Alexandros stopped to greet Flori and Konstantin and load the luggage in the back of the SUV.

"Emily, your fame precedes you. I admire women of action. In fact, I married one. I know you'll like Iola. She was an army nurse when I met her. Now I work for her. She runs the hotel and she also runs me," Alexandros laughed.

Emily doubted anyone told a guy who looked like Alexandros what to do. She watched as he helped secure Karl in the front seat.

Alexandros was of medium height and all muscle. The hair on his head was shaved completely off. He sported a day's old growth of beard that made his Adonis-like face appear even more masculine. Muscle bulged through the fabric of his shirt. Any hint of fierceness vanished as soon as he mentioned his wife.

"I've got buddies on guard tonight so you two can sleep without worrying. Jerry assured me that most of the threat should be gone by tomorrow or the next day. Still, we'll keep extra people around just in case."

They passed a sign 'Hotel Alexandros' as they drove up to the front door of a large white stuccoed building. A wheelchair was waiting at the front door. Konstantin helped Alexandros move Karl from the vehicle to the chair.

Alexandros pushed the wheelchair. Emily had to force her tired legs to move faster to keep up with him. She was trying to absorb everything, where they turned, the colour of the walls, the colour of the carpeting.

"Karl, I'm putting you and Emily in the big suite. It has two bedrooms, a living room and kitchenette. Iola's there getting everything ready for you."

Finally Alexandros stopped in front of a set of dark wooden double doors and slid a key card into the lock.

As soon as he opened the door he called out, "Iola, come say hello to our injured warrior and Emily."

A slender Greek woman appeared from the far end of the suite. Her eyes were large and dark. Her face creased into a welcoming smile. Emily liked her immediately.

Iola had a slight Greek accent when she spoke; "Hi, Karl, nice to see you again. Are you going to be a good patient this time?"

Karl smiled. "Iola, I have always been the most patient of patients."

Emily could well imagine Iola as an army nurse as she cheerfully took control of her patient. "Not always, Karl! You like to think you're ready to climb mountains when you should stay in bed."

"This time I have both you and Emily to make me behave."

Iola turned to Emily. "Emily, it's nice to meet you. Karl comes here anytime he gets wounded in action and I patch him up. He knows where to come for good care. By the way, I heard about your exploits today. You are quite the heroine!"

Iola was being kind but secretly Emily wanted to put the events of the day behind her. "I only did what you or any other woman would have done under the circumstances."

"I am sure you did. But brava to you for doing it!"

"Thanks, Iola."

"I run the hotel and double as the resident nurse. I'd like to check our patient before the two of you bed down for the night. You can use the other bedroom. Our patient will need a lot of rest until he's healed. Alexandros is bringing your luggage in now."

Emily excused herself and went to the small bedroom. She could hear Iola asking Karl questions about the trip over.

She's not going to find out anything from him, she thought. *He slept most of the way.*

She placed her suitcase on the bed and opened it. Maybe it was a good idea to come here after all. Her nerves were still jangling. She could use these days to relax and regain her composure and then she would return home as though nothing had happened. She unzipped her bag and found a note sitting on top of her clothes:

> *Dear Emily,*
>
> *Brava! Jerry told us all about your exploits when he phoned for your bags. Men always underestimate what we women are capable of.*
>
> *You are to come here after your stay in Patmos.*

Don't argue! You will stay a week free of charge. Plus I want to get some of your great fish recipes before you head back to Canada.

With love,

Pia

She climbed into bed ignoring her unpacked bag. That would wait until tomorrow. She closed her eyes and felt her body ease into the mattress. Memories of her days of hiding out with Karl rippled through her mind like a haze of warmth and sensuality. She felt the tiredness seep out of her bones as she thought about his arms around her.

She was knocked out of her reverie when she heard her name called. It was Alexandros' booming voice, "Emily, please come back in. Karl won't settle down unless he knows you are close by. It must be the shock of the surgery. Maybe it was too soon to move him."

She entered the larger bedroom and Iola motioned for her to sit on a chair beside the bed. Her golden warrior had been bathed and was anxiously looking around the room. She sat on the chair beside him. "Emily, you're not safe yet. You have to stay near me until the word gets out about the weapon. Finding it is one thing but getting the word out could take a while."

"Karl, stop worrying! I promise not to leave you. You're tired. Perhaps the trip was too much for you."

She felt Alexandros' hand on her shoulder. "He's in very good hands here. We'll look after him. Iola ordered some dinner for you. She'll feed him some soup then he'll sleep."

"He's quite pale."

Alexandros chuckled. "Don't worry about him. He's strong as an ox and recuperates quickly. Now relax and think of this as your home away from home while you're here. You're among friends!"

Iola came into the room with a pitcher of chicken broth for Karl. "No steaks for you tonight, Karl! Just broth!"

A waiter carrying a tray of food followed close behind her. Iola continued giving orders. "Kyros, Mrs. Clark can sit over there. You can set up a table for her."

When Emily uncovered the tray, the aroma of chicken and freshly cooked vegetables wafted up to fill her nostrils. She didn't feel hungry until she smelled the food. She took her first bite of the succulent chicken and smiled. She deliberately ate slowly, savouring every delicious bite.

After Iola finished tending to him and left, Karl sat watching Emily finish eating. "As soon as I get my strength back I plan to make love to you, lovely lady."

He was in the process of uttering these words as Alexandros reappeared in the doorway pulling a cot behind him. He gave no indication he overheard Karl's comment. "Emily, you can sleep here so Karl doesn't worry about somebody stealing you during the night."

Alexandros opened up the cot. "Happy now, Karl?"

Karl's response could best be described as a snore.

She kissed his sleeping face before crawling onto the cot.

FIFTEEN

Emily awoke feeling rested. It took her a few seconds to figure out where she was. She opened her eyes to see the morning sun trying to force its way around the edges of the drapery.

Karl was sitting up in bed smiling down at her lying on the cot. "Hope you slept well. Iola was in and left some breakfast for you in the kitchenette. She said to phone down if you want something more."

She climbed off the cot and walked over to examine him more closely.

"Iola tells me, I'm doing great. There's no sign of fever or anything sinister so take that worried look off your face."

"You can't blame me. This time yesterday, I thought I was losing you. You lost a lot of blood."

"I'm on the mend now. That's all that matters."

As though for the first time, she looked around the room. "Karl, this place is beautiful. Why didn't I see it last night?"

"Maybe you were too tired? Yesterday wasn't exactly uneventful."

The whiteness of the stuccoed walls was broken up by jewel-toned pieces of art. The effect was dramatic and beautiful. Emily threw open the curtains and opened up French doors onto a protected balcony. "Karl, can you come out here? It's lovely! It's sheltered so no one can see us. I'd like to eat my breakfast here."

He edged his way out of bed. She rushed over to help him but he pushed her away. "I'm fine. Just a bit slow moving, that's all."

"Do you need a blanket?"

"Emily, I'm fine. Iola does enough fussing over me. You're here for a rest-cure as well. So relax."

"I feel better already. I think it's finally sinking in that the weapon has been found and my worries are over."

"Think you're going to like it here?"

"So far I love it. I feel like I'm on vacation already."

For the next four days, neither of them mentioned the weapon or the ordeal they had been through. Instead they relaxed on their balcony and in the evening walked slowly around the hotel's garden area. Meals appeared in their suite as if by magic. They resumed their chess tournament and Iola began helping Karl exercise his shoulder.

Their sense of serenity was shattered by loud banging on the door late Friday morning. Jerry announced his presence in his usual stentorian voice, "It's me! Let me in."

He rushed in as soon as Emily opened the door. "I got a load of computer equipment and other junk. Can I come in and set up on that big table?"

Karl replied, "Sure, that's a good place. You ever do anything quietly?"

"Not my nature! By the way, I see you have a second bedroom. I'll sleep in there."

Shaken out of his tranquility Karl quickly spoke up, "Not a chance, Jerry! Get your own room."

He laughed feigning disappointment. "Thought you'd say that so I booked the next room down the hall. But I could cancel if you change your mind."

He looked hopefully at Emily. "Don't look at me, Jerry. I'm staying out of it."

"Got lots to tell you two love birds. While you were lovey dovey here, I was working! Man, I'm starving, got anything to eat here?"

Emily ordered three pikilia platters.

Jerry eagerly began relating his information.

"Wait till you hear what the officers found when they went through Ingrid Soll's house. For one thing, she had enough weapons to equip a small army. The place was spotlessly clean. Even her socks were lined up like little soldiers in her drawer. The woman was OCD in a big way and judging by some of the stuff in one room in her basement, she was into playing sexual games in a big way. There's no question she was Viktor. She had a scrapbook full of newspaper articles about her exploits as Viktor. The closet in one of the bedrooms was loaded with disguises."

Karl interrupted, "Were they able to access her computer?"

"Oh yea! Techs grabbed that as soon as they entered the place. They extracted all sorts of data. This is the best part! We now have enough to go after Alberto Rizzi."

Emily squeezed in a question: "Is that Rinaldo Rizzi's father?"

Jerry had the floor: "One and the same! Up until now, he was Mr. Smooth. Couldn't get anything to stick to the guy. But, now that's all changed. He paid Soll to take out a couple of the witnesses against junior last year. Soll videoed the poor sods before she killed them. Obviously it was for insurance purposes. No wonder she wasn't afraid to give young Rizzi the yo-heave-ho down the bank at Lucca."

Karl asked, "What was all the shooting about at Monterosso al Mare? We had to run for cover."

"The Italian police had quite a cleanup job to do there. It seems Viktor or rather Soll went on a shooting spree. My guess is she wanted to thin out the competition for the KZR weapon. Your man Rinaldo Rizzi brought a platoon of thugs with him."

He looked over at Emily. "They planned to grab you, my dear."

Before she could comment he quickly added with complete certainty, "Don't worry, Karl would never have let that happen."

Looking back at Karl he carried on: "Young Rizzi was trying to put people at every station to grab Emily. But Soll already knew you went to Monterosso del Mare, and followed you there. She opened fire on them. The body count was seven, counting your friend Ruth."

Room service arrived with their meal. As they sat around the table Jerry continued his recitation. "Young Rizzi and three of his men are still in hospital. Soll did some serious damage to Rizzi's spine. He'll spend his time in prison in a wheelchair sporting a bag. Couldn't happen to a nicer guy."

Karl probed some more, "So how many men did Rizzo have at Cinque Terre?"

"Rizzi brought at least ten guys with him. Plus there was the one who cut off my van on the highway. Old Rizzi was intent on getting his hands on the weapon. Six dead, three wounded in hospital and one other is behind bars! The police were also able to lay drug charges after they checked their vehicles."

"Did Soll give any reason why she didn't respond to my request for back-up?" Karl asked.

"Brushed it off. Showed us what looked like a bruise on her temple and said she'd been knocked out. All lies, of course!"

Jerry poured ales for himself and Karl and a glass of white wine for Emily.

"Emily, you'll be pleased to learn that Lombardi graciously accepted credit for killing Viktor. Don't know if you remember him. He was the young cop who was the first one to show up at Luigi's after all the ruckus."

"Don't remind me. It's a day I'd like to erase from my memory. But thanks, Jerry. I hope Lombardi didn't mind that."

Jerry let out a loud guffaw. "Mind all that attention! Bloody hell! In my opinion the guy was thrilled with it! Thanks to you, he's a hero. If you two lovebirds watched the newscasts, instead of mooning over each other, you'd have seen his beaming face plastered all over the telly. Apparently his notoriety has already gained him invitations to appear on talk shows and offers of marriage from three women. The guy is riding a high."

Emily smiled, realizing her family would never have to know about her close call with an assassin. "I am glad it worked out so well."

Jerry looked at his partner with a devilish grin. "Karl, Soll had a photo of you on her desk. Can you imagine? Ha! I think she had a secret thing for you. Boy, what a creepy thought!"

Emily wanted to be part of this. "I'm not surprised. When I first met her at Villa DiMattia, she was in raptures about how thrilled she was to be working with you, Karl." With a twinkle she added, "That's when I began to suspect she was crazy."

Jerry let out a roar of laughter. "Good one, Emily!"

Karl held up his good arm. "Don't worry. She wasn't my type. In fact I thought she preferred women."

Emily grinned. "She did like women."

Jerry was impatient and interrupted: "Let me continue!"

Karl took a sip from his cool drink and then grinned. His patient look indicated he knew his partner well. "Go on, Jerry."

Jerry continued: "Soll kept diaries. It'll take a while to go through them along with the other evidence. Hopefully it will give us a better idea of who else hired her to kill people besides Alberto Rizzi. We know there were others from her bank deposits. She used her high security position to gain access to all sorts of classified files."

Karl interrupted, "Jerry, how was she able to get her hands on some of those witnesses? That information exceeded her authority."

"As always, you're one step ahead, Karl. She was blackmailing people in high places. In a safe in the floor of her basement, they found files on all sorts of people. Several judges and a few high-ranking officers have already been arrested and that's just the beginning. This could have a ripple effect. Wait and see!"

Karl considered this and voiced what both he and Emily were thinking: "Strange no one picked up on her before."

"Karl, the people who knew about her, were scared to death of her. Much of her diary was devoted to her love of inflicting pain. She was a perverted sadist."

He was about to give more details when Emily stood up. "Please, not over lunch. As she wanted to make me one of her victims, I prefer not to hear this at all."

Karl gave Jerry a warning look.

Jerry looked penitent. "So sorry. How thoughtless of me. I promise it won't happen again."

In a low voice Emily asked. "Is it too soon to find out? Did she leave a list of any kind? I mean—"

Sometimes as a police officer you must deal with unpleasant truths. Jerry replied in a sympathetic tone, "I know what you're asking, Emily. The answer is yes, she kept a record."

"Was John's name on that list?"

Jerry responded, "I'm afraid so. He was one of her hits."

She replied almost in a whisper, "Thank you, I wanted to know for sure. It confirms what Ruth said."

She rose from the table and went into the bedroom.

Karl held up his hand, hushing Jerry. "Give her some time, Jerry. She's strong. You'll see."

"Now that we're alone, there's some other things. I popped in to see Konstantin before I came here. His agency informed him the alert level is still high."

"Why is that? Turner located the weapon. Emily should be able to ease back into her old way of life."

"Unfortunately, when the hunt for the weapon was on, someone posted a photo of Emily on the net. Whoever Clark was hiding her from, saw the picture and is now searching for her."

"Jerry, she has no idea Clark was protecting her or that someone continued the protection after his death. Does Konstantin know who this menace is?"

"All Konstantin knows is that it's someone high and mighty. Someone with a long reach."

"What are we supposed to do, Jerry? We're cops, not bodyguards."

"Konstantin beefed up security around here. He paid Alexandros to hire extra guards. We are to notify Konstantin any time Emily leaves the building and we are to keep her away from the shoreline."

"Is this because of Clark? Did being married to him entitle her to a lifetime of fear?"

"Anything is possible in this case, Karl. Nobody knew about her until Clark hooked up with her. Everyone concerned, meaning Turner and Konstantin's people, agree she is safer here than back home. I'd like to begin questioning her as soon as possible."

"Don't rush her, Jerry. She's been through a lot in the past while. Can you wait a couple days before starting?"

"I'm afraid not. I want to finish up here, so I can get back to the case we dropped when Turner phoned and begged us to get involved in this fiasco."

"If you're going to question her, there is something you should understand about Emily before we begin," Karl said. "She becomes loquacious whenever she is trying to work her way through something."

"She's a woman, Karl. Women perfected the art of talking. Most women can out talk the average guy any time of the day or night."

"No, you don't understand, Jerry. It's more than that! Whenever she appears to be rambling, she is sorting things out in a rather astute way. Let me explain."

He had Jerry's full attention.

"When we were in Riomaggiore it became clear several of the factions were preparing to make their move. As soon as I got her to Monterosso al Mare, she told me she knew Viktor was at the hotel and possibly part of the painting group. Then at Luigi's place she began to talk about some of the goings at Riomaggiore."

"What are you getting at?"

"Jerry, the afternoon before Soll attacked our hideaway, Emily wanted to use me as a sounding board because there were some things she was trying to sort out. She was within a hair's breadth of figuring out the identity of Viktor. She spotted things

I missed and as you know, I don't normally miss much. Not only that but she put the pieces together minutes before she pulled the trigger on Soll. She knew who she was going to shoot."

"Man, am I impressed. That's nothing short of amazing. In future, I'll be happy to sit and listen whenever she wants to expound."

"I generally grab an ale when she's in a talkative mood."

Jerry chuckled. "Works for me."

Jerry walked to the window, then turned to face Karl. "Remember how we always talked about opening up our own agency."

"You have more thoughts on the idea?"

"I'm thinking we should do it now. Don't say no again, hear me out."

"What's on your mind?" Karl asked.

"I'm thinking that maybe we found the perfect partner, Karl. I think Emily is a natural."

"Emily?" At first he chuckled then he answered more seriously: "Jerry, she has no investigative or police background. Chances are she wouldn't be interested in any case. Besides, her family lives in Canada. She'll want to go back home as soon as we leave here."

Jerry persisted: "Listen to me, Karl. What she lacks in background, she more than makes up for in brains and instinct."

Then he looked directly at Karl and in a loud voice added: "What do you mean, lives in Canada? How can you even think of allowing that woman to leave you?"

"That's something I'm trying to work out."

Jerry chuckled. Coming from his taciturn partner, that was quite an admission. He continued enthusiastically, "Think about this!"

He waited until Karl finished sipping his ale before continuing: "What novice would have figured out to lie in wait for Soll the way Emily did? You or I would have hidden in the kitchen behind that bar thing. She found the perfect spot beside the door. Not even a pro like Soll thought she'd be there. I love the irony of it. She killed the monster who murdered her husband."

Jerry was on a roll and continued with even greater enthusiasm: "Who discovered the identity of Viktor? Emily Clark did, no one else, that's who. And that includes yourself and my humble self who worked with Soll more than once. I'm not mildly impressed with Emily Clark's abilities, I'm a huge fan of what the woman is capable of. I think we should go for it."

Jerry continued his monologue as he paced around the room. "Pity she's so publicity shy. We could have capitalized on her shooting Viktor. That would have been the perfect drawing card. It would have given our new business incredible publicity."

Karl was cautious as always. "We still have a lot of work to do on this case. Let's see how this progresses before we mention anything about it. She may not have any interest in detective work. Jerry, not everyone eats and sleeps this stuff like you and me. Don't mention it to her. She has more than enough to contend with for now. Besides she's close to her family in Canada. I believe she'll want to go back home."

In too loud a voice, Jerry replied, "Bloody hell, Karl, don't let this opportunity slip away. Emily is a once in a lifetime find. If she isn't in love with you, she should get an award for acting. Open your eyes, man."

Cautiously Karl added: "I want to be sure Clark is out of her system. I don't want a wife who is still half in love with her late husband, especially a husband who casts such a long shadow. I mean, does it ever end with this guy?"

"I understand what you're saying. But, if I were in your shoes, I'd settle for whatever part of her, she was willing to offer."

"No, you wouldn't, Jerry. I know you better than that."

Emily returned to the room carrying a tray loaded with three cups of Greek coffee and some biscuits.

As Jerry accepted his cup he continued speaking, "Turner sent over a file with information from your paintings and other stuff. Do you mind if we begin questioning you now?"

"I knew I'd have to talk about my time with John, I just didn't think it would be so soon."

As if ignoring the import of what she said, Jerry continued: "We need you to tell us anything you can remember about your travels with Clark. Things that may seem insignificant to you, may not be insignificant to us."

"I'll do it but do you mind if I take a little time to collect my thoughts before we begin. I'd like to go for a swim."

Karl looked at her understandingly. "No problem! Take all the time you need."

Then he looked over at Jerry. "Let's go join Alexandros in the gym."

Looking back at Emily, he added: "We'll meet you back here in just over one hour."

Emily excused herself and went to the bedroom. She sat on the bed for a few minutes before donning her black bathing suit and cover-up.

As soon as she was out of earshot, Karl motioned to Jerry. "She's still fragile, Jerry. Don't rush her. Go easy."

"I can see that now. Konstantin wants to keep tabs on her. I'll drop by his room on the way to the gym."

Emily made her way to the pool area. No one was in sight. She'd have the pool to herself. She needed solitude.

Nothing was as she had thought. Her perceptions about John and their trips together had been wrong. Now Jerry wanted to questions her about events she barely understood herself. She swam lap after lap and slowly felt some of the tension drain out of her body. Then she held on to the side of the pool and allowed her body to float up to the surface. She started when a face came into view directly above her.

"Karl, you startled me."

"Sorry, I could see you were lost in thought. Jerry's back upstairs and chomping at the bit to get started."

"Is he always this impatient?"

"The short answer is 'yes'."

She climbed out of the pool and allowed Karl to wrap a towel around her.

"Let's go. The sooner we get this over with, the better," he said.

She chuckled. "I thought police officers enjoyed interrogating people."

"Not this time. I want you to myself. The sooner we get this over with, the sooner Jerry will leave."

Jerry was sitting at the table looking impatient when they returned. "The return of the mermaid!"

She smiled. "Was Karl careful with his shoulder at the gym?"

Jerry laughed. "Careful? You shoulda heard Alexandros! He was over him like a mother hen. He's too afraid of Iola to let anything happen to one of her patients. After witnessing that pathetic scene, I plan to stay single forever."

Karl was his methodical self. "Emily, you sit in the big chair so Jerry can see you as he works at the computer. With my one arm I can manage to go through some of the information Turner sent to us."

They arranged themselves accordingly and Jerry began the questions: "Emily, I understand your first trip with Clark was to Capri. You mentioned you saw Soll approach John Clark."

Karl stopped him, "Let's get a bit more background. Why don't we start with when you met Clark? Please speak into the microphone."

Emily gave details of her early days with John. Then they moved on to their trip to Capri.

Jerry asked, "Did Clark receive any phone calls or messages when you arrived at the hotel in Capri?"

"There was a large manila envelope waiting for him."

"You see what was in it?"

"I never saw him open it."

Karl took over questioning her: "How many days was he away from you on that trip?"

Meanwhile Karl gestured towards the minibar and Jerry nodded affirmatively and jumped up. He grabbed ales for both of them and poured a glass of white wine for Emily.

Emily took a sip of her wine before replying, unaware the two police officers were settling in to listen to a long dissertation if need be. She was focused on trying to remember details of a trip she took long ago. "As I recall he was gone when I awoke the morning after we arrived. He came back about three days later. We spent the rest of the week shopping and seeing the sights."

"When did you see Soll?"

"John took me to lunch on the patio just before we flew home. We ordered and were chatting when Soll came over to our table. I thought perhaps she was an old lover because John didn't introduce us."

Karl could see she was having difficulty dealing with this and spoke up, "Emily, there's no way you could have known otherwise. Any woman would have thought the same thing. Let it go. He was not about to introduce her as a fellow assassin."

"I overheard my roommate at Villa DiMattia say that Viktor had an affair with John's first wife and then murdered her. At the time I assumed Ruth was referring to a man. Do you think John knew Ingrid Soll killed his wife?"

Karl responded, "No, not for a minute! I think he was disgusted because he knew what kind of an animal she was. As it's Soll we're talking about, I'm certain he had good reason for his feelings. When did the two of you travel together again?"

"On our honeymoon."

She described her wedding in her back garden in Dundas. The renovations on the house were far from complete. She was disappointed John invited only one friend and not a single relative to attend.

"John took me to Paris for our honeymoon. I spent a year there studying at culinary school before I opened my restaurant. John knew I kept in touch with my friends there. He would come and go from our hotel during the three weeks we were there."

"Did he meet with anyone there? Tell me anything you can remember."

"Most days he went to his business meetings so I kept myself busy phoning friends and meeting them for lunch."

Jerry mumbled sarcastically, "Some honeymoon!"

Karl gave him a warning look.

"John wanted me to attend a reception at an embassy with him. We went to a massive house just outside the city. While John was busy talking to some people, I began chatting with a tall Arab gentleman. He was charming. He kept looking at me in such a strange way. I believe his last name was Al Fraih. John came and stood between us and introduced himself."

She stopped speaking and took a sip of her wine. "I was a bit intimidated because it was the first reception we attended together and we were so far from home. I guess I was annoyed at John for ignoring me up until then. But suddenly he seemed thrilled to be near me. Mr. Al Fraih called John some name like 'the Athenian' or 'the Armenian' and he invited us to his home for a weekend to meet his associates."

Jerry helped himself to two more ales. After handing one to Karl he poured a soda for Emily.

"We were driven to a small airport early one morning and flew out by private jet. It was similar to the one you and I flew here in, Karl. We landed in the desert. It was so hot I could hardly breathe when we got off the plane. We were driven to a palace that was the same shade as the sand."

She stopped again getting a visual image of the building and the general atmosphere. "Al Fraih greeted us at the door. He took John aside and they talked. The entrance hall was incredibly opulent. I was ushered to the women's section of the building and John went someplace else. I expected John to join me later but he never did. It was there I met Manaar. She brought my meals."

She stopped talking, giving herself time to manage her memories. "Later on, whenever John and I travelled in the Middle East, Manaar would come to our hotel, and take me on tours of the countryside. I was thrilled to get a chance to see so many ancient shrines. The tour guides were always archaeologists. We went to visit actual digs. It was wonderful. I often think about Manaar. I'd love to see her again."

"Tell me more about that weekend in the desert. Who did you meet there?" Karl asked.

She looked over at him but delayed answering while she tried to remember all the details of that weekend. "Nobody! Absolutely nobody! I stayed in the women's section the whole time. As I said, not even John came to see me. I was well treated. I remember having a massage and spending time in a swimming pool. The food was sumptuous. I remember wishing I had a list of the ingredients in several of the dishes."

She stopped for a moment, her eyebrows knitted together. "Wait a minute! I did see someone else. Someone I didn't expect to see. I can't remember."

"Emily, don't rush it. Do you want to stop now?" Karl asked gently.

"No, I want to continue. I remember Manaar telling me I was important because of my father. I have no idea what she meant because my father is the minister of a church in a small town. She must have confused me with some other guest."

Karl and Jerry exchanged glances.

Unaware of their unspoken communication, she continued her monologue: "When we left on the Monday evening, Manaar insisted I be fully covered up, including my face. Then she took me out some back way, not the front door. I was driven to a waiting plane. John was already on board. He told me he had a most satisfactory weekend but explained nothing more."

She pondered briefly before responding: "For some unknown reason, I didn't ask John any questions. I realize now that I should have but I didn't. It all seemed rather strange to me. I felt I was out of my league so I tried to make myself inconspicuous. It was all so new to me. We were only just married."

Karl held up his hand. "Stop the tape! Emily, I think you just gave us the name of, or at least information on your husband's handler."

He looked compassionately at her. "Try not to be so hard on yourself. I believe John Clark intended for you to be cowed. That would fit the profile for his type of behaviour. Shall we call it a day?"

"No, I want to get this over with," Emily insisted.

"Very well then, this event would have coincided with Clark's resigning from his law partnership. The timeline fits. What did he say to you after he first met Al Fraih at the reception?" Karl asked.

"When we got back to our hotel room that night, he picked me up and literally danced around the room holding me up in the air. He told me that I was his good luck charm and he wanted to take me on every single one of his trips from then on."

"If this man is who I think he is, you may not be entirely safe until he is dealt with. Hidden away in Dundas, you had a kind of anonymity but eventually he may have worried that you would remember too much about him. We must be very careful how we proceed. What do you think, Jerry?"

"I agree. This man could be the sleeping dragon Clark was worried about. I doubt he works alone. He's probably part of a consortium. You said he wanted Clark to meet with his associates. I wonder who else was there that weekend." Jerry replied.

"I wish I could be of more use. I can't seem to remember any more," Emily said.

Jerry was suddenly unusually enthusiastic. "Emily, your powers of observation and recollection astound me."

Then he boasted to his partner: "Told you so, Karl. We need her. We can teach her how to shoot."

"What on earth are you talking about?" Emily asked.

Karl interjected, "No, Jerry!"

Jerry became expansive. "Emily, Karl and I have talked for years about setting up our own investigative services business but we kept putting it off. After seeing you in action, I suggested we do it now and ask you to join us."

Karl interrupted, "Stop it now, Jerry. This isn't going to happen."

Jerry ignored him and spoke to Emily: "How did you figure out that woman you met in Capri was Viktor?"

"Actually it was thanks to you, Jerry?"

"Me? Bloody hell, I remind you of an assassin? Me?"

"Yes, you! When I first saw you at the Amsterdam airport, I noticed your scar."

"If I got plastic surgery, I'd miss all attention the ladies give me."

"Enough, Jerry!" Karl said. "Emily, please continue."

"Later when I met Jerry at the villa, I barely noticed it. When he smiled, it was as though the scar vanished. I no longer focused on it."

Karl asked, "What did that have to do with Soll?"

"When I met Soll in Capri, she had a long scar running down the side of her face."

Karl smiled. "She had plastic surgery."

"She must have. Karl, now that I think about it, I saw her one other time. She was in the swimming pool the first time Manaar took me for a swim. We had to turn back."

"When you were at the home of Al Fraih?" Karl asked.

"Yes, Soll was in the pool swimming when we got there."

"Did you actually go into the pool with her?"

"No, Manaar spotted her and took me back to my room. She called her an animal."

"She was right on that point," Karl replied.

"Karl, I'm tired. Can we stop now?"

"We can. Iola invited us for dinner. I'm sure Alexandros has a hundred stories to tell us. Care to join us, Jerry?"

"Not me! I've got a date with a rented scooter and then a round of darts at the pub."

"You found a pub here?"

"Karl, there are English pubs everywhere, even in Patmos."

"Have fun," Karl replied and then looked back at Emily. "Dinner isn't for a couple hours. Anything you want to do?"

"Karl, are you up to a walk around the village before dinner?"

With great pride in his voice, her lover announced, "Emily, my brave princess, there's nothing I would rather do. I've been to Patmos many times but never with you. I'd love to show you around."

He became more expansive as he continued, "In fact I want to show you the whole wonderful island. I hope you come to love it as much as I do."

The town of Skala was enchanting. The buildings were like something out of a storybook. Emily and Karl meandered along the narrow cobbled streets admiring the whiteness of all the buildings. Then they stopped at the old church.

"Karl, is it me or does this place have a mystical quality? I feel something."

He smiled. "Some feel it. I've heard people say that the minute they set foot on the island, they felt as though their souls had been here before. The apostle John lived here while in exile. Another day we can investigate the cave where he stayed. Strangely enough there are people who come here and aren't able to sense the spirituality. I always have and am glad you feel it too."

He stopped walking and looked down into her eyes. "You know, Emily, few people have the presence of mind to carry it off the way you did at Luigi's place. You had to be upset and possibly in shock when I was shot, but you carried on."

She tried to make light of it. "I wasn't about to let you bleed to death on the bedroom floor. Especially after the wonderful sex we enjoyed. I'd have to go hunting for another gorgeous man. They're hard to find."

"So it was all about the sex? I'm a sex object?"

"Yep!"

He laughed and bent down. Cupping her face in his large hand, he gently kissed her lips.

NEGATIVE SPACE

They returned to the hotel and dined on black sea bass, fresh from the Aegean Sea. Alexandros entertained them with funny stories and the evening passed by quickly.

At midnight Emily and Karl drifted back to their suite. Karl's shoulder was still bandaged but the pain was now manageable.

They began kissing lightly and soon found themselves in the thrall of passion. Why did this man excite her so? With only one touch, she felt as though she was on fire.

He whispered in her ear, "Bet you're glad you saved me now."

"Couldn't replace you if I tried."

"I feel the same way. We have to talk about that some time soon."

They made love twice more during the night.

They were jarred awake by the sound of loud banging. "Dreamers awaken!"

"Go away, Jerry!" Karl yelled back.

"Alas fair lovers, we must get to work!"

"Give us an hour. We need to shower and eat."

"Point taken! See you in exactly one hour. I need time to talk to my friend Konstantin, anyway. At least he's out of bed."

When Jerry returned all was ready and waiting for him. They sat down in their usual positions. Jerry began: "Emily, I'd like to go through your trips in chronological order, if that is all right with you."

"That is easiest for me."

There was a bang on the door and Jerry yelled out, "Who is it?"

"Hendryck!"

Jerry yelled back, "Bloody hell, we've got work to do. What are you doing here anyway, Hendryck?"

"I've come to see the fallen soldier. How is my big brother?"

"He's fine. Now go back home. We're busy."

"I've also come to approve of his lady friend."

"Already approved of her, so go back home, Hendryck. Take the hint! You're not wanted here."

"Karl, do something!" Emily admonished.

Karl rose and opened the door to a shorter, darker version of himself. "Careful where you hug little brother. I'm still sporting a sling. How was the trip over?"

The smaller version responded with a slightly more pronounced accent: "Trip was fine. I flew down myself and landed on Kos. I didn't want to wait for a ferry so I hired a helicopter to fly me to Patmos. The pilot was this interesting guy called Stefanos. He had the most amazing stories."

Karl grinned. "We know what you mean. Where's Greta?"

"Greta couldn't come so she sends her love. As do Julian and his wife."

Jerry pointed to Hendryck. "This is the evil twin. Julian is only slightly less evil."

"How long are you staying?" Karl asked.

"Just a couple days!"

Hendryck looked over at Emily and winked. "I'm going to ignore that grouch at the computer but I'm most eager to meet this beautiful woman."

Instead of shaking hands with Emily, he bent over and kissed her outstretched hand. "The lovely Emily, I presume. When I get you alone, I promise to tell you all Karl's secrets."

Emily laughed. She was delighted to meet Hendryck and loved the way he and Jerry teased each other. In fact, Hendryck seemed to want to tease everyone.

Karl was smiling broadly. "You can sleep in the spare room, little brother."

Jerry poked his head up with mock seriousness and said, "What? What about me? When I wanted to sleep there you both said no and now you're going to let him sleep there? That's not fair!"

Emily responded, "Oh Jerry, we do love you, but if we're going to be working together, don't you think we'd tire of each other if we all stayed in the same unit?"

Jerry grinned slyly. "Does this mean you are considering my suggestion?"

Emily and Karl responded in unison. "NO!"

Karl rose. "Hendryck and I are going to the café for an ale while you two work. Come join us when you feel like taking a break."

Jerry winked at Emily. "That means come down at lunchtime. They want enough time to get tanked before we arrive."

Emily sat while Jerry plied her with questions about her time in the desert. What did she remember of the building? Could she think back and remember who else she might have seen? Who drove them to the palace and who else met them at the front door? Did she see a guard? Did she remember the markings on the airplane?

She explained again she was kept away from all activity of the house. John didn't so much as send her a note. She kept herself busy sketching the intricate patterns on the walls and upholstery and talking to Manaar.

"I wish I could be of more help. I'm sorry I can't tell you more about my days there, Jerry. I didn't see much of anything. Only Soll, that one time, in the swimming pool."

"I'm curious. Let me pull up some old records."

He paused as he brought up Soll's file.

"Well, I'll be! Lady, you're right! Come look at this."

Emily peered at the photograph on the screen. "That's how she looked when I saw her before. Her nose and chin were different, but you can't see the scar."

He was quiet for a few minutes. "I have an injury report filed about eight years ago. She was in hospital for couple months. I can't seem to find the incident report. Maybe she wasn't injured in police action."

"Jerry, if Ingrid Soll was there that weekend, she should have met Al Fraih."

"What are you getting at, Emily?"

"The day the painting group went to Lucca, Soll and I had a cappuccino together at one of the cafés."

"Yes, I remember. I was on surveillance."

"She demanded to know the name of my husband's big client. If Al Fraih was the one giving John all the work, shouldn't she known that? She was there that weekend."

"Sounds to me as though John Clark outfoxed her as soon as he was inside the front door. He must have found out Soll was there and didn't want her near you. It's unlikely Hakim Al Fraih would invite you to his home and then intentionally stick you in a closet. I have a suspicion Soll and Clark were applying for the same position, and we both know who got the job. Also sounds as though the evil Soll was prevented from having an audience with Al Fraih."

"Pity I didn't figure out what was going on sooner."

"Never second guess yourself, Emily. I tried it once and it doesn't pay. No ordinary person could have figured out what John Clark was about. He was a very complex individual."

"Jerry, there is something I really don't understand."

"Only one something?"

She chuckled. "No many, but this is particularly perplexing. I grew up in a small town. I've never distinguished myself in any way and yet John, whose list of accolades went on and on, married me? We had so little in common. He travelled the world and was very sophisticated. And don't give me that baloney that he fell in love with me the minute we laid eyes on each other."

"He targeted you for a reason. That much is clear. He may have only meant to have a fling with you but realized you could be quite an asset to him. You present yourself well and have a genuine friendliness. It's possible he had another reason for wanting you. But I'd urge you not to rule out the possibility he loved you for yourself."

"Jerry, there's something else I want your opinion on."

"Ask away. I see these are things you're a little uneasy talking about with Karl around."

"I know people kill others in wars and I know you were a soldier. How do people deal with taking another's life?"

"Emily, a couple weeks ago, you shot and killed a monster. How do you feel about that?"

"Awful, but I did what I had to do to save my life and Karl's as well."

"Some of us have to kill in the line of duty. If evil didn't exist, Karl and I wouldn't have jobs. You have to do what's necessary. We have a good way of life and we want to preserve that."

"But from what I overheard from Ruth, John killed for money."

"Soldiers and policemen sometimes have to kill people and they're paid as well. I'm not being fair to you. You are assuming your late husband killed based on what you overheard from Ruth Zhou. I know the woman was right about Viktor, but let's wait before we condemn John Clark."

"But if he did kill people? How do people do that?"

"Professionals detach themselves from their killings. They have little or no emotion when they act. In other words, it's a job. Being a cop is a job."

"But Ruth went on and on about all the people he killed."

"Don't rush to judgement. You're basing everything on what one woman had to say. In police work we look at mountains of evidence before we draw conclusions."

"But Ruth said . . ."

"Didn't Karl tell you Ruth Zhou was Po-Ling Yanmei, a fugitive from China."

"Yes!"

"She also had a rap sheet that included prostitution and extortion and then she was hired by a sleazy detective agency. She was not a nice person. Turner got a court order for the agency and is processing their files. They apparently did some work for John's first wife on some of her divorce cases. They also received payments from John himself. Turner's people found payments going into a numbered company, which corresponds to one we found in Soll's files. So they may have been the intermediary who hired her. We can only speculate. We know very little."

"How many others in my painting group were working with Ruth?"

"Several! Both Edgar and Turner knew who they were from the get-go. All the people who signed on late were connected with the detective agency. However, one of the original group gave the list of participant's names to the agency."

"Any idea who?"

"Not my problem! The important thing is to figure out who hired them. We aren't interested in the low life forms. We want to find out who was paying them."

"So Ruth was paid to cozy up to me. She was convincing. Karl told me not to trust her and he was right."

"Karl had more of the facts than you did, Emily. Besides, when you're up to your ass in alligators, you grab onto any stick that's offered to you, even if it's the tail of another alligator."

"I'm not sure I like that analogy but I get your point."

"According to our files, you have a step-son. Tell me about Clark's relationships with his son and daughter-in-law."

"When John and I first got together I sensed that John had been too busy to pay much attention to Paul while he was growing up. That changed after they moved to Dundas. John was very supportive of Paul when he decided to go to medical school. He also insisted on paying for the wedding when Paul and Laura got married. The wedding and reception were held at our home. John bought the old stone house on Brock Street for Paul and Laura as a wedding gift, and when Ardi was born a year or so later, John was over the top. It was the only time I've ever seen him with tears in his eyes."

Jerry interrupted her. "What did you say the baby's name is?"

"John insisted on naming him. His name is Ardian Dalmat Clark but we call him Ardi."

"Ardian Dalmat! Perhaps they are family names."

"Are you sure I was part of John's cover, as Ruth put it when I overheard her?"

He replied, "Emily, the more I learn about Clark the less certain I am about anything relating to him. The man is a paradox. Anything is possible but what you've described is a devoted family man, not some murderer."

"He had a lot of weapons hidden in the basement."

"You think too much, Emily. It is entirely possible he liked to collect weapons. Weaponry is not a hobby that excites everyone but loads of guys are really into it. There are even magazines for gun fanatics."

"I gather, you're not one of those fanatics."

"I like a good piece and I admit to owning a few revolvers."

"I don't understand why he needed so many," she replied.

"Emily, stop this. Turner is still working on the theory that Clark was an agent under deep cover. Just because Ruth Zhou, a woman who went around setting off bombs and killing innocent men, women and children in China, called him a murderer, doesn't make it so. Can we work with evidence, not hearsay? Why are you so set on condemning Clark? Was your life together that horrible?"

"My God, Jerry! I am condemning him, aren't I? I know it sounds irrational but I was so angry at him for dying, for leaving me alone. And then when Greg Turner told me he was passing on information regarding terrorists to him, I was even angrier because he deliberately put his own life in jeopardy. John doesn't deserve the way I've been condemning him. He treated me like a princess. We were happily married. Mom and Dad loved him. My life has been so empty without him."

"I may be wrong but I think we'll find there's a logical explanation for the KZR weapon episode. The unfortunate thing is, he didn't tell you to check your wedding ring for secrets."

"It was right there in front of me all the time. Why have I been so willing to believe the worst about John? He was only ever good to me?"

"Fear! Actually, terror! That's what it does to people's minds. Remember when you were with Edgar at the airport in Amsterdam."

"Yes."

"You spotted me keeping an eye on things."

"Yes, I did. I was afraid of you."

"Admit it, Emily, it went beyond that. Edgar told me, you envisioned me as the reincarnation of *Jack the Ripper*."

"Was I that bad?"

"He finally had to tell you I was on your side."

"Why didn't he say so in the beginning?"

"He was trying to make the two of you look like an average couple travelling alone. Two men and a woman together and people are more apt to notice them. But the point is when you're terrified your thought patterns get turned upside down. That's what happened when you overheard Ruth Zhou. You were already terrified so everything she said became magnified in your mind and you believed her."

"Why was I so ready to accept her as a friend and believe anything she said?"

"Fear! You wanted someone, anyone to make you feel safe. Chances are, if you'd met her under different circumstances, you'd have spotted inconsistencies in her spiel right away."

"I'm rather ashamed of myself."

"Don't be. We see this thinking in whole countries. Terror is a very effective tool for manipulating people's minds. Do you still think Clark would have slit your throat if you had found out about his other activities?"

"No! I think we would have talked about it the same way we talked about everything else in our lives. But I probably would have asked him to retire."

"That sounds more reasonable," Jerry replied.

"Karl told me you were very perceptive. In fact, he said you were almost uncanny in your ability to work things out. I can see what he meant now."

"I don't do compliments. Let's go grab some lunch?"

"I'd love to."

"While you freshen up, I want to make a phone call."

"Konstantin, I'm trying to keep you posted. We're headed to the restaurant down the street. Think it's the one on the corner. Karl and his brother Hendryck are out there already. Hendryck is not a risk."

He hung up as Emily came out of the bedroom. She now wore her large floppy sun hat and blue linen jacket.

The brothers were sitting at a table under a large umbrella and beckoned Jerry and Emily over. They had obviously enjoyed several beers and were looking entirely too relaxed.

"Why the long faces?" Karl asked.

Hendryck cut in, "Spending time with Jerry would depress any woman."

Jerry rose to the bait, "I'll never tell what went on while we were alone."

Karl was about to jump to his feet when Hendryck stopped him, "Can't you see he's trying to get a rise out of you. Sit down and let's order lunch. After that Emily and I can go for a walk while you two cops work."

Jerry responded, "Yea, Karl, I could use a hand with some of this data."

Hendryck eyed Emily. "And I could use a nice long walk after my trip here. What do you think, Emily? Karl tells me you love to hike the trails back in Canada."

"Hendryck, I'd love to go for a walk. But right now, I'm starving and all I can think about is food. I think I'd like a salad with some calamari and some of that wonderful bread. A cold beer would be great too."

She spotted Konstantin and Flori sitting at a table not far from them. "Jerry, why don't you invite your friends to join us?"

"They're not really the joining type. I'll have a chat with them after lunch."

Over lunch Hendryck described some of the antics he and his two brothers engaged in as kids. Like all healthy boys they didn't lack for imagination when it came to getting into mischief.

After lunch Karl and Jerry joined Konstantin and Flori before returning to the suite.

Emily and Hendryck embarked on their walk. They checked out some shops.

Hendryck spotted some scooters for hire. "Ever drive a scooter?"

"No, Hendryck, I would probably fall off and land on my head."

"Can you drive a bicycle?"

"Yes, but a scooter goes faster than a bicycle."

He laughed mischievously, "Why not try it? We'll rent a big one and you can ride on the back and hold on to me. I'll drive slowly."

She felt like doing something daring after the emotional morning she spent with Jerry. She smiled at him and shouted, "Let's do it!"

Hendryck was already making plans. "We'll drive to the Kalikatsou Rock at Petra Bay. I think we can get a good view of the rock from Grikos. It's not far from here! The island is so small, nothing is far from anywhere. However, the distance varies depending on who you ask for directions."

They rented a bike and were soon on their way. Emily held onto Hendryck's torso with determination.

Hendryck slowed down. "Emily, I need to breathe. Ease off. I'll drive slowly until you get the hang of it."

They drove slowly and gradually she felt more confident. She began to relax and enjoy herself. "I'm fine now, Hendryck. Go faster."

They made their way down the ancient road towards Grikos. White cube houses dotted the landscape. Emily wondered how many generations of Patmians had lived in each of the square white buildings. After a while Hendryck pulled over to the side of the road and helped her climb off the scooter. They looked down at the famous Kalikatsou Rock.

Hendryck was a cheerful sort of man, far more outgoing than his older brother. "One of my boys is a budding geologist. I want a picture of the rock for him."

Hendryck snapped the photo with his cell phone and sent it to his son in Belgium.

They decided to walk down to the sea shore to get a closer look.

"I think you'll want to come back here to sketch this big thing. Artists seem to love it."

She was feeling more relaxed. "Let's walk along the beach."

"Good idea, I think I'll take off my sandals. I love the feel of sand between my toes. Hold on, my cell is ringing. It's Karl."

He stopped to talk while she continued walking slowly down the beach.

"Hey big brother, you miss me already?"

"Get the hell off the beach!"

"How'd you know I was on the beach? You got X-ray vision now?"

"There's a speed boat circling not far off shore."

"What's that got to do with anything? We're just strolling along the beach."

"Hendryck, I swear I'll wring your neck if you don't stop arguing. Get Emily off the beach right now."

"She's way ahead of me. I see Jerry's friends Konstantin and what's-her-name talking to her. Funny seeing them here! Guess they wanted to have a look at the rock as well. Catch you later."

Hendryck ran down the beach. "Emily, wait up!"

She turned. "Hendryck, I want to introduce you to Konstantin and Flori. They're Jerry's friends. We flew here together from Italy."

After exchanging pleasantries, Hendryck said, "Emily, we passed a nice pub not far back. Interested in stopping in for a nice cool ale?"

They walked back up the hill toward the town. "Emily, I'm glad we finally have few minutes to chat. I wanted to tell you a bit about our family."

"But Hendryck, Karl and I are friends, nothing more."

"Not from what he told me and not from what I can see every time he looks at you. In any case, Karl can be a hard guy to understand so I thought I'd fill you in."

"Very well."

"Karl's wife Marta left him a wealthy man when she died. He invested most of his inheritance in the business Julian and I started. Julian is younger than me by three minutes. The business has worked out well. The door is always open if Karl ever wants to be more hands-on but so far he seems to like what he's doing."

"He's very good at what he does."

"He still owns the old estate near Brussels. The place has been pretty much empty since Marta and his two young boys were killed. It was in Marta's family for centuries. She was the last of her line."

"That's very sad, Hendryck. Karl has never talked about the family he lost. It must still be painful for him to think about them."

"He changed after the accident. He became withdrawn and buried himself in his work. Today I saw the old Karl again. He's happier than I've seen him in years."

"He's had time to relax both in Italy and then here in Greece. Perhaps that accounts for it."

"When Jerry phoned us from the hospital to tell us about Karl's injuries we were all so worried. He was injured before in the line of duty but when we heard that this time it involved that Viktor character we all said a prayer of thanks he was still alive."

He looked at her warmly and actually seemed surprised at her embarrassment. "Emily, you're the first woman Karl has shown any real interest in since Marta died, and believe me, many women have tried hard to get his attention. The real reason I came here was to meet you. We were all thrilled when he told us about you and how you saved his life."

"That's very kind of you. I don't know how much he's told you, but Karl has helped me work my way through a personal crisis and I'm very grateful to him for that. Whether he or I want to carry our relationship to the next level is still up in the air. I am very fond of him."

He stopped walking and looked at her seriously. "Hope you're not planning to run away back to Canada."

"So much has happened, I haven't had time to give conscious thought to making any decisions."

"Please don't break his heart. That's all I ask."

They spent the rest of their time together talking about the differences between growing up in Belgium and Canada and found they had a lot in common. Both of them had grown up in small towns that were suburbs of large cities and small-town life had a certain pattern to it.

They meandered through Grikos. She ordered tea and a pastry and he ordered a beer at a café.

Unlike his more taciturn brother, Hendryck loved to talk. "Belgium considers itself the beer capital of the world. Wherever I travel I like to check out the competition, but I consider ours the best in the world. One restaurant in Brussels lists over four hundred Belgian beers on its menu."

"Have you tried them all?"

He laughed out loud. "Not yet! Have to save some things for when I retire."

They began their drive back to Skala at a faster speed. Suddenly Hendryck stopped the bike and climbed off. "You're going to drive and I'll sit on back." He showed her how to use the pedals. "Ease your way onto the throttle. That's it!"

He climbed on behind Emily. She drove at an excruciatingly slow speed until Hendryck announced he would like to get back to the hotel in time for dinner. She sped up little by little until she gained more confidence. As they approached Skala, Hendryck urged her to slow down.

He was laughing merrily, "I know the natives drive through these narrow streets like the devil is on their tail, but I don't recommend that for you or me. Let's just take our time and arrive in one piece."

Karl and Jerry were both waiting when they drove up to return the scooter. Karl was looking volcanic and Jerry wasn't far behind.

Jerry pointed at Hendryck. "You did it this time, Hendryck, my boy."

"What are you two so uptight about? My God, we're on an island. There's hardly any place to go. I mean, what can possibly happen on an island this size?"

Jerry offered, "Suggest you and I mosey over to the pub for a cool one while Karl takes Emily back to the suite."

"Always game to try a new brew," Hendryck volunteered.

As they walked away Jerry continued: "There's a few things, I got to explain to your small brain. I'll probably need a few drinks after that. My first drink is on you! You should have seen Karl when Konstantin phoned telling us where you took Emily. He's got it bad. Maybe I can be best man at their wedding."

"Why would they want you when I'm available?"

"Hendryck, they'd elope before they'd have you as their best man. No, I'm the one."

Emily was bewildered. "I don't understand, Karl. We were perfectly safe. All we did was drive down to look at Kalikatsou Rock and walk along the beach. Besides, all the nonsense with the KZR weapon should be behind me by now."

"Don't worry about it. Let's go back to the hotel and grab a bite to eat. We won't hear from those two all evening. They'll be trying to outdo each other in everything. This goes on every time they get together. Watch tomorrow morning, they'll both be nursing good sized hangovers."

"You've seen them in action before."

"Oh yea, I'm glad Julian isn't here. He adds to their mayhem."

"I never had brothers. I envy you."

"You'll think differently in the morning when Hendryck and Jerry are grumbling around the suite."

They ordered their dinner, and sat on the balcony to enjoy it. Emily began to wonder what tragedy had befallen Karl's wife and two young sons. How horrible to lose not only your spouse but your children as well!

If they were to have an honest relationship, should she consider bringing up the tragedy? Could she comfort him? In the end she decided to let the matter drop. It was Karl's personal affair. She would let him choose the right time to talk about it.

She need not have worried because Karl brought up the events surrounding the death of his family on their regular evening walk through the village.

He recounted the story of his earlier life. He and Marta married not long before his first deployment with the army and their children were born within a year of each other.

He told her how his wife was forced off the road on a mountain in Switzerland on the way home from a ski trip. The culprit was a drunken fool who had been partying at a nearby hotel.

"I would have murdered him if he hadn't gone over the edge with them. I can't imagine the panic she must have had when she knew none of them would survive," he said in almost a wail.

She slipped her hand into his much larger one as she listened.

"I blamed myself. I know Marta was a careful driver but the conditions were icy. I wish she had waited until the roads were in better shape. I had taken some leave from the army and she wanted to be there when I arrived. If it hadn't been for me, maybe they'd be alive today."

"How old were your sons when it happened?"

"Niels was eleven and Lucas, a year younger when they were killed. They were excellent skiers as was Marta."

"Tell me about Marta."

"Our fathers were both doctors. They were like brothers. Both our parents encouraged the match. Marta's father was a baron. They had a long and noble history and Marta was the last of her line so they were eager for her to marry young. As soon as Lucas was born, they insisted we move in with them. Marta had a hard time carrying Niels and decided she didn't want any more children. I couldn't blame her."

"Did you love her?"

"In a way, yes! Our families wanted the match. We made it work. We were both doing what was expected of us."

"Is that what you feel bad about?"

"Maybe. No. I was in army intelligence at the time. I was in love with my work. I should have been home more. I didn't spend enough time with my sons or Marta."

"Isn't that the sacrifice every soldier makes for his country? You had a calling and you followed it. Was she angry you were away so much?"

"No. Marta kept busy, she was involved in all sorts of charity work and had a very active social life. When I'd come home, I used to tell her I had to book an appointment just to take her out for dinner."

"She sounds fulfilled to me. Were the boys happy?"

"Julian and Hendryck were always taking them places when I was away. They sort of adopted them. Their letters to me were filled with their adventures with Uncle Julian and Uncle Hendryck."

"Sounds as though your sons had two father figures while you were away."

She continued, "Karl, I know you miss them terribly but to carry around so much guilt for so long isn't good for you. Are you still close with her parents?"

"The Baron and Baroness were with them when they were killed. There had been a storm in the mountains and they were trying to get home for her parent's anniversary party. Everything was arranged for that night. Hundreds of people were invited. That's why I took time off and flew home."

"So she wasn't hurrying home to see you. They wanted to be back in time for a party. How far is the drive from the ski resort to your home in Brussels?"

He paused for a minute. "It's a six to seven-hour drive in good weather."

"Is it possible they were trying to make time?"

"You mean, were they speeding?"

He paused and then continued: "It had been snowing hard for two days. The accident happened just after noon. If the roads were clear, they would barely have had enough time to make it back for the dinner. Marta was a good driver."

"But if she hit a patch of ice at high speed . . ."

"She could have lost control. She had to be speeding. They were rushing to get back home for the party. They had planned to leave two days before but weren't able to get out because of the storm. I phoned her that morning and she told me it had turned very cold during the night. She said that as soon as the wind died down they planned to head out."

"Could they have cancelled the party?"

"Not without great expense! It was to be a gala affair. The baron had invited friends from all over the continent. The baroness gloried in this sort of thing. Even Sunday dinner at their place was an event."

"So, Marta was under pressure to get them back in time for the celebration?" she asked gently.

"They should have cancelled it, I see that now. Funny how I can be so analytical about the cases I'm involved with, but I couldn't reason my way through this."

"You were standing too close, my love."

Emily lit some candles and placed them on the balcony. They sat there and enjoyed a glass of wine before going to bed.

After Karl fell asleep, Emily returned to the balcony and sat thinking about Karl's life with Marta. Now she understood why Hendryck rushed to Patmos to meet her. He and Julian had been both mother and father to two boys whose mother was too busy with her own social life to bother with them. She couldn't find time to have dinner with her husband when he came home on leave. Hendryck knew what Marta was all about. That's why he came to Patmos to tell her not to break Karl's heart again.

She loved him too much to do that.

SIXTEEN

The temperature soared to 37°C, so they decided to take the afternoon off. They were back working again and Emily watched as Jerry wiped perspiration off his forehead. Judging from the telltale signs under the armpits, the man was fast dissolving into a puddle. She rose and turned on the air-conditioning and closed the door to the balcony.

On the way back to her seat, she grabbed a can of beer from the fridge and delivered it to him. "Hope this will help."

"You don't mind the heat?" he asked.

"So long as I don't have to stand in the sun, I love it."

They sat quietly watching Karl who was examining a photocopy of Emily's painting from Barcelona.

"Emily, I want to deal with your trip to Barcelona first. The letters on the back of the painting are MQ/AQ. Considering how methodical Clark was, I thought there should be more information, so last night I e-mailed Turner and requested he take a closer look at the frame. As I recall, you said Clark took your work to Toronto to be framed."

She nodded.

"We should hear back from Turner, shortly. In the meantime I want you to tell us anything you can remember about that trip."

"It feels like so long ago, I don't know how much I'll remember, but I'll do my best."

"Do the names Mateo Quintanilla or Antonio Quintanilla mean anything to you?" Karl asked.

"Yes, I remember them. John told me Mateo was in banking and that they were doing some business together. I have no idea what sort of business. But I remember he invited both John and I to his brother's birthday party. Both Mateo and Antonio were extremely charming. After the party they suggested we spend a few days with them at their country house near Monserrat. We planned to go but John was called away on business so we had to decline."

Karl responded, "According to the Barcelona police report, Mateo Quintanilla's body was found on Saturday morning at the bottom of a cliff during the time you and your husband were there. His brother, Antonio was discovered sitting in the driver's seat of Mateo's car on the road directly above. He was reeking of alcohol and had blood spatter on his shirt. He claimed he had no recollection of how he got there or where the blood came from. Both men showed signs of bruising as though they'd been in a scuffle. In addition, Mateo had a knife wound just below the rib cage. A bloodied knife with Antonio's fingerprints was found at their cottage. The following year, Antonio was convicted of murdering his brother. Strange, he didn't offer a defence. He pleaded guilty."

"I can't comment. The only time I met them was at the birthday party."

"Karl, I hate to interrupt but I've have an e-mail and with an attachment from Turner," Jerry said as he watched the monitor.

"In the e-mail, Turner says they found a small flash drive hidden inside the frame. They had to smash the frame to get at it. They downloaded the file and sent it to us. He says he wants us to call him later today. He wants to talk to Emily."

While Jerry reviewed the contents of the file, Karl asked Emily to continue.

"The party was at Mateo's home. They were wealthy judging by the house and gardens. It was an all-out lavish affair. There was a band. I remember the flowers and the food. It was a lovely evening. John told me a lot of the who's who from Barcelona was there."

Jerry interrupted again: "I opened the file, Karl. Want a paper copy of it?"

"Just give me the gist of it. We have enough paper already."

Jerry watched the monitor. "There's a long file on Antonio Quintanilla, the plastic surgeon. There are 'before' and 'after' photos of his patients. He was good at what he did. You'd hardly recognize some of these people after he worked on them. He did a lot of work for the underworld. Looks like he was helping people establish new identities. This file alone would be worth a fortune to a blackmailer."

"What about the other brother, the banker?" Karl asked.

"Mateo Quintanilla was another bad boy. There's a report from the bank's internal auditors dated two days before he was killed. Not only was he embezzling from his employer but there's evidence of writing off a large loan to some guy who belonged to a Basque terrorist group. There are a bunch more questionable loans he wrote off, mainly to women.

"There's a forensic report on Mateo's vehicle. That's the one found at the scene of the incident. There was blood found in the back seat and the trunk. Wait, this report is done by a private lab and it predates Mateo's death by three days. Blood match is to someone called Jean Cameron McGrath.

"There's a photo and police report on the death of Miss McGrath. Her decomposed body was found six months earlier in the same spot as Mateo Quintanilla's body was found. There's six other names here, all women.

"There's a memo from a local detective who worked on the McGrath's case. All six women disappeared within the prior five years. They all were blond and two had plastic surgery at Antonio Quintanilla's clinic. The names of two others are on the other brother's write-off list at the bank. What do you think?"

Karl replied, "If this evidence is to be believed, then, one of the bastards deserved to die and the other can rot in hell."

"I think they're the real thing. I know the officer who wrote the report on the missing women. It appears the police couldn't get enough on either of them to lay a charge. The Quintanillas were well connected, almost untouchable until this.

"It also appears that if Clark was involved in this and helped fate, shall we say, he had enough proof to justify whatever ever involvement he had. We don't know that he did anything. All we know is that he was in Barcelona at the time. Antonio Quintanilla doesn't sound like a choir boy to me. He was alive and kicking when Clark left town and he didn't point a finger at your husband, Emily."

"So John didn't go around murdering people like Ruth said."

Karl replied, "Emily, if this is an example of what Clark was involved with, I don't want to know about it. Someone, perhaps a family member of Miss Jean McGrath was willing to pay an enormous amount of money to see justice done and I applaud him for it. What do you think, Jerry?"

"I think it's poetic justice. The guy's body was found where they dumped one of their victims. I'm with Karl, this case is closed for me. I don't want to know anymore. I'll get back to Turner and tell him. I know he'll agree."

"I can't tell you what a relief this is," Emily whispered.

"It's not the sort of thing a man would want to share with his wife, Emily," Karl said.

"I can see that now." She nodded.

"I've got another e-mail from plclark," Jerry announced,

"That's Paul, my step-son. Can I see the message?"

"I'll read it. 'Mrs. DiMattia from your hotel gave us this e-mail address. Everyone is here now. Can we talk to you on Skype?'"

Jerry grinned. "I'm going to answer in the affirmative. Give them a few minutes."

Laura was the first to speak. "Mom, where are you? Are you all right?"

"I'm fine, darling."

Emily turned up the speaker so Karl could hear.

Laura continued, "Mom, we phoned Villa DiMattia and a woman called Pia told us you'd gone to someplace called Patmos. She said you were safe with some guy called Karl. We're all worried. What did she mean by safe? Mom, what's going on? We thought you were in Tuscany painting with Edgar."

Emily gave a reassuring laugh. "Nothing to worry about! I assure you, I'm fine."

A small dark-haired woman came into view beside Laura. "Emily, sweetheart, we're all at the old house for a barbecue. Your father and I miss you!"

"Hi, Mom! You and dad are there too! How wonderful! How is Wellington? Is he behaving himself?"

A short balding man came into view, carrying a tan and white whippet. "Hi sweetie! Here's your pup! He's been on squirrel patrol since you left town."

"Hi dad! Is my dog driving your crazy?"

The jovial man laughed. "Not for a minute! Though we may not want to give him back. By the way where exactly are you? We're all dying to find out."

"I am on a Greek Island called Patmos. One day I promise to bring all of you here. You'll love it."

Jerry was smiling as he listened to the conversation. He purposely stayed out of range of the lens realizing his presence could elicit more questions.

Then a tall fair-haired young man came into view. Karl and Jerry exchanged looks.

Emily reacted excitedly. "Paul, how are you?"

He flashed a familiar smile, "Hey, Mom! We miss you. We all started to worry when you weren't at Villa DiMattia. You OK?"

"Yes, Paul, I'm fine!"

Paul questioned her: "Tell us all about this Karl guy, Mom. We're all eager to find out who he is and how the two of you hooked up so quickly."

"He's right here. I met him at Villa DiMattia and we've become good friends."

Karl waved into the camera.

Laura was concerned. "Mom, be careful, you're a wealthy widow. The world is full of scam artists. You could end up broke, then what would you do? Besides, Dad has been dead for less than two years. What are you thinking?"

Paul spoke up, "Laura, listen to yourself! Stop this immediately."

Emily's mother was about to say something but Paul cut her off.

Paul continued, "To begin with Mom owes Dad nothing. I told you how she changed him. Before they got together I always thought he was arrogant but I realize now that maybe he was just plain lonely. After he found Mom he became the man you came to know. She worked magic on him. He was the happiest I'd ever seen him."

Paul wasn't finished: "Not only that but I don't ever want to see Mom sitting in the house crying her eyes out day after day. You saw how she mourned Dad. She's entitled to get on with her life."

Then he looked back into the monitor. "Mom, if Karl is a good guy, you go for it."

In a more serious vein he added: "But I'd like to meet him and check him out before you do anything serious. You understand?"

"Yes, Paul, I understand."

Laura added, "Sorry, Mom."

"Laura, there's nothing to be sorry about. I know you only want the best for me."

They could hear the voice of a toddler in the background.

Paul reached down and lifted a towheaded boy into his arms. "Ardi has something he wants to tell you."

He turned the toddler around to face the screen. The boy's hair was almost white blond and his eyes were a very pale jade green.

Paul told Ardi to look at the computer screen and speak in his loud voice. "Grammy, I see you!" he giggled and looked up at this father. "Wellington was bad. He stole a whole box of cookies and ate them all. Then he threw up all over Nana's new rug. Boy, was she mad!"

Emily fought back her tears. She missed the little tyke so badly. "Oh, I'm so very sorry, Ardi! Is Wellington better?"

The boy waved at her as he continued his story: "Yes, Wellington is better. He loves scaring squirrels. Yesterday, he chased away a big cat."

Emily concluded the conversation by announcing that she and Karl would return to Canada together at the end of the month.

Then there was a round of goodbyes and the picture disappeared.

Karl and Jerry, who were both accustomed to living alone, sat in stunned silence.

Finally Jerry said, "I don't think I'll ever be brave enough to get married and have kids after hearing all that ruckus."

Karl chuckled. "Jerry, we're both jealous. With that crew near you there would never be a dull moment. Emily, they seem like a very caring family."

"Oh, Karl, they're wonderful! I'm so blessed. They are all hard working and caring. Who could ask for more? My parents are the gentlest, sweetest people in the world and my little grandson is adorable."

Jerry looked at her seriously. "Tell me, Emily, are your features quite common where you live?"

Emily smiled embarrassed. "You mean skinny freckled girls with green eyes? I never thought about it."

Jerry looked at her closely. "It's more than that, Emily!"

"What are you getting at?"

"We'll talk about it later. Right now we have evidence to consider. Turner sent a report on the contents of the safety deposit box. There's also a letter I'll print out and leave for you to read in privacy."

"Was the letter written by John?"

"It was written by your late husband and it's rather personal, Emily. If you don't mind I want to go through the other items first because I'm thinking of catching the ferry to Athens tonight."

"You have more questions for me?"

"You know me too well. I'll soon be finished. Does the name Emily Engleston mean anything to you?"

"Emily Engleston was a famous Canadian journalist and writer. But she was quite young when she died."

Jerry looked over at Karl as he continued speaking to Emily. There was an unspoken communication between the two of them. "Her last will and testament was in the safety deposit box. John Clark and Peter Shandman were named as executors. According to Turner they were working at the same law office at the time. Turner is contacting Mr. Shandman to find out what this is about."

Emily answered, "Peter Shandman and his wife came to my wedding but I never met Emily Engleston. She died about twenty years ago, I believe. She was always on the newscasts reporting from some faraway place. That's your only question for me?"

"That's my only question. Turner is sorting out the documents from the deposit box and wanted to find out how much you know before he talks to Shandman."

"Now on to other things, namely the KZR weapon! This is exciting! The weapon looks like a cellphone and weighs about the same. As you already know it uses face recognition technology. What you don't know is this: it can shoot at three targets in extremely quick succession, its accuracy is uncanny and it hones in the area just below the nasal bone. If that cannot be easily accessed then it will aim for either the left or right temple. The nail-like projectile carries two charges. The first charge ignites and fires the projectile out of the device, while the second charge ignites approximately ten seconds after impact. Plus the projectiles have homing devices built in and will actually track the movements of the intended victim once released."

Karl was impressed and walked over to examine the information on the screen.

Jerry continued excitedly: "In other words, the projectile explodes inside the victim's head. No wonder Soll wanted to get her hands on the thing. I think Clark realized the impact it would make if it fell into the wrong hands and decided to mothball the thing. It's potentially worth a fortune."

"Have Turner's people tested out the weapon?" Karl asked.

Jerry continued eagerly: "They tested it using dummies. First they photographed a dummy's face with the camera in the gadget. They then placed five different looking dummies in the room and fired the weapon from behind a protective barrier. The accuracy of the little weapon is uncanny. The projectile fired off perfectly and then found its way to the right dummy and entered the dummy's head through its nose. Within ten seconds the second charge fired and the whole head exploded. There was a supply of twenty projectiles so they decided to conserve them until they're certain they can understand the blueprints."

Karl was more sombre as he considered the possibilities for the weapon. "The weapon sounds deadly. How expensive is it and ammo to manufacture?"

"Turner has a bunch of nerds trying to decipher the blueprints. That's as far as they want to take it. Production is another matter."

"It's innovative. I'm amazed at the small size of it," Karl mused.

Jerry was still enthusiastic. "The weapon is revolutionary and very complex. Liu Wong had to be a brilliant engineer to design this."

Karl responded thoughtfully, "Maybe the question should be, do we really want more of these in circulation?"

"Karl, it's out there. You saw what happened when Clark tried to mothball it."

"I must admit, I'd love to have a chance to try it myself," Karl replied.

"Emily, I printed a copy of that letter from the safety deposit box for you. Turner wants you to call him before you read the letter. I'll get him on the line now?"

"Go ahead, Jerry."

"Do you mind if I put him on speaker phone?" Jerry asked.

"Not at all, I want you and Karl to know everything."

Greg Turner's voice came over the line: "Are you there, Emily?"

Jerry responded, "Yes, she's here. Mind if Karl and I listen in?"

"Listen in, if you like. Emily, it's about the weapon. The weapon does not belong to KZR. As heir to your husband's estate, it is yours, Emily. There was a memo in the safety deposit box indicating where to find the blueprints. I am now in possession of everything. Your husband commissioned the weapon himself. He hired Liu Wong, the KZR engineer to work on the shell, only. It works somewhat like a camera. The missiles were made according to John Clark's design by an engineer in Germany. It's the missiles that are revolutionary considering their size and accuracy. Emily, your late husband was a genius."

Karl looked at Emily as he spoke. "If Emily doesn't mind, I'd like to respond."

Emily nodded so he continued: "What about getting a patent for it?"

"That's in the works thanks to Kenneth Zachary Reid himself. The great man phoned me from his ivory tower in London. He got wind that some of his people in Canada were taking aggressive action to get their hands on it. When I explained that we found all Clark's design papers, he agreed to help patent it in Emily's name. He wanted to meet and talk to Emily but I put him off. He's a high powered guy, Emily, and I thought you had enough to deal with for now. I can phone him and give him your number. Just say the word."

"I've read about him and his family in the newspaper and magazines. I have no desire to meet the man. No, Greg, please don't give him my number."

Karl asked, "Any insight into who ordered the hit on Clark?"

"I do but I want to check on a few things first."

They hung up and Jerry handed Emily a copy of the letter from the safety deposit box. After nodding to Karl, he left the room.

She began to read:

Dearest Emily,

(Tears welled in her eyes.)

The weapon in this box is for you in the event I am no longer here to protect you. It is for your safety. Don't be fooled by its small size, it's quite powerful but easy to use. I left instructions for its care and maintenance with my uncle Armend Berisha, in Toronto. He will release my information to you. I trust him implicitly.

Finally, dear one, I want to but cannot tell you how very much you mean to me. You gave my son and I unconditional love and I thank you from the bottom of my heart. Until you, I really didn't know the meaning of loving and being loved in return.

I knew as soon as I saw you I didn't deserve you, but I couldn't stop myself. I searched for years to find you and when I did, I didn't do my duty. There is so much I haven't told you about your real mother and father.

Please forgive me!

Always remember, I will love you into eternity,

John

Karl sat beside her as she read the letter aloud. It was written just days before John's death. The man suspected his days were numbered and was trying to set some things right.

"What is this about your mother and father? I saw them on the screen very much alive?"

"Karl, I was adopted at birth. I never thought or cared about my birth mother or father. I had a happy childhood. As far as I'm concerned Moira and Reverend Alex MacLean are my real parents."

Finally tears began to fill her eyes. She had managed to keep her emotions in check during all the tumult of the past few weeks. At last the floodgates opened up.

Karl held her as she cried. She cried some more and he rocked her gently in his arms. Finally, he led her to their bed and tucked her under the covers.

He ordered tea and a bottle of brandy from room service. Iola delivered them personally to their suite. He explained what was happening. She listened with great sympathy and finally said, "Karl, it sounds to me as though she has kept too much inside her far too long. Give her some tea with brandy and be there for her."

He held her while she drank the hot tea laced with brandy. She cried some more. When she had exhausted herself she slept peacefully in his arms.

When Jerry called him to come into the hall he gently laid her sleeping form on the bed.

Jerry whispered, "It's about time she shed a few tears. She's kept too much bottled up inside. She's one brave lady."

"She'll be fine. I'll look after her."

"Karl, I want to head back to Villa DiMattia. Edgar was left with a hornet's nest. Those people who signed on late for his tour are giving him trouble. We all thought that once Turner found the weapon, those clowns would disappear, but they haven't and there's already been a couple incidents. Edgar thinks they're up to something."

"Edgar obliged and helped us when we needed him. I think we should return the favour. By all means go to Villa DiMattia and give him a hand. He wouldn't ask for help if he wasn't worried. The two of you worked together before so if anyone can help him, you can. I must admit, I didn't like the look of some of those characters, myself. I'll see you at the villa around the end of the month."

"Before I go, I'll check in with Konstantin. Do you want to come with me?"

"I don't want to leave in case Emily wakes up in the next few minutes. Tell Konstantin I'll drop by a bit later."

Karl pulled a chair up beside the bed. Emily was lovely in repose in spite of her tear-stained cheeks and the puffiness around her eyes.

Their time together would end soon.

The question was, could he live with himself if he let that happen?

At what point had he fallen in love with her? He couldn't remember making a conscious decision about it.

It began with the call from Turner imploring him to drop everything and go Villa DiMattia. He refused until Turner mentioned his informant. It's safer to reveal the identity of a dead informant, even a murdered one. It was pay-back time. Jerry agreed. They dropped what they were working on and packed up their bags. Jerry flew to Amsterdam to meet Emily's plane and he to Florence, not long afterwards.

He spotted her talking to Edgar in the dining room the night before they met. She looked like a sad angel. He was attracted to her even then. Too attracted to her. He decided it would be prudent to put her in Soll's hands. He had enough to focus on without the distraction of a woman.

They met the next morning in Russ's office. She stood her ground. Man, did she ever stand her ground. Her looks are deceptive. He couldn't ever remember being put in his place as neatly or effectively. Then she left him standing there, facing his three friends. Capitulation was the only course of action.

She was ghost white the day they went to Cinque Terre. Damn Ruth Zhou!

She worked her magic on him at Luigi's place. Every morning she would reveal some heart wrenching detail of what she'd overheard from Ruth Zhou. He could see it was tearing her apart. He insisted she get it over with, first thing each day. The rest of the time was theirs and theirs alone until the last afternoon when she began to put the pieces of the puzzle together.

Even if she left him at the end of the month, there were moments in their days at the safe house, he would carry within him forever: her delight when she beat him at chess, how she looked at him when she was sketching him, her smile when she served one of her gourmet meals and that moment she whispered she loved him when he was lying bleeding on the floor.

Maybe Jerry was right about encouraging her to do detective work.

What was he thinking? That wasn't the way to keep her close to him?

He wanted her in his life. He'd filled enough emptiness with work. He loved her. Hell, he wanted to marry her.

He watched as she moved slightly in her sleep.

Did she love him enough to leave her family and move across the ocean? She lit up the minute she connected with them on Skype. He would have to make some changes in his own life. He'd probably have to resign his position at Europol. Jerry's offer of a partnership was looking better and better. Or he could work in the family business. Either way, he'd find time to make regular trips to Canada with her.

She awoke and looked up at him.

"You were here the whole time I was asleep?"

He nodded.

"How long did I sleep?"

"Just a short while."

He handed her a small glass of brandy. "It is for medicinal purposes. How do you feel?"

She obediently sipped on the drink. "Drained. I'm sorry. You must be disgusted with me crying like a baby."

"Anything but. Are you happier now that you know Clark wasn't an evil villain?"

"Yes, I'm ashamed of myself for thinking that. I've even come to terms with the fact he kept me in the dark about so much."

"You've forgiven him?"

"I have."

"It's the first step in getting on with your life."

"I was stuck in the past, wasn't I?"

"Only a little bit."

"I'm over it now."

She needed to feel him. She reached up and threw her arms around his neck. She began kissing his neck and nuzzling him gently. She undid the buttons on his shirt and ran her hand over the coarse blond hair on his chest. She'd come to love this beautiful golden body. She reached down and felt the stirrings of his erection. She smiled and gazed into his cerulean eyes.

He gave her a playful grin. "Are you going to finish the job?"

That was all the incentive she needed. She unbuckled his belt and finished undressing him. She pulled off her own clothes and after pushing him down on the bed, made love to him. Karl smiled the whole time. She felt her bones dissolve.

Later they strolled into Skala and had dinner under the stars. They ordered a bottle of white wine and feasted on an Aegean fish stew. They sat sipping a second bottle of wine and talked until the restaurant closed.

Hand in hand they wended their way back to the hotel.

With the help of a couple extra glasses of wine she was a bit tipsy.

"Karl, there's no one around the swimming pool. Let's go for a dip."

She ran ahead of him.

He caught sight of her peeling off her clothes beside the pool. "Emily, what are you doing?"

"Going for a swim, of course!"

The normally staid policeman was completely taken by surprise as he watched her nude body dive into the pool and then surface five metres away.

"Jump in, Karl. It feels so good!"

"Emily, I refuse to skinny dip at my age."

She swam past him doing the backstroke. "Karl, try it. The water feels absolutely divine. Besides, do you see anyone around? We're completely alone!"

He doubted that, considering Konstantin was never far from them. Any time they walked out the front door of the hotel Konstantin and Flori shadowed them.

The water in the pool became still. He couldn't see her or hear her. Concerned about her safety considering the amount of wine she'd imbibed, he reacted quickly. He shed his clothes and with lightning speed dove into the water.

He still couldn't see her.

"Emily, where are you?"

"Over here! I climbed into the hot tub. Come on in. It feels wonderful with no clothes on. It's so liberating."

"Emily, I've never done anything like this. What if someone turns on the lights?"

"Nobody is around. Just relax and enjoy it."

They sat in the hot tub for five minutes and then decided to cool off in the pool. They floated their way to the other end of the pool.

A peal of deep laughter erupted from above them. Alexandros was standing on the edge of the pool. "Well, well, well, what do we have here? A little skinny-dipping in the moonlight?"

Karl roared, "Alexandros, don't you have someplace else you should be?"

Alexandros' deep voice resonated in the quiet around them. "Not a chance! I'm enjoying myself too much right here."

"Go away!"

"No way! I'm having too much fun. I'll have to add this to my list of stories. Trouble is nobody is going to believe I found Karl Busch skinny-dipping in my pool at midnight."

"Alexandros, you're ruining a very romantic evening!"

Alexandros relented. "You're right about that, my apologies."

Alexandros still couldn't contain himself. He gave a loud guffaw.

"Emily, I congratulate you for getting my old friend to let down his guard. How'd you manage to get this guy into the water in his birthday suit?"

She answered him with another question, "Alexandros, tell me you weren't watching us on some hidden monitor all this time."

He laughed again. "Actually, my staff spotted two after-hours pool hoppers and called me. When I realized who it was, I ordered some towels, wine and snacks for you and then turned off the monitor."

He looked up at the hidden camera and announced, "And the monitor should still be off!" He turned back to them. "Take your time and enjoy your swim. Can't wait to tell Iola about this one." With that, he gave another deep-chested laugh and ran off.

After Alexandros left, Karl and Emily climbed out of the pool and wrapped themselves in towels and burst out laughing. The incident made them feel like carefree youngsters again.

They devoured the treats Alexandros had left behind. Karl opened the bottle of wine and poured out a glass for each of them.

He smiled at her in the moonlight. "Emily, I'm not given to flowery language, but I want to tell you how very much you've come to mean to me. Please don't run back to Canada and leave me."

"You're not getting rid of me that easily."

"Would you consider being my lover for the next fifty years?"

"I might consider that."

"It comes with perks."

"Perks? I like perks."

"Yes, you get to wear a ring on that finger. It also comes with a large Belgian family."

"I like the sound of that."

She threw her arms around his neck.

"Are you comfortable living so far away from your family? I would offer to live in Canada but my work is here in Europe."

"I think with a little planning we can work something out, don't you?"

"Emily, I know we can."

"But I'd like one more perk," Emily said.

Karl replied, "Just one? Then you'll agree to marry me?"

"Without hesitation!" she replied.

"I hope it's something within my power to provide."

"I think it might be."

"What do you want, my love?" he asked softly.

"Children."

There was silence. Emily couldn't see his face in the darkness. She was becoming uneasy.

"You're quiet," she said.

"I'm etching this moment into my memory so that if I live to be one hundred and ten years old and all my other memories fail me, this one will still be there."

"Then you agree?" she asked.

"Wholeheartedly!"

They kissed in the moonlight. Their images reflected in the stillness of the water.

He whispered, "I'd like to begin working on that last perk tonight."

"I hoped you'd say that."

They returned to their room and savoured the taste of each other. Then they talked until they fell asleep in each other's arms. The silvery moon lit up their glistening bodies as they slumbered.

They awoke late and showered. Emily sat on the balcony watching Karl finish his breakfast.

"Karl, I want to phone my family and tell them about our wedding plans."

"You made wedding plans already? When am I getting married?"

"I hope the same time as I am, my dear. It's just that I can't keep a secret like this. I have to tell them."

"I'll give you a few minutes of privacy so you can break the news to Paul and your parents."

"Don't you want to call your family and tell them?"

"No need! Hendryck told me not to come home without you."

"What if I'd said no?"

"Don't even go there. You met Hendryck, and there's another one identical to him back home. Sometimes I wonder if their brains aren't somehow connected because they almost think the same thoughts."

"I can't wait to meet Julian. Your mother must have had lots of fun trying to raise the two of them."

"You'll like my mother. I promised Jerry I would drop in on Konstantin. Be back in about five minutes."

He kissed her lightly on the forehead as she dialled the phone. Then he locked the apartment door behind himself and walked down the hallway.

Flori opened the door. "Mr. Busch, we've been expecting you. Where is Mrs. Clark?"

"She's phoning her family. Don't worry, I locked the door behind me."

Konstantin beckoned him inside. "I spoke to Jerry before he left and he told me you and Mrs. Clark plan to join him in Tuscany by the end of the month."

"Emily is eager to see her friends at the villa before I take her home to meet my family in Belgium."

Konstantin responded: "I've been informed that a trip by sea is perhaps the safest at this time. If you are agreeable, you and Mrs. Clark will board a vessel in two days' time and travel to Livorno. We will arrange transportation from there to the hotel in Tuscany and then to your home in Belgium."

"Are you and Flori coming with us?" Karl asked.

"I believe so, although they might arrange for replacements for us."

"I have to sell this to Emily. She doesn't need any more uncertainty. She has no idea Clark hired protection for her and now is not the time to break it to her. If I could tell her you invited us to travel with you again, she'd accept that easier."

"Give me a minute," Konstantin urged as he dialled his cell phone.

Karl thought he had a working knowledge of most European languages until he heard Konstantin talk to his cohort on the phone.

"It's been arranged. We'll come with you," Konstantin informed him.

"Good but what language is that?"

"Flori and I are from Albania. Our agency was hired by John Clark as soon as he married Mrs. Clark."

"If she didn't have such a rough day yesterday, I'd tell her why you and Flori are here. It would make your job easier."

"She's one of the easiest subjects we've had to protect," Konstantin replied.

"Come back to my suite with me for a cup of coffee. While you're there, I'll tell her you invited us to cruise back to Italy. I hate to do it this way but as soon as I can, I'll level with her. She has a right to know why you're here with us."

"I'll let you handle it," Konstantin replied.

Karl unlocked the door and yelled in, "Emily, we have guests!"

She came rushing to the door. "Karl, I wish you'd been here. I spoke to Mom and Dad and they're so happy for us. They can't wait to meet you. I spoke to Laura as well."

She paused as she noticed Konstantin and Flori. "My apologies! I was so wrapped up in my own excitement, I've been rude. Please come in."

Karl led the way into the living room area. It had been tidied up following Jerry's departure.

Emily was still glowing with excitement. "Flori, would you like a cup of tea? I found some sideritis in one of the local shops. I also have regular tea and coffee."

"My mother used to give us sideritis anytime we were sick. I think I'd prefer a coffee."

Emily brewed up a fresh pot of coffee and handed Flori a cup and sat opposite her. "Are you enjoying your holiday, Flori?"

"Yes, very much, the island is beautiful."

"Flori, you make me feel like I'm at home. You sound so much like Maria Deralla when you speak. She and her husband look after my house in Canada. My late husband hired them as soon as we were married."

"Perhaps they are from Albania as well."

"Emily," Karl interrupted, "Jerry's friends are going on a week-long cruise aboard a private yacht. They've invited us to join them."

Emily looked at Flori. "You own a yacht?"

Konstantin responded, "The yacht belongs to a good friend. He offered to take us back to Italy. We'll be at sea for a week and then dock in Livorno."

"What do you think, Karl? Do you want another week off or are you ready to head back to work?"

"My shoulder is still healing. I'm not eager to rush back to work and risk an injury to it. I'd really enjoy a week on a yacht."

"I would as well. When do we leave?" Emily asked.

Konstantin replied, "We leave the day after tomorrow. Be ready to board at 9pm."

"We'll be ready," Emily replied.

After Karl showed Konstantin and Flori to the door, he turned to Emily, "I hope you don't get sea sick."

"I'll have you know I've crewed many times for Paul. The winds in Hamilton Bay are my old friends," she replied.

"Quite the pro, aren't you? I think I'll check my e-mails. Jerry should be back at the villa by now. He promised to keep me posted."

As he looked at the monitor, he said, "We have one from Turner. He wants you to be available for a conference call this afternoon. We can order room service for lunch so we don't miss him."

The call came in the early afternoon.

Greg Turner spoke first. "Emily, I have someone here who wants to talk to you. His name is Peter Shandman and he is a lawyer who worked with your late husband."

"I'd be happy to talk to him."

"Hello, Emily. My name is Peter Shandman. John Clark and I go back as far as law school. John was always at the head of the class and I was always second. We met briefly at your wedding."

"I remember you and your wife. How wonderful to talk to you again!"

"Emily, I'm calling about your mother's estate."

"Mr. Shandman, my mother is still alive. In any case she is the wife of a minister. There's not much of an estate to talk about."

"Let me clarify. I'm talking about your birth mother Emily Engleston, and her estate."

"Emily Engleston, the journalist, was my mother? I had no idea. I've never known anything about my natural parents."

"Nevertheless she was your birth mother and she provided for you in her will."

"How is that possible? How did she know who I was? If she went to one of those agencies to find me, I was never contacted."

"Let me explain. Your mother Miss Engleston, came to John just after she gave birth to your brother"

"Brother? I have a brother? A real brother?"

"You do indeed. But let me continue. During her pregnancy, your mother was diagnosed with breast cancer. She refused treatment and by the end of the pregnancy the cancer had spread. She didn't want the father contacted so she asked John to help her find a good home for her son. She also asked him to act as executor for her estate. To make a long story short, Emily, John adopted the boy himself."

"Are you telling me Paul is my brother? Why didn't John tell me?"

"I know this must be a shock to you, but let me finish, Emily. Miss Engleston wanted half of her estate left to the child she had given away earlier. She was at the height of her career when she gave birth to you and as a rising star, she didn't want to take time off to raise a child. She was an international correspondent and travelled constantly. She felt it wasn't right to raise a child in some of the places she went to. The minister of her church helped place you. He assured her you would be put in a warm and loving home."

"Which I was."

"After Miss Engleston died we tried to find you. The minister had died and we had no idea where he'd taken you or what lawyer he used or even if he used a lawyer. Then one day one of John's clients came into his office and spotted Paul's photo. He thought the boy looked like the fair-haired lady who ran a restaurant in Dundas. That's how he found you."

"Why didn't John tell me about the will? He never so much as told me Paul was my brother."

"I know he wanted to tell you but once he met you and fell in love with you, he wanted everything to stay the same. You have to know what John went through to understand. He never talked about his childhood but I know he had a rough time. Then he married Helen while he was still in law school. She was an aggressive woman. As soon as she finished law school she set up her own practise as a divorce lawyer. She was always campaigning for clients and fighting with everyone around her. Then she found this Italian girlfriend and decided she wanted to have a relationship with her. John offered her a divorce but she didn't want that. The two of them carried on for years with Helen flying back and forth to Italy once and sometimes twice a month. Just before Paul turned fourteen, Helen announced she was leaving and going to live with her girlfriend in Italy. She demanded a million dollars from John and he paid it plus her share of the house. He had her sign the separation agreement, stating she would have no further contact with Paul or him. A year later she was back on his doorstep and she was very ill. Judging by some of her injuries, it appeared she had be part of a consensual sexual relationship that had gone terribly wrong. He took her to the hospital right away and they discovered she was full of cancer. John flew her to a special cancer clinic in the US but there was nothing they could do for her. All her savings and all the money he gave her was gone. She barely had enough money to pay for her plane fare back to Toronto."

"Poor John, she treated him terribly. He and Paul never talked about Helen. All of this had to be painful for both of them."

"John was very concerned about the boy."

"I can understand why. John had to be quite young when he adopted Paul," Emily replied thoughtfully.

"It was two years after he graduated from law school. He loved the boy but Helen wanted nothing to do with him."

"Tell me something. You and your wife were the only ones John invited to our wedding. I was disappointed he didn't invite more people."

"Emily, after all the fiasco with Helen, he wanted a change. Helen was the consummate self-promoter. I can tell you she had great parties because I went to a few of them, but John wanted to leave it all behind."

"Why did he resign from his law firm?"

"He did that after the two of you got married. He was fed up with the long hours and wanted to spend more time with you and with his son. He felt he had neglected Paul. He kept an office here. He told me he was content to work on a couple clients so he could be home for dinner every night. Didn't he tell you about that?"

"I'm afraid not."

"Typical John! He always played his cards close to his chest. Emily, I would have seen to this estate sooner but I owed John a favour. About fifteen years ago I took on a client I shouldn't have. He wanted me to do things that amounted to outright fraud. Then he began threatening my family unless I co-operated. I was so edgy, I think the whole office thought I was going to have a breakdown. One day, John came in my office and closed the door and demanded to know what was going on. He told me to leave everything to him. Emily, it went away. Within a week, it all went away."

"How did he get rid of the client?"

"Emily, I don't know. Don't want to know. My family was safe and that's all I cared about."

"Peter, did Emily Engleston tell you the name of my father?"

"She told John. John never mentioned his name to me."

"Do Paul and I have the same father?"

"That much I do know. Yes, you have the same father and mother."

"Have you spoken to Paul yet?"

"As soon as I'm off the phone with you, I plan to drive to Dundas to meet with him."

"Tell him to call me after you talk to him."

"I'll do that, Emily. When you're back in Canada, we should meet and wrap up this estate. Bye for now."

She clicked off the phone. A glass of red wine appeared in her hand.

"Want to talk about it?"

"Yes, I do. Can we sit on the balcony? If we're here for only a couple more days, I want to spend my time there."

"What are your thoughts?"

"In a way I'm surprised Paul is my brother but in another way I'm not."

"How so?"

"Karl, the first time John brought Paul to see me, we connected. I mean there was something that drew us together. Paul was seventeen at the time but I know he felt it. I'm furious at John for not telling us. He should have told us. We both had a right to know."

"Emily, anger does no good. I agree he should have told you. I can't believe it didn't cross his mind a thousand times during your time together but he couldn't bring himself to do it. It certainly would have complicated things. For all you know your biological mother may have forbidden him to reveal your father's name."

"But now I'll never know who my real father is?"

"A day ago, you didn't care and didn't want to know who either of your birth parents were. As I recall you told me you considered Rev Alex and Moira MacLean your parents. Does it really matter anyway?"

"It doesn't matter at all. I've lost a step-son and gained a brother. That's not a bad deal! I can live with that. Wait till Mom and Dad find out. They'll be thrilled. I'll phone them after I talk to Paul."

After talking to Peter Shandman, Emily was ebullient. When Karl suggested they go to the gym, she jumped at the chance.

Alexandros watched as she worked the machines, smiling all the while.

"Karl, I've seen happy before but never this happy to work out in my gym."

Karl chuckled. "She's over the top and she's got two good reasons."

While Karl stood there smiling watching Emily work out, Alexandros said, "Come on, give! You're all smiles as well. What's going on?"

"Number one: Emily has agreed to be my wife."

"That explains the look on your face. But what's the second thing?"

"Emily was adopted. Today she found out she has a brother. It means a lot to her."

"My God, I should hope so. No wonder she can't stop smiling."

"I plan to take her home to meet my family and maybe get married there."

"Great! Iola will want all the details. I'll feed her some tidbits first, you know, I'll give her some hints and that'll drive her crazy."

"You can be an evil man, Alexandros."

"Like to have fun!"

They returned to the suite twenty minutes before Paul phoned. Karl sat in the armchair watching Emily. Her enthusiasm was almost contagious. She and Paul were like two young children as they went to the internet to get details about their mother's life.

Emily Engleston spent her life as a foreign correspondent covering stories in as many war-torn areas as her time on earth permitted. She had written several books, one of which was still in print.

The more they learned about her, the more excited they became. They decided that Paul resembled their mother much more than Emily. His hair was sandy and his eyes were blue like their mother's had been.

As soon as she hung up, she wanted to fill Karl in on any details he may have missed.

Karl asked, "Was Paul upset Clark didn't tell him you were his sister?"

"He told me his first thought was that Helen wasn't his mother. He said he could have kissed Peter Shandman when he told him that. It's the first time he ever wanted to talk about Helen and I think it did him a lot of good to open up to me about her. We both agreed John did a wonderful thing bringing us together, albeit in his own rather unorthodox way."

"I must say, you're both very forgiving."

"Like you said, anger solves nothing. Besides, it's more fun having Paul as a brother than being his step-mother and it means that Ardi is more mine than before. Now I know why his eyes are the same colour as mine."

Karl surmised, "Now that I'm beginning to understand Clark better, I have a feeling that he intended this to be a pleasant surprise for both you and your brother. The weapon was in the safety deposit box and it was to be a gift to you. No doubt he thought you'd find the safety deposit box when you went through all his other assets as soon as he was gone."

"Which I would have done if he had mentioned the numbers inside my wedding ring."

"Emily, the man was focused on his work."

"But why didn't he tell Paul, he was adopted. My parents told me when I was young."

"From what Shandman said, I would guess Clark was busy putting out fires with his first wife. Shandman described Helen as being combative. I think we can safely assume in view of what you overheard from Ruth Zhou, that Soll was the Italian girlfriend."

"I thought the same thing. Considering the injuries Helen Clark sustained at the hands of Ingrid Soll I'm not surprised John was so upset when she approached him in Capri."

Karl replied, "That would do it for me! In fact, he was amazingly restrained considering the circumstances."

He paused a moment and then chuckled before continuing: "It really had to gall Soll when out of the ashes of her own carnage, you arrive in Italy right under her nose and she is the officer put in charge of seeing to your safety. Not only that, but she wanted the weapon for herself and you were the only one with access to it. No wonder she couldn't say your name without stuttering."

"I wish I could erase her from my memory."

"The memory will fade in time, my dear."

"From what Peter Shandman said, John came to Dundas to tell me about my mother's will but he didn't do that."

Karl grinned. "Emily, I believe when he met you, he found someone he wanted to be with. Then, after the two of you began dating, it was too late to say, 'Oh, and by the way, my dear, I really meant to tell you about your mother!' He lost that opportunity when he looked into your eyes. I know exactly how he must have felt."

"What are you talking about? When I met you, we had an argument because you wanted Soll to act as my bodyguard. The very idea!" she replied.

"You have to understand my position. First of all, you can't deny that when we first saw each other in the dining room, something passed between us."

"You felt that too?"

"I did indeed. So I had to make a choice. I knew if I was the one guarding you, I wouldn't be able to focus on the case and there was no way in hell, I was going to allow Jerry near you for a whole month. So believe it or not, Soll sounded like the perfect solution at the time. Mind you, she behaved herself when we worked together on previous occasions."

"I'm glad I stood up for myself."

"So am I, my dear. So am I."

He reached down and kissed her on the forehead.

"John was a good man."

"He was a very good man, Emily."

"Ruth was wrong about him."

Karl agreed. "Yes, she was. Interesting how she was right on the money with regard to Soll, but couldn't have been more wrong about John."

"I believed her. Why did she think such terrible things about John?"

"People see what they want to see. Besides if Clark didn't confide in you, I seriously doubt he would have done so with Ruth Zhou," Karl replied.

"But to say such terrible things?"

"Emily, if I remember correctly, you told me Ruth called Clark's first wife 'a real bitch' and seemed almost delighted when she described how the woman died."

"Yes, that's precisely how she sounded."

"Then she saw fit to denounce you as being incredibly naive. Am I not correct?"

"Yes, she seemed angry that John kept me away from all of them. She also seemed angry that John settled down after he married me. She said he was 'a real swinger' before he met me."

"Turner sent a copy of the note they found in your basement so we could compare it to Ruth's handwriting. I thought the note was suggesting a degree of intimacy on her part."

"My God, Karl, you're right. She mentioned the restaurant where I brought John on the day he came to see me. He enjoyed the omelet so much, he obviously told her about it."

"Emily, she signed the note 'R' again trying to denote a degree of intimacy that existed in her own mind. She was jealous of you. She had aspirations of having Clark for herself after his first wife died."

"But John was widowed two years before we met."

"He had no interest in her, darling, he loved you. So her revenge was to concoct a story about his being a contract killer."

"You make Ruth sound terrible."

"Emily, she was a woman without a conscience, a sociopath."

"Can we talk about something else?"

"Gladly!"

"Paul thought I should be the one to tell Mom and Dad. I think I'm ready to tell them now."

"I'll sit on the balcony and enjoy a cold beer while you talk to them. That'll give you a few minutes of privacy."

There were tears as Emily and Moira MacLean talked.

"Emily, it was old Bishop Campbell from Toronto who brought you to us. He knew I couldn't have children and then one day he phoned telling us about this little baby girl. He said your name was Emily, after your mother. Do you remember Bishop Campbell? He used to come here a lot when you were young. But then he died when you were about eight years old."

"I remember him. He would preach in the church and then stay for dinner. Did he tell you the name of my father?"

"Emily, I am about to pull out the paper I wrote out when he brought you here. I wanted to remember everything right in case you asked one day, but you never did."

"I never cared, Mom. It never mattered. I was happy."

"We did the best we could for you. Ah, here's the paper I was looking for. It says here that your mother was a professional woman. Her parents died when she was in her late teens and she was an only child."

"Does it say anything about who my father might be?"

"Bishop Campbell told us he thought the man was married. He also said he thought he wasn't from around here. Guess we'll never know."

"It doesn't matter, Mom."

"You know honey, there's some things we're better off not knowing."

"I know what you mean. I have no desire to pursue it. You and Dad are all I ever wanted."

"We feel the same about you, sweetheart."

Emily hung up and found Karl still sitting on the balcony enjoying his second beer. He pointed to a glass of red wine on the table. She picked it up and smiled.

"Happy?" he asked.

"Very! I'll always be their daughter no matter what any document says."

"Sounds like a good choice to me."

"My father says that if I plan to 'skulk' around this side of the ocean with you . . ."

"Skulk?"

"My father's word, but he said he is going to adopt Paul if I'm not going to be around much."

"From what I saw when they Skyped you, he and your mother already have."

"We'll visit them often?"

"Every chance we get, darling."

"It's wonderful to feel safe again. I had no idea what it was like to feel hunted and I hope I never have that feeling again."

"Emily, did Clark ever talk to you about security?"

"Never, but when Greg Turner had my house searched for the weapon, his people found an invoice for security for me in John's hideaway in the basement. I don't know what that was all about."

"Did he ever tell you about the people he hired to look after your house?"

"Oh, you mean Maria and Steve. He didn't want me having to worry about cleaning such a big place so I could be free to travel with him."

"Did he tell you who they are?"

"I know who they are. They came from Macedonia and John hired them as soon as they immigrated to Canada. They look after the gardens and everything. They're wonderful. Why do you ask?"

Karl wanted to tell her Clark had hired round the clock security but clearly now was not the time. In any case, he had no idea who Clark was protecting her from.

He'd let her enjoy the high she was feeling in discovering she had a brother.

He responded, "No reason. It's a beautiful evening. Let's enjoy it."

SEVENTEEN

Their last day on Patmos dawned with winds and cooler temperatures. Everyone breathed a sigh of relief. It was mid-morning before Karl turned on the computer.

"Emily, there's an e-mail from Turner. I'll read it to you. 'Please tell Emily, I located John Clark's uncle. His name is Armend Berisha and he is eager to talk to her. Would she be agreeable to meeting him on Skype?'"

He looked at her as he continued, "I know Turner met with Berisha to get the papers on the weapon. The guy must be all right if Turner wants you to meet him."

"Karl, please tell him I would love to talk to John's uncle."

"Just did and he sent an e-mail with a bunch of information he wants you to review before you talk to the uncle."

"Can you print it out for me?"

"I'd rather go through this with you, Emily. I'm familiar with some of it."

"I'm ready whenever you are."

"Ever heard of the Albanian blood feuds? They're regulated by customary law known as Kanun."

"Never heard of any of it. Certainly it has nothing to do with John? He was born and raised in Toronto."

"I'm afraid not, Emily! According to Berisha, John was born near Shkodra, Albania, the youngest of three boys. His birth name was Ilir Kadare. He was the son of Dafina and Jorgji Kadare. His older brothers were called Dalmat and Ardian."

Emily gasped when she heard the names of his brothers. She flew out of her seat and rushed to the computer. "Oh my God! Ardi's names are Ardian Dalmat. John insisted on naming him when he was born. He called Ardi after his brothers. That explains so much."

Karl asked, "What does it explain, Emily?"

"He named Ardi in honour of his brothers. It was the only time I ever saw him with tears in his eyes. He told Paul, that he and Laura could name the rest of their children, but he wanted to name the first one. I had no idea until now why it meant so much to him. I'll explain this to Paul and Laura."

She began pacing back and forth.

"Emily, if this is too upsetting for you, we can stop. You don't have to do this. There is really no need for you to talk to Armend Berisha."

"No, I can handle it. Please continue."

He waited until she was sitting before he continued.

"Their father was a mechanic and their mother worked as a seamstress. Clark's father, Jorgji Kadare, repaired a car belonging to a local businessman by the name of Ndrepepa. Within a week of the repairs the vehicle went off the road, killing all four occupants. The owner of the car and his brother both blamed the mechanic even though there was clear evidence that Ndrepepa's wife, the driver at the time of the accident was speeding.

"The Kanuns sanction blood feuds and regulate them. They established the rule that whoever kills will be killed. Blood is avenged with blood. The Albanian name for blood feud is *gjakmarrja*, meaning blood. Within a few months of the accident John's father and two brothers were murdered by Ndrepepa and his family. John's mother Dafina, was left with only her youngest son Ilir, and was terrified of losing him.

"The way the Kanun law works is that each death is avenged and four people were killed in the accident. Dafina knew that either she'd have to keep her one remaining son hostage in her home or risk losing him. She wrote to her brother Armend Berisha who was living in Toronto with his wife and pleaded for his help. Armend flew to Albania and brought them to the Canadian Embassy, hoping to get them refugee status. He was successful in that. He then brought them to Canada."

Karl stopped while he grabbed an ale from the fridge. He extracted a bottle of white wine and poured a glass for Emily. He paused only a moment longer to take a long sip of his ale before resuming his monologue, "When they came to Canada, they lived for a while with the uncle until Dafina found a job. She still feared for her son and insisted he adopt an English sounding name. She wanted him to become thoroughly Canadian. She was paranoid the Ndrepepa family would find him.

"The boy was ten years old when they immigrated and quickly picked up English and all things Canadian. He was at the head of every class through school and law school, but Dafina was obsessed over the loss of her husband and two other sons. She saved her money to send her son back to Albania to avenge her loss."

Emily was listening intently. "Poor John! What a terrible way to spend your childhood!"

"The summer John turned eighteen he returned to Albania. Times were tough in the old country. He went back to his old neighbourhood and looked up his best friend from when he was a boy. The family welcomed him and took him in. He didn't have to tell them why he was there, they knew. Ndrepepa had become the local magistrate and had acquired a fancy young wife. John and his friend watched Ndrepepa's house day and night and finally they came up with a plan. As soon as they realized Ndrepepa's younger brother was a frequent visitor to the house, they knew what to do. They sent Ndrepepa an anonymous letter saying that his wife and his brother were having an affair. It turned out to be the truth. Ndrepepa came home early the next day and shot both of them dead. But it didn't end there. What followed was a family bloodbath where the brother's oldest son killed Ndrepepa. It didn't stop until all the men in both families were dead."

"John went through this at eighteen? It sounds like he was put in a terrible position. I can't imagine a mother doing this to her son. He was so young."

"Emily, this childhood experience may explain how he became the man he was. He spent his life righting wrongs for other people."

"He did, didn't he? I am beginning to understand why he risked so much to pass on information on terrorists. It puts a whole new perspective on things."

"Yes, it does."

"If I had known about his past, I would have . . . I would have . . ."

Karl smiled understandingly. "You would have done what, Emily? Closed the restaurant business you worked so hard to build up so you could devote yourself to him? Become the mother his son never had but longed for? You would have lived your life ready and willing to travel with him at the drop of a hat and then spend endless hours in strange hotels waiting for him to return from his countless meetings, leaving you to worry where he was and if he was safe? Would you have done those things?"

"That's what I did."

"I think you treated him very well considering you never knew where he was or what he was doing most of the time."

"I felt he needed someone to be there for him, to be waiting for him. He was always grateful to see me. It wasn't an act. It was real. Even when he arrived home at night, he'd park the car and then rush in and hug me. It was as though he feared I might not be there waiting for him, but I always was."

"Any idea why he was worried about your safety?"

"What are you talking about? We lived in a safe community. He wasn't really worried about me. It was just a little romantic game he liked to play. That's all it was."

Karl considered her reply. *It was the second time he had tried to broach the subject of her security. She had the right to know that everywhere she went, she was being followed. Why the hell didn't Clark tell her? Now it fell to him to tell her but she wasn't ready to listen. Perhaps now was not the time. He would wait for a better opening and then try to bring the subject up again.*

The more he came to understand Clark's mind, the more he could see there was a purpose for everything the man did. If Clark didn't tell Emily he was worried, no make that, 'terrified' for her safety, there had to be a damn good reason. There was something Clark didn't want to have to explain to her unless or until, he had to.

She looked at him with raised eyebrows. "You're quiet. I'm sorry, I didn't mean to snap. It's just that I don't want to hear anything more about security. Now that all the horrible things are over, I can return to a life of peace and quiet and that's what I plan to do."

"Armend Berisha wants to explain more to you, Emily. Are you still interested in talking to him?"

"Definitely! I'm beginning to understand why John kept so much to himself."

Karl thought, *He kept a lot more to himself than you know,* but he said, "Turner says they'll be on line in a couple hours. That gives us time for lunch and a quick walk around the village. I need to stretch my legs."

"Sounds perfect. I want to put on my jacket and hat."

As soon as she went into the bedroom, he phoned Alexandros. "Hey buddy, we're leaving by ship tonight. Need the bill including nursing services."

"Yes, I was hoping you'd invite us for dinner. It has to be early. We leave at nine."

Then he dialled Konstantin's room. "I'm taking Emily for lunch at the café and then a quick walk around the village. We'll have an early dinner with Alexandros and Iola."

Emily came walking behind him. "Who are you talking to?"

"We're invited to have dinner with Alexandros and Iola tonight. That OK with you?"

"I'd love to. I want to find a little gift for Iola. She looked after you so well."

"We can go to the jewellery store after lunch. I'm sure you'll find something there."

Konstantin and Flori were sitting at a table in the corner when they arrived. They were carrying on an animated conversation with a dark-haired man sitting with them.

Emily and Karl sat at the table nearest the street. They both ordered moussaka and a glass of wine and sat chatting.

A scooter came racing down the cobbled street. The young driver lost control as he approached the tables at the café. Karl tried to jump up and grab Emily before the scooter hit their table but his injured shoulder hadn't yet regained its full mobility.

He felt himself being pulled back. The scooter hit the table with such an impact, it flipped over, umbrella and all. His chair was mangled as the scooter hit it head on.

He looked around to see Konstantin standing behind him. "Thanks! I really appreciate that. My shoulder is still stiff."

"That was a close one. How are you?"

"Emily? How's Emily?"

"See for yourself." Flori and the dark-haired man were standing on either side of Emily. Konstantin reassured him, "She's fine. Flori spotted the guy back there. Good thing I was close enough to reach you in time."

"Was the driver injured?"

"Don't worry about him. I want you to take Emily back to the suite and keep her there until it's time to board the ship."

"That's probably a good idea, but she wants to buy a gift for Iola at the jewellery store. Maybe she's too shaken up to do that now."

Konstantin chuckled. "Women and their gifts! I guess it wouldn't hurt. We'll have to come along."

"By all means, come with us."

"I'll bring your food up to your room. I can't allow Mrs. Clark to be exposed like that again. The guy with us is Jak Luga. He's the head of our firm and a childhood friend of John Clark. He was most eager to meet Mrs. Clark but I had to explain that she still doesn't know she's being guarded. He feels it's time she is told. So I tried to explain how you have attempted to tell her several times."

"I plan to tell her as soon as I get the chance but this business with the weapon opened up a whole new chapter in her life. She's planning to talk to Clark's uncle this afternoon so I'll have to wait for another time."

"Let's get Mrs Clark out of here, Jak will question the driver of the scooter. We need to know if there's something more going on here."

After a quick trip to the nearby jewellery store Karl and Emily returned to their suite. As promised Konstantin delivered their moussaka. They finished eating and sat on the balcony waiting for Turner to call.

"Are you sure you want to put yourself through this?" Karl asked.

"I know where you're coming from, Karl, but rest assured this is part of healing process. I want to put the past behind me. I decided to come on this trip because I knew I'd fallen into a hole and I was struggling to dig my way out. Paul and my father knew it as well. Dad was the one who pushed me to get away. He told me, he believes in honouring the dead but what I was going through was unacceptable. And then all this business about the weapon arose and clouded the issue. I needed to close a door but when I overheard Ruth calling John a murderer, I felt that door could never be closed. However, as soon as I knew she was wrong about him, it was over. I am now ready to get on with my own life."

"It sounds as though you needed more information in order to close the chapter on Clark."

"You're right, I did. Agreeing to talk to his uncle is really a way of honouring John. His uncle wasn't there for the funeral and no doubt he needs to pay his respects. Maybe talking to me will help him do that. I want to know why John never introduced us. Paul never mentioned this man either, which makes me wonder if Paul ever met him."

"Emily, surely by now, you know enough about John Clark to realize he had a reason for everything he did or didn't do. And judging by the bit of information Turner sent us about his childhood, it's not surprising that he learned to keep secrets from a very young age."

"You're right, of course. I always over think things."

"That's not necessarily a bad thing. I have an e-mail from Turner, they're getting ready to go on line now."

The detective's familiar face appeared on the monitor. "Hello everyone! How's the weather in Patmos?"

"Warm! What's it like there?"

"We're in for some stormy weather! But let's get to the business at hand. Emily, as you already know we located John Clark's uncle. He's been most co-operative in helping us understand some of what transpired. I gather the two of you have yet to meet. May I present, Armend Berisha. Armend, this is Emily Clark."

The face of an older dignified gentleman appeared on the screen.

He spoke with a pronounced accent and seemed a bit nervous. "Hello, Emily, how are you? I have a photo of you and my nephew Ilir, sitting on my mantle at home."

Emily looked at the face in the monitor. Unconsciously she was searching for some resemblance to her late husband. John's long dark face and chiseled features were echoed in the old man's countenance. "Hello. I am deeply honoured to meet you. May I call you Uncle Armend?"

The old gentleman spoke slowly and deliberately: "I would be most honoured if you did, my dear Emily. I have heard so much about you, I feel as though I know you already."

"Why did you never come to see us?"

The old man continued to speak slowly. "It is a long story but I will try to explain. Mr. Turner told me that they explained to you about *gjakmarrja*, the Kanun or blood feud in our native Albania."

"Yes, that was explained to me this morning."

"Let me give you some more of Ilir's background and then you will understand everything."

"Take your time, Uncle Armend."

The old man gave a sad smile. "It was because of his mother's desire for revenge that he helped destroy those people who murdered his father and brothers. Ilir did not possess any hatred or anger but he loved his mother dearly. She was all he had left of his family. He detached himself emotionally from the act so he could please his mother, but that was not enough for the woman."

The old man pulled a handkerchief out of his pocket and wiped his eyes. "After Ilir avenged his father and brothers, I'm ashamed to admit that my sister Dafina, went around boasting to others in our community about Ilir's cleverness and skill. Before long others come to him begging and pleading with him to avenge their relatives."

These were very obviously painful memories for the old man, but he continued: "There were many who came to Canada to get away from the Kanun—those were the lucky ones. Ilir took on cases out of compassion. He always ensured that some other guilty party would be there to take the blame, so the police never looked for him."

He stopped and loudly blew his nose. "My nephew, Ilir really was the cleverest of men. But he had his troubles. In law school that dreadful woman attached herself to him. She harassed him to marry her. She never loved him. She didn't even give him children. He had to adopt. He brought her around once and I told him not to bring her back. Then he told me she had another lover and he did what he always did, he put up with it. None of us were sad when she died. No one was sad!"

Then the old man brightened. "Then one day he appeared at my door and told me he found you. He was so very happy. '*Kam takuar një engjëll*,' he said. I have met an angel. He was the happiest I have ever seen him. That angel was you, my dear Emily! He raved about your beauty, your lovely hair, the unusual colour of your eyes and, above all, your sweetness."

He drank some more of his coffee: "From the moment Ilir met you, he swore that nothing from his past would intrude on your life together. He was determined to shield you from every unpleasantness. When you and Paul took to each other so well, he was amazed and he began to see the boy in a different light. He no longer looked upon the boy as part of his first marriage but began to see him through your eyes and really care for him."

He looked directly into the monitor. "You showed him the way, my dear. He wanted to be everything wonderful for you. I remember laughing out loud when he told me about buying a dog and proudly walking it through the streets with you. He finally had a real home life and was loved for himself. He would phone me at night when he took that funny looking dog out for a walk and he would tell me all about you and what he was working on."

She wiped tears from her eyes. "We all loved him dearly, Uncle Armend."

"Mr. Turner wants me to explain more about his work. As I said before, Ilir did not allow himself any feelings whenever he was involved in such things. His mother forced him to do it the first time. It was definitely not his choice. His mother was totally to blame. He used the money he made to put himself through university and even bought his mother a new house. Once he got started he found the money was so good he didn't want to give it up. But if he could have found an easier way to make such good money, I'm sure he'd have stopped then."

"I thought he was making his living practicing law, Uncle Armend."

"He did very well in his law practice but that horrible woman he married wanted to be on all the society pages. There was never enough money to satisfy her. That woman loved to flaunt herself, but that was not like my dear Ilir, as you well know. Both of them were successful lawyers but he was miserable. He worked such long hours. It took him years to find you. One of his clients told him about you and so he found an excuse to go to Dundas and see you for himself. I remembered how overjoyed he was at the time. He told me how much you look like his boy.

"When you introduced him to that fancy Arab man on your honeymoon in Paris, he was over the top. He kept saying how he knew you'd work out for him. After that the people he worked for were good people. They were against crime and terrorism. I know he tried to negotiate with people who were involved in aiding criminals. He tried to prevent funds or arms from getting into the hands of bad people. If he could not talk sense into them, he would take action."

The old man was tiring but insisted on continuing: "Ilir believed in what he was doing. He abhorred violence for its own sake. He would never hurt innocents. He left me with what he called a flash drive to give to you, only you. He told me it would explain everything I've just told you. I'm not allowed to pass it on to anyone else. When we meet I will give it on to you as Ilir instructed me to do. I've hidden it away and the police could search forever but will not find it. He was always firm about passing it on to you alone and one does not meddle with the wishes of the dead, does one?"

"Absolutely not, Uncle Armend!"

"Emily, this is Ilir's story, not mine to tell."

John's uncle stopped to rest. Emily took the opportunity and interjected, "Uncle Armend, you can't imagine how happy I am to meet you. I only wish he'd felt safer about bringing you to our home in Dundas, but now I understand why he took such precautions. Thank you for explaining it all out to me."

He smiled. "My poor Ilir took too much upon himself. I miss his visits so very much."

"Uncle Armend, I expect to be in Toronto next month. I hope we can have a nice visit together. I wish John had trusted me enough to tell me all that he had gone through."

"Emily, you were a new beginning to him. You gave him the only measure of happiness he'd ever known. There was no way he wanted to taint that with what he had lived through. He would not have done anything to risk losing you or upsetting you."

"Thank you so much, Uncle Armend."

"Thank you, *engjëll*."

The camera switched over to show Detective Turner again.

"Emily, when are you coming back here?"

"Let me talk it over with Karl and get back to you."

A huge grin spread across Turner's face. "Pia and Russ told me something was brewing between you two. I'm delighted to hear it. I'll have good news for my wife tonight. The woman can't stand to see any man without a wife. She should have been a matchmaker."

Karl spoke up, "Enough with the broadcasting! We'll be there soon. I'll give you an exact date after we book flights. We promised to visit with Pia and Russ, then we're heading to Belgium so Emily can meet my family."

Greg signed off and was gone.

"What do you think of Uncle Armend?"

"Karl, I thinks he's wonderful. I want to introduce him to Paul and my parents."

"Do you think that's a good idea, Emily?"

"I think so. Why wouldn't it be?"

"Berisha knows about, shall we say, Clark's secret side. I'm not sure you want Paul or your parents knowing anything about that."

"How did you get so wise?"

"Years of working in law enforcement! All us cops are brilliant. Ask any officer you meet."

"Enough, you're starting to sound like Edgar."

"Nobody sounds like Edgar. Nobody can keep up with him."

"So we'll be travelling for a while. When do you plan to return to work?" she asked.

"I'm taking Hendryck's advice and resigning from the force." He pulled her into his arms, "It'll give me more time to spend with you."

"Any idea what you want to do?"

"Not yet, but I'll have loads of time to think about it on our cruise."

EIGHTEEN

Dinner with Iola and Alexandros was a lively affair. One of Alexandros' many stories was about a tourist who sounded as though he was having an orgasm every time he lifted weights at the gym.

"Sure you know that sound, Alexandros? Let me hear it," Karl asked.

"What? You want a lesson, Karl?"

"I know the sound. It's you I'm worried about."

"Actually, I'm a silent lover. Aren't I, Iola?"

Iola laughed. "In your dreams, Alexandros. I'm surprised Karl and Emily haven't heard you all the way upstairs in their suite."

Then Alexandros began describing some of his experiences with his massage therapy clients. "Some of them start snoring as soon as they stretch out on my table. Others want to use me as their psychiatrist. One day last year I gave a massage to a man and then to his wife. My next two clients were his lover and then her lover. Unfortunately they crossed paths in my waiting room. What a free-for-all!"

Iola added, "If Alexandros was a blackmailer, he could be a millionaire."

Karl began to reminisce about their army days. Alexandros joined in. The men regaled them with stories about their adventures. Some stories were funny and some very sad.

After dinner, Emily and Karl returned to their suite to finish packing.

"I promised Konstantin we'd be in the hotel lobby by 8:30. Are you ready?"

She took one last look around the suite. "Karl, when we come back here, I want to stay in this suite. Even if we have to reserve it months in advance, I want to come back here and sit on the same balcony again."

"That's easily arranged. Let's get moving."

Konstantin was standing at the front desk when they came downstairs. "I have a car waiting out front. The yacht is moored close by."

They drove to the Skala marina and boarded a zodiac. They rode out into the darkness for four minutes, and veered to starboard and made their way around a small island.

Konstantin informed them, "The island is called Tragonisi. The ship is anchored on the far side of the island."

As soon as they rounded the island, they spotted the lights from a sizeable vessel.

They pulled alongside and climbed a ladder to board. It was difficult to make out very much in the darkness. They watched as the inflatable boat was lifted onto the back of the yacht.

A small dark-haired man of indeterminate age welcomed them aboard and introduced himself as Aza and then led them to a dark, wood panelled bedroom. The room was not large. A king-sized bed covered in a creamy white spread took up a good bit of the space.

As soon as Aza closed the door, Emily jumped on the pristine bed.

Karl laughed at her playfulness. "You'll have a whole week of peace, my dear. It'll give you a chance to relax and do some thinking."

She climbed off the bed and put her arms around him. "Thinking is not what I have in mind at the moment."

"And just what do you have in mind?"

"Turn out the light and come find out."

"This what you had in mind?"

"Um hmmmmm."

A sense of serenity settled over both of them as the gentle rocking of the ship helped lull them to sleep later that night.

Their days and nights soon fell into a comfortable routine. Daytimes, they spent on deck under a large canopy. Emily sat on a large cushioned chaise and sketched while Karl availed himself of the yacht's well-stocked library. They played chess and napped. Aza poured hot tea into tall thin glasses and quietly saw to all their needs.

Flori and Konstantin joined them on deck at lunchtime and for dinner. All four of them made use of the small gym.

The fifth night out as they were approaching the southern coast of Italy, Karl woke up and looked at the clock. "You awake?"

"Yes, what's that noise? Could that light be any brighter?"

"It appears a helicopter is landing on the back of the ship."

A few minutes later they heard the sound of the rotors lifting off.

"We have a visitor. Wonder who it could be? We'll probably find out tomorrow. Go back to sleep."

They joined Konstantin and Flori on deck for breakfast.

While the two women chatted, Karl asked, "Konstantin, any idea who came on board the ship last night?"

"The owner of this vessel is now on board."

"You've never mentioned his name. Who is he?"

"Mr. Hakim Al Fraih, I am told."

"I see, I assume he wants to talk to Emily."

"My understanding is, he would like to speak with both of you early this afternoon."

After breakfast they worked out in the gym, and then returned to their stateroom to shower. In early afternoon Aza came to them and announced, "Mrs. Clark, Mr. Busch, please come with me."

Aza lead them to a set of double doors. He knocked and then opened one of the doors. A tall gentleman with a sculpted beard rose from behind an ornately carved desk.

His face creased in a warm smile. "Emily Clark, do you remember me?"

"I believe I do. It was long ago. We met at a reception in Paris. Mr. Al Fraih, I believe."

"Very good! But must we stick to surnames. Please call me Hakim. Emily, I feel as though I know you well because John spoke about you many times."

"Hakim, this is Karl Busch. He looked after me during a recent crisis."

"I know about your crisis. I've spoken with your Mr. Greg Turner in Canada. Let's get down to business, shall we. We have much to talk about."

They sat down and waited while Aza poured glasses of hot tea. Then he bowed and left.

"I trust you have been comfortable while on board."

"Yes, very comfortable, thank you. But I don't understand, I thought the ship belonged to Konstantin's friend?" Emily responded.

"You have been kept in the dark far too long, Emily. Have patience and all will become clear. Your late husband thought you fragile and wanted to protect you from any possible harm. But in the past month, you've shown yourself not only to be strong but very resourceful."

"There were a lot of things I could have done better."

"Never look back, my dear. I want to explain some things to you. Let us begin with the time you spent at my home a number of years ago. When John brought you to my door you were taken to the women's quarters. It was for your own protection, Emily."

"I don't understand."

"There was much going on when you arrived. The council was meeting and my home was full. I invited John hoping they would hire him and they did."

"Hakim, I know John was pleased about something but he shared very little with me."

"And with good reason! He was not permitted to reveal anything about his work with us. But I feel it is time you understood. Let me begin. John was an incident expert. He could make things happen. He agreed to work for the council provided they understood he would never take the life of an innocent person. Anyone using him had to provide proof. You see Emily, sometimes heads of countries and even executives find themselves in untenable positions. I'll give you an example. The president of a country, which will remain nameless, discovered one of its diplomats was molesting young boys. The miscreant had an insurance policy, which was a photograph proving an indiscretion committed long before he became head of state. It was really quite minor but it could have been enough to perhaps ruin his career. He asked John for help. No one knows exactly what happened. But we do know this: John paid a visit to the embassy and the man promptly disappeared. He resurfaced a month later in Mexico and resigned his post from there."

"John didn't kill the man?"

"One resorts to death only in extreme circumstances. And that had to be approved by the whole council. It has never happened."

"I had no idea. I'm ashamed to admit there was a time not long ago when I thought the worst of my poor dead husband."

"When you were terrified for your life, I understand that was when you learned much of what John Clark was hiding from you?"

"Yes!"

"It was perhaps wrong of him to keep so many secrets from you but you must understand that secrecy is key to all of us on the council. Telling even you would have been a breach of his contract with us."

"I'm beginning to understand."

"There is much that should be explained to you. On the weekend you spent at my home, your husband did me a great favour. Emily, I am a wealthy man. With wealth comes power. Someone within my own family wanted what I had. Before you arrived, there was a serious attempt on my son's life. I told John about it the night we met in Paris and he agreed to help me. John set a trap using me as bait. It turned out the traitor was my own nephew. His mother is a very greedy woman. She was greedy as a child and will never change. I sent him and his mother away. I asked John to name a price for his services but he refused to accept money. He asked me for one thing only."

"One thing?"

"Yes, one thing! He asked that I see you were protected and safe should something happen to him. As soon as I got word he was dead, I began covering the cost for your protection. Konstantin and Flori Cana are part of the agency John hired, as are Maria and Steve Deralla who look after you at home."

"I don't understand, Hakim. I live in a very safe neighbourhood. Maria and Steve aren't guards, they look after my house and garden. Nobody has guards in my neighbourhood."

"You do, my dear. When I met you in Paris, I knew immediately who you were. I also realized you didn't know."

"I grew up in Dundas. My father is the minister at a local church."

"No, my dear, your father is Kenneth Zachary Reid and your mother was Emily Anna Engleston, the journalist."

"Kenneth Zachary Reid, the industrialist is my father? I beg your pardon. That can't be possible."

"John collected a sample from Kenneth that weekend and compared it to your own DNA just to be certain. Your mother had told him Kenneth was father to both her children."

"Does Mr. Reid know about Paul and myself?"

"I believe he has only just found out about you."

"But he has a wife and sons. Stories about them are in the tabloids all the time. I don't want to be near people like that.

A man like Kenneth Reid would not have any interest in me in any case."

"Emily, John brought you to my home at my suggestion to introduce you to your father. It was meant to be a special surprise for you and for him. Your father carried on a secret affair with your mother for years."

"Did you ever meet my mother?"

"She interviewed me once in connection with a book she was writing. She was a fiercely independent woman. If I were to describe her, I would say that she lived life on her own terms."

"I wish I had known her."

"The weekend John brought you to my home a very unfortunate occurrence took place. Kenneth brought Ingrid Soll. He was new to the council at the time and I believe he misunderstood our purpose."

"Soll was in the pool when Manaar took me for a swim."

"Ah Manaar, my cousin! Yes, she agreed to care for you when I explained things to her. She is very fond of you. So much was happening that weekend. After Kenneth presented the council with Soll's resume, there were threats by other members to have him thrown off the council. We decided it was wiser and safer not to make an enemy of the man. I suggested he transport Soll off the premises as soon as possible, which he agreed to do."

"Did you know I killed her myself? I had no choice."

"Ironic, isn't it? You did the sane world a great favour. But let me continue. Reid ordered his pilot to fly Soll back to Italy and then return with his own family. John Clark was astute. After they arrived he talked to Kenneth's wife and sons at dinner to draw them out. As I said earlier, where there is great wealth, there can be great avarice. We both realized that exposing you to your father's family would have led to a life of chaos for you and we knew our plan to introduce the two of you had been a mistake."

"Kenneth Reid probably wouldn't care anyway. I'm not from his world."

"Don't be too sure. He was very fond of your mother. From what I understand she was, shall we say, the love of his life. He would want to provide for you and he knows what his sons are all about. The man is no fool, Emily."

"Is this why all the security for me? John was afraid of Kenneth Reid?"

"John's work came with its perils. He was happily married, Emily. He didn't want anything to interfere with the life he made for himself. He knew the minute Kenneth or any of his family found out there was another potential heir, your life would change and not for the better. Kenneth occasionally travels to Toronto on business. John kept you away from the Toronto social scene for that reason."

"And you kept up the security after he was killed?"

"It was our agreement. He saved my son's life and in return I kept my end of the bargain."

Karl spoke up, "Sir, if I may interrupt."

"Yes, Karl, please, I welcome your comments."

"Is it necessary to continue with the security for Emily? John Clark grew up in very difficult circumstances and chances are he was insecure about losing someone he loved."

"You're suggesting all this concern for Emily's safety is unnecessary."

"It does sound a bit over the top considering who we're dealing with. I mean Kenneth Zachary Reid isn't some member of the underworld committing heinous crimes. He's an upstanding member of the business community."

"There is nothing upstanding about his two sons or for that matter about his wife," Al Fraih responded.

"I know the sons are tabloid heroes for their rich boy antics, but there's never been talk of anything sinister," Karl countered.

"Kenneth has paid dearly to keep it that way. I will not go into details with a lady present."

"That bad?"

"Yes, and Kenneth's friends refer to his wife as Lady MacBeth."

"That is a rather chilling comparison."

"Lady Catherine Atwater Carmichael Reid is one of London's great hostesses. She is the daughter of an impoverished earl. Her family had country houses but no money. She married Kenneth to shore up her family's finances. Women who pursue her husband have the misfortune of facing social disgrace and sometimes worse."

"She wants to protect what's hers," Karl replied.

"Two months ago, Jason, her older son was involved in a serious car accident. Kenneth rushed to the hospital to donate his blood for a transfusion. They were not a match. Jeremy, the younger boy was a match to his brother but not to his father."

Emily responded, "He's not their father? I don't understand!"

"Emily, John raised your brother and he was married to you so he was intimately familiar with both of you. Jason and Jeremy are several years older than you. When John met them for the first time, that weekend at my home, he immediately suspected that neither of them was related to you or your brother. He went so far as to request that I help him obtain samples of their hair, which I did. They are definitely not related to you."

Emily answered, "So John knew eight years ago. But Mr. Reid may not be their biological father but both are legally his sons. Should it matter?"

"It matters! Believe me it matters!" Al Fraih looked at Karl hoping he would explain.

Karl obliged. "Emily, Clark was protecting you because he knew this day would arrive and he didn't want to be caught flat-footed. I would have done the same thing. It wasn't your father he was protecting you from, it was your father's family. Your father's estate is probably worth an enormous amount. From what Hakim has told us, his wife and sons are motivated by money. It's how they value themselves."

"Hakim, has he shut off the tap, yet?" Karl asked.

"I understand he consulted his legal firm as soon as he found out," Hakim responded.

"Have you told him about Emily?"

"I would not betray John Clark but somehow with this business regarding the weapon, he saw your photo, my dear. It took him the same amount of time it took me in Paris, to figure out you were his child," Hakim replied as he smiled at Emily.

"John knew all this when he designed the weapon for me? Do you know anything about it?"

"He kept me informed as he designed it. He felt many women were nervous about using guns so he designed a small lightweight weapon that a woman could carry in her purse to protect herself. Even an inexperienced person can fire it because you don't have to aim it at a target. You simply photograph your prey and the weapon does the rest. I am interested in procuring one for myself."

"I had no idea he had such skills."

"I believe if you talk to his uncle, you'll find that John acquired a knowledge of weapons when he was still very young. He liked to modify weapons. In later life it became a kind of hobby for him."

"I had no idea John could create something so complicated."

"The most complex part of the design was the missiles. I put him in touch with an engineer in Germany who understood what he wanted. The mechanism that holds the missiles is a redesigned camera. He hired a Toronto engineer to work on that. That was the simple part. "

"Did you know my husband was passing information on terrorist activities to Greg Turner?"

"Yes, I did know that. Most of his information came from a retired British agent. Anytime you're dealing with terrorists, you put your life at risk. He knew that."

"He was a special man."

"He was that," Al Fraih replied.

Al Fraih focused on Karl for the first time. "And you, sir, are with Europol?"

"I'm sure you know more about me than I do about you. It's like having the tables turned on yourself."

Al Fraih chuckled. "Well put! We haven't filled John's position. You may be interested."

"I read the file on the Quintanilla brothers from Madrid. I'm not interested in tossing live bodies off cliffs."

"I remember the file. It was John's first assignment with us. We were all interested to see how he handled it. Refresh my memory. One brother was a plastic surgeon, I believe."

"Yes, Antonio was a plastic surgeon. His brother Mateo was in banking," Karl replied.

"I believe a dead body was tossed off the cliff and not by John. John was with the brothers the night of the incident. He plied them with copious amounts of liquor. He put a folder with the internal audit report from the bank and photos of the dead girls on the table and excused himself claiming he was unwell. He stepped outside. The brothers did the rest. John did set up the situation at the cliff. Antonio offered no defence for the charges against him. More importantly Miss McGrath's family felt justice had been done."

"From Clark's file, we assumed this pair were responsible for the deaths of those other women," Karl answered.

"The Quintanilla brothers had money and prestige and were very cunning. The police couldn't get enough for a warrant."

"So Clark helped end it."

"Precisely!" Hakim replied.

"Emily had the misfortune of sharing a room with Ruth Zhou at Villa DiMattia. She overheard Ruth talking to one of her co-workers. She alleged that John was a contract killer working around Europe and the US."

Al Fraih looked compassionately at Emily. "You poor dear! All this because of a weapon, John created for you."

"I woke up early one morning and overheard Ruth saying horrible things about John. She knew his first wife. I was already terrified so I panicked. I was trying to come to grips with the idea that John had a secret life," Emily replied.

"I doubt much of what she said was true. I think you'll find this Ruth was part of what John described as his clean-up crew.

He talked about Dave Rowe's team. He said it was like dealing with a group of devils but they did a good job and kept their mouths shut. Rowe's team would come on the scene after the fact and help John stage a scene or clean up a hotel room. John wanted no trace of himself left behind. We knew from the beginning he intended to use them but I can tell you without hesitation, he never took any of them into his confidence. John worked very much alone."

"So when Ruth said John went around killing people?" Emily asked.

"John was an incident expert. He set people up, yes, but he didn't kill them. This Ruth person was creating fiction, I assure you."

"I'm relieved to hear you say that," she answered.

"Where are you two planning to go after you visit your friends near Lucca?"

Karl replied, "I want to introduce Emily to my family in Brussels. We will hopefully be married there and then we'll visit Emily's family and friends in Canada. We plan to live in Europe."

"I think it might be wise if you avoid Emily's home at least until Kenneth has his family situation under control. John went to great lengths to prevent those two young men from meeting Emily. I suggest we continue as we were."

Karl looked at Emily. "It's your decision, dear. If you feel you absolutely must go back home, I'll be happy to make the arrangements, otherwise I'm happy to fly your family to Brussels."

"Does Kenneth Reid know about my brother?"

Al Fraih replied, "Not to my knowledge!"

"As far as the world knows, Paul is my step-son, not my brother. It might be wise to keep it that way. What do you think, Karl?"

"Again it is your decision. Clark went to great expense to give you both a good life. I'm not sure any change is in order."

"The question is whether I should even tell him Kenneth Reid is our father," Emily mused.

"Would he be happier knowing? Ask yourself, are you happier knowing?" Karl asked.

"In a sense it closes a loop. I now have ancestors like other people."

"You don't have to decide everything today. Give yourself some time," Karl urged.

Al Fraih interrupted, "How safe is your home in Brussels?"

"Access to my place in Brussels is easy to restrict. It shouldn't be too difficult to keep unwelcome visitors at bay. My days with Europol are over. My brothers will be pleased because I was shot twice in the past three years. I may go into the family business or start a detective agency with my partner from Europol."

Al Fraih smiled. "You have a lot to think about. Konstantin has arranged for your transportation from Livorno to your hotel in Tuscany. He and Flori will travel with you to Brussels. I suggest you use their agency to secure your home in Brussels. John found they were very good. You will find Jak Luga, the owner of the agency, easy to deal with."

Karl replied, "I'll keep that in mind. Konstantin grabbed my cellphone when we came on board."

"We have a secure line on the ship. Feel free to make calls. I'd prefer your presence on board this ship be kept quiet."

"I'll bear that in mind."

"Karl, if you and your partner decide to open up a detective agency, let me know."

Emily stood up. "No, you don't. I lived with one husband who kept secrets from me. I don't want that ever again."

Al Fraih smiled. "This, from the woman who killed a professional assassin. Maybe they should hire you, my dear."

Karl stood and shook hands with Hakim Al Fraih. "We are in your debt, sir. If there's anything I can do for you, let me know."

"There is one thing. Think about my offer."

"I promise to do that. I will discuss it with my partner at the first opportunity."

They excused themselves and went to make their phone calls.

Jerry's phone was off-line so they called Greg Turner.

"Where the hell have you been, Busch? Been trying to contact you for days."

Karl replied, "We've been hiding out. Just wondered if there are any new developments."

"Loads of new developments. Is Emily there?"

"She's here beside me. I'll put you on speaker phone."

"I have news for you, Emily."

"I'm listening, Greg."

"My first bit of news is: we arrested the wife of Liu Wong and charged her with murder."

Emily replied, "She murdered John?"

"No, but she was complicit in his death and the death of her own husband. Hope you got a few minutes."

Karl replied, "We do. We're both listening."

"This case has tentacles. Jiao Wong came storming in here a couple days ago claiming her husband invented the weapon and therefore it belongs to her. When they couldn't shut her up, they brought her to see me. She claimed her husband was the mastermind behind everything. Needless to say, she couldn't produce any proof. I questioned her and became curious so I got a warrant to check her phone usage and discovered there were several calls to KZR the morning her husband disappeared. The woman is a woodpecker. If she wants something she keeps pecking away to get it. The bottom line is we had enough to arrest her this morning."

Karl asked. "Did you get a confession?"

"Jiao Wong would implicate her own mother if there was something in it for her. She bent over backwards to negotiate a deal for herself. I'll give you the short version, if there is such a thing as a short version of this. Man, can that woman talk."

Karl laughed. "Sounds like you were having fun with her."

"I'd rather take my chances with a rattlesnake. The problem arose because Clark was still acting as council for KZR and would frequent the executive offices on a regular basis. Liu Wong assumed he was part of the woodwork there. When Clark wanted to hire an engineer to construct the case for his weapon, he knew Liu Wong could deliver, so he hired him. Are you with me so far?"

Emily responded, "You're saying that Liu Wong thought John worked as an employee for KZR."

"That's right! Clark wasn't exactly known for spreading information around, as you well know. He hired Liu Wong, and paid him out of a numbered company. However, when the job finished Jiao Wong didn't want the gravy train to end and made her displeasure known to KZR. She phoned KZR and began stirring things up, trying to drum up more special work for Liu. KZR had no record of any special work and after repeated calls from Jiao Wong to the head of research, they figured out Clark was involved. Clark had an informant at KZR who let him know there was a problem and that he was being watched. So he told Liu there was to be no more communication between them. "

Karl replied,. "We're not missing a word. Go on."

"We know Liu Wong met John Clark just before he died and judging by the timing and what we learned from John's informant, we believe Mrs. Wong provided the impetus that got him killed. As soon as Clark found Wong waiting for him at the cafe in his building, he had to know something was very wrong."

"Mrs. Wong sounds like a nasty piece of work," Karl said.

"Jiao Wong wasn't finished. Fast forward to a month ago. She was still complaining about their lack of funds so Liu told her how he helped build a revolutionary weapon and lamented he didn't get a piece of the action. He figured it would be worth a fortune. So Jiao started phoning his bosses at KZR once again and demanded her due. One day later Liu Wong disappeared and as you know, we found his body floating in the harbour."

"I see what you mean by a tangled web. Is Mrs. Wong getting bail?"

"Judge turned her down. He considers her a flight risk."

"I'm not surprised," Karl replied.

"Jiao Wong is pointing fingers at everyone at KZR but at the moment she doesn't have a lot of credibility. She'd implicate me if she could."

Karl responded, "You've made a lot of progress. I'm impressed."

"I'm not finished. Had a long talk with John's uncle. Armend Berisha was a mentor to his nephew when he was growing up. Every Saturday morning the two of them would head into the woods to practise target shooting. Berisha told me his nephew was a natural marksman. I assume his love of weaponry began to develop then. We noticed when we examined his arsenal in Emily's basement that many of the weapons had what appeared to be repairs but were actually modifications. He decided to design the little weapon for Emily because of what his mother had gone through when he was a child. She was defenceless after she lost her husband and would cower inside her house, terrified of even a knock on the door. He worried about what would happen to you, Emily, if he was no longer around to protect you."

"So it was a labour of love in honour of his mother," Emily replied.

"Considering what his family went through, I'm not surprised he was so concerned with your security," Turner replied.

"If weapons have names, I'd like it to be named after his mother."

"I'll relay your message," Turner said.

Karl asked, "That it?"

"Nope, one more thing! My last news is this. Kenneth Reid was instrumental in hiring John Clark to act as counsel for KZR and he feels responsible for what happened. He closed down his Canadian plant and has now put the building up for sale. He's prepared to offer Emily one million dollars in compensation for the loss of her husband and another million for the aggravation she suffered because of all this business about the weapon. I get the impression he's willing to negotiate upwards if you will meet with him."

Emily replied, "Please thank him on my behalf and tell him that I'm not interested in payments of any kind, though it is kind of him to offer. I'd prefer not to meet him at this time."

"I'll relay your message and don't worry, Emily, I'm an expert stonewaller. Your privacy is safe with me."

They both thanked him as they hung up.

Karl put his arm around her shoulder as they went upstairs for a stroll on the open deck. "Case is solved. Life is good. Let's enjoy it."

"Karl, the case is only somewhat solved. We don't know who hired Soll. Mrs. Wong wouldn't have done that."

"Emily, I'm sure Turner knows who ordered the hit, however, he's not going to give you any information until it's in the bag. And I might add, he's not going to arrest anyone until he has enough solid evidence to get a conviction. No man wants to think about his widow having to go through the chaos you've just experienced. When Turner has all his *i*'s dotted and his *t*'s crossed, his first phone call will be to you."

"Actually that sounds very much in character for Greg. You know him well."

"We go back a ways. May I treat you to dinner on the deck tonight?"

"Sounds like a plan." She laughed. "Now that I know you plan to marry me in Belgium, I think we should talk about that. When were you planning to tell me?"

"I realized when we were talking to Hakim that I'm not the patient man I once was. I'd marry you this moment if I could."

"I love you, Karl Busch."

"I love you too, my dear. But to be perfectly honest with you, I have to admit that my brothers wouldn't allow me to leave Brussels alive without marrying you."

"So it's a question of your survival? That's why you want to marry me?"

"Precisely!"

"Then I'll have to marry you to save your life."

"I hoped you'd say that," he replied.

"But it'll cost you."

"How much?"

"I want a dog." She tried to appear stern.

"What about Wellington? I was thinking of bringing him to the wedding along with your parents and the rest of your tribe."

"I love you, Mr. Busch."

NINETEEN

Two mornings later the yacht anchored in a small cove down the coast from Livorno. The sky was overcast and the wind was moderate but not enough to cause any alarm. Konstantin and Flori were already waiting to disembark when Emily and Karl came on deck.

Suddenly the wind whipped up into a frenzy and torrents of rain came rushing at them as though the heavens had turned on a tap. Within seconds they were drenched. Emily's favourite sun hat hung like a limp rag in her hand.

Aza beckoned them back inside. "It's not safe to lower the zodiac. Please return to your cabin and I will see to your wet clothing."

The ship was pitching badly as they made their way back to their cabin.

Once inside, Karl handed her a towel. "Aza said to put all our wet clothes into a laundry bag and leave it outside our cabin door. They'll have everything ready for us in an hour."

Emily stripped out of her clothes and handed them to Karl. She wished she hadn't boasted about never getting seasick. This was not her finest moment. She felt as though the world was spinning around.

"Karl, why were you keeping secrets from me?"

Karl who was trying to maintain his equilibrium while he towelled himself off, looked at her in surprise. "Secrets? What secrets?"

"You knew Konstantin and Flori were security people and you didn't tell me."

He finished towelling himself and threw on a terry bathrobe. Her back was to him and her hair was hanging down in long wet pleats. "You're worried about that, now?"

"How can I marry someone who keeps secrets from me?" she continued as she tried to dry herself.

As he approached her, he realized she was shivering but she continued speaking in a shrill but shaky voice. "Ignore that. How can I marry another someone who keeps secrets from me?"

"You're putting me in the same category as Clark?" He was sorry the minute the words came out of his mouth. It wasn't what he intended. Memories of one's late spouse were sacrosanct.

She seemed not to notice as she continued, "I'm angry. You should have told me. How long have you known?"

"I tried to tell you several times." As he turned her around and examined her, he realized her skin tone was approaching the shade of her green eyes. "Emily, look at me."

"I can't." She ran into the bathroom. He followed her and held her while she wretched.

Then he wrapped her in a bathrobe and grabbed another towel to dry her hair. She was shivering badly as he cradled her in his arms. He was concerned.

Aza picked up the phone on the first ring. "Aza, Mrs. Clark has motion sickness. Do you have anything?"

Aza was at the door a minute later and handed him a small blister pack of pills. "As soon as Mrs. Clark is able to walk, bring her up on deck. I'll be back in a few minutes."

"I made a fool of myself again, didn't I?" Emily whispered as he cradled her in his arms.

"Emily, dearest, you are precious beyond words. Even guys who make their living on the sea get seasick at times. You need air. I'll take you up top as soon as you're able to stand."

Five minutes later they met Aza in the hallway. He examined Emily and said, "Please follow me. Mr. and Mrs. Cana are both sick. You can join them. There's an area out of the wind near the aft cabin. I'll bring you some tea."

Still wearing their robes, Emily and Karl huddled beside Konstantin and Flori. Flori looked no better than Emily felt. Aza brought tea in large mugs instead of the usual tall thin glasses.

As the winds began to ease off, Aza brought more hot tea and some biscuits. "I suggest you return to your cabins within the hour. The captain says it'll soon be safe to lower the zodiac."

Their clothes had been cleaned and dried and were lying on their bed when they returned to their stateroom.

As soon as she changed, Karl came over to her. "Emily, you're right, I should have told you. Turner found out you had protection while I was in the hospital. He told Jerry about it and Jerry called them to see if they would transport us to Patmos. Until we talked to Hakim Al Fraih, none of us had any idea what it was all about. But you're right, I should have told you sooner. The only thing I can say in my own defence is that every time I tried to tell you while we were on Patmos you seemed to be in the midst of some dramatic discovery about your family or Clark or his uncle. Once we came on board, I saw you relax for the first time. I wanted to spare you some worry. I know that's rather a lame excuse considering how well you've coped with everything. Please forgive me."

"No more secrets."

"I promise! No more secrets."

They followed Aza to the zodiac. Flori was already on board. Both men helped Emily climb on board the little boat. The water was far from calm.

Konstantin pointed to the shore. "Our driver should be waiting for us over there. This delay put us at a disadvantage."

Karl responded, "You and I should go ashore first."

"No, you stay with the women. I'll go."

As soon as they reached shore, Konstantin climbed out of the zodiac. "Give me five minutes." He looked at Flori, "You know what to do."

He disappeared into the trees. They waited. Flori checked her watch after four minutes and stood up.

Konstantin came running down the embankment. "You'll have today only at Villa DiMattia. We'll move you out tonight."

Karl asked, "There's a problem?"

"Reid is in the area. We don't know his present location. Follow me."

A beige Range Rover was parked among the trees nearby. They stowed their luggage and climbed in.

Karl phoned Russ when they were within a kilometre of the villa. Russ and Pia were both standing in the courtyard as they drove up the hill. The sun had come out and was already beginning to dry the stonework in the courtyard.

Pia ran to the car. "Emily, I'm so glad to see you again."

Karl introduced Konstantin and Flori as friends and explained they would be all staying for dinner only.

Russ stayed behind with Karl while the others went inside the building. "I'm not stupid, Karl. That couple with you are muscle."

"Play along with me, Russ."

"You always were a man of few words, Busch, but I get your meaning. Let's forget about everything for one evening. Come and enjoy yourself."

"Suits me!"

They followed the women upstairs to Russ and Pia's apartment. They could hear laughter as soon as they opened the door.

Edgar sat with his arm draped over Mary Cominski's shoulder. He didn't need to say he was pleased with this turn of events. It was written in the broad grin on his face.

Edgar began, "So, Em, why did I hear that you killed that viper and now this Lombardi guy has his mug plastered all over the media claiming he did it?"

Jerry was standing by the fireplace with a glass of ale in his hand. "Like you'd want your lady love's face plastered all over the rags! I don't think so, Morris."

Edgar continued: "That guy is really eating up the publicity. He's on talk shows and has had his face in the newspaper every day for the past few weeks. Now they're saying he wants to be a talk show host."

Emily laughed. "Better him than me!"

"I need another cool drink then I'll tell you my news!" Jerry boasted in a loud voice.

After grabbing a bottle from the fridge, he looked around the room making sure he had everyone's attention.

Russ asked, "If this is important news, shouldn't you wait for Vince and Toni to arrive so they can be in on it?"

"I'm not waiting to make my announcement."

He waited until all eyes were on him again before continuing and then he took a slow sip from his glass just for effect. "The three of us are opening our own detective agency. Karl and I have resigned from the bureau."

Russ said, "Congratulations! Sounds like a great idea!"

Edgar looked up at Jerry. "You said three of you. Who is the third?"

Jerry explained, "Why Emily, of course!"

Edgar was clearly surprised. "You're turning into a snoop, Em? Aren't you coming back to Dundas with me?"

Karl answered for her before she could open her mouth. "Don't listen to Jerry, Edgar, he's two-thirds right at the most. I have resigned from the bureau but I assure you, Emily is not about to become part of any detective agency."

Pia looked from Karl to Emily. "Wait, something's going on. Where are you rushing off to? You're not going back to Canada with Edgar, are you, Emily?"

Emily shook her head. "I'm going to Brussels to meet Karl's family."

Pia began yelling as she rushed over to hug Emily, "You're getting married, aren't you?"

Emily and Karl betrayed themselves with their wide smiles.

Russ announced, "This calls for a toast! I'll open a bottle of champagne."

A champagne bottle appeared and glasses were quickly filled.

Jerry toasted them with his glass of ale and yelled in a louder voice, "Here's a toast to our new detective agency!"

Russ asked, "Will you be able to get enough business to support yourselves?"

Karl replied, "I'm looking at some possibilities. Haven't had a chance to discuss things with Jerry yet."

Vince and Toni arrived. In his usual musical voice Vince took the floor. Vince's every word ended with an 'a' sound. "Sorry I'm late, I had to pick up my new car. Someone shot my other new car full of bullet holes. What is with you, Karl? Every time I lend you something you blow it up or shoot it."

With a glass of champagne in hand, Vince was enjoying himself. "You shoulda seen my cousin Luigi's house. The front door was shot full of bullet holes and then kicked open, almost off its hinges. Not only that, the downstairs was all shot up. Even Luigi's coffee pot was shot dead. If that wasn't enough the upstairs window was shot."

Karl in his usual deliberate manner of speaking, responded, "Not to worry, Vince, the state will cover all costs for the clean-up." Karl tried to continue, but there was no stopping Vince once he was on a roll.

Vince was laughing. "You drank all Luigi's good wine. He'll cry when he finds out you drank all his Mandarine Napoleon."

Karl responded calmly in an even tone, "Told you I'd pay you for everything." Then he looked at Vince suspiciously. "I didn't drink all the Mandarine Napoleon. Emily and I savoured a tiny drink one night. Vince, you can't blame that on me."

Vince ignored his comment and jumped out of his seat waving papers in the air. "Toni found these drawings hidden away in the kitchen. What was going on there, Karl? Thought you were guarding the woman not stripping naked for her." He held up the sketches Emily had drawn of Karl while they were hiding out at Luigi's house.

Karl was out of his seat in a flash and grabbed the sketches before Vince could utter another word. He threw the papers on his chair and sat on them.

Vince laughed. "Don't worry everybody, I made lots of copies!"

Karl looked over at Emily and winked.

Nancy Moore

Nancy Moore was born in Nova Scotia. She attended McGill University, graduating with a BSc. She qualified as a Chartered Accountant and worked for many years in public accounting firms and then as a sole practitioner. *Negative Space*, her debut novel, explores the quest of a woman who, while still attempting to come to terms with the death of her husband, discovers that he was a man with many secrets. This mystery thriller carries atmosphere and tension from the opening chapter, and will keep the reader turning pages until the very end.

Negative Space is the first book in The Earth Tone Mystery Series.

CPSIA information can be obtained at www.ICGtesting.com
Printed in the USA
LVOW09*1237221114

414797LV00001B/4/P

9 781460 255940